Tikiri

Copyright

This is a work of fiction. Names, characters, businesses, places, events and incidents are either the products of the author's imagination or used in a fictitious manner. Any resemblance to actual persons, living or dead, or actual events, situations, and customs is purely coincidental.

The use of any part of this publication, reproduced, transmitted in any form or by any means electronic, mechanical, photocopying, recording, or otherwise or stored in a retrieval system without prior written consent of the publisher—or in the case of photocopying or other reprographic copying, a license from the Canadian Copyright Licensing Agency—is an infringement of the copyright law.

. . . .

THE GIRL WHO RAN AWAY
The Red Heeled Rebels Series
Book One
All rights reserved.
Copyright ©2020 Tikiri Herath
Edition: 2020
www.RedHeeledRebels.com[1]
Library & Archives Canada Cataloging in Publication
ISBN: 978-1-989232-24-8[2]

. . . .

AUTHOR: TIKIRI HERATH
Publisher: Nefertiti Press
Copy Editor: Stephanie Parent
Cover Design: Angela Oltmann
Back Cover Headshot: Aura McKay

---

1. http://www.RedHeeledRebels.com

2. https://www.collectionscanada.gc.ca/ciss-ssci/app/index.php?fuseaction=logbook.edit&publication=625966&lang=eng

The Girl Who Ran Away

Book One
Red Heeled Rebels Series

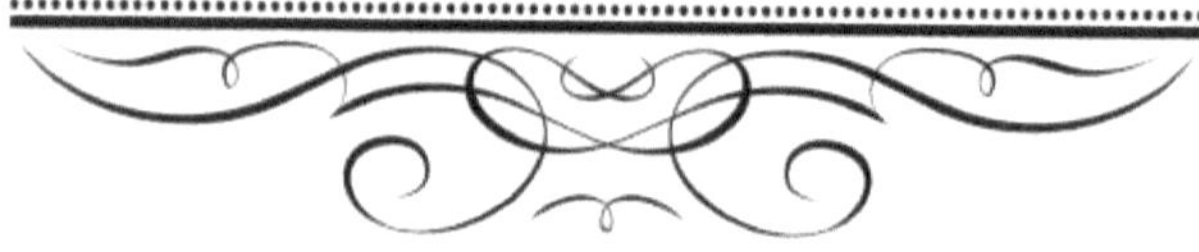

Formerly titled BETRAYED / DISOWNED

Other Titles by Author

· · · ·

<u>The Red Heeled Rebels Thriller Novels</u>[3]
The Girl Who Crossed the Line
The Girl Who Ran Away
The Girl Who Made Them Pay
The Girl Who Fought to Kill
The Girl Who Broke Free
The Girl Who Knew Their Names
The Girl Who Never Forgot

· · · ·

The Accidental Traveler
An anthology of short stories based on the author's sojourns around the world.

· · · ·

The Rebel Diva Nonfiction Series[4]
Your Rebel Dreams: 60 Days to discover your purpose and passions and power up your life.
Your Rebel Plans: 30 Days to create a masterplan for your career and life change.
Your Rebel Life: 100 habit hacks to transform the ten most important pillars of your life.
Bust Your Fears: 3 easy tools to conquer your fears and upgrade your career and life.

· · · ·

---

3. http://www.redheeledrebels.com/

4. http://www.RebelDivas.com

Collaborations
The Boss Chick's Bodacious Destiny Nonfiction Bundle
Dark Shadows 2: Voodoo and Black Magic of New Orleans

A Gift

There's a gift for you in here for picking up this book!
If you'd like to know what inspired the Red Heeled Rebels series, in particular this novel, you can read **The Girl with No Hands,** a short story by the author.
The download link for your personal copy is at the back of this book.

Part ONE

Two hands yanked me out of the crumpled car. My back scraped against the mangled steel, but I felt no pain.

I looked around in a shocked daze.

Everything was a blur of smoke.

I heard shouting nearby. A police siren. The man in the Tanzanian patrol uniform let go of me and doubled over coughing. It was a rough, gagging cough. His face was glowing, not from sweat but from the reflection of fire.

That was when I felt the heat.

The grass around us, tall enough to hide a fully-grown African elephant, was ablaze. The fire was climbing the acacia tree we'd hit moments earlier, its leaves curling inward in pain. I gazed in horror at our small Fiat, engulfed in flames. There was a familiar shadow inside. A darkened head collapsed forward. Another shadow leaned against the steering wheel, now a ring of fire.

"Oh, my god!"

I struggled to my feet.

"Get back!" someone yelled.

"Mama! Papa!"

I had to get to them. Save them.

Before I could do anything, the officer grabbed me by the arm and pulled me through the hot grass, half carrying, half dragging me like a rag doll. I kicked at the dirt and struggled all the way, almost losing my precious red sandals.

"Lemme go!" I screamed. He dumped me on the asphalt and flopped down beside me, one hand tightly on my shoulder, the other wiping his face which was drenched in sweat.

The crackle of fire and the blaring of sirens were getting louder. I felt hands pull me onto a stretcher. People were shouting at each other and at me. Someone was forcing me to lie down, hands on my shoulders pinning me down.

"No! Let me go!"

I fought to get up.

"*Hatari!*" a sharp voice said behind me. "Danger!"

The man who'd pulled me out of the car came over and reached for my hands. *"Huwezi kwenda nyuma,"* he said in a soft voice, shaking his head. I didn't understand and not because I didn't know the language.

"But we've got to go back! Do something!"

I lunged forward. Hands clamped me down. The officer sighed and shook his head.

"Pole, pole," he said.

I stared at him through the smoky haze. I knew enough Swahili to understand he'd just said "sorry."

I collapsed. My mind was heavy, foggy. *This isn't happening. This is a nightmare. I'll wake up soon.*

But the fire was all around us now. I couldn't see our car anymore.

Then, the world went black.

Chapter Two

"What did the police say?" a female voice whispered in the dark.

"Tight-lipped, they were," another whispered back. "I overheard one of them say it was a good thing a highway patrol was on the road, or it could have been worse."

Who's talking? I couldn't see a thing, but the voices kept going.

"How much worse could it have got?"

"I don't know but it sounded serious, from the way they were saying."

"I tell you what I think, Rosa. These foreigners just don't know how to drive here, but nobody wants to say that."

"Tell me about it." A big sigh. "Every time we go on those safari roads, I tell my husband somebody should put up signs or someone will get killed one of these days."

"If we had signs for lions, do you think tourists would stay away? They'd follow it with their fancy cameras, I tell you."

"Only the white *muzungus* will do that."

"Have you not seen those buses full of Chinese these days? Even the *Wahindi* are running around with their cameras, I tell you."

"Well, the good Lord was looking over this little *Wahindi*. She'll heal."

"Why don't we call that hindu priest to come and talk to her?"

"How do you know her church? Maybe she's buddhist, or christian or maybe even muslim. You never know these days."

"Well, we need *someone* to bless her parents."

Bless her parents? I pried my eyes open and was immediately blinded by a fluorescent light. I shut my eyes back tightly.

"The girl's up!"

"Call the doctor!"

I opened my eyes cautiously this time, to see two Tanzanian nurses in starched white aprons and stiff caps standing on either side of my bed. They were staring at me like I was an alien. I stared back. They couldn't have looked more different from each other. One was short and stout, and the other was thin and tall.

I looked around. We were in a small, windowless room. I was on a hospital bed with beeping machines surrounding me. On the wall in front was a wildlife calendar with a photo of a sandy-colored impala leaping over a bush, its long, black horns leading the charge. I did a double take. That reminded me of something, something urgent, but for the life of me, I couldn't think of what it was.

A shiver ran through me. This place was cold, sterile, and smelled of disinfectant like they'd scrubbed everything down with bleach. Something nipped at my arm. I looked down to see a gangly plastic tube sticking to my forearm. *What's this?* I pulled my arms up and instantly, a searing pain rushed through my body.

"Aaargh." I struggled to get up. "Where am I?" I spoke but heard only a strange, raspy sound. I put my hand on my throat. My back hurt and my legs felt heavy. Something somewhere was hurting badly, and tears welled up in my eyes.

"Now, now, take care, my dear," the stout nurse said, coming closer and putting a hand on my shoulder. Her hand felt warm to the touch.

"Don't pull on these," the other nurse said, fixing the IV bag. "These are for your own good. See, you're already feeling better, no?"

"Where's Mama?" I croaked. My throat was drier than the Sahara.

"Relax. No talking. You need rest," the plump nurse said, pushing a button on the side of the bed to bring it upright. In her hand was a plastic cup with a bent straw in it. "You'll be just fine," she said, pushing my long hair back. "This'll help. Drink."

I reached for the cup with shaking hands and put my lips on the straw. As they watched me silently, I took a tiny sip of the water.

The black phone by the door rang. The skinny nurse ran to pick it up and talked into it, nodding every few seconds, saying, "Yes, Doctor. Yes, Doctor." The plump nurse started to bustle around the room, taking readings from the screens and writing on charts.

I sat motionless with the cup in my hands, trying to make sense of what had happened, why I was here. Suddenly, a fiery image sprang to mind. It was of our green car in flames with the shadows of my parents inside. Unconscious.

My body went numb. Panicked thoughts came rushing in like a sandstorm in a desert, roaring, swirling, filling every crevice of my mind.

Mama! Papa! Did they get away? Are they okay? Oh, my god. Where are they?

My mind reeled. I remembered how I'd begged them to go on this safari, how I'd sniveled like a spoiled brat. I remembered the day before, how my best girlfriend, Chanda, and I had disappeared for hours in the Uhuru market and worried them sick. It was also that morning I'd committed a crime, my first crime, a misdeed only Chanda knew about and one I'd regret for the rest of my life.

Mama always said karma never forgets.

The plump nurse turned and noticed my ashen face.

"Where's my mother?" I squeaked the words.

She set her chart on the side table and walked a slow deliberate walk toward my bed. Something in her face told me I didn't want her to answer my question. I didn't want her to speak. I pulled back. She leaned in and wrapped me in a hug. When she told me I wasn't going to see my parents again, I wanted to cry, scream, but I couldn't even breathe.

I made the accident happen. I'm the one who made them die.

I pulled away and threw up over the side of the bed. I didn't care I was spraying my sickly vomit on her pristine white skirt.

"She's just a child," whispered the voice of the plump nurse, whom I knew as Nurse Elizabeth now. "Think of that before you make the decision."

I sat up in bed and looked around me. I'd just woken from a drug-induced sleep and was still drowsy. The voices were coming from the room next to mine, where the nurses kept their medical and bandage supplies and had a desk to write their charts and reports.

"This is not my decision, mesdames," a man replied.

I recognized that voice. It was Mr. Mudenda, the children's psychologist assigned to me. He was a small man with a pleasant face who'd visited me every afternoon for an hour, for the past two weeks. He was the only person, other than the cleaning lady, who came without a stethoscope around his neck. He shared stories about his family and told me about his eldest son, Peace, a year older than me, who went to a public school in town.

Sometimes, when Mr. Mudenda didn't have time to drop his son off at home, he'd bring him in, together with several books they'd picked out for me from the town library. As Mr. Mudenda inquired about my health, Peace would sit quietly on the bench outside the room, engrossed in his own book, his oversized spectacles threatening to fall off at any moment.

When I asked about the boy, Mr. Mudenda regaled with pride that Peace was at the top of his class, a chess prodigy, and even two grades ahead of his age group. I wished Peace would come in and chat but he never did. Other than an initial hello, he kept to himself. Instead, it was Mr. Mudenda's soothing voice and stories that put me to sleep every night.

Though I'd known Mr. Mudenda for only two weeks, he was all I had now. That first day, he came over with a book and sat next to my bed and read while I slipped in and out of consciousness, throwing up every few hours till I could vomit no more.

The nurses had their hands full with patients in far more serious conditions than I was. They didn't have time to pay attention to a child who felt worse in her heart than in her body, so it was Mr. Mudenda who stayed with me till dawn the next morning. After a few days, I came to trust him so much that I almost told him my terrible secret of crime.

"The police are still investigating, you know," Nurse Rosa, the thin nurse, was saying. "They'll want to talk to her."

My heart skipped a beat. *They know what I did?* I strained to listen.

"It's the police telling me to send the girl away," Mr. Mudenda said. "Besides, she can't stay here forever."

"But you can't ship off a little one just like that," Nurse Elizabeth said.

"It's for her own safety," Mr. Mudenda replied.

What does that mean?

"This is not the first time they had trouble," he continued. "Remember the dead Swedish scientist they found in the desert last year? He worked for Environ Africa as well, and he complained about the same problems in his letters to the newspapers. There will be an investigation, and it's going to be up to the commissioner now."

"Oh, my, my," Nurse Elizabeth said. "What's the world coming to these days?"

"The mining companies have long hands, and they don't like it when others meddle in their affairs," Mr. Mudenda said.

"They have all the money," Nurse Rosa said in a disapproving voice. "And we know where half of that ends up, don't we? Right in the pockets of our politicians."

I no longer followed the conversation. I shook my head from side to side to clear the heavy fog of drugs from my mind.

"What's her official status?" Nurse Elizabeth was asking. "Didn't she say her father's Indian and her mother's from Sri Lanka or somewhere like that?"

Their voices were getting lower. I leaned toward the door.

"According to the documents I received, she was born in Kenya," Mr. Mudenda said, rustling papers.

"A Kenyan citizen then?" Nurse Rosa asked.

"From what the police sent me, the parents were expatriate contractors." Mr. Mudenda spoke slowly as if he was reading something. "They moved around the region, but they had no residential papers from anywhere. The only things we have are copies of their passports kept at the company."

"What about a birth certificate?" Nurse Rosa asked.

"They've asked the Kenyan authorities, but that will take time. In the meantime, she doesn't belong anywhere, I'm afraid."

"Tsk. Poor girl. She must be ten, not even," Nurse Rosa said.

"Eleven, I think," Mr. Mudenda said. More rustling of papers.

Hey, I'm twelve now and that's almost thirteen.

I peeked over the bed. My ruby red sandals, the last birthday gift from my parents, were still there. They looked worn and dusty now, though I'd only got them a few days ago.

"What about school? Doesn't she go to the international school?" Nurse Rosa asked.

"That's a boarding school, isn't it?" Nurse Elizabeth said. "Maybe she can stay there for a while."

My heart dropped. I detested being at school during the day. I hated being the odd one out, the one everyone picked on. I couldn't imagine living there around the clock, especially without my parents to escape to. I shook my head silently. *No, please no.*

"Who's going to pay for that expensive school?" Mr. Mudenda asked. "The company promised only to take care of the funeral arrangements and her trip back."

Trip? Back?

"She tells us her home is here," Nurse Elizabeth said. "Let's see what a foster home could do, at least."

A wave of nausea washed over me. I pulled the blanket to my chin and curled my legs under me. Part of me didn't want to hear this anymore. Another part wanted to run into that room and demand to know what they were planning to do with me.

"Mesdames," my social worker said. "She does have a family, and as far as the authorities are concerned, that is where she has to go."

"Hmph!" Both nurses snorted at the same time.

"Didn't they say they didn't want the *half-breed*? That is what I heard," Nurse Rosa said with a huff.

"Yes, think of that now, Mr. Mudenda," Nurse Elizabeth said.

"Whether they like it or not, they'll have to take the girl," Mr. Mudenda said. "And Asha will have to adjust."

Adjust to what? My head was hurting.

"Habari!"

Someone else had entered the room. I heard the usual Swahili pleasantries and a man's deep voice, a voice that was in charge.

"Did you tell the kid it's an accident?" the man barked.

I craned my neck to look, but couldn't see a thing.

"Don't worry, sir. I'm handling this the best way I can." Mr. Mudenda sounded strained now.

"Funeral arrangements will be made here by the company, two days from now," the man said.

"I'll take the girl with me," Mr. Mudenda said. "She will need company."

"Shouldn't we send the bodies back to the family?" Nurse Elizabeth asked.

"They do not want them," the man replied.

"Oh!" Nurse Elizabeth gasped.

"Tsk. Tsk. Tsk." Nurse Rosa always clicked her tongue when she wasn't happy.

I looked at the impala calendar on the wall where Nurse Rosa checked the days off every day. My parents would be buried on a Sunday.

A flood of memories came to me.

Sunday was our family day. It was the day my mother baked and I became her sous chef, piping creamy swirls onto little cakes. I'll never forget the heavenly baking smells that wafted through our home those quiet Sunday mornings when we'd brew cups of steaming Ceylon tea and sit at the kitchen table with my father to taste my mother's latest creations.

No matter how bad the week had been, Sundays made the world all right again.

"What kind of family is this, you have found?" Nurse Elizabeth's angry voice came from the room.

"Don't be so quick to judge," Mr. Mudenda said. "They've been in Africa for the past twelve years. Probably no one even knew this girl was alive."

"We can't fly the bodies anyway," the strange man said. He didn't seem to be making any effort to lower his voice. "I was at the mortuary when they brought them in. Oh, man. Not something you want to see, I can tell you that."

"At least the commissioner said he will look into this business," Mr. Mudenda said. "I just hope the company doesn't start lobbying like they always do."

"Those bastards," the man said. "Always interfering with our investigations."

Silence.

"Are you going to escort us to the airport after the funeral?" Mr. Mudenda asked.

"We're going to drive you there, my friend," the man replied with a chuckle. "Only the president gets an escort."

Not I, nor anyone else can travel that road for you.
You must travel it by yourself.
It is not far. It is within reach.
Perhaps you have been on it since you were born,
and did not know.
Perhaps it is everywhere - on water and land.
Walt Whitman

Chapter Four

I t had been the longest flight of my life.

I'd spent the whole time curled into a tight ball, staring out the tiny window, not seeing anything, my head buzzing. *Why are they sending me there? Who'll be on the other side? Am I going to see my home again?*

Throughout it all, one conversation had played in my head repeatedly.

The caskets had remained closed at my parents' funeral. All my parents' colleagues and friends from Environ Africa had come, as well as Nurse Rosa, Nurse Elizabeth and Ms. Stacy, my teacher at the international school.

The only people I hadn't known were the five uniformed officers who stood silently, with their sunglasses on and hadn't talked to anybody. I wondered why they were there, but no one was answering my questions that day. Not even Mr. Mudenda.

When I'd asked to see my parents, he'd stammered something about it being a tradition that we weren't supposed to open funeral caskets. But I'd noticed how he avoided my eyes when he said that.

Nurse Elizabeth, who'd overheard me, gave me a big hug and asked me to go sit in the armchair in the funeral home director's office. She left me there with a book and a cup of tea while the adults conferred next door where the coffins lay side by side.

Later, neither Mr. Mudenda nor the faceless officer in shades who'd sat in the backseat of the police car answered any of my questions on our way to the airport.

Mr. Mudenda kept trying to reassure me. He kept saying I was finally going home to a family who'd take care of me, that I was about to start a new life in an exciting country, and I must focus on school from now on and make new friends there. He promised I could visit when I got older and that I could come as often as I wished then. I noticed him wiping his eyes when he said this.

I knew he was being kind, but my gut was tightening into a knot that told me something was very wrong. Something inside me knew he wasn't telling the whole truth.

I'd clenched his hand at the departure lounge. I hadn't wanted to let go. Other than Nurse Elizabeth and Nurse Rosa, he'd been the only adult who seemed to care. I'd wished he'd adopt me and let me go to the local school with his son, Peace, instead.

Just before walking through the security gates at the Dar es Salaam airport, I handed him a piece of paper on which I'd been scribbling for a few days. It was my goodbye letter to Chanda, which I'd written on hospital letterhead that reeked of Lysol.

"You'll find her at the market, won't you? Promise?" I'd asked. "She's my best friend in the whole world. I want her to know where I'm going."

"I promise," Mr. Mudenda had said, squeezing my hand. "Go now, child. They're waiting for you."

• • • •

AFTER THE PLANE LANDED, I stayed crouched in the cocoon of my seat, even after everyone had taken their bags and walked out. Whatever was waiting for me outside terrified me. The last few people getting off glanced my way with funny looks, but I didn't care. I curled up and waited—for what, I didn't know.

A flight attendant came and leaned over the seats toward me.

"Namaste," she said with a pretty smile, "you're home."

Home? I looked at her blankly.

"Everyone's leaving. You have to as well, sweetie."

I shook my head. *No, I don't want to go out there. I don't want to go anywhere.*

"You have family waiting for you in that building." She pointed through my tiny window to the airport terminal. "You don't want to keep them waiting now, do you?"

Family?

"Come on, sweetie." She plucked my bag from the overhead bin and beckoned.

I looked outside the window. *Didn't they say they didn't want a half-breed?*

I couldn't go back to where I came from, and I didn't want to go where I was supposed to. The stewardess reached down and pulled me up gently by the hand. I didn't have a choice. I uncurled my legs and stood up, feeling shaky. Holding my hand, she led me to the stairway of the plane.

"There," she said, "what a beautiful day it is today in Goa, isn't it?"

I looked out with fearful eyes.

"Go on, now. I'm right behind you."

I took a timid step and licked my dry lips. The first thing that hit me was the heat—a heavy, humid, tropical heat that clung to my body for the rest of my stay in this country.

The stench of jet fuel mixed with rotting garbage and the sweat from a billion people wafted into my nose. I almost gagged. The inside of the plane had been much nicer, but the stewardess was gently nudging me forward, down the stairs and onto the tarmac, step by step.

There was a constant hum around us. Was it the rumble of jets taking off? Or the roar of ocean waves? I looked through the glass windows of the main airport terminal. Inside, all I saw were people—people, people, everywhere. The whole of India, it seemed, had descended on Goa's International Airport that morning.

Two young women were waiting for me at the arrival gate.

One of them was a girl, just a few years older than me. She looked like me, but different. I remembered Mr. Mudenda's preparatory words at the Dar es Salaam airport. *That must be my cousin Preeti.*

Her skin was the color of milk chocolate and she had long black hair and dark brown eyes just like I did, but she wore a white school uniform and had a strange black dot in the middle of her forehead, both of which were foreign to me.

Next to her stood a beautiful young woman wearing baggy pants and an oversized shirt that went down to her knees, the salwar kameez that my mother used to call the "Indian pant dress." *That must be Aunty Shilpa.*

The two stood close side by side, with shy, embarrassed smiles on their faces. Preeti was carrying an awkward brown cardboard sign with "ASHA" written in squiggly letters. I didn't know it then, but that was the first time either of them had stepped inside an airport.

I stared at my newfound family. They stared back. The three of us stood apart, shifting from one foot to the other, unsure of what move to make next. It took me a whole minute to step toward them.

Taking the bus to their home was a frightening experience.

All those people I'd seen at the airport were now crammed inside the bus, I was sure. I didn't need to hold on to anything because the jam-packed bodies kept me upright, so much so I could barely breathe. I couldn't see much except for a man's white shirt on my right, an unknown yellow sari in front, and Aunty Shilpa on my left.

My suitcase had been precariously tied to the top of the bus with a ton of other luggage, baskets, and bags. With every swerve and jolt, I wondered if mine would fall off if it hadn't already.

In between strangers' arms and waists, Aunty Shilpa held on to my hand and squeezed it now and then, to make sure I was still there. Preeti had been separated from us by a few people, but every few minutes, whenever an opening came up, she'd tilt her head to give me a curious smile. I smiled back. In relief.

I began to relax a bit. Every time someone got off the bus and made some space, I got on my tiptoes to peek out the window and get a glimpse into this new and unfamiliar world.

Outside, vehicles of all types and sizes were fighting for space on dirty streets. The pavement was overflowing with people. *Where are they all coming from?* When several people got off the bus, I glanced out to see a line of coconut trees swaying against a tropical blue sky, promising peace in this mass of crowds and confusion.

My heart quickened.

It was exciting to be in this peculiar new city, yet heartbreaking to know I'd left behind the only home I knew, back in Africa. It was reassuring to meet these new relatives of mine, yet devastating to know my parents were no longer with me.

I seesawed between grief and fear, between curiosity for the new and dread at being in this strange land. And in the pit of my stomach lay that heavy knot that had formed after the car crash, that knot that told me what happened was wrong. Very wrong.

Back at the airport, conversing in a mix of broken English and Konkani, together with hand gestures and facial expressions, Aunty Shilpa and Preeti managed to explain that we were going to my father's old hometown of Vasco de Gama, where they lived.

My new family comprised my grandmother, my cousin Preeti, the daughter of my father's oldest brother, and Aunty Shilpa, who was my father's youngest sister. I didn't have to ask why my grandmother hadn't come to the airport. I'd overheard Nurse Rosa and Nurse Elizabeth whispering in the little anteroom when they thought I was sound asleep.

"Who asks for a bribe to take care of a grandchild, ha?" Nurse Rosa had said with a huff. "The company had to pay, can you imagine?"

"That woman cares more for money than her own blood," Nurse Elizabeth had said.

I already knew I wasn't going to be my grandmother's favorite.

But I was glad to get off the crammed bus and onto the streets. We didn't have to walk far to their one-bedroom apartment in a gray government complex.

I smelled the heavenly scents of spices before I stepped through the door. Inside the apartment, squatting next to a stone fire stove was an old woman in a faded yellow sari and a gray bun on her head. Her face glowed from the fire.

She barely looked up as we walked in, and when she did, her squinting eyes settled on my half-naked feet, strapped in my red sandals. With a loud snort, she turned back to her pot again.

I stared at my new guardian.

She was a small woman with shriveled-up skin that made her look like a human grape left to dry in the sun too long. Holding a wooden spatula in one hand and a fistful of herbs in the other, she stirred something that made my mouth water and my stomach rumble. She looked up again for a second to spit out, "Show the orphan where she'll sleep," and went back to her pot with a scowl.

We tiptoed to the furthest edge of the room where Preeti put my bag down. Aunty Shilpa squeezed my shoulder and walked over to help our grandmother at the stove. I stood in the corner of the room, uncertain of my role, waiting for someone to give instructions on what I was supposed to do in this brand-new life thrust upon me.

Aunty Shilpa rolled out a square bamboo mat and placed a stack of warm rotis in the middle. Preeti filled four glasses with water, and our grandmother piled the delicious-smelling curry into small plastic bowls.

One look at the bowls and the roti and my stomach rumbled. I hadn't eaten anything on the plane or the day before for that matter. I suddenly realized how hungry I was.

Our grandmother picked up a bowl with a grunt and passed it to Aunty Shilpa. She picked up the second bowl and passed that to Preeti. Then, she picked one for herself and squatted on the mat to eat. That was when I realized she'd filled only three bowls.

I stared at the big pot simmering with the yellow curry, wondering what to do. With a sigh, Aunty Shilpa took an empty cup from the drawer, scooped a spoonful of the curry into it, and handed it to me with a soft smile. I nodded my thanks and took it gratefully with both hands.

Preeti and Aunty Shilpa ate silently, heads down. I sat cross-legged on the floor behind Preeti and dug into the curry with a piece of the warm roti. I took the first bite expecting to savor my first Indian meal, but I tasted only rejection.

Chapter Five

If I'd believed my new school would save me, I was wrong.

Aunty Shilpa had told me that in India, white symbolized purity, innocence, and goodness. And that, I was told, was why our school monitor wore a white sari to school every day. But to me, she was anything but.

The monitor was a tall, thin woman with bony hands and a crooked nose, who answered to no one, other than the principal himself. Her face reminded me of a witch in one of my old storybooks, the one who almost had Hansel and Gretel for supper. She ran the school like an army boot camp. Even our teachers feared her.

On my first day, I followed Preeti to the schoolyard where the teachers and students were lining up in rows. On a silent cue from the monitor in front, everyone took a rigid pose and began to sing the national anthem, followed by what I later learned was the school's official song.

The girls' youthful voices rose in unison as they sang a cappella in harmony, the sound pleasantly bouncing off the school walls. I stood with my back straight and arms glued to my sides. I didn't know the words to either song, so I put a serious look on my face like a soldier at attention.

When the singing ended, an uneasy quiet fell over the school grounds.

We must have been a hundred girls and teachers, but no one said a word. A few daringly shuffled their feet. Others glanced around anxiously. How strange it was to stand in silence, as the India I was beginning to know was notoriously noisy, a place where everything was declared at the highest volume, clamoring for the world to hear.

The girls stood quietly in their rows, stiff as the queen's guards I'd seen on TV. Each skirt pleat had been ironed into knife edges. Each shirt had been perfectly pressed. Everyone had the same hairstyle, separated in the middle, done up in plaits, and kept in place with coconut oil, which I could smell all around me.

In contrast to the whitewashed military rows of the students, the teachers' line in front was a dazzling rainbow of multicolor and sequins. While these new teachers of mine were striking, they were nothing like the larger-than-life women of the Uhuru market in Tanzania.

My teachers looked more like my mother—skinnier and shorter and more subdued. Their dresses weren't made of the bold kanga of the savannahs but of satin-soft fabric from Asia. Draped in scarves and saris that flowed to their toes, these teachers sashayed in their rows, golden nose rings glittering in the sun. I watched them in rapture, dreaming of the day I'd get to dress like that.

The school monitor was walking down each row of students, stopping to inspect a pleat, a shirt collar, a hair plait. If anything was amiss, she rapped the girl's knuckles with a long steel ruler, while the rest of the girls winced, thanking their stars she hadn't picked on them.

She noticed me halfway through my row. Ignoring the other girls in line, she marched toward me, holding her steel ruler up in the air like a samurai sword. She stopped in front of me with a snort that echoed off the school walls. My heart started to beat fast and my palms began to sweat.

What does she want with me?

The other girls stood silently, eyes straight ahead. The monitor's beady eyes looked me up and down and stopped to give a penetrating look at my hair, which I'd done up exactly like every other girl in school that day. Her gaze went down to my shirt. I was wearing one of Preeti's old uniforms. Though Aunty Shilpa had ironed it the night before, it had become wrinkled from squeezing into and out of a crowded bus that morning, but Preeti had helped me get most of the creases out by hand.

The monitor's eyes ran down my legs, widening as they settled on my feet. I had on my precious red-heeled sandals. These were the last things my parents had bought me and after all I'd gone through, they were what kept me grounded, what linked me to my former life. I only took them off to get into bed at night.

The school monitor pointed at my hands and beckoned me to give them to her. With a feeling of dread, I opened my palms. I heard the steel ruler hit before I felt the cruel sting. She hit me not once, not twice, but seven times.

Once the parade inspection was over, the girls got into small groups and wandered toward their classes, talking in muted tones. Preeti ran toward me and gave a gentle squeeze on my arm.

"Are you okay?"

I nodded, trying to hold back tears. The humiliation in my heart hurt far more than my throbbing hands.

"I'm so sorry," Preeti whispered. "Should have checked your shoes. Taking care of you is my duty. This is my fault."

I tried a weak smile and shook my head. "No, it's fine," I croaked. This had been my doing, not hers. And I'd paid the price.

The school bell rang. Preeti squeezed my arm quickly again before running off to her classroom. I knew she couldn't be late. I couldn't either. I turned around and walked to my classroom alone, my face flushed.

That was my first day.

More often than not, I found myself alone in the back of the classroom during lunch. Preeti tried to get me to join her during breaks, but I couldn't stand the whispering of the others. My cousin, a year older than I, had been coming to this school since grade one. She was also a popular girl here. Her hair was shiny, and blacker than midnight. Her kohl-lined eyes were large and round, and the dimple on her cheek was as endearing as her nature.

Preeti knew what to say and do, when to say and do it, and to whom. And she was always reminding me: "Put that away, good girls shouldn't eat in public." "Stop skipping on the sidewalk. Girls don't do that." "That skirt's too short. You can't go out like that." "Remember, I told you not to look at strange men. They'll think you like them."

There were so many mind-numbing rules, I couldn't remember them all. Next to the poised and cultured Preeti, I was a bumbling, odd curiosity—strange and alien, like the ugly duckling, but one that would never metamorphose into something better.

Everyone called me "the foreign girl," even the teachers. I thought I'd finally fit in, now that I was in India. I looked like everyone else around me, unlike at the international schools of Africa, but whenever I approached a girl to chat, others would stare and whisper, and some would point like I had chickenpox or something.

It didn't help that the school monitor made me her primary target.

I left my red sandals behind and wore an old pair of white canvas shoes that belonged to Preeti after that first day, but she gave me no slack. If it wasn't my shoes, it was my hair. If it wasn't my hair, it was because I'd reverted to English, which happened whenever she came close.

My brain stopped working when I got frightened, and the only language I could articulate was the one I'd grown up with. But as far as it concerned her, I was disobedient, so the steel ruler came out again and again.

There was no place to hide, not even a quiet library like at my old international schools.

There was one dusty shelf in a dark corner of my classroom, so during breaks, I'd sit on the floor and go through the books, teaching myself to read in languages I hadn't known existed a year ago. Since my father's language was Konkani and my mother's was Sinhalese, English was their common lingo. While I knew a few words of Konkani and Tamil and could understand simple sentences, I struggled in class. I wished I'd asked my parents to teach me their languages. I wished they were with me. I missed them badly. I even missed my old school.

But even those colossal African elephants couldn't drag me back to my past.

Chapter Six

A shrill whistle rang through the air, almost making me drop my books.

"Hey, you! Com'ere! Wanna show you something. Haha!"

We'd just come across a group of young men squatting next to their motorcycles in front of a bike store. They called out as soon they saw us. Preeti immediately bowed her head, and Aunty Shilpa grabbed her hand and mine and pulled us across the street. I hurried to keep up with them, not daring to look back at the leering men making lewd gestures.

Strolling through town with Aunty Shilpa and Preeti was a nice change to staying stuck in the dreary apartment with an unwelcoming Grandma. But one thing bothered me, and that was how the men stared. They stared until we disappeared from view, so we ended up walking stiffly like we had bull's eye marks on our backs and there was nothing we could do about it.

Sometimes, the men would come close and brush against us. After a few times, I recognized the difference between an accidental bump on a crowded street and a deliberate, unwanted touch. When any of this happened to any of us, Preeti and Aunty Shilpa would cross the road hurriedly, pulling me away with them.

I found it strange to be catcalled by men who were old enough to be my father. "Is this normal?" I asked them on my tenth day in Goa.

"Happens every day," Preeti said, with a defeatist shrug.

The next day, Aunty Shilpa decided it was time to teach me Indian street smarts.

It was a Sunday, the day when Grandma went to her various worshiping places and the three of us had the apartment to ourselves—the day when Preeti and Aunty Shilpa's faces softened and their shoulders relaxed.

The reason Grandma never took us with her was because girls were considered "dirty" and forbidden to enter religious places when menstruating. Not bothering to plan around our periods, Grandma went alone, which was perfectly fine with us.

"Listen carefully now," Aunty Shilpa instructed me in an officious tone. "When you walk outside, first, you cover your chest with your bag and hold it tight."

"Next, shove your elbows out and walk like this." Aunty Shilpa did an exaggerated strut in front us, her plastic bangles jingling with every step. Preeti and I collapsed on the sofa laughing.

"You look like a constipated chicken, Aunty Shilpa," I said when I finally caught my breath.

"You laugh, eh?" she said, with a mock stern look. "If you follow my instructions, no one will be eve-teasing you."

"Eve-teasing?" I asked. That was a new word for me.

"Don't you know anything?" Preeti said, throwing her hands in the air.

"Is that when girls pick on you, like at school?"

"No, it's when boys follow you, call you, and touch you everywhere," Preeti said, making a face, her beautiful eyes squinting in disgust.

"You're not a child anymore, Asha," Aunty Shilpa said, looking serious. "Stay away from crowds. That's where they corner you and you'll get stuck." Her voice broke, and she stopped to cough, holding her chest. She looked unwell, I thought.

"And don't look at men or boys in the eye," Preeti said, pointing a finger at my eyes, almost poking me. "Because they'll think you're loose."

"Loose?" I frowned. My parents had used that word to describe what happened after we'd had some bad food at a roadside stall. "I'm feeling really loose," my mother would warn my father in the front seat. "Find a restroom quick. That food had been lying under the sun all day." *Surely that can't be what Preeti means, can it?*

"And if Grandma ever finds out a boy likes you, she will *kill* you," Preeti said.

I knotted my forehead, trying to figure this out. This new protocol was as perplexing as it was complex.

"Yup," Preeti bobbed her head from side to side, the Indian nod I was becoming familiar with, "last year, she beat me with the broom because the boy next door said hello to me. Aunty Shilpa grabbed the stick away or I'd be gone by now."

I stared at my cousin with my mouth open.

"The most important thing to remember," Aunty Shilpa said, wagging a finger, "is if anyone tries to talk to you, or tries to give you a ride, or says they have a nice present for you, walk away quickly. Walk away. Do you understand that?"

I nodded.

"Or you'll disappear like Pushpa and Maya," Preeti said.

"Who's that?"

"They used to live upstairs," Preeti said, pointing at the ceiling.

"Where are they now?"

"They got sold," she said.

"*Sold?*"

"Uh-huh." Preeti nodded. "A man from Mumbai came one day and said he had jobs for girls in a factory in the big city. He said they'll make lots and lots of money and can send it to their families. Pushpa and Maya's family signed them up. They wanted me to go with them, but I wanted to finish school first."

"What happened to them?"

"A few months ago, our neighbor told us Pushpa was sold to a rich family in Dubai and Maya was sold to a family in Kuwait. They're slaves now."

"*Slaves?*" My eyes widened. "Can't they get out and come back?"

"It's not that easy," Aunty Shilpa said, shaking her head. "Terrible things happen to girls who go to the Middle East. Even Lebanon, Qatar, and even Saudi Arabia." She gave a shudder after that last name. "They treat girls worse than how we treat street dogs. They work day and night till they die or till someone kills them."

"Don't you read the newspaper?" Preeti asked me.

I shook my head. I was learning to speak the language but couldn't read fully in Konkani yet, and I'd never heard such crazy stories when I lived in Africa.

"They sell Sri Lankan girls to work in rich Arab houses, don't you know?" Preeti seemed eager to share more of this horrifying news with me. "They're kicked and beaten, and they have to serve the man at night too."

"What do you mean?" I asked.

Preeti ignored me. "If anyone finds out you're half Sri Lankan, they'll get you too."

A cold shiver went down my spine.

"The thing is, don't believe strangers who make wonderful promises, okay?" Aunty Shilpa said. "Remember, no one can save you after you're taken."

The cities of India seemed far more dangerous than the jungles of Africa.

"Just be careful," Aunty Shilpa said, seeing my fearful expression. "It's different here."

Yes, things were different.

The sky, the ocean, the people, the markets—even the cows were different. I felt as lost as Alice when she fell down the rabbit hole. In Goa, I was at a Mad Hatter's tea party. Every. Single. Day.

I remembered, on road trips in East Africa, how I saw cow herds grazing in fields that stretched to the horizon. They munched on grass, flicking flies with their tails, while their spear-wielding caretakers hovered around, keeping an eye out for cheetahs and hyenas.

In contrast, the cows of India were lonely souls, vagabonds who loitered through the dusty streets with nothing to do but chew on rubbish. They sauntered unceremoniously in front of swanky hotels, surprising tourists. I felt sorry for these sacred cows, but it was the elephants that grabbed my attention.

I'd seen the elephants in the vast savannah lands on safari trips with my parents. Watching the smaller Indian elephant haul logs on the streets one day, I wondered if anyone had succeeded in taming their wild cousins back in Africa.

The thought of a skinny Indian mahout in a loincloth scampering up a thirteen-foot tusked African beast with ears flapping like giant sails made me laugh out loud. Preeti gave me a funny look. I smiled a sheepish smile and looked away. She'd never believe me if I told her about the extraordinary animals of Africa. My birthplace would be as strange to her as hers was to me.

If Africa was big and bold with open skies, India was a claustrophobe's nightmare. It was a constant tidal wave of colors, smells, and noises that rushed in and drenched me to the bone. The brightly colored saris of women walking by clashed with the brown rags of the beggars on the streets.

The sharp, acrid smell of incense burning mixed with the tang of marigold garlands strung together to be offered as gifts to the gods. Then, there were the honks from buses, toots from rickshaws, rings from bicycles, and the incessant sound of people everywhere. The cacophony was deafening and there was no escape.

Preeti, Aunty Shilpa and I spent every Sunday afternoon together when Grandma was busy worshiping her many gods and Aunty Shilpa didn't have to work. We'd sit cross-legged on the beach, licking pineapple ice pops to keep cool, with Aunty Shilpa's scarf acting as a thin beach blanket. While we people-watched, we kept an eye on the time so Grandma wouldn't get mad at us for coming home late.

We'd watch European tourists in Speedos stroll along the beach next to locals in full-length dress pants, shirt, and tie, looking good but sweltering under the tropical sun. Local women would dip into the waves fully clothed in silky saris right next to tourists in micro bikinis.

We didn't dare go in the water ourselves, partly because the ocean terrified Aunty Shilpa and partly because they told me Grandma would beat us if she got a whiff of the seasalt on us.

So instead, we'd cross the street to the market, ducking double-decker buses, concrete trucks, three-wheelers, two-wheelers, and even the occasional stray cow. Here, we'd discover sidewalks covered with brassware, children's' toys, cheap mobile phones, and T-shirts made at the nearby garment factory.

Some vendors put bamboo mats outside their stores to dry red chilies, which made me sneeze if I got too close. Woven baskets lined the streets, filled to the brim with sweet-smelling guavas, papayas, mangoes, rambutan, and passion fruit that made my mouth water every time I walked by.

Enchantments awaited us inside the mysterious spice stores where mounds of gold saffron were piled on tables like miniature pyramids. The one thing I didn't find in the stores of Goa was gulab jamun balls sprinkled with gold dust, real gold dust, those luxury sweets Shanti from my international school in Tanzania had boasted about. I never stopped looking for them.

Every little shop we walked by played transistor radio music, each song blending into the next as we strolled along the street. The songs I heard were not the sonorous African drumbeats that made your heart thump and the ground shake. They weren't the soulful Bollywood tunes where the hero and heroine wrapped themselves around a tree and looked achingly into each other's eyes, either.

The music of Goa was fast, light, and fun. It made me want to jump up and wiggle my hips, like the Sri Lankan *Baila* my mother used to listen to as we baked on Sunday mornings.

Everywhere we went, we saw tourists. Some looked like they'd just arrived. Others looked like they'd come decades ago, still dressed as they did in the sixties. While my father had badly wanted to escape Goa, this place seemed to be where everyone in the world was escaping to.

And why wouldn't they?

The skies above were permanently painted iris blue, speckled with puffs of cotton candy clouds. The water was an exquisite indigo hue and enchanting coconut mangroves littered the bays that curved along the city.

Aunty Shilpa told me Goa was where the Portuguese had come hundreds of years ago but had never left. In Goa, East and West blended so you were never sure where one ended and the other began. Snow-white, staid cathedrals stood proudly next to multihued Hindu temples, their facades covered in half-dressed figurines doing impossible poses. A mishmash of architecture. A mishmash of religions.

Grandma, like everyone else, went for catholic mass and, on her way back, stopped by the hindu temple to offer a flower garland to the other gods. When she got home, she'd light an incense stick for the shrine above her bed that contained a statue which looked suspiciously like a big-bellied buddha. It was all very confusing.

Though she worshiped at several churches to many gods, none of them seemed to soothe her angry heart. She found fault in everything. She lashed out at anyone about anything on a moment's notice, and she saved her worst wrath for me.

On my first day, I learned my job was to help her cook and do the kitchen work. I smiled when I heard about my chores as I couldn't have asked for anything better. This also meant I was being useful. I felt, maybe, just maybe, I'd soon belong.

But I learned quickly that wouldn't be easy. On my second day, she gave a stinging slap on my cheek for taking too long to bring in water from the outside tap. The next day, she slapped me harder for not putting enough salt in the curry. The day after that, she slapped me for dropping the big black pot. I hadn't been prepared to feel the heat of the iron cauldron on my fingers, but that was only an excuse for her.

Grandma was strong for a small woman. When she slapped me one day, because I'd mistakenly picked a roti from the communal plate using my left hand, I reeled back and tripped over the stove, making my curry bowl spill to the ground. There I sat, too ashamed to move, shaking while she shouted and called me a "savage girl." She made me clean it all up and go straight to bed without supper. That night, I swallowed my sobs.

It was nights like these I remembered the old times, life with my parents. I'd stare up at the ceiling and bring up long-forgotten memories, my mother's sweet smile, my father's kind words. I imagined the car crash as a nightmare I'd dreamed up on a sleepless night.

Though I knew in my bones they were gone forever and in a terrible way yet unknown to me, my mind conjured up images of them being alive back in Tanzania. Some nights, I even pretended they were coming to join me in Goa. One day. Soon.

Despite the leering men and Grandma's sharp slaps, Goa was exhilarating, overflowing with sounds, colors, smells, life. What at the beginning of my stay had felt overwhelming, was now invigorating. Though I didn't know it then, my stay in this country would be short-lived. But at the beginning, it was a welcome distraction from ruminations over my parents' deaths.

But I hadn't seen the dark underbelly of this town. Yet.

Chapter Seven

I'd just got off the school bus when I heard the commotion.

I whipped my head around and saw three teens surrounding the beggar woman at the bus station. I stopped and watched with a feeling of dread rising in me. I'd been in Goa for more than a year now and had seen these mob scrums before, but this time, something told me it was worse than usual.

"Oi! Weirdo!" one of the boys said to the beggar, almost spitting in her face.

"Sicko!" said the second boy, making an ugly face.

"You twisted freak!" the third boy taunted, pretending to punch her head. The woman ducked, her eyes wide in fear.

"Freak! Freak!" they hooted. The boys whistled and danced around her while she crouched low, shielding her head.

This beggar woman was what Grandma called a "dirty *hijra* from the north." When I described her to my teachers, they told me she was "most probably a transgendered person relocated from Delhi."

She'd arrived in town two months ago, and sat cross-legged in a corner of the station in her pink sari, playing haunting melodies on her bamboo flute. From the way she closed her eyes and the way her chest moved up and down when she played, I could see her soul was wrapped around that music. I wanted to close my eyes too, whenever I heard her play.

Against all advice from Preeti about talking to strangers, let alone beggars, I started chatting with her while we waited for the school bus to arrive. One morning, as Preeti was greeting her girlfriends at the bus stop, I walked over and said hello. She responded in kind. She told me she was from Mumbai and her name was Meena.

Meena's voice was rough and low, and her shoulders, visible through the sheer sari wraps, were muscular, but her face showed another side. Her black lined eyes were soft and her heavy lipsticked smile was warm, and through it all, it was clear she wasn't much older than Aunty Shilpa. She wore cheap makeup on her face, but that didn't cover the scar on her cheek. "A knife scar," Preeti explained, before going on a monologue about how good girls don't go talking with street beggars.

That evening, I saved up a roti from my dinner plate, wrapped it carefully in newspaper, and hid it in a corner of Grandma's kitchen. The next morning, I packed it quietly in my school satchel and brought it with me to the bus station. I never forgot Meena's smile when I handed it to her. The roti was nothing more than a few dry bites, but I knew it wasn't the food that made her smile.

I was as foreign to this place as she was, and that formed an unspoken bond between us.

The teens harassing her were a mainstay at the station and had been there ever since I started school a year ago. We usually found them squatting like vultures hunkering for prey on the concrete barrier at the station, under the big yellow sign that said, "Good and Fast Immigration Broker."

Some days, they threw pebbles at incoming buses to get a rise out of the overworked, short-tempered bus drivers. Other days, they used slingshots to shoot pebbles at schoolgirls disembarking from the buses. The worst was their hollers to "come closer," be their "friend," or "touch this."

All three boys lived in our apartment compound so we knew who they were, but Preeti and I gave them special names. The oldest was Nuthead, the biggest of the three. He wore a dirty, oversized sarong, a square piece of cloth wrapped around the waist and hiked up to the knees to make it easy to walk.

In that neighborhood, what you wore showed how close you were to manhood. Shorts were for boys, pants were for teens, and sarongs were for men. In my mind, though, none of these juveniles were close to becoming men anytime soon.

Scratchy liked to rub himself between his thighs whenever he saw girls. He was as thin as a rake and was always holding his ratty pants up with one hand. "Doesn't he know what a belt is for? What a twit," Preeti had said in exasperation one day when Scratchy had been particularly annoying. He heard her and hollered right back, "It's to thrash you girls to a pulp, that's what!" That day, we ran home so fast, I got a cramp in my thighs.

Fartybag was the short and chubby one, and with his curly mop of hair, he looked younger than his friends. He always wore a faded Rambo T-shirt and had a tendency to urinate on the concrete barrier in public view. Even while doing so, his head would swivel around looking for girls to whistle at, while we tried to scurry out of his view.

No one complained or called the authorities about these boys. The other girls didn't seem to notice anything. Whenever the boys catcalled, they clutched their books against their chests and hastened their steps to duck under the bus shelter, eyes downcast—like good girls were supposed to.

They pretended nothing was happening, but they got picked on too—on the street, at the school, at the bus stop, even inside the bus. The worst was inside the bus.

Some days, when I got stuck in the middle of a sweaty, smelly crowd, I'd feel a slimy arm rub on my chest, or worse, a hand crawl up my leg underneath my skirt. When that happened, I'd scrunch my body and stop breathing. I'd feel like I wanted to puke. I'd pretend it wasn't happening. I'd pray for it to stop. I knew I needed to say something, cry for help, but every time, my voice disappeared.

The minute the bus lurched to a stop or people moved even one inch, I'd push through the walls of sarongs and saris to get away from the creepy hands. On those days, I'd walk home feeling sick to my stomach, angry at the world until I got home and buried the nauseating memories under my pillow.

The three teens at the bus stop were getting louder.

"You dirty thing!" Fartybag yelled at the beggar woman.

"I will show you how to be a woman!" Scratchy shouted, making Meena crouch lower.

"I will trash you just like a woman!" Nuthead said with an ugly laugh.

Normally Preeti would be with me, but that day, Aunty Shilpa had forced her to stay home to recover from a bad flu. The other girls had walked away quickly as soon as they'd seen what was happening. I wanted to say something, but I didn't know what.

I looked around. There were adults near the station. They saw but took a wide berth to avoid the commotion. Three bus drivers on their breaks were squatting nearby, playing cards, absorbed in their game.

I ran up to them.

"Excuse me," I said. "Please?"

One of them looked up and squinted.

"Those boys are shouting at Meena," I said, pointing. "Can you do something?"

The men snickered.

"They said they're going to hit her!"

"What business is that of yours?" One man waved his hand dismissively.

"Go home, girl, and stop bothering grown-ups," another said, not looking up. He slapped a card down with gusto. "Aha!" he said, and the others turned back to the game like I wasn't even there.

I looked up to see Nuthead punch Meena on the head. For real, this time.

"Aii!" she screeched, her face contorted in fear as Nuthead's arm went up for another blow.

"Hey!"

The blow came down, harder this time. Meena quivered on the ground.

"Stop that!" I yelled running toward the group, my arms waving. "I said, stop it!"

The boys turned and stared.

"Leave her alone!" My voice was firm. My legs were solid. My hands were fists.

Fartybag was looking at me, his mouth open.

"Huh?" Scratchy said, his hand paused in the air, forgetting to scratch himself for an instant, making his pants fall a few dangerous inches lower.

"*What* did you say?" Nuthead asked with a scowl.

"I said, leave her alone!" It felt good to stand up to them, to tell them how I truly felt for once.

Fartybag snorted.

"Oooh. Stop it," Scratchy jeered.

"Stop hitting her or I'll tell my monitor!" I said, looking at each of them right in the eye.

"Is that right?" Scratchy said. "I'm so very scared of your m-o-n-i-t-o-r."

"She'll show you," I said. "You big, fat bullies!"

Nuthead's face turned dark. "I'll teach you to talk to us like that," he said in a low warning voice. He took a step toward me.

"No!" It was Meena, gesticulating behind him. "Run, Asha, *run!*"

I watched in dread as Nuthead strode toward me. Suddenly, I didn't feel so solid anymore.

I was trying to decide which way to run when a series of loud pops came from Fartybag. He'd surprised Preeti and me on more than one occasion with his personal noises. Normally, we'd cover our mouths and walk away, snickering, but I didn't feel like laughing now.

But that stopped Nuthead in his tracks. He and Scratchy turned and looked at Fartybag.

"Wowzer! That was a big one!" Nuthead said, crinkling his nose.

"Ha, ha, ha!" Scratchy laughed. "You'll stink us to death!"

"You're all so disgusting," I said, without realizing I'd said it out loud. With all the laughing around me, I didn't hear Fartybag race toward me. Faster than a cheetah, he was within inches of my face, backing me against the station wall.

I looked at him in surprise. He normally shuffled when he walked, always behind the other two, slow to move and slow to think.

"Don't you laugh at me, girl!" he shouted, pointing a stubby finger at me. His face was beetroot red, either from the exertion of running the few steps or from the fury at being made fun of.

"I wasn't laughing at you," I said, looking at him squarely. "It's your friends who're laughing at you."

Behind him, I could hear Meena beseeching him to leave me alone and for me to get out *now*.

"You talk back to me?" Fartybag said. "I'm gonna punish you!" His black eyes bored into mine.

"Back off!" I said, looking straight back into his eyes. My blood was pumping through my veins and my breath was coming fast and furious. Something strong, something like a steel thread, was weaving through my spine.

Fartybag's friends were hollering behind him.

"Get her!"

"Show her who's boss!"

"She's only a stupid girl."

Fartybag thrust his hands up and slammed me against the wall. "I'll teach you to make fun of me!" he said. I could smell his breath, a vile mixture of cigarettes and curry.

That steel thread had become stronger. Without hesitating an instant, I clenched my right hand into a fist and swung my arm up. I

punched Fartybag's nose, just like I'd learned in my martial arts classes at the international schools.

Upper hook. Right on that soft target.

Fartybag gave me a startled look.

I raised my arm and punched again. Harder.

He clutched his nose and backed away groaning.

I stepped forward, fist still in the air. He stepped backward, still
holding his nose, staring at me confused.

There was silence as his friends took in what had happened.

I stood immobile, staring at my clenched hand in surprise. *Did
I just hit him? Twice?* I looked fearfully at the other boys, who were
now staring at me in shock. Behind them, Meena was on her feet, her
hands on her head, looking at me in a mixture of awe and confusion.

"She-dog who came out of the back of a mongrel," Fartybag
mumbled, glaring at me.

They're going to kill me.

I was about to run when Nuthead blocked me. I turned and
bumped right into Scratchy.

"Where you going?" he said, with a nasty grin on his face.

"You think we will let you go after you hit our friend?" Nuthead
said. He was standing with his arms crossed, smiling, but it wasn't a
nice smile. Before I could blink, he pulled the satchel off my shoulder, ripped it open and threw my books on the ground.

"Hey!" I said, grabbing my empty satchel back. "Give that back!"

He picked up my history book, tore it, stomped on it, and spat
on the ripped pile of paper. "Go tell your monitor now!" he said,
while the other two surrounded me, howling with laughter.

I bent down to pick up my books. Just as I stooped, I felt a sharp
kick on my thigh.

"Ouch!"

Someone tried to pull down my skirt. I heard it rip.

"Hey!" I straightened up quickly, clutching my skirt. "Get away from me!"

"Ha, ha!" The boys were enjoying the show. That's when Nuthead grabbed my chest.

"Booby! Booby!"

"Stop that!" I let my books fall to the ground and hugged myself to stop them from touching me.

They laughed.

I ducked around Nuthead before he could grab me again.

And, I ran.

I ran out of the station and onto the main road, my heart pounding like mad.

"Get her!" I heard Scratchy call out to his friends.

"She's mine!" Nuthead yelled.

I doubled my speed.

Chapter Eight

"**O**y!"
I stopped and bent over, hyperventilating.

I prayed it was a police officer, a teacher, someone in authority. I'd have been happy to see our school monitor, but the voice was coming from an obese, middle-aged man, wearing nothing but a faded blue sarong.

"Oy!" he shouted again.

I froze. It was the candy store man whom Preeti and I saw as we passed his store on our way to school every day. His shop was dark and dank, with see-through candy jars on the counter and a million forbidden knickknacks on the shelves. Pictures of Hindu gods hung on the walls, and long incense sticks stuck out of glass jars filled with sand, their gray smoke swirling up and around the gods, making them look ethereal.

The candy store man had a huge handlebar mustache that covered his entire upper lip, and his face was pockmarked like someone had gone digging on his skin. Though his sweets looked tempting, we didn't dare step into his store. Preeti, who'd do anything for a candy bar or piece of chocolate, wouldn't even look his way. His shop looked like just the place where our nightmares would come alive. And he looked exactly like the bogeyman of our imaginations.

He was standing at the doorway of his confectionery shop now, a grass broom in his hand and a scowl on his face. I'd dashed right through the dirt he'd carefully swept out of his shop, scattering dust, food crumbs, and loose paper all over the place.

"Oh!" I said, seeing the mess I'd made. "I'm so s...sorry."

He glared.

Behind me, I could hear the boys getting closer. I looked around desperately. Before I could make a move, the candy store man stomped out of his shop and grabbed me by the arm.

"Hey!" I yelled. "Let go!" I struggled, my empty satchel falling to the ground and making the dust fly.

He pulled me inside the store. I wriggled, trying to get away, but he was too strong. He heaved me toward the store counter and plunked me on a wooden stool. The smell of incense was so strong, it choked me. My heart was beating so loudly I felt my chest would burst open.

"Konkani?" the man said, stooping down till he was level with my eyes.

His mouth was dripping with red juice and smelled of something putrid. I pulled back in disgust. From the red gobs and splats of spit all over the streets of Goa, it seemed every man in this city was addicted to the betel nut. Right then, it looked like blood. His hairy arms and chest made him look like a gorilla from the jungles of the Congo. I was sure I was about to be devoured. My throat went dry. I barely managed to shake my head.

"You not from here?" he said, more to himself than me. The boys were at the store now. I could hear them whooping outside, which meant they'd found my satchel. I wasn't sure which was worse, being chased by the boys outside or being held captive by the bogeyman inside.

"Found you!" Scratchy came inside first, followed by his friends, all short-winded but smug.

"You're so dead," Fartybag said.

Nuthead sauntered in behind them like he owned the place.

My heart started to pound like mad.

The boys were looking at me with hideous smirks on their faces. I turned to look at the candy store man, who was regarding the boys like they were an infestation of insects. I was trapped. I glanced around quickly. The back of the store looked scarier. *Who knows what's back there?* The steel in my spine was still strong. I had only one thought in my mind. *I'm getting out of here alive.* I jumped from the stool and grabbed the broomstick from the candy store man's hands.

"Hey!" he said, startled. "What're you doing, girl?"

"Get away from me!" I yelled at him. His eyes widened in surprise.

Holding the broom like a spear, I jumped toward the boys. They jerked back.

"Oi!" Nuthead yelled.

"Whoa!" Scratchy said, holding his hands up.

"Stop!" Fartybag covered his face.

"No, *you* stop!" I shouted, reverting to English, the only language that came to my tongue when I was cornered. "I'm sick of you lot!" I shouted, slashing the air with my weapon. "I'm sick and tired of you picking on us. I'm sick and tired of you yelling at us every day. You bunch of creepy perverts!"

No one said a word. They just stood and gaped.

"You picked on poor Meena. I can't believe you hit her. She's a *beggar*! Just a poor beggar and you *hit* her! How could you do that? How dare you? You horrible, donkey-brained, stupid turkey-cowards!"

I'd run out of expletives, so I glowered at them instead, my broomstick still aimed at their necks. I was sure they hadn't understood a word I'd said, but when I took a step forward, the boys scrambled over each other and bunched up in a corner of the store.

"Ha ha ha!"

I turned around to see the candy store man laughing, head thrown back, his belly jiggling like Jell-O. "Oooh," he said finally, holding his stomach with one hand and wiping his eyes with the other. "Oooh."

He reached a hand toward me in slow motion. I watched him warily. "Give," he said, pointing at the broom. I didn't budge. He motioned at the door and gave the Indian sideways head nod. "You, go."

It took me a few seconds to release my grip on the broom. He leaned over and plucked the stick from my hands.

"Go," he said with that sideways nod again.

Keeping an eye on him and the boys, I stepped backward, toward the open doorway. When I got to the door, the candy store man thrust the broom up, like our school monitor held out her steel ruler every morning, and turned toward the boys.

Their eyes widened with fear.

"You boys!" The candy store man raised his voice. "If I see you run after little girls again, I'll whip you so hard your hide will remember my broomstick for the rest of your life. You understand?"

Scratchy's face went white, Nuthead didn't know where to look and Fartybag slinked into the wall.

"This is how you treat your sister? Huh? Your cousin? Your mother? You ignorant idiots!" The candy man gestured dangerously with the broom. "You think you're so smart to run after little girls? I will teach you smart!" He took a menacing step forward.

Fartybag squealed.

I didn't wait to see. I stepped out of the doorway, picked up my satchel and raced home like the wind.

Chapter Nine

"Aunty Shilpa! Preeti!" I crashed through the doors of our apartment, panting loudly. "Oh my god, you've no idea what just happened!"

Preeti was lying on the sofa and gave me a weak smile. Aunty Shilpa was pressing our school uniforms in a corner of the room and Grandma was hunched over the fire, as usual, stirring a clay pot that was sizzling with spicy potato masala, making the whole apartment smell divine, quelling any other odors coming our way.

My father's family had moved out of the slums and into this government-built complex a long time ago, as part of a program to give slum dwellers a better life. "A Change for the Better," was the program's slogan, Aunty Shilpa told me.

Their new apartment was on the ground floor of the complex and wasn't far from the communal toilets. Some days, the smell was overpowering, but at least, Aunty Shilpa said, there was a tap with running water outside, a roof over their heads, and four walls, though part of it was already crumbling. "They just wanted our votes," Grandma grumbled every time something stopped working.

Living here was a change for me too. After having had only two parents to fight over one bathroom every morning, I now waited in long lines with the women and girls of the ten other families on our floor. All for a two-minute cold shower that trickled brown water, and for the use of the dirty hole in the ground that was our common toilet.

I turned to Preeti. "You know those boys at the bus station—"

Grandma looked up sharply. "What boys?" She turned and glared at me. Her eyes were milky white with cataracts, but sometimes I swore she saw better than any of us. "Are you talking to boys now?"

"No, Grandma, I didn't talk to them. They were being really mean to me, so I told them off."

"Told them off?"

"Did you do anything naughty now?" Aunty Shilpa asked.

"No, they started it. They were shouting at Meena. They even hit—"

"Who's Meena?" Grandma snapped.

Preeti sat up quickly and shot me a warning look. "She's a girl in our school."

Preeti was sitting on the frayed sofa that doubled as our bed at night. She looked pale from the flu she'd been fighting all week. On her lap was her secret diary, a small pink book with hearts all over the cover. She told me it held her dreams. No one was allowed to touch it, not even Grandma. She took it with her everywhere she went, to school, to the beach, even to the market.

Preeti was a shy girl who stuck close to her friends. Her mother had died in childbirth and her father, my father's oldest brother, had been crushed by an errant machine at the stone quarry where he'd worked. Unlike me, she didn't seem to miss them much. Maybe, it was because she never had a chance to know them well.

For Preeti, school and books were everything—her whole life. She had a brain and dreamed of becoming a pediatrician, or a "baby-doctor" as she called it. I was sure she'd succeed as she was always first in her class in all subjects, except for English. I held that honor now.

The adrenaline from my scrimmage with the boys was still hot in my veins. I was bursting to tell my story to someone. Anyone. I plopped down next to Preeti on the sofa bed.

"You know those boys who pick on us every day?" I said. Preeti nodded. "When I got off the bus today, I saw them hitting Mee...I mean, that girl. She looked really scared and no one was helping her, so I shouted at them and told them to stop."

"You didn't!" Preeti said, drawing in a sharp breath.

"They came after me too. Nuthead pushed me and Fartybag tried to hit me, but I hit him first, right on the nose." My voice has gotten louder. "I hit him twice!" I suddenly realized what I'd done and grinned to myself. *It feels good to fight back.* "I hit him really, really hard."

Aunty Shilpa was staring with her mouth open. Grandma was staring too, but her look was of severe disapproval.

"What's this nonsense you are talking, child?" Grandma asked.

"They were awful, Grandma," I said. "They threw my books on the floor and pulled my skirt. It was horrible. They called me bad names and I shouted at them to stop but they didn't listen." My words tumbled out haphazardly, and it took some effort not to revert to English. "I ran away and when I got to the candy store, I took the candy store man's broom and stuck it to the boys. The man helped me even."

"You mean the *bogeyman?*" Preeti asked, eyes as wide as saucers.

"Yes, but he's a good man. You should never judge someone by how they look, Preeti," I admonished my cousin. "Anyway, he tried to help me. And the boys got really scared."

"I tell you!" Grandma banged the pot with her spoon, making us jump. "What's wrong with this girl?"

"You're just making this up, aren't you?" Aunty Shilpa said quickly, her eyes steady on mine as if trying to tell me something. "You're just telling us a story, right?"

"No, no," I said, shaking my head vigorously. "It really happened, just now. I swear. Look at my skirt. Look at what they did." I pointed at the rips on my clothes and the red scrapes on my knees. "It was a big fight."

"Fight?" Grandma spat.

"I had to defend myself," I said. "There were three of them."

"My Lord, have mercy on this idiot of a girl. She knows nothing about honor," Grandma said to the ceiling.

"Honor for what?" I said.

"Honor for *what*?" Grandma looked flabbergasted I'd even asked the question.

"I don't know what you were taught in those African schools, but it is different here," she said. "Good girls don't go running around in the streets talking to boys. A girl always bows to the gods and sadhus of the temple, then to her parents, and then to her husband. That is how she becomes respectable. If you don't know that, you are as good as a mongrel on the street."

I looked at Aunty Shilpa and Preeti. Both had eyes downcast.

"That is our culture." Grandma jabbed the potatoes violently. "Listen to me and learn to become a good Indian girl for once."

Grandma owned India's culture. There was only one way, and that was her way.

"I told you about eve-teasing, Asha," Aunty Shilpa said in a soft voice. "You just need to be more careful, dear."

Aunty Shilpa was the careful one.

She was also our aunt and therefore, responsible for us girls. She was my father's youngest sibling and only sister, barely twenty when I met her. She looked like an older Preeti with her long black hair framing her heart-shaped face. Her midnight-black eyes and long eyelashes made it look like she was wearing makeup, though she couldn't afford any. Her hair was done in one thick braid that hung down to her knees.

If Preeti was pretty, Aunty Shilpa was beautiful. Though she had lines on her brow and calluses on her hands from overworking, men were always following her on the streets.

Her much older husband had died six months earlier. Childless and husband-less, she was now as good as a leper. No one wanted her near their home for fear of the bad luck she could bring. Normally, a family would never accept a widow back into their home, so she had been one of the lucky ones, I was told. Back in the village, she told me one day, she'd have been burned the same day they cremated her husband. I took a sharp breath.

"You mean like Princess Aouda?" I asked.

"Who's this Princess Ooda?" she said, wrinkling her brow.

"Oh, no one special," I said, remembering Aunty Shilpa couldn't read. "Just a story I read a long time ago." The stories in my father's favorite book, *Around the World in Eighty Days,* had been so fantastic I was sure they lived only in the wild imagination of its author. To learn something so ghastly happened in real life was shocking.

"That would have made me respectable and revered," Aunty Shilpa said wistfully.

Burnt and dead too, I thought with a shudder. "But it wasn't your fault your husband died," I said. "It was an accident, so how can they blame you?"

"That's not the point," Aunty Shilpa said, looking at me with sad eyes. She sighed. "You're just a child. You'll understand when you're older."

"I still think it's wrong," I said. "Fogg thought it was wrong too."

"Who's this fog? You think too much about these things, Asha," she said. "Only the gods can know what's right and wrong."

"Then how can they let girls burn like that?"

Aunty Shilpa paused and bit her lip. Maybe she realized how strange her statement had been.

"And how come the police don't stop this sort of bad things from happening?" I asked.

Aunty Shilpa sighed loudly. "If you have enough money, you can pay them to not see anything." She paused. "They don't work for poor people like us."

"Are you serious?" I said.

"If it makes you feel better," she said, with another sigh, "the ashrams take in widows these days. They don't burn them anymore, at least in the city."

Yes, I'd seen these women and their children begging near the temple. Whether in a village or in a city, a widow's life ended at her husband's pyre. But Grandma had been kind. She'd taken Aunty Shilpa in even though she was almost an untouchable. That Aunty Shilpa had found a job cleaning toilets in a luxury hotel right on the beach, one teeming with rich Western tourists who liked to give big tips, wasn't such a bad thing.

Aunty Shilpa was the only breadwinner in the family and Grandma knew exactly which side her chapati was buttered.

"Always talking back, always running around and blackening our family name," Grandma was talking angrily to her pot now. "What will the neighbors think? They will spit on me one of these days." She banged the spoon on her pot again, making us all jump. "That is what happens when you take in a foreign girl. A good Indian mother would teach her these things. The problem with this girl is she has too much of her mother's blood. *That* is the problem."

I pulled back like I'd been stung.

"Sri Lanka's not like India," This time she looked at me as she spoke. "No rules, no traditions, no respectability. Savages. That's what your mother was."

"How can you say that?" I blurted out. "Stop disrespecting my mama!"

"Oh, Lord Vishnu!" Grandma cried as she stood up, her old bones cracking with every move. She walked toward me, holding her curry-soaked wooden spoon high. "Oh, my Lord, save this girl!"

I watched her come close in dread. Grandma bent down and slapped my thighs hard. I winced.

"When will this stupid girl learn?" She towered over me, waving her spoon. "Look at your skirt! Like those tourist girls who come here wearing next to nothing. Are you going to start running around naked like them?" She glared. "You think you're a white girl? This is why the boys follow you and talk to you. Because you make them."

"*Make* them?" I asked.

"I should make you stay home and learn to cook and clean like all the other little girls. Maybe it's time to stop you going to school!"

I stared at her. *Didn't she hear anything I'd said?*

"If you were a boy, I would already give you a proper beating!"

I looked up at Grandma, standing in front of me with her hands on her hips and a frown on her face, looking like she'd grown into a giant over the past few minutes. I'd been preparing to tell her about my schoolbooks, the ones on the ground at the bus station, dirty and spat on, but decided this wasn't the time for that news. I glued my knees together and sat straight, just like a good little Indian girl.

"But Grandma," I said in my most respectful voice, "I was only trying to defend myself."

Ignoring me, she walked back to her pot, muttering to herself, "It's time to take care of this footloose girl for good."

Chapter Ten

I f anyone had been footloose, it had to be my father.

My father had always dreamed of seeing the world. He never talked about his childhood, but I knew it had been very different from mine.

The fastest way to annoy him was to beg for pocket money. "You are spoiled, my child," he'd mutter, doling out a few shillings. "There were days when I didn't have anything to eat when I was your age."

Is that really true? I'd wonder but didn't dare ask.

My father wasn't much of a talker—unless he was preaching to me about school. Those Sunday mornings when I baked with my mother were the best times to ask my burning questions.

"Why didn't Papa have enough food to eat when he was a kid?"

"Is India really hot? Is it like the Kalahari desert?"

"Can we visit Sri Lanka one day?"

"Did your mama teach you to bake when you were a girl?"

"Have you ever eaten a gulab jamun with real gold sprinkles?"

Little by little, between sifting flour and mixing dough, my mother told me about herself and my father, how they met, their childhoods, and their lives before me. When she told me her stories, I listened enthralled, only paying half attention to my baking chores.

As a young boy growing up in India, my father used to watch the enormous ships that came into the harbor. He stared in wonder at the strange pale-skinned travelers who spilled onshore with their cameras and wide-brimmed hats. He would have given his soul to join them, to board one of those shiny ships and sail beyond the horizon.

His friends mocked him and his siblings teased him. His parents made a living growing vegetables along the railway tracks near the slums, and had a hard time feeding their five children.

My father, his brothers, and his sister, Aunty Shilpa, had worked since the day they learned to walk. No one believed a grubby boy from a low-caste family from the outskirts of a shantytown could travel outside the city. Journeying outside of Goa, let alone India, was an unthinkable extravagance. A childish fantasy.

Over time, though, and with help from newfound friends at tourist cafés and shops where he hung around in his spare time, my father taught himself to read in English. He was a keen student, and eventually put himself through the local shantytown school, but it hadn't been easy.

His brothers thought he was being lazy. His mother accused him of being selfish. His father gave him a good beating more than once, for neglecting his duties and disappearing to school.

My father, though, had a dream and wouldn't let go. He saved scraps of paper reeking of dead fish, stolen from fishmonger stalls, so he could write. He swiped any pen or pencil left unchecked at store counters, and he dove into garbage dumpsters at the back of bookstores, cafés and schools to unearth the one thing he treasured most: books, especially books about adventures in far-off, exotic lands.

The dumpsters behind international hostels where young Europeans and Americans stayed offered the best selection of all. Sometimes he found trash, but there had also been gems, like the day he discovered the tattered copy of Jules Verne's *Around the World in Eighty Days*. He had found it without a cover, ripped, and smeared in fish oil. He'd cleaned it, taped back the pages, and carried it with him for the rest of his life.

But the greatest mystery of my childhood was how my parents had got married.

Every once in a while, I'd ask for the hundredth time, "Mama, how come Papa is from India and you're from Sri Lanka?"

It took a long time before my mother opened up on this. It was three months before the car crash and we were making cakes for my father's thirty-eighth birthday. To the twelve-year-old me, he was as ancient as the baobab trees of the savannah.

"Papa's getting old," I said to my mother as I poured the batter into blue cake liners. We were making his favorite cakes that day, chai fairy cakes, a rare treat for us all. She laughed. "He's not *that* old, honey."

Like good chocolate and fresh strawberries, loose chai tea leaves were not easy to find in East Africa at that time. My mother got her baking supplies from an Indian store in town.

It was a musty shop that sold outdated Bollywood videos, samosas smothered in oil, and illegal fifty-kilogram bags of rice with the blue UNICEF logo still on them. They even exchanged local currency for US dollars for a hefty fee, which you had to do if you ever wished to buy something from the fancy duty-free store downtown. At the back of this old shop was where the owners kept the special ingredients my mother ordered in advance.

My parents rarely squabbled, but I knew this was an issue between them.

"How can you go to that place?" my father would say. "You're encouraging the black market, don't you know?"

"That's the only place I can find the ingredients I need," my mother would reply in defense.

One day, I jumped in. "Everyone in school goes to the duty-free store or to Jo'burg," I said. "Even Shanti's family."

"We can't afford to go to Johannesburg to buy groceries, or anything else for that matter, honey," my mother explained. "We're not rich like Shanti."

So, we baked using the out-of-date ingredients from that musty store. Still, I remember the cakes tasting delicious, and my father's birthday cakes were no exception.

That day, while we waited for the cakes to rise in the oven, my mother decided it was time to tell me their story.

My parents had met at a university in England. They'd been on a program that gave scholarships to students from Commonwealth countries, students with high grades but with no funds to finish school.

It was the day my father returned home in the last summer of university that everything turned upside down.

His overseas education had initially turned him from self-absorbed son to local superstar in his shantytown, but no one was prepared to hear his announcement the day he came back.

He was planning to marry a girl he'd met in the UK, a *foreign* girl at that. The whole family, including grandparents, uncles, aunts, distant cousins, and neighbors, shunned him. "Even the lowest-caste families have standards to uphold," they murmured to each other, shaking their heads. "Doesn't he know these simple facts? What good is an education if he doesn't understand the basic principles of life?"

"My good god!" my grandfather had cried. "Marrying a non-Indian? May Lord Vishnu strike you for the shame you bring us!"

"You abandon your own family like this? You're no longer my son!" Grandma had said when he asked her permission to marry the woman he loved.

"We told you so," the sages of the neighborhood had said, nodding wisely. "This is what happens when you let your children go to school. When you allow them to go abroad, they lose all respect for our traditions."

My father went from hero to outcast within a day.

It had been much worse for my mother, who'd also returned home with this news. She was the youngest of four daughters of a poor but up-and-coming family living on the outskirts of Colombo.

Over the years, her father had progressed from selling cinnamon sticks on the streets to carrying mail for the post office, a substantial jump in income and social status, a jump their mother never let anyone forget. Each of her four daughters had graduated from secondary school, a first in a community where women didn't finish school but stayed home to cook, clean, and have babies. It was progress but old beliefs prevailed.

On my mother's return, within minutes of intense cross-examination, her family discovered, to their utter horror, my father's background.

"What kind of children do you expect to breed with this dark-skinned Tamil?" my eldest aunt said, spitting on the ground.

"Konkani," my mother had tried to explain.

"No matter," her sister had replied, "he's not our kind."

Kind? That always perplexed me.

I never noticed the differences between my parents or those of my classmates and teachers at my international schools. I knew they came from many countries and different backgrounds, but their "kind" was never something that came to mind. What I always remembered was how they treated me and how they made me feel.

I knew my father was color-blind; he had a hard time telling the difference between a blueberry cupcake and a mint one until he took a bite. Maybe, I thought, I was becoming color-blind too. They say it's an inherited condition.

"This is what happens when you leave the village," my mother's mother wailed, beating her chest. "You get corrupted by foreigners. *Aiyo Bodhisattva.* What to do now?"

"If you leave with him, you leave us forever," my eldest aunt had said, dismissing her sister with a wave of her hand.

"Ané," cried the more compassionate of my aunts. "My young sister, what is this you're doing? Let us find a good Sinhalese man for you."

"But he loves me and I love him," my mother said. "Can't you understand?"

Her pleas fell on deaf ears. My mother had cried for days, knowing she had to make a choice between the man she loved and her family. I cried, too, when she shared this story with me.

In the end, my parents had followed their hearts. They moved, leaving behind their families, their friends, their pasts.

They used their newly acquired degrees to find work overseas. Their journey over the years hadn't been easy, but they had made a new future together. Not an extravagant one, but a far better one than either could have imagined in their poverty-ridden childhoods.

I didn't know it then, but my parent's actions had left an indelible impression on me.

Part THREE

Who wants to die?
Everything struggles to live.
Look at that tree growing up there out of that grating.
It gets no sun, and water only when it rains.
It's growing out of sour earth.
And it's strong because its hard struggle to live is making it strong.
Betty Smith

Chapter Eleven

We never saw it coming. Not even Aunty Shilpa.

It was twelve months after my confrontation with the boys at the station. That evening, Grandma asked me to cook dhal curry and coconut roti for supper, a chore I was getting good at.

I kneaded and flattened the dough on a chipped plate and flipped each roti on the flat iron pan. Grandma turned the fire low. "So the flavors will work hard and mix well," she said. I sat next to the warm fire with a wooden spatula in my hand, mesmerized by the sizzle of the onions, coconut, coriander, and semolina as they worked hard to make our delicious dinner.

As much as I hated Grandma dictating my life, I loved cooking. It was one reason she tolerated me and didn't throw me out of her home, I was sure. Every afternoon after school, I sat next to her in the kitchen, watching carefully, taking notes in my head, amazed at how simple things like flour, honey, fruit, and spices could come together and make mouthwatering treats. As I learned to cook over time, her yells and slaps became less frequent.

Playing with ingredients consumed all my attention. I mixed and stirred and fried and broiled, worrying of nothing other than what I wanted to add next, how long I needed to stir, or when to move the pan from the fire. When I focused on my cooking, the world receded around me. I forgot about having lost my parents and having left my birth home. I forgot I didn't have any friends in school and how men harassed me on my way to school. Most of all, I forgot I was a stranger in this strange land. When I cooked, I felt I'd found home.

Aunty Shilpa was ironing her hotel maid uniform in the corner. Supper was ready, but Grandma wanted to make an offering of the food to her Kali Ma goddess statue before we ate. While she prayed, I cleaned the kitchen and joined Preeti on the sofa bed to finish my homework. She was writing a letter to a penpal on pretty pink paper, fully absorbed in her task. The smell of the coconut oil on the roti skillet hung in the air, making me feel full and drowsy. My chemistry book was laid out in front of me, but I was having a hard time keeping my eyes open.

In Goa, I had to learn every one of my textbooks by heart. Night after night, I read and reread books on history, religion, biology, and language, memorizing every word, every paragraph so I could regurgitate it the next day in front of my class or on an exam. That evening, I was getting ready for the chemistry exam, writing out equations over and over again.

I had no clue what they meant. They could have been a cure for cancer or a concoction to change the color of cabbage juice, but it didn't matter because the best grades went to those who remembered the most. Not those who tried to understand or inquire more deeply. It was very different from the international schools in East Africa where I learned to ask questions, rethink ideas, and never take anything at face value. I was nodding over my chemistry book, my pencil almost slipping from my fingers, when Grandma walked over, her prayers finished.

"Asha, my dear granddaughter," Grandma said.

I sat up and blinked. Preeti looked up with a frown.

Grandma bent down and gently pulled the pencil out of my hand and closed my book. She reached to caress my hair. I pulled back like I was about to be bitten. Preeti, Aunty Shilpa, and I instinctively went on guard whenever she became nice, which didn't happen often. Something was up.

"In a few months, you will belong to the Kristadasa family. They will take good care of you, my dear."

Grandma gave me a beatific smile fit for Mother Theresa. A chill went down my spine. I was fully awake now. Other than the noise of water running in the communal washroom nearby, no other sound could be heard in the apartment. I realized all three of us had stopped breathing and were staring at her.

"What do you mean?" Preeti asked, looking first at me, then at Grandma, her forehead knotted.

"This is a very auspicious thing that is going to happen," Grandma replied, nodding her head the Indian way.

Whatever it was, it didn't feel good.

"Mother," Aunty Shilpa said in a hesitant voice, "I thought you said you wouldn't—"

"I spoke with the marriage broker yesterday," Grandma spat out, cutting her off. I drew in a sharp breath. "He had some good choices. Some boys came with good horoscopes, but the one I chose was the best fit. I am sure Asha will make a very good wife."

"Wife!" I shrieked.

"You're marrying Asha off?" Preeti said, sitting up.

"The Kristadasa family will treat her very well," Grandma said.

"Kristadasa?" My ears were pounding. *Did I hear that right?* I looked at her in shock. "You're marrying me to *Nuthead*?"

"No, silly girl. Oh, my good Lord, no. Not that block of a boy." She patted the sofa and slowly eased in between Preeti and me. We quickly moved aside. Sitting near Grandma was like being next to the African black mamba. One move and you're gone for good.

"It is his father who is interested," she said.

"*His father*?" I squealed. "That smelly old man with red eyes and hair growing from his ears? He's even older than Papa!"

Grandma slapped my thigh. "Watch your language, girl. He owns a good rickshaw business and is the richest man in the complex. You should be happy he even thinks of you."

I sat stunned.

"Mother, this might be not the best...," Aunty Shilpa spluttered in her corner. "What I am trying to say is, he's already married."

She gave her mother a cautiously stern look. "We were going to talk about this."

Grandma, in turn, gave Aunty Shilpa a nasty look. "There's nothing to talk about."

She turned to me. "I have already made the decision. This is your duty. Your husband will teach you well, and you will stop running around like a half-breed savage from Africa. It's time to learn to be a proper woman. I talked to the sadhu and checked your horoscope. The planets are aligned. They all agree with this union." She sounded like she was giving me a gift. "When my poor heart gives out one of these days, you will be taken care of well."

"Is this a joke, Grandma?" I asked.

"I don't do jokes," Grandma said, putting on her preachy voice. "You know men. They want a big family to show off their manhood. He is looking for another wife and is not asking for any dowry. He will pay for part of the wedding. Such a generous man he is. Who will marry a dark foreign girl like you, tell me that, ha? You should be so very lucky, Asha."

She smiled at me.

I struggled to not throw up. Preeti's face had gone ashen, and in her corner of the room, Aunty Shilpa had started a coughing fit.

"Mother," she said, once she'd recovered. "Asha is only fourteen." I could see her hand, the one holding the iron, was shaking.

"What are you going on about, girl? Didn't I marry you off at fourteen? I was married at twelve, as soon as I got my period, mind you. I had my first son at thirteen and I gave my husband four boys," Grandma said, pointing her index finger in the air and making it sound like a feat for which we should congratulate her. I noticed she hadn't mentioned Aunty Shilpa, her one and only daughter.

"Let the girl finish school," Aunty Shilpa said in a soft but firm voice. "She's doing well. An A-plus student, even. Once she is done, we can find her a suitable boy. She is already in grade ten, almost finished."

I looked over at Aunty Shilpa. Her face, steamed up from the coal iron, looked pale. By then, I knew Preeti and I went to school because she had insisted. Insisted and insisted. To Grandma, school was a complete waste of time when we could be working at the hotel making money or staying at home where we could be cooking, sewing, cleaning, and learning to be good future wives.

Though Aunty Shilpa thought school was important, she could barely read herself. I once caught her going through my history book, a finger tracing the lines, her lips moving laboriously, trying to read a paragraph about India's independence. I took the book from her and read the passage out loud. Her eyes shone with delight with every word. Though it was only a boring textbook, she laughed and repeated my words with glee. From that day on, I read to her whenever I could, whether it was on the beach, in the kitchen, or on the steps of our apartment complex.

"Who cares if she's in grade ten or grade twenty?" Grandma said with a snort. "What good will school do? Teach a girl to cook? To be a good wife? What kind of man wants to marry a girl who went to school, huh? Answer me that."

I sat up angrily. "Papa would never let this happen! He told me the only job girls have is to finish school. You can't make me break my promise to Papa."

"You think your father knew everything because he went to school? That son of mine lost his way the day he married that mother of yours. Heh!" Grandma pretended to spit on the ground.

I stared at her in shock.

"Why are you looking so glum?" Grandma said, throwing her hands up in the air. "You will get a new sari and silver bangles. You should be happy, I tell you."

"I don't want a sari," I said, choking on my words. "I don't want bangles. I don't want any of this!"

"Have you gone mad, girl?" Grandma said, sitting up. "I work so hard to help you and this is how you show your gratitude? I gave a good life for you, you foreign girl. Now, you will have food to cook and eat and you will bear many children for a good husband. What more do you want? Everything I am doing is for you!"

Grandma was getting agitated, her cloudy eyes darting back and forth, her mouth quivering. "All my sons ran away. They left their own dear mother, who taught them how to walk, who cooked and fed them, and took care of them when they were sick. They took their wives and left to Mumbai and Delhi. Why? To make money. When is money more important than your own mother? I tell you."

No one said a word. I looked at Grandma's crusty eyes. They flashed angrily. Her lips were set in a grim line.

"What am I left with now, I ask you?" she cried out. "I'm left with the burden of three girls. Three girls. Three mouths to feed. Three dowries. Three *curses*. That's what you girls are. You, Shilpa, you had to go and have your husband die on you. What am I supposed to do now? Tell me!"

"I can do this, Mother," Aunty Shilpa said in a quiet voice. We turned to look at her.

"What is this you're talking?" Grandma asked suspiciously.

"I can take care of the girls like I do now," Aunty Shilpa said. "I can ask for more hours at the hotel, so Asha is not a burden."

"What? A widowed, childless cripple like you?"

It was like Grandma had turned a blowtorch on her. Aunty Shilpa withered like a leaf on fire.

"You are very lucky the foreigners are giving you work," Grandma said, shaking a withered finger at her. "Wait till they pass the hotel to the locals. You think they will let an untouchable like you near them? They will sack you before you know it. Then what are you going to do? Go beg near the temples with the rest of the widows?"

Grandma glared at her. Aunty Shilpa cowered like she'd been beaten.

"Oh, Lord, why did you curse me to suffer like this?" Grandma threw her arms to the heavens and cried out. "Does the Lord not have any pity on me? Why me? Why me?" She wrapped her sari around her shoulders and rocked back and forth.

I wished I could disappear into the ground. I wanted to speak, but I'd lost my voice.

It was Preeti who spoke up. "My teacher said no one can force anyone to marry anyone anymore. It's against the law, she said."

"You keep quiet, girl," Grandma snapped. "You're next!"

Preeti's face went white.

Chapter Twelve

The next night, a loud knock sounded on our door.

Preeti and I looked up in surprise. It was almost bedtime, and no one visited our apartment at night. Grandma shot Aunty Shilpa a warning look.

"Girls, take your books and go outside," Aunty Shilpa said, quickly gathering up our pens and pencils and closing our books, despite our protests.

"Now?" Preeti said, grabbing her pen back. "But I want to finish my homework."

"Do what Aunty says, girls," Grandma said, hastily removing a dishcloth from a chair.

The knock sounded again. Louder. Imposing.

Grandma waddled to the door and opened it. In walked a gray-haired man carrying a cane and a black briefcase. In a traditional white sarong and shirt, and with white chalk marks on his forehead, he looked like a mix between a respectable businessman and an even more respectable sadhu from the local temple.

Preeti and I stared at him wide-eyed. He surveyed the room with a haughty look on his face.

"Marriage broker," Aunty Shilpa whispered to us.

"Namaskaaru." Grandma brought her hands together and bowed her head in greeting. The man gave her a nod. He didn't notice us girls huddled in the corner.

"Where's your respect?" Grandma snapped, turning to us.

I felt a slight push from Aunty Shilpa on my back. Preeti and I walked toward the man. He stood ramrod straight, like a king in front of his subjects.

Watching my cousin closely from the corner of my eye, I followed her prompts. Hands together, bend all the way down and touch his feet, then get up and say *"Namaskaaru,"* with a slight bow of the head. I didn't dare look in this man's eyes.

That morning, I'd gone to school trying to forget Grandma's ugly words, pretending the conversation of the night before had been only a surreal nightmare. But here was my nightmare alive and well, standing in our living room, staring me in the face.

I heard Aunty Shilpa say something from behind me. Preeti took me by the arm and led me out the door. I followed her meekly, head bowed, shoulders hunched. This was the real bogeyman. If Preeti hadn't been there, holding my hand, I'd have thrown up on the spot.

We walked out of the complex and sat under the coconut tree near our building. Neither of us said a word. Preeti drew shapes on the sand with her toes. My body was too numb to move, my mind too paralyzed to think. I sat quietly next to my cousin in the waning light, my heart heavy, wondering what was going on inside the apartment.

It was an hour later when we saw the marriage broker walk out the front doors of the complex. He walked with his chest out and a self-satisfied look on his face. He glanced at us momentarily but looked away as if we were not worth acknowledging. We waited for him to disappear into the streets before heading back inside. Grandma and Aunty Shilpa were busy cleaning up in the kitchen, putting teacups away.

"You girls need to get to bed now," Grandma said as soon as we walked in. I glanced at her wallet lying open on a chair on top of a pile of papers.

"What happened?" I demanded. "What did you do?"

Grandma snorted but said nothing else.

Aunty Shilpa didn't look up.

"Tell me what happened!"

No one spoke.

It wasn't until the following week I learned the destiny they'd planned for me.

Chapter Thirteen

I'd just come home from school to find Grandma having her afternoon nap. Aunty Shilpa hadn't come home from work yet and Preeti was nowhere to be seen.

Ever since the marriage broker had visited us, the apartment felt claustrophobic, like the air had thinned and the walls had closed in. I felt nauseous just walking through the door.

Aunty Shilpa appeared more and more downcast. She may have won a few battles here and there, but she had no power to win this war against Grandma. There were days when she stopped looking me in the eye.

Preeti got absorbed in her books. She stopped going to the beach, listening to music, or eating pineapple ice pops with me. She kept her nose firmly planted in her textbooks, eighteen hours a day, at school, on the bus, and at home. I found myself on my own more often than not.

In one night, I'd lost my two closest friends.

I threw my satchel on the sofa and decided to go to the beach alone. Still in my uniform, I slipped outside and pulled the doorknob gently behind me. The last thing I wanted was for Grandma to wake up and ask where I was going.

"Where you going?"

I jumped and nearly banged the door shut.

"Oh!" I said. "Sorry, I didn't see you... um... er...Uncle Kristadasa."

In India, it was customary to address anyone old enough to be your parent as Uncle or Aunty, even if they were strangers. It was a matter of respect, I was told. I stood by the door, confused.

What do I call someone older than Papa, but who's planning to marry me? Uncle? Brother? Cousin? Preeti and Aunty Shilpa would have known the right thing to say, but they weren't here.

The man towered in front of me, his bulbous nose bigger than ever, his belly hanging out of the top of his dirty pants. As usual, he reeked of *feni*, the vile liquor sold at night at the corner coffee shop where I'd seen him loitering with the rest of the men from our housing complex. Aunty Shilpa said I'd go blind if I ever drank that stuff.

Kristadasa was looking at me with bloodshot eyes, and I couldn't help notice the hair popping out of his ears like black thickets.

He cleared his throat loudly and spat phlegm on the floor. I quivered in disgust.

"What you doing going outside alone?"

"I...I, er, was going to join Preeti and Aunty Shilpa," I said.

"You come with me."

I looked at him, startled, and shook my head.

"You come upstairs," he said, louder this time.

I glanced behind him at the corridor. The place was deserted. The neighbors were having their afternoon naps or out doing chores. The kids in the complex were probably playing in the dust patch outside. This man lived just above us. All he had to do was pull me up one flight of stairs.

I felt a shiver go through me.

"Sorry, but I've got to go back to school," I lied.

"Now?" he asked.

"Yes," I said and looked away. I never could lie well.

He shook his head as if he'd caught me up to mischief. He looked down at my school uniform and leered. "Just like foreign girls, no? Running around in short skirts by yourself."

"I'm not a foreign girl," I replied in a defiant tone that surprised even me. I was tired of everyone calling me foreign. *Isn't this my father's hometown? When am I going to belong like everyone else?*

"Yes, just like foreign white girl." He leaned in and put his hand on the door. "But I own you now." I felt the weight of his arm on my shoulder. His face was inches from mine. He was scaring me now.

"I have to go," I said, ducking under his arm. Within half a second, I felt my body slam against the wall. He'd pinned me with his body, my face squished against his disgusting belly. I struggled to push him away, but he was too strong, too big; it was like the weight of India was on me.

I heard his belt slither out of his pant loops and I felt him undo his zipper. He pulled up my skirt. I opened my mouth to scream but a hefty hand clamped down on my mouth.

I desperately moved my head from side to side. I struggled to pull away. I tried to scream. But he had me pinned down tight. There was no way out. That was when the feeling of steel started to weave through my spine. His dirty, greasy fingers were over my mouth. I pulled back my lips, bared my teeth, and bit down. Hard.

"Oy!" he yelled, pulling his hand away.

I wasn't done.

I pulled up my knee and hit him squarely between his legs—*Slam!*—with a *kiai* cry, in exactly the way I'd done so many times at my martial arts classes at the international schools, long ago.

"Aaargh!" he said, clutching his crotch. He dropped to his knees in front of me, his hair standing straight like he'd been given an electric shock.

My heart was pounding, fear, anger coursing through me. I lifted my knee again.

"Nooooo!" he screeched, shielding his body with his arms and shuffling back on his knees.

I aimed for his thigh instead. *Wham.*

As soon as I made contact, I slipped out. He howled, either in pain or shame, I wasn't sure. I didn't care.

"You witch!" On his knees, still clasping his groin, he turned, his face flushed red in rage. "I will trash you to pieces!" His roar blew back my hair. By now, he'd have woken Grandma and everyone else in the building. "Wait till I get my hands on you!"

I didn't wait to find out. I turned around, pulled our apartment door open, stepped inside, and slammed the door shut. I stood staring at it for a few seconds, shaking like a jellyfish, until I realized I hadn't locked the door. *Oh, my god.* I turned the latch quickly, thankful he hadn't come barging in.

After a few seconds, I put my ear against the door and listened but only heard my heart beating like a hammer. Then, I heard heavy footsteps dragging outside. Loud cursing. A door slamming. Then quiet. Not another sound from the corridor.

"Grandma!" I screamed, turning around. "Grandma!" I ran toward the bedroom.

My legs felt like they'd give way any minute. My heart was thumping like crazy. *What just happened? Why did he try to attack me?*

Grandma was lying on her mattress in the room she and Aunty Shilpa shared. "What is all this banging and shouting, girl?" she said angrily, looking up. "You will give me a heart attack, I tell you."

"Grandma!" I plopped down beside her. "Kristadasa tried to hurt me!"

"What are you talking about?" Grandma said, sitting up and rubbing her eyes.

"He pushed me on the wall. He pulled my skirt up. Just now. It was awful! He tried to—"

"What is this sacrilegious thing you are saying?" She stopped and stared at me through her cataract-white eyes.

"Right outside our door! Just now! He pushed me on the wall and tried to attack me, but I bit on his finger and—"

Smack.

I sat stunned for a few seconds, then slowly brought my hand to my cheek. My face was throbbing in pain. I looked at her in shock.

"Grandma, why did—?"

"You say bad lies like that and I will disown you from this family. You understand?" she hissed.

"But, but... I'm telling the truth..."

"If I ever hear you make up dirty stories like this again about your future husband or anyone else, you will sleep on the street, do you hear? You will live in the dump and pick garbage with the untouchables. You won't be part of this family anymore."

Grandma's voice was steady.

This wasn't the angry scoldings or slaps I'd felt before. Her mouth was set in a straight grim line. Her white-washed eyes were cold, hard.

"I won't have this kind of behavior ruining our family's honor."

I stared at her with my mouth open.

"Shut your mouth, girl. That is not attractive for a bride." She got up from the mat and fixed her sari. "This is all your stupid mother's fault," she said, throwing her hands in the air and giving me a scowl. "You don't know basic decency."

Grandma walked out of the room muttering to herself, but I heard her. "What was he thinking, that son of mine, marrying a foreign girl? Should have disowned him years ago."

A chill went through my spine.

Chapter Fourteen

I walked out of the apartment like a zombie.

As soon as I got outside the complex, I picked up my pace and walked faster. I began a mindless jog. Then, I broke into a run.

I ran past the bus station. Past the markets and all the stores and streets that were so familiar now. I ran until I could run no longer, until I felt my feet slither on sand.

I stopped to catch my breath. I was on a stretch of the beautiful white beach, next to a line of coconut trees swaying in the afternoon breeze.

I leaned against a tree and stared at the ocean, still panting, my mind buzzing like I had live electric wires in my head. I listened to the waves crashing on the shore, a soothing sound in contrast to the hammering of my heart.

Far away, a bright yellow sun was slowly sinking into the horizon. It winked at me as I watched. I stared at this scene, not sure what to think or how to feel.

It was karma raising its ugly head again, I was sure.

It was karma punishing me for stealing those ruby red sandals for Chanda back in Tanzania, long ago. *Haven't I paid my dues with my parents' deaths? Is karma so insatiable?*

Grandma's threat to cast me out of the family hurt far more than what Kristadasa had tried to do. If he'd been waiting outside the building afterward, I'd have made easy prey. My fighting blood had cooled. My thoughts had been elsewhere.

Why didn't Grandma do something? Why didn't she believe me?

Part of me felt guilty for being angry at her. This was the woman who'd taken me in when I had no one else in the world. She'd put me through school, fed me, and gave me stability when I'd felt utterly alone. *But how can she blame me for what happened?*

The waves crashed and pulled away in rhythm, crash and pull away, crash and pull away, as if to tell me no matter what happens, life goes on.

Yes, life goes on. But I didn't want *this* life to go on.

The sky was changing into vibrant maroon and purple hues like it was preparing for a party that evening.

Around me, I heard the sounds of people finishing their daytime lives and starting their nighttime ones—men hauling fishing boats up the beach, friends laughing over supper at a nearby food stall, a transistor radio cranked up, children playing their last play before being called to bed.

The long fronds of the coconut trees waved gently with the wind, mocking me, taunting me. The more the trees swayed, the worse I felt.

I could no longer keep track of my emotions. Anger. Guilt. Shame. Fury. Guilt again. It was Kristadasa who had attacked me but for some reason, I felt like I had committed an unspeakable crime.

I slid down to the sand and put my head in my hands.

That afternoon, Goa lost its luster. Like my father of long ago, all I wanted to do was escape this place.

Chapter Fifteen

"Cheap service. 15,000 rupees for first immigration filing. No problemo is the motto."

I had noticed the garish yellow sign above the bus station before but hadn't thought much of it.

This time, I marched toward it with only one idea in mind. I ducked under the banner and walked up the dingy, narrow stairway that smelled of urine and diesel. I was headed for the offices of the Good and Fast Immigration Broker.

All week, I'd been either lingering at the bus station or ambling mindlessly at the beach after school, biding my time until supper, dreading going anywhere near our apartment complex.

The three teens had moved away from the station after the incident with the candy store man. It was a relief not to hear their catcalls when we got off the bus. Though after the encounter with Kristadasa, their harassment seemed trivial.

Meena, though, was still there, her melancholy music giving respite in the middle of the bus station's chaos.

Until then, I'd only made small talk with her, but the day I ran to the beach, I'd walked back up and had squatted next to her on the pavement. She'd put her flute down and listened patiently, with a warm hand resting on my shaking shoulders. She hadn't looked shocked. It was like she'd heard this kind of story before. Maybe she'd even experienced it.

When I finished, she'd wiped the tears from my cheeks and said, "Your heart will tell you what you have to do now." She hadn't said much more and instead played a song for me. But I knew she would approve of what I was feeling in my bones.

I wanted so badly to tell Preeti and Aunty Shilpa what had happened with Kristadasa, but every time I tried, my mouth refused to open. It was like a five-ton hippo had settled on my shoulders, and had also taken control of my tongue. I had a hard time looking them in the eye that evening, feeling sure they'd blame me for what happened. Just like Grandma did.

But I didn't have to worry because they hardly talked anymore. Preeti burrowed herself in her books and Aunty Shilpa worked back-to-back shifts at the hotel. Whenever she was home, she slept, and Grandma wouldn't allow me near her. "She's working hard every day to pay the marriage broker. Don't you dare wake her up."

My mind went over the incident again and again and again.

If only I'd stayed home that afternoon like Grandma said I should have done. If only I'd been a good little Indian girl like Grandma said I should. It was my fault for trying to go out alone. Maybe Grandma was right. I wasn't a good girl. I deserved it. *Maybe, maybe...*

All I knew for sure was Grandma had banished me, Preeti had become distant, and Aunty Shilpa was almost never home. For the first time since my parents died, I felt completely alone again.

"The vegetable shop is downstairs," said the man behind the desk at the Good and Fast Immigration Broker. He didn't even look up from his newspaper.

I glanced around his office.

On one wall were outdated travel posters of the Eiffel Tower, the Red Square, and the London Bridge with a double-decker bus on it. Above all these hung a large white cross. Another wall was dedicated entirely to miniature statues of all the Hindu gods in the world. They posed on wooden shelves that ran the length of the wall.

Directly behind the main desk where the man sat ignoring me were three framed pictures. At the bottom was a yellowed black-and-white photo of an old woman in a sari. Above her was a cheap print of Lord Vishnu in all his blue glory, standing on a lily pad in the middle of a river surrounded by beautiful, half-dressed maidens. Flower garlands and gold necklaces decorated his neck, and a halo made of live cobra heads surrounded his bejeweled head.

Above this mythical image was a poster of Rambo. I did a double take. Yes, it was a faded poster of the movie *First Blood* with a muscled-up Sylvester Stallone carrying a gigantic machine gun.

The Good and Fast Immigration Broker was located on top of the station so I could hear the buses rev in and out. The smell of gas fumes and the heat from the station rose up and stagnated in this room. There was another faintly familiar smell—not a pleasant one. *How can anyone breathe in here?*

"Excuse me, sir," I said loudly, so the man could hear me over the buses. "I want to go overseas, and I want to take my cousin Preeti and Aunty Shilpa with me."

The man laid his paper on the desk and looked surprised to find me. His eyes slithered over me, from my head to my toes. He was a slim man in an ill-fitting gray suit with a pencil-thin mustache above his lips. The V-shaped white dust mark on his forehead told me he'd recently visited a local temple.

I stood in front of him with my satchel in one hand, feeling like I was in front of our school principal.

"What do you want?" he barked.

"I want to take my family abroad, sir."

"And where does this girl, with her cousin and her good aunty, all want to go?"

I didn't hesitate one second. "Tanzania."

Silence. The man burst into laughter. "Ha- ha- ha!" His uneven, yellowed teeth made him look like a hyena under the subdued light. A gold-colored tooth glinted momentarily. "Why on earth do you want to go there?"

"Because my parents are buried there."

He stared at me intently. I stared back.

Mr. Mudenda had told me my parents would always live on Tanzanian soil. He'd also told me I was welcome to visit when I got older. I was now old enough to travel, I was sure. Besides, I wanted nothing more than to sit at my parents' graves.

The knot that had formed in my stomach after the car crash had never gone away. It sat there, heavy and bloated, interfering with my digestion and sleep now and then. I had many questions about their death, and I felt it was my duty to go back home.

"*Tanzania?*" the man asked squinting at me. "Are you sure?"

"You want to go see *black* people?" Fartybag's voice came from a dim corner of the room. I spun around. There he was with his mocking grin, loafing on a broken rattan chair. He was sucking on a mango and watching a grainy version of *Rambo* at low volume on a black-and-white TV.

Large letters scrolled across the bottom, almost obscuring the movie. "Violation of movie copyright is a serious federal offense. If you see this message, please call 1-800-259-1009 immediately." I hadn't seen Fartybag when I'd walked in, but that was the smell I'd noticed earlier. He grinned at my surprise.

"What do you know about Africa?" I asked.

"I saw *Cannibal Attack* on TV," he said, pointing a mango-juice-soaked finger at the small screen. "If you go there, they'll chop you up and eat you. Everybody knows that."

"What're *you* doing here?" I asked, frowning.

"I'm the right-hand man. The second in command, assistant in chief," he said, sitting up and puffing out his chest. "Why don't you get out like Appa said, or I'll punch you in the nose."

"Like how I punched you?" I shot back.

"Hrmp." Fartybag turned back to his TV with a scowl.

"Enough!" the man snapped. "What do you want?"

"I want to leave this place," I said, turning back to Fartybag's father. "Can you help me?"

"Okay, let me see what I have," he said, thumbing through a book on his desk. "I have a first-class ticket to have tea with the queen of England. How about that? Ha! Or maybe you want to visit the president of America? Go and see the splendid White House?" His face broke into a broad smile.

"Good one, Appa!" Fartybag said from his corner, slapping his thighs.

"Ha-ha!" His father joined in.

I waited until the laughter died down. The man picked up the newspaper again and Fartybag went back to his TV.

"Please help me, sir," I said, putting my hands together like I'd seen Aunty Shilpa and Preeti do whenever they talked to our school principal or a priest at the temple. "I want to get away before they make me marry Kristadasa."

"Ah!" The man's eyebrows shot up. He sat up and gave me a keen look. "So you're the foreign girl they're giving to Kristadasa."

"No one's giving me to anybody," I said, my voice steady.

"She's not from here, Appa," Fartybag said from his corner, not taking his eyes off the TV. "That's why she's so weird."

"All I want are tickets and a visa," I said, ignoring Fartybag.

"If you want to travel anywhere in this world, you also need lots of rupees," the man said, brushing his suit. His face said *stop bothering me*.

"Tons," Fartybag said with a smirk. "Tons and tons of rupees."

"I have money, sir," I said, my mind whirling.

Mr. Mudenda had handed me my parents' bank account papers in a sealed envelope just before I'd got on the plane. I'd opened the envelope on the plane and looked through it. Though the papers were in English, all I could make out were pages and pages of small print with difficult words, strange numbers, and convoluted sentences.

I'd handed the documents over to Grandma, as Mr. Mudenda had instructed, but he hadn't known she couldn't read, let alone read in English. She'd thrust the papers back at me and said I should bury them under the sofa mattress with my passport, which was what I did, until the night the marriage broker visited us.

That night, taking care to not wake Preeti up, I slipped my hand under the mattress and pulled out the papers. An outside street light and a conspiring moon had given me ample light to read them by the window. Though I hardly understood much of what I read, I was sure there was money in a bank in England left by my parents for me. I may not have any rupees, but what I had could be changed to rupees. I was sure.

"I don't take pocket change from useless little girls," the man said, waving me away.

"Yeah, get out," Fartybag said. "We're busy people."

"But I have money," I said. "It's in a bank. A foreign bank."

"A bank!" the man said, throwing his head back in laughter. "You think any bank will do business with *you*? What a jokester!"

"Ha-ha-ha!" Fartybag joined in. "What a stupid girl."

"Oooh," the man said, clutching his sides. "I haven't laughed this hard since the day your uncle got hit by that cow on his scooter."

I waited for the laughter to subside.

"I'm serious," I said, standing my ground.

The man leaned forward, his eyes sharp and unfriendly. "Enough of this nonsense. Stop wasting my time!" He banged on his desk, making me jump.

"Yeah. Get out or I'll bash your lights out!" Fartybag shouted from his corner.

I looked at the man, who was glaring at me now.

"Get out!"

Chapter Sixteen

I stumbled home, my shoulders stooped and my heart heavy.

The images of my parents floated to mind. I wished I could ask them for guidance. *Is there such a place as heaven, and can they look down to see what's happening?*

I remembered how I'd had a real family at one point, where all I felt was warmth and love. I remembered how we'd spend every Sunday baking cakes and having fun. I remembered how we'd pile into our green Fiat every Saturday to go to the market to visit Chanda and sell my mother's cakes. I stopped as an idea dawned on me. *Maybe, just maybe there is a way out.*

I didn't wait another second. I ran home as fast as I could.

First, I wrote down my plan in my school notebook to make sure I wouldn't forget the details. Then, I convinced Aunty Shilpa to lend me ten rupees to start my "biziness," as she called it. It took almost two days, but she finally relented to stop my begging.

The next day, I walked to the market after school and bought two cups of flour, a small bottle of coconut oil, rice milk, a cup of sugar, a can of baking soda, a tin of cocoa powder and a tiny but expensive stick of vanilla bean from a fancy shop I'd never stepped into before.

These last two items were beyond my ten-rupee budget, so I had to buy them on credit after much pleading with the shopkeeper. She gave them to me right away after I accidentally switched to English while beseeching her. For some reason, that seemed to give her reassurance.

At the pawnshop at the street corner near the bus station, I found a rusty twelve-cup baking tray they were throwing away. I cleaned and scraped it for hours to get it back to cooking-ready status. That evening, I made my own cake wrappers using aluminum foil.

At first, Aunty Shilpa watched me with curiosity, then she came over and squatted next to me, to help. She still didn't say much, but her quiet companionship was all I needed to know I wasn't alone as I'd thought.

That night, I made a dozen fairy cakes—a dozen because that was all I had ingredients for. I didn't have a recipe book to follow, so I baked from memory.

I revived old memories of my mother in her blue pants and floral blouse in our kitchen back in Dar es Salaam. I remembered how I'd measured ingredients as she'd instructed, handing her a cup of flour or a spatula. I'd watched carefully as she sifted and mixed while explaining, chatting, and telling me stories. I walked down memory lane, recalling feelings, details, and brought my mother's cakes to life.

The next day at lunchtime, instead of hiding near the bookshelves in the corner of my classroom, I walked over to the school canteen with my first batch of cakes. I lined them up on a wooden bench at the back of the room. Then, I sat behind my cakes and ate lunch by myself, as I always did.

Every time someone walked by, I looked up and smiled. I even smiled at the girls who made fun of my accent. One by one, the girls came over after finishing their lunch to see what the foreign girl was up to. Preeti's best friend bought my first cake, then her other friend bought my second. Soon, I was sold out.

The next day, with the money I made, I doubled to twenty-four. A teacher tried one of my cakes and came back for one more. The following day, another teacher came by and bought two at once.

After a month, I'd made enough money to add icing swirls on top. I baked late into the night after doing my homework and brought in thirty-six cakes to school every day after that.

Then one day, my classroom teacher asked me to bring fifty-five fairy cakes for the principal's birthday party. With the money I'd made from the first two months of sales, I paid back Aunty Shilpa's ten-rupee loan, paid off my credit at the fancy store and bought more baking supplies. After the principal's birthday, I took fifty cakes to school every day. I had to. Everyone was asking for them.

For the first time, a few girls started to talk to me. Some began sitting with me at the back of the canteen while I kept shop. They didn't seem to care anymore that I'd been born in a strange land far away, that I spoke in a funny way, or the monitor picked on me often.

Maybe it was because the teachers came to visit with purses in their hands and smiles on their faces. I put an extra cake in the bag whenever the school principal or the senior teachers came along, a tip I'd learned from the market women back in Africa.

Little by little, the school monitor stopped rapping on my knuckles in the morning. More and more often, I found her scrawny claw hovering over my cakes at lunchtime, trying to decide which flavor to pick that day.

Best of all, Grandma approved.

Kristadasa had gotten greedy and was asking for a dowry now and the marriage broker's fees were higher than expected. This meant my wedding was postponed for twelve months, twelve months for Aunty Shilpa to make more money and twelve months for me to prepare for my future.

Though Grandma grumbled about the foreign sweets, she took it as a sign I was becoming domesticated, that it would make me a good wife. She stopped blaming my mother and my background and happily gave me time on the stove after supper every evening.

And that was all I needed.

I handed over a tiny portion of what I made to Aunty Shilpa to satisfy Grandma's curiosity. What she didn't know was after I paid for my baking supplies and ingredients, I squirreled everything away in my pillowcase.

I did this every day for eleven months. And soon, I found myself with four weeks before they took me away to become the wife of Nuthead's father. Four weeks before I lost my freedom.

Part FOUR

Robert Browning Hamilton

"Hello sir," I said, after clearing my throat. "I can pay for my ticket in rupees now."

I was back at the Good and Fast Immigration Broker's office, the sole travel agent in my neighborhood. Fartybag was in his usual smelly corner watching a Rambo film. His father was at his desk, frowning at me over his newspaper.

But this time, I had cold hard cash in my hands, not in some foreign bank with indecipherable words and numbers on paper that needed sorting out. There was no way he could refuse me now.

"What do you want?" Fartybag's father barked.

He'd already forgotten me.

"I want to buy visas and tickets to go to Tanzania."

"What?" His frown deepened. "And who do you think you are?"

"I'm Asha," I said.

He gave a blank look.

"I came to see you last year about an airline ticket." I opened my school satchel and took out a wad of Indian rupees. "See, I can buy it now."

He put the newspaper down slowly, his eyes not wavering from the money in my hands.

"Where did you steal that from?"

"I didn't steal this. This is mine."

"Where did you find it then?"

"I made it from selling fairy cakes at school."

"Fancy cakes?" He squinted at me.

"No, fairy cakes," I said. "I have enough money to go back to Dar es Salaam now." I didn't have enough cash to take Preeti and Aunty Shilpa with me, but a plan was hatching in my head on how to get them there too.

"*Dar es Salaam?*" the man asked, looking at me bewildered.

"Don't you remember her, Appa?" Fartybag piped up from his corner. "She's the crazy foreign girl. I told you she's nuts."

The man's eyes cleared. "Ah!" A smirk grew on his face. "You also have a passport now?"

"Yes, sir."

"Really?" he said, his eye widening. "Where is it?"

"Under my mattress."

"Under your—?" He paused. "Where did you get it from?"

"Papa gave it to me. I've had one since I was a baby."

"Oh?" The man put his paper down and sat up. He looked at me silently with an interested glint in his eye. "So, your parents, they travel?"

"They traveled all over Africa. They even went to London."

"London, eh?" The man's voice had softened. "What your parents do, pray tell? They work for big company?"

"No, they don't," I stammered. "I mean they did, but they died when I was twelve." I looked down at my shoes. I felt something stick in my throat. I swallowed it quickly.

"Where did they used to work?"

"At an NGO." Unknowingly, I had switched to English.

"NGO?"

"Non-governmental organization."

The man was silent for a long time.

"Which NGO, miss?" he said, switching to English as well.

"Environ Africa."

"Where exactly did your esteemed parents work, miss?"

"Dar es Salaam, Nairobi, Lusaka, Gaborone, and some other places, but I've forgotten now."

"If your parents worked good jobs, why do you make fancy cakes?"

"Fairy cakes."

"Didn't your parents leave you anything when they passed away?"

"Yes," I said, shuffling my feet. "I'm not supposed to touch those papers until I'm eighteen. Mr. Mudenda said that's really important to remember. I've read them but they're a bit hard to understand. I want to use it to help my cousin and aunty join me in Dar es Salaam."

"Who's this Mudenda?"

"My social worker who helped me after...after my parents died."

Silence from the man.

Then, he stood up, brushed his suit, cleared his throat and to my surprise, almost gave me a bow. "Come, come, sit down." He rolled a chair toward me. "Sit, sit now, miss."

I walked over to the offered chair and sat down, my feet barely touching the floor.

"Normally, I don't talk to anyone who come without appointment," the man said, getting behind his desk. "I only take referral, miss, but I will make extra exception for you because you need of a lot of good help. Lots of good help." He smiled.

"Thank you," I said in relief.

"If I knew you were an orphan, I'd never have turned you away. Never say no to an orphan in need. That is what I say. I try my best to be most pious you see." He pointed at the colorful Lord Vishnu picture behind him.

"Thank you, sir," I said with a nod, not knowing what else to say. I had expected a fight hard to buy my tickets and visa. But he seemed rather cooperative, especially considering he was Fartybag's father.

"Now, now miss. No need to call me sir. My name is Fanibhusan Sardindhi." Fartybag's father smiled again, showing a row of crooked, yellow teeth. "But you call me Franky. Much easier, no?"

I nodded.

Franky turned to his son. "Oy! Get up and make yourself useful, boy. Stop stinking this place like hell and get two sweet chais."

Fartybag got up with a scowl, walked out and slammed the door behind him.

Chapter Eighteen

"**H**ave you gone completely mad in the head?" Preeti hissed at me.

It was well past midnight. We were huddled under the thin blanket on the sofa bed. Grandma and Aunty Shilpa were sleeping on their shared mat in the bedroom, a few feet from us, but Grandma's loud snores were reassuring. I knew it would be safe to nudge Preeti awake.

"Grandma's right," she was saying in a fierce whisper. "You make so much trouble."

I stared at her for several seconds before whispering back. "I can't believe you want me to sit and wait for her to marry me off to Nuthead's dad."

"It's your destiny."

"How can you say that?" I said louder than I'd intended. "What kind of life is that? I'd rather be dead."

If there was one lesson I'd learned recently, it was that nothing was predestined. I no longer relied on anyone to take care of me, not even the gods, though I had to admit the ones in Goa were impressive with their jeweled crowns and golden halos. My life was in my hands alone.

"It's your duty!" she hissed.

"I thought you were on my side!" I replied, giving her an accusing look.

Preeti lowered her eyes. "You must think of your family's honor. That is the most important thing."

"But *you* said it was wrong!" I said, throwing the blanket off me in exasperation. "You even said it was illegal!"

With a loud sigh, she gently pulled the blanket back over me. "Go back to sleep and stop this silliness."

"No!" I kicked the blanket away. "I'm getting out of here. And I want you and Aunty to come with me so we can get away from this place and these people."

She shook her head and gave another sigh. "You're not a child anymore. It's time for you to become a woman. You can't go around disrespecting elders like this."

"Mama and Papa left me enough money," I said lowering my voice. "He said he can help me. He can help all of us."

"Who said that?"

"Franky."

"Who's that?"

"Fartybag's father."

"How can *that* man help?"

"He owns the Good and Fast Immigration Broker. He's not as bad as you think—Franky I mean, not Fartybag. Fartybag's still mean. Franky promised to help get me out of this wedding."

"You've been talking to Fartybag's father about this? This is a private family affair! How can you trust him? He's a disgusting man."

"And Nuthead's father's a horrible pervert!" I whispered furiously back.

Preeti gave me a disapproving look. "Respect your elders."

I put my head in my hands. I had to tell her what happened the other day, but pulling those words out of my mouth meant tackling the colossal hippo that had made itself comfortable on my shoulders, draining my strength, my voice, my power.

Aunty Shilpa had told me Nuthead's father had had his eyes on me ever since I'd arrived, and this wasn't the first time he'd approached Grandma. I remembered seeing him staring from his doorway when we walked to school, even before we heard from the marriage broker.

Preeti had noticed him watching and always lowered her eyes and walked away quickly when he was around.

I shivered in disgust. Then in anger. *Why can't she see what's going on?*

"I've got money now," I said, turning to look Preeti directly in her eyes. "And Franky will help to get you and Aunty Shilpa out too. He knows how to take money from Mama and Papa's account and get visas and passports and tickets and all that stuff. I don't have to be eighteen to get my money anymore."

"This is madness," Preeti said, shaking her head. "Even if we don't agree with her decision, we must obey Grandma. It's our duty. You have to honor Grandma's wishes. Why don't you understand this?"

"Grandma's a dictator!" I blurted out.

"Shhhh..."

I lowered my voice back to a whisper. "If she really loved me, she wouldn't do this."

"You really don't understand, do you? She's ashamed she can't take care of you like your parents did. She thinks Kristadasa will give you at least half the things you had before. Don't you see?"

I sat quietly trying to take this in.

"She loves us," Preeti said, putting an arm on my shoulder. "She's trying to make a better life for all of us."

My stomach turned. *No, I just can't do this.* I elbowed the fat hippo off my shoulder. I almost heard it grunt as I pushed it off. "Preeti, there's something I need to tell you."

"What is it now?"

"He attacked me."

"Who?"

"Nuthead's father." I gulped and looked away. There. I said it.

Preeti stared at me silently. I waited for what felt like forever, wringing my hands and my heart. *What's she going to say? Will she think it's my fault? Just like Grandma did?*

"What do you mean?" she asked, finally.

I looked down at my hands. "After the marriage broker came, he found me outside the door. I was alone, and he pushed me against the wall and...and...he tried to attack me. He tried to tear my...skirt. It was awful. It was horrible." My voice faded and my heart rate quickened as I'd remembered the terror I felt. "He tried to attack me but I ran away."

"Is this the truth?"

"You know I can't lie."

"Did he hurt you? Did you see blood?"

"It happened so fast. I pushed him away. I hit him hard. Then I ran away."

"You *hit* him?" Preeti stared at me for a whole minute before she spoke again.

"Asha," she said, shaking her head.

I swallowed.

She let out a sigh. "Why do you have to be so melodramatic? Grandma's right. She's always saying you have such an imagination."

I looked at her with my mouth open.

"He's a respectable man," Preeti said pulling the blanket around her. "He's going to be your husband soon. You should never talk badly about him like this. That is such a dishonorable thing to do."

Didn't she hear what I just said? "But he's a monster!"

Preeti put up one hand. "Please don't say these things. This man has promised to take care of you, Grandma, me, and Aunty Shilpa. We're all going to become part of his family. As your older cousin, I forbid you to disrespect him. You really need to learn how to—"

"But I can't marry him!" I was beside myself. "You're wrong about him. I'm never going to—"

"Stop acting like a little girl. This is not even your decision to make."

"But..."

"You're wrong about him. You're wrong about Grandma. She cares a lot, and she's trying her best to take care of us. Besides, you have no choice."

"Why not?"

"Because Aunty Shilpa's sick."

I stopped for a moment. "What do you mean?"

"She's dying."

I looked at her, speechless.

"Don't you hear her cough all the time?"

I'd heard, but I'd thought it was because she worked too hard and was always tired.

"Haven't you seen her cough blood in the shower?"

That, I had not. I put on my invisible cone of privacy as soon as I entered the washrooms, never looked more than a few inches in front of me, and ran out as soon as I was done. I hadn't seen because I'd never looked.

"What's wrong with her?" I asked in a whisper.

"She was sick before she came to live with us. Everyone says her husband died at the quarry, but he died spitting out blood. They told us he got AIDS."

"Oh!"

"I think Aunty Shilpa's sick in the same way."

"Oh, no."

"Aunty doesn't want everyone to know, so don't go around blabbing, okay?"

"Why can't we do something about it?"

"Do you think we can afford to help her?"

I had no answer to that.

"Grandma already spent all our savings at the clinic, but they wanted more. We had to pay extra to the government official to get an appointment, then we had to pay extra to the nurse to take her temperature, and then we had to pay extra to see the doctor. You know the money they gave us when you came here? We gave that to the doctor to pay for special medicine from America, but they never gave it to her. They chased Grandma away when she went to find out what happened to her money. They stole it from us. We're not made of cash, so we can't fight these big people."

I sat motionless. My mind was a whirlwind.

"When you marry Kristadasa," Preeti continued, "he promised to help Shilpa. She won't have to break her back working. Maybe she can stay home and rest, even get medicine. See, little cousin, Grandma's not a dictator. She's trying to help all of us. It's not her fault she's stuck with three girls. She has to find a dowry for you and me and then take care of Aunty Shilpa for the rest of her life."

Something didn't ring right. I spoke up. "But isn't Aunty Shilpa the one working right now to pay for the dowry—"

"I'll have to get married soon, too," Preeti continued without hearing me. "I wanted to be a doctor so I can help Aunty, but that may be too late. What's the difference if my marriage happens now or later? It's our destiny. At least this way, Grandma will stop worrying, and we can get help for Aunty Shilpa."

I stared at her.

"Stop thinking about school and all these other crazy things. You'll make a really good wife. You cook so well," she said, squeezing my shoulder. "Now stop talking and go to sleep, my little cousin."

She gave me a sad half-smile, turned away, lay down on the sofa and curled into a ball, as she always did when she went to sleep.

I lay back against my pillow and looked up at a brown patch on the ceiling, a permanent reminder from when the floor above had flooded years ago. I stayed awake, feeling numb, gazing at it till early morning.

Chapter Nineteen

"How do you know this will work?"

Aunty Shilpa was frowning at the piles of paper scattered in front of her. Her face was paler than usual and the lines on her face were more entrenched. I sat close to her, making sure her teacup was always filled.

Franky went over the forms, forms which had taken him three weeks to sort out with the banks. I'd learned quickly that between a visa, an air ticket and "government and administrative fees," the money I'd made from selling my cakes wasn't enough to get away to Dar es Salaam as quickly as I'd planned.

I had no choice but to dip into my parents' account. Each day of waiting for Franky to work his way through the "damn bank bureaucrats," as he called them, made me more and more nervous. And now, I had seven days before my wedding day.

When he finally had everything in order, he read the papers out loud to Aunty Shilpa and me. The documents were written partly in English and partly in Konkani, both of which I could read but the language was far more complex than anything I'd learned so far.

Just when I thought I understood one sentence, the next would start with "notwithstanding the above, it must be duly noted that...and that...and that...," and I felt hopelessly lost.

"This is the language of businessmen, not girls," Fartybag said with a condescending sniff from his corner when Aunty Shilpa and I stopped Franky for the hundredth time to ask a question.

"I see the company paid Asha's parents in British pounds and American dollars to a London bank," Franky said, licking his lips. "All we're going to do is make simple transfer of money from Asha's parents' account in London to new account in Goa, and we're converting it into rupees. Nothing more, nothing less, madam."

"How do we know there won't be any problems?" Aunty Shilpa asked.

"No problemo is my motto, madam," Franky said, flashing his yellowed teeth. I wished he wouldn't do that.

Aunty Shilpa looked even more skeptical.

"Let me assure you," he said, taking off his glasses and speaking slowly to make sure we'd follow. "You have absolutely nothing to fear. Positively nothing. I know exactly what I am doing. As I have explained to you already, you will *really* have a big problem if you leave the money in these foreign banks until Miss Asha is eighteen. Are you willing to trust these foreign banks, madam?"

Aunty Shilpa looked unsure. I wasn't sure either.

"Are you willing to make her lose everything to foreign fees, and taxes, and even expropriation?"

"What's that?" Aunty Shilpa and I said together.

"They can take your money and run away anytime. You will never know. Never know. Who knows how much they've already taken out without anyone knowing, huh?"

"Won't they write to me or something?" I said. "I'm sure Papa and Mama wouldn't put their money in a bad bank."

Franky sighed. "You are a very smart young lady, Miss Asha, but I must humbly say, also little naive. But then, you are still young. Never trust these foreign banks, that is what I say. Worse than vipers. Vipers, I tell you. I know because I am forced to do business with them on a daily basis. At the Good and Fast Immigration Broker, that is all I do, fight with these banks. English banks, American banks, Australian banks, even Japanese banks. Thieves, I tell you."

A loud, smelly pop came from Fartybag's direction. We ignored him.

"Best thing to do now is to take everything out and make sure you put it in safe place right here in India where we can see it. And put it in rupees, not this foreign money. Then you can decide to do whatever you want with it." Franky nodded his head sideways. "That's the smart thing to do, no?"

"I guess so," I said slowly. Aunty Shilpa was still frowning at the papers.

With my parents' money, I could pay off the marriage broker and pay those "extras" to Aunty Shilpa's doctors, nurses, clinics, and other people in between, as needed. I could also whisk everyone away—Preeti, Aunty Shilpa, and even Grandma if she'd come—with me to Tanzania, where I remembered life as being much safer.

There were no school monitors or marriage brokers over there, no men who drank *feni* and attacked girls. There were no boys who harassed girls at bus stops either. For the first time in my life, I felt I had all the answers.

"First, we need to pay off the marriage broker to stop the wedding and make sure there's enough left for emergencies and such," I said, giving Franky a discreet nod. He didn't nod back. The day before, I'd told him, in no uncertain terms, that we must not talk about Aunty Shilpa's sickness in front of her. I prayed he remembered that conversation.

"I'm afraid, miss," Franky said, shaking his head, "that will need a lot of money and it is not all that simple. Nothing is simple these days. I did my calculations. Your parents had money, but not enough to stop a wedding and all the peripheral and emergency things, I am so sorry to say."

"What's all this perife...peri....?" Aunty Shilpa stuttered.

Does he mean there's not enough to pay for Aunty Shilpa's health costs? I peered at Franky, but his face was blank.

"How much do we need for the emer... to help, I mean to stop the, er, wedding and all that?" I said, struggling to find the right words.

"Ten lakhs," Franky said.

"Ten lakhs!" I exclaimed.

"Why do we need that much?" Aunty Shilpa asked giving Franky a dubious look.

"If your mother didn't already sign the legal papers with the marriage broker, madam, this would be very easy thing to do. Now, it is not going to be cheap to break the contract."

"Maybe I can't read, but I know a lakh is a lot of rupees," Aunty Shilpa said.

"What will happen if we don't pay the broker?" I asked.

"Marriage is serious business in this country," Franky said in a firm voice. "That is why we men take care of these things. It is not like the haggling for vegetables at the market that you women do every day. The broker can take you to court for breaking a contract, and then you will pay millions of lakhs. Your parents had money, but not that much, Miss Asha."

I listened with a sinking heart. Banks accounts, contracts, business arrangements, and courts were a whole new world to me. Judging from Aunty Shilpa's face, they were to her as well. I wished I could ask more frank questions off Franky, but I also needed Aunty Shilpa here to sign the papers, and I didn't have much time left.

"In this country," Franky was saying, "it is major offense to break a marriage contract. I can assure you that you will be held in the highest legal liability. Liability, I tell you. It will definitely mean prison."

"*Prison?*" I looked at Franky with wide eyes, wondering what Grandma had got us into.

"How much did Asha's parents have?" Aunty Shilpa asked. We'd been asking this question all morning. Franky said the money was held in several accounts in different currencies, so he had to add them all up, and it was all rather complicated.

"Ah, that is a very good question," Franky said, picking up his oversized calculator for the tenth time that morning. He stared at it for a moment, scratching his head. He took his notepad and scribbled numbers on it, mumbling to himself, and he punched numbers into the calculator, one by one, as if he was afraid he'd miss the correct button. After a few hmms and umms, he put his calculator away and looked up with a sigh.

We looked at him expectantly.

"Well?" Aunty Shilpa asked.

"I am really sorry to say that you will need to find another way to pay off the marriage broker in full."

"Oh, no!" I said.

"Not to worry," Franky said, rubbing his forehead. "My job is to think of options. My motto is no problemo. There is always a solution, that is what I say."

He shuffled the papers around and picked one up. Leaning back in his chair, he read it silently to himself, moving his lips as he went through each line while we waited quietly.

In the background, I could hear Rambo's booming voice and machine gun fire coming from Fartybag's corner.

"The problem," Franky said thoughtfully after a few minutes of intense reading, "is that Kristadasa's family wants to expedite this wedding. He is my neighbor, you know. He told me that he is very anxious for this marriage to take place sooner than later. Plus the marriage broker is a very respectable and powerful man in town. This does not make it easy for us."

He put the paper back on the desk and leaned forward. Aunty Shilpa and I leaned toward him.

"So?" Aunty Shilpa asked.

"We will have to act fast and quietly if we want to succeed. You only have seven days left, miss."

"What do we need to do?" I asked, panic rising inside me.

"Do you really want to stop this arrangement?"

"Yes!" I said. *Why is he even asking?*

"Here, first let's have a cup of tea," Franky said, passing Aunty Shilpa a teacup. He looked at me expectantly. I shook my head impatiently. This was no time for tea.

"This is serious business we're talking about now," Franky said, pouring himself a cup. "We must make these decisions mindfully, and with the blessing of Lord Vishnu, we will solve your problems. That is what I say."

Aunty Shilpa took a sip of her tea with shaking hands. She was a nervous wreck.

It had taken me days to convince her to come and speak to Franky. Fartybag's father had been specific. I had to find a relative over the legal age of eighteen if I wanted to access the money my parents left me.

Aunty Shilpa had not at all been happy when I told her I was getting help from the Good and Fast Immigration Broker to escape from my impending wedding. She'd refused to be part of my plan until I rustled up the courage to tell her of the day Kristadasa attacked me.

Her face went dark as she listened to my story. She sat motionless for a whole minute with her head hung low. I stood quietly by her. When she looked up, I saw tears running down her cheek.

"Don't worry, Aunty," I said, reaching out to squeeze her hand. "He didn't hurt me. I got a tiny scratch on my arm. That's all. I hit *him* and ran away in time."

"I remember my wedding night," Aunty Shilpa said in a soft voice, her eyes far away. "It was the worst night of my life. I was only fourteen. I was so scared. Mother was in the room next door. Aunty Patel was in the next house. I thought if I screamed loud enough, they'd come and rescue me, but no one came."

I listened silently.

"He left me on the bed with my thighs covered in blood," Aunty Shilpa continued. "I cried all night."

"Did he beat you?"

"Yes…in many ways," she said, hesitating. "He came home drunk every night and he beat me inside and out, on my face, my back, my head even. One day he beat me so hard and I bled so much I had to throw away the sheets. I bled the next day, too, and when I went to the hospital, the nurse said I bled a baby out of my stomach." She looked down, unable to meet my eyes.

I reached out and put my hand over hers, feeling numb. I may not be able to take away the memories or the pain, but I could at least hold her.

"Every night was the same," she said in a distant voice. "I wished I was dead. That is what happens when you marry an older man. That was my life. That is the life you will have."

I'd squeezed her hand tightly, the same way she'd squeezed mine on my first bus ride home in Goa.

"It's okay, Aunty Shilpa," I said. "That's not going to happen. Everything's going to be okay. I promise we'll find a way."

"Your grandma knew all along what she was putting me into," Aunty Shilpa said, looking at me with sad eyes. "She never said a word, not before or after the wedding. When she found out I'd lost a baby boy, a *boy,* she said I was trying to sabotage the family. My husband hit me the hardest that night for losing a son."

I listened in shock. I had no understanding of these horrors she was describing but I knew in my bones I was never going to face these same things.

Aunty Shilpa wiped her tears. "Oh Asha, you are much too young to understand. You shouldn't be hearing this."

I leaned over and gave her a hug. Whatever nightmares she was reliving, there was no going back and changing them, but I knew one thing for sure. I was not going to marry that monster who lived upstairs. No matter what, I was going to get away. And I was going to take Aunty Shilpa and Preeti with me.

"So," Franky said, putting his teacup on his desk. "Here's what we can do, my dear ladies. I can take out a bank loan on your behalf and add it to Asha's parents' funds. You can then use that to pay off the marriage broker, and anything else you need, er, emergencies and all that, including keeping Kristadasa off your back legally."

"That's good," I said, feeling relieved.

"Yes, but how are you going to pay the loan back?" Franky said, giving me a serious look. "No one gives money away for free, miss. That is a problem we have to solve."

"I'll take another shift at the hotel," Aunty Shilpa said. "They need help and they like my work."

"No, Aunty, you can't do extra work. Not in your con—" I swallowed quickly.

She turned and gave me a puzzled look.

"Because—" I grasped for words. "Because I'm going to make fairy cakes. I'll make hundreds and hundreds. The girls at school love them, even my principal likes them."

"Ha, my dear ladies. I am afraid that working at the local hotel and making fancy cakes will not be enough. It will take a lifetime to pay off this loan and even then, you won't be finished."

We looked at him in dismay.

"But, not to worry." Franky broke into a grin again. "What I want to tell you is that I have a solution."

"Like what?" Aunty Shilpa gave him a suspicious look again.

"I have connections all over the world." Franky spoke deliberately as if he was about to reveal a big secret.

He paused. We waited.

"What are you trying to say, Franky?" Aunty Shilpa said warily.

"You see, madam," he said. He took a sip of his tea and paused. "I can send Asha to work for a very rich family, overseas."

Chapter Twenty

"**N**ever!" Aunty Shilpa jumped from her chair. "Never, I tell you!"

"But madam—"

"What nonsense is this!"

"Calm down, madam," Franky said, motioning with his hands. "Take your seat, *please.*"

"How can you tell me to calm down when you tell me you will sell my niece?" Aunty Shilpa was furious. I looked at her in surprise. I'd never seen her this angry before.

"Madam," Franky said, in a serious but calm tone, "am I offering you any money?"

Aunty Shilpa was too agitated to hear him. "This is blasphemy!" she cried, waving her arms in the air.

"Am I offering you any cash, Madam?" Franky repeated louder.

Aunty Shilpa glared at him.

"If I was offering you money for Miss Asha, then, yes, you would definitely be selling her. What I am proposing is only to broker a contract for her to work as a contractor. Then she can make enough good money to solve all of your problems." He paused before adding, "All of your problems. I am only trying to help you here."

I cleared my throat to speak, but Franky continued quickly.

"She speaks English and she is very good in school. She will make the perfect candidate. Not to worry, this is nothing like those mangy dogs on the street who steal girls and sell them to the rich Arabs. I am a good businessman. I only work with professionals."

Aunty Shilpa didn't say a word. She was watching Franky like a wary cat would watch a Husky walk toward her.

"What I am proposing is a serious and formal business contract that we will sign and that will be upheld in any Indian court."

Franky's smile widened. "Miss Asha will be paid very well to work for a respectable family. A very good family. I will assure you of that."

Aunty Shilpa was still standing, but her face wasn't as red as before. "Madam, *please* sit," Franky pleaded with his arms outstretched. "Sit and have another cup of chai and we can discuss this."

He turned to his son in the corner and raised his voice. "Oy! Go get two more sweet teas for these ladies." Fartybag shot us a nasty look and got up reluctantly.

Fartybag no longer bothered me. He sat in his dark corner watching pirated movies and pretending to ignore us, but I knew my presence bothered him. His father was treating me like an adult, and I was no longer "the stupid foreign girl" but "Miss." I didn't rub it in Fartybag's face, but I made sure to only drink the tea if Franky had poured it into my cup. I didn't want to take any chances.

Aunty Shilpa sank slowly back in her chair. I could see she was shaking.

"I am only trying to help your good family, madam," Franky said, giving her a pleading look, his palms open, his shoulders reverently hunched. "Just trying to do the right thing."

"What will Mother say?" Aunty Shilpa asked, worried. "I won't be able to live with myself if Asha leaves us."

"Even if she goes back to Tanzania?" Franky said.

"Tanzania?" I said, sitting up. "Are you serious?"

"No!" Aunty Shilpa said, half standing again. "Not back to Africa."

"Why not?" I said, turning to her. "That's my home."

"That *was* your home. Your home is here now," Aunty Shilpa said, giving me a stern look. "Besides, you're only fifteen. Still a child."

I stared at her. "Grandma says I'm old enough to marry that nasty old man and have tons of babies. How come I'm not old enough to travel to my home country? How come, huh?" I spoke with more force than was needed.

Aunty Shilpa had nothing to say to that. She covered her face with her hands. Franky watched us with a slight smile curled on his lips.

"What about school?" I asked, remembering my promise to my father.

"Ah, but this will be a short break for you. Only for one very short year away from school, miss," Franky said, leaning toward me. "You're such a smart girl, you won't even realize you missed a year. In fact, let me tell you the work you will be doing will be like getting a degree. You will come back even smarter than your classmates. How good will that be?"

I sat back in my chair to consider this. Taking a year off to save Aunty Shilpa and myself wasn't breaking any promises to my father. All I was doing was slightly stretching time and for a good cause. Plus, it sounded like the experience would move me further ahead in school.

I nodded. This proposal was good, any way I looked at it.

"Will you promise the wedding will be stopped and *all* those other things will be taken care of if I do this?" I asked. "One hundred percent?"

"Two thousand percent." Franky nodded vigorously. "I will personally have a talk with Kristadasa and everyone else myself. They will listen to me. You can rest assured of this."

"This is great!" I said, getting excited at the thought of returning to my homeland. I turned to Aunty Shilpa with a wide smile, my heart beating a tick faster. "I can do this, Aunty! This is such a great idea."

She didn't smile back.

"Miss Asha is the best person for the job, madam," Franky said. "She can even read and write in English. She has traveled all around the world. She has even her own legitimate passport. She has qualifications that everybody wants. Finding a well-paying job will not be a problem at all. You're, in fact, very lucky to have her. She will be paid well and treated well, I can very much assure you of that, madam."

"I know what happens to girls that leave India," Aunty Shilpa said in a quiet voice. "They become slaves. They get beaten. They die."

"Not in Tanzania," I said, shaking my head. "I never saw bad things happen there. Except for my schoolmates, everybody was super nice. It's the best place in the world."

"What kind of job is this you're talking about?" Aunty Shilpa asked Franky.

"Not to worry so much, madam. It is like office work for a family business," Franky said, bobbing his head from side to side. "She doesn't have to dirty her hands like a lowly maid, and they will take care of her very well. And if Miss Asha wants to return any time, she can do so. But I am sure she will stay and do a very excellent job and make a lot of good money for you."

"Of course, I will," I said quickly.

My heart had begun to beat faster and faster as the conversation played out. My mind whirred. I'd left a part of me on the African continent and I couldn't wait to go back. I'd get to talk to Mr. Mudenda again and ask what truly happened to my parents, a worrying question that kept me up at night. I'd get to see Chanda. I'd get to visit the market and get my hair done by Mrs. Ngozi again and eat her delicious pumpkin stew.

Most of all, I'd get to visit my parents' graves and give them a proper farewell.

"Imagine, madam," Franky said with a wide yellow grin. "In one year, you will not only be relieved of this marriage burden, but you will be able to send the girls to school, get new uniforms, get a fancy big television even. You will not need to work at the hotel anymore. Think about all this before you say no."

"Who will take care of her in Tanzania?" Aunty Shilpa said, turning to me with a frown.

"Mrs. Ngozi," I replied. "She's my best friend's mother. She said I can come and stay whenever I wanted. I also know Mr. Mudenda from the hospital. He's the one who arranged Mama and Papa's funeral. He said I can come back anytime too. They're the nicest people you will ever meet."

"She will make in one month what you make at the hotel in ten years, madam. Do you really want to let this chance slip?"

"I don't know about this."

"Look, her own parents went to Africa to build a better life there, and they did very well," Franky said.

"Mama and Papa loved it there," I said. "Once I've settled in, you and Preeti and Grandma can join me."

Franky got up and picked up one of the teapots Fartybag had just brought in. Fartybag had got fed up being asked to troop up and down the stairs for us, so he was bringing two teapots now. Franky poured a cup for Aunty Shilpa.

"You are worrying too much, madam. All you have to do is sign and I can take care of it all for you."

"How do I know *you* won't take the money and run?" Though illiterate, Aunty Shilpa was no pushover.

"How can you even think that, madam?" Franky said, throwing his hands up in the air with a look of distress. "How can you say that to your own good neighbor? I am a god-fearing Hindu. I attend the temple ceremonies every day, I tell you, every day. I even go to church. I have been in this business for twenty-five years and every year I give something back. This is what I live for."

Franky stood up.

"To show you my full, honest integrity, I will swear on my dead mother's grave," he said, turning to the pictures behind his desk. He brought his hands together and bowed in front of the faded photo of the old woman on the wall. "I swear by my dead mother's grave I will do my best to help these young women."

"Now," he said, clearing his throat. "I will also swear on the shrine of our great Lord Vishnu." He turned to the poster of the blue Vishnu god behind his desk and bowed deeply. "May you throw a thunderbolt on me if what I am proposing does not help these ladies in any way whatsoever."

A thundering sound rattled Franky's desk. I looked up in alarm. Franky looked petrified.

"Oh, Lord Vishnu!" Aunty Shilpa cried, bringing her hand to her chest.

"It's a bus, Appa," Fartybag said from his corner. He was looking out the window. "The double-decker bus."

Everyone sighed in relief. Franky took out a white handkerchief and wiped his brow.

"As I was saying," he said, after clearing his throat. "I swear by all the ten thousand gods, Lord Shiva, Lord Vishnu, Lord Ganesha, Lord Devi, Lord Surya—"

"What do we have to do?" I snapped. "Just tell us. I have seven days before my life ends and I become a beaten wife."

Next to me, I felt Aunty Shilpa flinch at my words. She shook her head and gave an unhappy shrug like she was stuck between two difficult decisions, like she couldn't stop the inevitable.

With a self-satisfied smile, Franky rustled through the papers until he found what he was looking for and turned to Aunty Shilpa.

"All you have to do is press your thumb right here."

Aunty Shilpa stared at him wordlessly.

"If you will permit me to hold your finger, madam," he said with a slight bow and reached out for her hand.

Franky dipped her right thumb in the ink jar and pressed it delicately on the paper to create a bright purple smudge.

Chapter Twenty-one

The orange henna twisted around my ankles like barbed wire.

I sat quietly, trying not to move as the old woman squatting in front of me created her artwork. She didn't look at my face nor did she talk to me. I was just a nameless canvas on which she did her ritual work.

When she finished, she offered a toothless grin to Grandma, who in turn offered her betel nuts and money. I looked at my hands and feet. To Grandma, this was the traditional beautification of a bride before an impending wedding. To me, it was a cobweb designed to entangle me.

Grandma was ready for the wedding scheduled for the next day. She'd bought my special sari, a long piece of cheap fabric in a garish red and yellow, a cocoon in which I was going to be entombed. She'd even made me prepare plates of sweets and desserts to take to the groom's family.

What she didn't know was I had other plans for my wedding day.

Before the sun was even a glimmer in the sky the next morning, I slipped outside our apartment and caught the earliest bus back to the place I'd first arrived in this city. There, I waited, hiding inside the main airport bookstore. I lurked behind the bookshelves, praying no one would see me, waiting for Franky to arrive, my stomach in a knot, my mind filled with anxiety.

The only person I'd said a proper goodbye to was Meena at the station, just before I got on the airport bus. It had been a hurried and whispered goodbye. When I glanced back from inside the bus, I saw her face, a mixture of sadness and worry, like she was responsible for what I was doing.

I waved as the bus pulled out. She put her hands together and bowed the traditional greeting. I hoped to see her again one day. One day, when I'd be free again.

Franky's instructions had been clear. "Pack your bag before dawn and take the first bus to the airport. I'll come with your passport and ticket. Don't breathe a word to anyone, not even your Aunty Shilpa, if you want to help her too."

The day after Aunty Shilpa signed the bank documents, I returned to the Good and Fast Immigration Broker to make sure Franky had understood the urgency of her health situation.

"Not to worry, miss. I will take good care of it. The doctor will already be calling her and she won't even know of this arrangement," Franky had said, passing me a cup of chai. "With the money your parents left you, you're going to be killing three birds."

"Killing birds?" I'd looked at him, horrified.

"What I mean to say is," Franky had said, holding up his fingers, "one, you will get out of this unwanted marriage, two, you will help your Aunty get better and three, you will help Preeti finish school even. Three good birds. Not bad, no?"

I let this sink in.

"That is exactly what your good parents would have expected you to do, miss."

I nodded. That was true. They'd always told me to help others who were in greater need than I was. "I miss them."

"Your esteemed father and mother would have been proud of you, miss," Franky had said, leaning back in his chair, cradling his teacup. "They were very smart. They even went to school."

"University."

"That is exactly what I meant. I only wish I had a chance to meet them. What a loss. They were highly respectable, not like the riffraff you bump into around here."

I had to agree. His own son, Fartybag, was one of those riffraff, but I couldn't tell him that.

"Your grandmother was wrong to try and marry you off. She means well, so do not resent her. She is not educated like your parents, miss. Marrying off a girl child is tradition. But now, it is practically child abuse, that is what I say." Franky had slurped loudly from his cup.

That's true.

He leaned in and said almost in a whisper, "Now, if you were my own daughter, I will give you one piece of good advice. Is that fine?"

I sat up. "Sure."

"If your grandmother finds out what you're trying to do, she will stop you immediately, and your aunty will not be able to help you. She may try to stop you herself."

"But Aunty Shilpa signed the papers. She's not as bad as Grandma. She's much nicer too."

"That is true, but she is an illiterate. She doesn't think like you and me, you see." Frankly had tapped his head. "Who knows? But I am only telling you for your own good."

He had a point. Aunty Shilpa couldn't even read the cartoons in the children's section of the daily newspaper. I read them out loud to her every week. Though she was kind, she knew little about the world and its ways.

"You can't educate everyone. What can you do? That is life. That is our karma," Franky had said. "All I can ask is for you to do your job, so I can do my job to help you."

I'd stepped out of his office that day, feeling like everything was finally falling into place. I was no longer afraid of the future.

Late after midnight that night, when Grandma and Aunty Shilpa were sound asleep, Preeti gave me my wedding gift. It was a pair of beautiful beaded ankle bracelets she'd bought at the market. I couldn't tell her my plans, so I'd just hugged her and cried.

She'd tried to comfort me, saying it's typical for girls to cry before they marry, but she hadn't known mine were not bridal tears. Mine were farewell tears. I was going to leave her, all my remaining family, and this country in a few hours.

I clasped one of the bracelets around my ankle, then, choking back a sob, I got on one knee to clasp the second one around hers. She agreed after some protesting, only after I told her it would be our forever link. What she hadn't known then was it would be my forever link to her, to India, wherever in the world I might be.

That anklet was now clinking with every step and the man in the airport bookstore was getting annoyed. I picked up the book nearest to me, pretending to browse. *Sunil Looks for a Good Indian Wife*, the title said. *How fitting.* I sighed and put the book back. The man was still glaring. I gave him a courtesy nod. I now knew how to do a bobblehead nod like a true Indian, but his frown only deepened. I'd been lurking in the store for half an hour now. *Maybe it's best to wait at the gate.* At least I wouldn't look suspicious.

At fifteen, I was just above the mandatory escort age of Air India. A year younger and I'd have had to get an adult to sign for my travel, and I'd have been escorted by an air steward throughout the trip. I was lucky.

I stepped out of the bookstore.

"Asha!"

I looked behind me to see Aunty Shilpa.

"Aunty!" I ran to her and threw my arms around her.

"I am so glad to find you," she said, hugging me back.

"What are you doing here?"

Part of me surged with happiness to see her, while another part of me felt slightly sick. *Is my plan in jeopardy?* But I held on to her tightly. I'd begun to feel lost in this big, busy airport, and it hurt I hadn't said a proper goodbye to her or Preeti. It hurt more, knowing I might not see them for a full year. *Remember why you're doing this,* I'd kept telling myself, whenever a lonely thought had crept into my mind.

"Did Franky tell you I was here?" I asked.

"I've been looking everywhere for you," she said, pulling me away from the corridor and into a quieter corner. She looked like she'd been crying. "You have to come home with me."

I looked at her in surprise. "But it's my wedding day. And Franky said—"

"That man is lying. Don't listen to him."

"What do you mean?"

"He's cheating us, Asha. And he's cheating your parents." Aunty Shilpa pulled a sheaf of papers from the folds of her sari. "See? He's doing this to take your parents' money. He doesn't care about us."

"But...but he used the money to buy my ticket and visa, and to get me out of the wedding contract. You were there with me, remember?"

"Oh, yes, I remember that very well. He was really good, wasn't he?"

"Aunty Shilpa—"

"Asha, please don't argue. You need to come home with me now!"

"You're starting to sound like Grandma. I'm doing this to help me, and help you too." The words slipped out before I could catch them. I swallowed, a little late.

"*Help me*?" Aunty Shilpa said, drawing back. "I don't need any help."

Now I'd said it, I'd have to say it all. "Yes, Aunty. You need a doctor. Preeti told me all about it."

Aunty Shilpa looked crestfallen. "What did she say?"

"She said you were very sick." I couldn't get myself to say "dying."

"Oh, my child, oh, my child...." She put a hand to her chest and started hyperventilating. "Oh, my Lord, oh, my Lord..."

I reached out and touched her arm. "It's okay. I can make enough money to help you. Franky promised to find the right doctor for you. That's why I'm going overseas. Please don't worry, Aunty."

"Listen to me," Aunty Shilpa said, pointing a shaking finger at the papers. "Look at this. I showed this to my manager at the hotel and he said Franky's sending you overseas to—"

"Hey!" A sharp voice came from behind us.

We turned around to look.

Chapter Twenty-two

"What're you doing here?" I asked Fartybag.

"What're *you* doing here?" he snapped, glaring at Aunty Shilpa.

"Where's Franky?" I asked.

"Appa can't come. He has important things to do with some very important people," he replied, puffing his chest. "I'm his deputy, you know."

He looked different today. His torn Rambo T-shirt and tatty pants were gone, and in their place were a brand-new pair of jeans and a blood red T-shirt with the words "The Boss" written across it. On his right hand dangled a set of car keys.

He had a swagger in his step and was no longer shuffling or huffing. He didn't let out one pop, at least none I could smell or hear. He looked like someone had cleaned him up and made him into one of those prep boys who hung out at the local college downtown.

"What do you want with us?" Aunty Shilpa hissed.

"Appa warned me about you. I'm not here for *you*." Fartybag sneered at her.

"Did you buy your new suit with Asha's money?" Aunty Shilpa snapped right back. "Shame on you!"

"I have a good father who takes care of me. Not like you two who have nobody," he said.

That stung. Aunty Shilpa looked away.

"That's really mean," I said, shaking my head. He'll never learn, I thought.

"Here," Fartybag said, thrusting a white envelope in my hands. "Appa said to give this to you."

I opened the envelope. Inside were my passport and a long white stub with an Air India logo. I pulled them out.

"Hey, this is not for—"

"Something came up at the last minute, and he said he had to make changes."

"What changes?" I spluttered. "Why?"

Fartybag shrugged and turned to gawk at a couple of young women walking by.

I looked at the Air India ticket again.

"Let me see this," Aunty Shilpa said, grabbing the paper from my hand. She peered at it. "What does this say, Asha? What does this say?" She held it up, desperately, to the light, but that didn't help her read.

"Maybe the lions won't eat you after all," Fartybag said, sounding genuinely disappointed.

"But I want to see my parents and Chanda and Mr. Mudenda and...." I trailed off, not sure what to say.

"He's tricking us," Aunty Shilpa said, fluttering the ticket in Fartybag's face. "I don't trust your father or you. You're tricking us again!"

"You can believe your illiterate aunty or you can read the papers," Fartybag said, ignoring her. "Appa said he's sending you to a place where you can make real money. Real dollars. It's right there in the new contract."

"New contract?" I pulled everything from the envelope. A legal-sized paper stated my new destination. It came with an official red seal at the bottom, next to a signature in purple ink that looked exactly like Franky's. I stared at it.

"He said you can make more money there. Then maybe you can visit your precious Africa after that. You should say thank you to us. Most people don't get to fly. They go in a dirty boat for days with no food. Don't know why Appa's doing all this for you, because you're just a stupid foreign girl."

"That's because you want to steal all her money!" Aunty Shilpa shouted at him. "You're thieves!"

"Shut up, you cow," Fartybag muttered.

"Hey!" I glared at him. "Don't you dare talk to her like that!" He looked away like he still remembered the punch I'd given his delicate nose.

With shaking hands, I opened my passport. There was a brand-new visa glued to a page at the end. I looked at it closely. The paper shimmered, a shiny red sticker and the word "visa." I turned the booklet to see it in better light. Franky was sending me to a faraway place I'd heard of before but had never dreamed of visiting.

Aunty Shilpa tugged at my sleeve. "Come, Asha. Leave this nonsense behind. This was a terrible mistake. We need to talk to Franky and get your money back."

Fartybag stepped in between Aunty Shilpa and me.

"Appa said if you don't get on the plane, Kristadasa will find you and thrash you to a pulp."

Visions of Kristadasa's looming *feni*-soaked face came to mind. I shook my head. *No! I'm not going back to that.*

"And you'll lose all your money." Fartybag pointed at the papers in my hand. "It's in the contract."

"So *now* you're worried we'll lose money," Aunty Shilpa said, her face flushed.

"Are you going to stand there like an idiot or are you going to go?" Fartybag said to me. "Your plane's leaving soon. If you don't go, Kristadasa will come and get you and then you'll see."

I stared at him. "Where's your father?"

"Appa said he can't help you if you don't go. He told me he wants you to do your job so he can do his job." He gave me a pointed look. "You can go now or stay behind and lose everything, including helping your aunty."

"Don't you dare do this!" Aunty Shilpa said, shaking her finger at him, her voice filled with rage. "Don't you dare!" She turned to me. "Don't listen to this boy!"

"You can't even read the ticket," Fartybag said to her with a sneer.

I looked up at the airport TV screen in the corridor. It was noon. It was close to the "auspicious" hour—the time the gods had decided was best for the wedding, at least according to the marriage broker. Visions of Kristadasa waiting for me flashed across my mind. I shuddered. I had to think quickly.

I turned to Aunty Shilpa. "I can't help you if I stay here and get married to that drunkard. I can't do that, Aunty Shilpa. But if I can make money, I can help you. I can find a way to help all of us. I promise. I can't go back now."

She looked like she was about to burst into tears. "You can't go, my child. You can't trust these people. You can't go."

"You're late," Fartybag said, poking my arm. "Look, they're calling your flight. You better hurry or you'll miss it."

I gave Aunty Shilpa a desperate look.

She let out a wail. "This is my mistake! How could I let this happen?"

"Aunty," I said, showing her the legal paper. "Look. This comes with a red seal. I've seen this before. Mama and Papa used this to make their job contracts official. This means we can trust these papers. Even if we can't trust Franky, we can trust a contract. I know this."

"Oh, my child...oh, my child."

"It's going to be okay, Aunty. I'll be back sooner than you realize. I'll write to you and send you money. Everything will be all right. I promise."

I reached over and gave her a hug, squeezing her as tightly as I could, while she stood stiff like a zombie, tears streaming down her face. "I'm doing this for all of us, Aunty. I want you to get better."

"They're calling your plane number now," I heard Fartybag say. "You're totally late."

I tore myself from Aunty Shilpa and picked up my bag.

Without looking back, I ran toward the check-in counter. I knew Aunty Shilpa was just a few feet behind, watching. I knew she was devastated. But I couldn't sit back and do nothing while she faded to death. And getting married to anyone, let alone that evil man, was unimaginable. My heart ripped a little with every step I took, but I kept moving.

Just before turning the corner, I glanced back.

Seeing Aunty Shilpa's face made my heart feel like it was rupturing into a thousand pieces. I was always leaving someone behind—my parents in Tanzania, and now Aunty Shilpa and Preeti in India. *It's only for a year,* I said to myself. *Only one year.*

I blew her a kiss. She stood like a heartbroken statue in the middle of the corridor, people bustling around her. She was crying, I could see. I choked back a sob. *If I don't leave now, I'll never leave.* I gave a final wave and turned around.

I stepped up to the flight desk. My worn Indian passport with stamps and visas from all over meant I'd traveled before. My shiny new visa impressed them. They glanced at it quickly before handing it back. I sailed through the security check. I'd just picked up my bag when the PA system crackled to life.

"This is a final boarding announcement for Air India Flight Three-Six-Seven to Toronto. All passengers must now be at gate seventy-two for departure."

That was my call.

Part FIVE

A journey of a thousand miles starts with a single step.
Lao Tzu

Chapter Twenty-three

I stumbled across the tarmac in a daze.

Instead of going east to Africa where my parents lay buried, I was heading north. It was like being in a surreal film, like one of those Swedish science fiction movies my father loved to watch.

I found my seat at the back of the plane, settled in, and opened the white envelope Fartybag had given me. I was about to tuck my passport and boarding pass inside when I noticed something else. A reedy-thin beige paper stuck to one side of the envelope. I pulled it out and carefully unfolded it on my tray. It was a letter in crooked, almost illegible handwriting like a market scribe in Goa had drafted it.

I squinted to read.

Dear Miss Asha, it began.

With you gone, your grandmother will no longer be bound by the contract to the marriage broker. You are saving your entire family and especially, of course, your own dear Aunty. You are a true loyal daughter, one that your parents would have been proud of. Very much.

I stopped. Something had caught in my throat. I swallowed, took a deep breath, and continued reading.

I want you to know that it took me a very long time to find the perfect family for you. This was really not an easy task and it was fraught with many problems. In the end, my lead in Tanzania did not turn out. I am utterly apologetic about that.

However, I have very good news. I took all the effort to convince Mrs. Rao in Canada to take you in for a year. She wanted the best girl in India, and I said I could surely help her in that regard. Now that she said yes to taking you, you will need to show her that you are the absolute right person for the job. This means you must prove you are a very diligent worker. There will be House Rules to follow. If you break any of these Rules or if she thinks at any time that you are not the right person for the job, she will send you back.

Alas, if you return before the contract is up by the end of the year, we will no longer be able to hold off the marriage contract between you and Mr. Kristadasa. I trust that you will use the high intelligence that your esteemed parents have bequeathed you and understand the right thing to do. In any case, you must not violate the arrangement. And I know you will be a good girl.

By the end of the year, I will send you a one-way ticket for you to come back and reunite with your family. Now doesn't that sound good?

I must warn you about one thing. Kristadasa will not be happy about the breakup of his wedding and will try his best to take revenge. Be careful of anyone asking questions. Do not speak with anyone, including the police or anyone who comes knocking on your door. Kristadasa and his men will try all kinds of trickery. Don't talk to any strangers. You must tell anyone who asks that you are none other than Mrs. Rao's lovely niece, an orphan, and that you are adopted by her.

Mrs. Rao is very frail, well into her age. She will be your sponsor, your family. A more wonderful woman you will never meet. She will be like a kind old aunty to you. She is, however, quite feeble, and will need all the help she can get around the house. With your abundant skills and talents, she will surely appreciate having you in her home and treat you very well, that I can assure you.

She will pay a weekly wage, which she will send directly here to Goa. I will use 40% of it to pay back the marriage broker, 40% to find that good doctor for your dear Aunty Shilpa, and put the remaining in a bank account for you in Goa so you can do whatever you want to do with it when you get back. I know for a fact that they all will appreciate your sacrifice very much, and that is all that I have to say.

God bless.

I turned the page, but all the other side had were ink blotches that had seeped through. The letter had no heading or signature, but the purple ink was unmistakable. It was the same ink Aunty Shilpa had dipped her thumb in to sign the bank account transfer documents.

I leaned back in my seat and wondered if I'd done the right thing. Fartybag's presence at the airport troubled me. But I'd had no choice. Or had I?

I was helping Aunty Shilpa get better and was getting myself out of a horrifying future, a nightmare I didn't even want to begin to imagine. Aunty Shilpa's sweet face flashed to mind. Tears welled in my eyes. The plane hadn't taken off yet and I'd already begun to miss her and Preeti, and even Grandma. I turned toward the window and cried silently, thankful no one was sitting next to me.

It took a long time to dry my eyes and sit up in my seat. Outside the window, wistful cotton clouds swam about, worry free. I watched them mindlessly, wishing I could be like them, wondering what awaited me on the other side of the ocean. I felt a stab of fear go through my heart. It was the fear of the unknown. The doubts of my decision. I took a deep breath. I could twist myself into a sniveling pretzel or I could prepare myself for my future. I took a few more deep breaths and tried to remember everything I knew about my soon-to-be new home.

The only Canadian I'd known in my entire life was Ms. Stacy from the International School of Dar es Salaam. She was friendly but didn't talk much about her country—too busy asking everyone else about East Africa. Her host continent fascinated her.

The one day we explored Canada was the day Ms. Stacy read a book by William Parry to the class. It was the first chapter from a diary written by a man who'd traveled to the Arctic a hundred years ago. It was a story about the most remote and barren place on earth where exposed skin froze in seconds. I shivered just thinking of it.

"Hey, Ms. Stacy, do you live in an igloo?" Tanya had asked, interrupting Ms. Stacy's reading.

"No, Miss Harding, I do not."

"Where do you sleep?"

"We have regular homes like anywhere else."

"Have you ever seen a polar bear?" It had been Shanti this time.

"No, Miss Brahmin, I have not." Ms. Stacy had looked like she'd heard these questions before. She'd tried to get back to her reading, but the girls were not finished.

"Father told me Canadians eat seals for dinner," Bethany had chimed in. "Baby seals too. Is that true?"

"Little baby seals?" Sophie had said, horrified. "That's disgusting." Seeing her face, I'd wondered for a moment if she felt the same about the children forced to work in her parents' mines in Africa.

"Well," Ms. Stacy had hesitated, "It's certainly a traditional delicacy in certain regions, but you won't see that at—"

"Is everyone in Canada fat?" Shanti had interrupted. "Like those Eskimos on TV."

"The correct word is Inuit, Ms. Brahmin, not Eskimo," Ms. Stacy had said in a firm voice, though her face was now flushed. "And we come in all sizes, like everywhere else." She'd let out a loud sigh.

"They're fat because they eat seal blubber," Anne had said, giggling.

The others had joined in the laughter. These girls attacked in a pack.

"You eat seal blubber?" a boy at the back of the class had asked.

"Have you ever eaten seal heart, Ms. Stacy?" another boy had asked.

"How about a walrus?"

"Gross!"

"Fatsos!"

"Jelly belly!"

"Blubber eaters!"

The whole class had erupted. "Blubber eaters! Blubber eaters!"

"Settle down, everyone," Ms. Stacy had said. Her plump cheeks had turned bright pink now. She'd picked up her book and begun to read the next chapter out loud, trying to drown the heckling, her voice wavering.

I folded the letter carefully and put it back in the envelope. I was on my way to the land of icy cold winds, polar bears, and possible blubber eaters.

I wasn't at all ready.

Chapter Twenty-four

Franky was dead wrong. Mrs. Rao was anything but feeble or frail.

I was standing near the airport pickup line with the worn suitcase Mr. Mudenda had picked out of the lost-and-found bin at the Dar es Salaam hospital. It was the same one I'd brought with me to India, a lifetime ago.

This new country I'd flown into was frigid. I felt the cold that seeped through my clothes, my skin, right into my bones, leaving me covered in a tingle of goose bumps. It was like I'd walked into an enormous outdoor fridge. Everyone around me was in T-shirts or simple blouses, chatting, checking phones, and hanging around like it was just another day. I shivered visibly.

"First time here?" asked the man behind me in line.

I looked up at the stranger and nodded, my lips too frozen to speak.

"Visiting?"

"No...um...I'm staying for a while," I mumbled, remembering Franky's warning in his letter. *Don't talk to strangers.*

"It's pretty cold for ya, eh?"

I nodded again.

"This is not cold. No siree. Real cold is when the river freezes and there's snow on the ground," he said with a wink and a kind smile. "Don't you worry. You'll be alright. Everyone gets used to it."

I hugged myself closer. *Freezing rivers? Snow on the ground?*

Just then, a sleek black Cadillac drove up with a swoosh and stopped right in front of me, sending more of the chilly air my way. It was the biggest, blackest car I'd seen in my life. The driver's door opened and a stout woman looked out. She glared at me. I stared back in surprise. She was Indian, obviously. She seemed as wide as she was tall, and dressed in a chic skirt suit. *Is this—?*

"Asha?" the woman barked in a voice deeper than a man's.

I straightened up. "Yes," I said in a meek voice.

"Put your bag in the back." With that, she slammed the door shut. It took a few seconds to collect my thoughts and pick up my bag.

Though her appearance had been brief, Mrs. Rao instantly reminded me of a warthog I'd seen during a safari trip at the Serengeti. Her dark brown hair was cut bob style. On top of her head had been a pair of enormous sunglasses attached to a chain that went around her chubby neck. Her thin lips were painted blood red. Stout, with heavy-set jowls, Mrs. Rao looked as formidable as a warthog. It would take me some time to discover those tusks of hers.

I put my suitcase in the trunk and opened the passenger door. And just as quickly, I pulled my head back.

"Are you getting in or not?" Mrs. Rao said sharply. "I don't have all day."

The inside of the car was suffocating with expensive perfume. I took a deep breath of the fresh outside air and got in, and promptly sank into the soft leather seat.

I couldn't believe my eyes—the plush interior, the wood paneling, the heated seats. Wasn't this how Bollywood movie stars got around? Hanging from the rearview mirror was a crucifix necklace made of ivory. On the dashboard was a framed photo of an Indian man in a smart white jacket. I turned to look at the backseat, which seemed a mile away. A well-groomed ball of black-and-white fur with its tail tucked in lifted its head momentarily to give me a condescending growl. Mr. Raj Kapur didn't think much of me from the start.

We drove in silence for a while.

"Thank you for picking me up, Mrs. Rao."

Not a word from my companion.

"One of my teachers was Canadian." I wanted to be friendly, to make a good first impression. "Do you know a Ms. Stacy from Toronto?"

Mrs. Rao grunted. Just like a warthog would.

"She used to teach at the International School of Dar es Salaam."

"I don't know your teachers," Mrs. Rao said brusquely. I guessed she wasn't much of a talker.

I looked out the window. Everything was crispy clean here. Unlike the streets of Goa, which were like a teen's messy, dirty room, upheaved by a tornado, this place looked like the waiting room of a posh beauty clinic.

I saw no cows on the road, no litter on the streets and no beggars on the pavement. No rickety rickshaws, no honking cars, no yelling street vendors, no festooned buses with dozens of people hanging on doorways. The asphalt was smooth as if the roads had been built yesterday. Cars stayed in their lanes, and to my surprise, all the traffic lights worked—each and every one of them.

We drove for miles along a quiet, landscaped boulevard. The road looked deserted. The city seemed uninhabited. The few people I saw were waiting in lines at bus stops or at zebra crossings.

"Where *is* everyone?" I asked loudly in spite of myself.

Not a word from Mrs. Rao.

If it isn't a holiday today, there must be a football match or a new film showing somewhere. Or a national emergency Mrs. Rao isn't aware of yet. I gave a sideways glance at my sponsor. She was looking dead straight ahead, her red lips set in a thin line.

Just then, a police car dashed by, with its sirens wailing. The siren didn't sound like the ones in Goa, but it was unmistakable. Franky's letter was still fresh in my mind, and I instantly ducked in my seat, praying Kristadasa hadn't found me already. The police car with lights flashing whizzed by us and disappeared as quickly as it had appeared. I slowly unscrunched myself in my seat, my heart still beating fast.

I glanced over at Mrs. Rao.

She hadn't even blinked. She kept driving as if nothing was unusual. But this time, there was a faint smile on those thin lips of hers.

Chapter Twenty-five

As soon as she parked the car in her driveway, Mrs. Rao scooped up her dog from the backseat and marched inside through a side door without a word.

I sat in the car wondering what to do. *Do I follow her? Do I wait for her to invite me in?*

I looked at the building in front of me in awe. Mrs. Rao didn't live in a normal house. It took a few days to realize she was the sole occupant of this magnificent mansion. In Goa, a place such as this would have housed thirty families. At least.

When I finally realized no one was going to invite me in, I walked inside, trailing my bag behind me. Inside, I found Mrs. Rao hand-feeding pink pills to her dog in the kitchen, cooing, "Eat it, my sweet. Papa would be very unhappy if you don't. These are good for your heart, my pup."

I walked in quietly, set my bag down, and stood next to the fancy kitchen counter, gaping in wonder. The sparkling stone counters. The gleaming stainless steel. The beautiful crown moldings. The futuristic lighting. I didn't know what half the gadgets on the kitchen counter did. This kitchen was twice the size of Grandma's apartment. I was sure I'd died and gone to kitchen nirvana.

"Passport, please," Mrs. Rao said, turning to me. I stared at her blankly for a moment. She snapped her fingers. "Now." I quickly opened my bag and handed it to her.

"Franky said you can cook. Is that true?"

"Yes, Mrs. Rao." If there was one job I could do and do well, this was it.

"Can you make a list?"

"Sorry?"

"I'm going to the washroom to freshen up. When I get back, I want a list of everything you can make."

"*Everything?*"

"Do as I say, please."

Without another word, Mrs. Rao spun around and stomped out of the kitchen with her Shih Tzu tucked under one arm, taking my passport with her.

I looked at the blank pad she'd pushed in front of me. I pulled out one of the plush kitchen chairs and sat for a few minutes lost in thought. *Does she want me to cook for her? Didn't Franky say I was supposed to do office work here? Work that would get me ahead in school? Maybe I start off with cooking and then graduate to other work?*

Taking a deep breath, I began to scribble the names of the cakes I'd made with my mother and the meals I'd cooked under Grandma's supervision.

Once finished, I sat back and glanced at the beautiful chandelier twinkling above me. I wasn't sure if the crystal pieces were truly diamonds, but I wouldn't have been surprised if they had been. The weariness of my journey faded, enough to let in a pang of excitement. The idea of working in this wondrous kitchen seemed like heaven even if it meant I'd not be doing the work Franky had promised me. *In this kitchen, I can make miracles happen.*

I picked up the pen again and wrote down the names of all the stews, curries, stir-fries, breads and sweet desserts I'd heard or read about in my entire life. I didn't know all the recipes, but I was sure I could figure them out.

"Done?"

I looked up. Mrs. Rao was back.

"Yes, Mrs. Rao."

"Good. Here's what we're going to do." She stood with her hands on her hips, looking every bit like a stout warthog. "Every Sunday night, I'm going to make a menu for the week. Your job is to give me a list of ingredients you need to make the meals. Then, I want you to cook for me. Do you understand?"

"Yes, Mrs. Rao."

"I need you to make me dinner starting tonight. Use whatever's in the fridge. Show me what you are capable of, understood?"

"No problem, Mrs. Rao. I can bake, too."

"Bake?" She paused. "Like pies?"

"My best are fairy cakes. My mama's own recipes."

"What in the world is a fairy cake?"

"They're small and round." I cupped one hand to show her.

She raised an eyebrow.

"They're sweet and tasty," I said.

"You mean muffins?"

I shook my head. "They have frosting on top and are fluffy like cakes. Everyone likes them, especially for birthday parties."

"You mean *cupcakes*?"

"My mama called them fairy cakes."

"Make a list. And remember, we call them cupcakes here."

And that was the beginning of my new life.

The list of my cupcakes and other meal ideas went up on the door of Mrs. Rao's stainless-steel fridge, held by a magnet that said *Welcome to Toronto*. Every Sunday, she made a menu for the following week, taking ideas from my list, others from elsewhere. If I didn't know the dish, she'd point at her library near the living room and say, "Go find a recipe book, girl. Don't bother me with details."

She didn't say much and made a habit of ignoring my questions. It took a while for my new situation to sink in.

Cooking was only one part of my job. I had to clean the house and yard as well. One night, exhausted after a full day of cooking and cleaning, I flopped onto the tiny bed in my basement room and looked up at the naked light bulb above. Oddly, it felt satisfying. It was a good-tired feeling. Every sore muscle and aching bone were worth it—well worth it to help Aunty Shilpa get better, make sure

Preeti got to finish school, and get myself out of a horrible arranged marriage.

The cleaning was a chore, of course, and I wished I could do office work to learn new things, but my work in Mrs. Rao's opulent kitchen was my reward. I hummed as I cooked lavish meals, knowing when I was done at the end of the year, Franky would send me a one-way ticket back to Goa, back to a healthier Aunty Shilpa, back to a happier Preeti, and back to school.

That was the year I learned to cook every type of meal on the planet, from hot curries, stews, and pies of all types, to pad Thais and noodles and biryani rice dishes.

I made all the desserts I could figure out, from dark chocolate rolls and, marble pound cakes to sweet sponge cakes filled with blueberries and peaches. Fruits that had been out of my price range in the duty-free shops in East African cities or the fancy stores in Goa—fruits I'd never tasted in my life but I'd seen in my mother's cookbooks—were accessible to me now, courtesy of Mrs. Rao's wallet and her expanding appetite.

Best of all, I had all the spices I wanted in the world. From cardamom to cinnamon, cloves to nutmeg, and saffron to turmeric, Mrs. Rao's spice shelves stocked everything I'd dreamed of. The world had become my culinary oyster.

Except for Saturday nights, Mrs. Rao dined alone. When she did, she sat at one end of her beautiful mahogany dining table. Across from her, all the way at the head of the table, sat a gold-framed photograph with an ivory crucifix necklace draped over it. The photo in it was of a serious Mr. Rao, in a black suit and tie.

When I first came to this house, I was sure Mr. Rao was hiding or lost in one of the many rooms of this mansion. Then, I learned he'd died years ago, but his spirit seemed to live on in this house.

Mrs. Rao was a pack rat.

She kept everything, including her dead husband's clothes in the closet and his shaving kit and toothbrush in the bathroom. The gold-framed picture of her husband never moved from its spot at the head of the table. One of my jobs was to dust it and make a fresh garland of flowers from the garden to put on it every day.

After I started to make fairy cakes every week, I noticed she propped the biggest one in front of the picture, like the offerings I'd seen Grandma give her goddess Kali in Goa. That cake would sit for days drying up, getting moldy, until I made a new batch, and a new cake would take its place in front of the frame. I wasn't sure whether to be freaked out or feel sorry for her.

I made whatever Mrs. Rao asked me. But there was one dish I wasn't able to make—the gulab jamun balls described by Shanti at my international school a long time ago. I could make the sugary balls well enough. I made them big. I made them small. I made them dry. I made them syrupy. But when I added "gold sprinkles" to my shopping list of ingredients, Mrs. Rao crossed it out with a fine-tipped red pen. It was then I realized Mrs. Rao might be rich and live in a mini castle in Toronto, but she wasn't the Brahmin daughter of an Indian High Commissioner.

There was one other dish I couldn't get myself to make. Spicy rotis reminded me too much of life with Preeti and Aunty Shilpa.

I missed them dearly. Though my last year in Goa had been like living under a darkened monsoon sky waiting for it to pour down on me, I ached for the smell of the tropical ocean. I ached to feel the warm Indian sun on my skin and to see everyone again. I especially wanted to give a big hug to Aunty Shilpa and tell her not to worry, that everything was fine, that I'd be back soon.

I wondered how she was doing back in India.

M rs. Rao entertained every Saturday night and it was a curious crowd she had over.

Saturday was the only day that broke my routine. On all other days, I mopped miles of tiles, vacuumed room after carpeted room, scrubbed the long granite kitchen counter, and cleaned three bathrooms, each with golden taps and marble tubs large enough to soak an elephant. I even took care of the outdoor pool, her cars, and the garage.

I didn't normally get to bed until one in the morning. I got lost in my work and days became weeks and weeks quickly became months. I felt grateful though. While Mrs. Rao's words were short and sharp, she didn't slap me like Grandma.

When she had dinner guests, I had to wear a uniform. It was a short black dress and a white apron. Being only five feet tall and ninety pounds, everything was usually too large for me. But this uniform was clearly made for someone exactly one size larger and it looked used, which made me wonder if someone else had done this work before me.

Because her guests expected nothing short of luxury, Mrs. Rao opened her entire library to me. "Find me the best menus that will be the talk of the town, you hear?" she said before stalking off with Mr. Raj Kapur in tow.

Mrs. Rao never used her library, but to me it was it was a treasure trove. When I slipped my fingers along the books on that first day, I discovered dust on every shelf. No one had touched these books for months, if not for years. It was the same with the mountains of fancy magazines she left strewn over the coffee tables and floor, still in their plastic dust jackets. I ripped off the covers to these magazines—ranging from travel to home decor to fashion to gourmet cooking—and devoured them in the kitchen while waiting for a cake to rise or a broth to boil.

And this was how I discovered Chef Pierre. His baking magazines had beautiful, mouthwatering photos for every recipe, and his articles were written with so much warmth, it was like reading letters from an old friend. Chef Pierre's magazines slowly became my baking and cooking bible, from which I tried every recipe I found.

Chef Pierre was a renowned pastry chef with luxury cafés around the world, cafés that catered to royalty—both true royalty and those of the film and fashion variety. I flipped through his glossy magazines, enthralled at the pictures of beautiful guests, red awnings, tables draped in white-and-red tablecloths, and plush red chairs. The photos of his cakes looked so genuine I felt I could lick the icing off the pages.

In the photos, Chef Pierre looked like someone I'd bump into at any corner bakery, a rotund man with a happy and friendly baker face that said, "I'm the best baker in the world. Come on in and have some sweets." How could anyone resist? I dreamed of meeting this man who'd begun with nothing and become everything I wanted to be. Independent. Free. Appreciated for my culinary creations.

He came from a poor background, just like me. He was born into a family of coal miners in southern Belgium. His mother had died when he was born, and it was his grandmother who'd taken care of him. I wondered if she'd slapped him around like mine had. It was when Chef Pierre discovered his passion for baking and cooking, he changed his predestined path that would have led to the dirty, dank mines where his father worked.

I consumed his story, his pictures, his recipes. *If he can do it, why can't I? One day,* I told myself. *One day. Just you wait, world.*

Very soon, I began to experiment, blending my mother's recipes with ideas from Chef Pierre's magazines, creating blends of East and West. I sprinkled cinnamon, cardamom, cloves, and nutmeg into my batter to get those earthy flavors my mother used to create. I learned to make spiced-up creations of all kinds of sweets, from maple-vanilla ice cream and strawberry-and-cream tarts to lemony cheesecake and triple-chocolate red-velvet cakes. I loved to bake. Mrs. Rao and her guests loved to eat.

Every Saturday afternoon, I designed menus, cooked, baked, prepped dishes, and set the table. When Mrs. Rao buzzed me from the dining room or the patio on warmer evenings, I'd bring out the dinner plates, two by two, for the seated guests. I lived for their *oohs* and *aahs*. I didn't speak with anyone, no matter what they asked or how much they cajoled. "Just nod and smile," had been Mrs. Rao's strict instructions.

One particular guest had a nose like the proboscis monkeys of Borneo and liked to pinch my behind whenever I walked by him. "My cupcake girl," he'd say with a glint in his eye, oozing sleaze. I always made sure to stay a foot away from him, even if it meant reaching across another guest and making them duck under my hot dishes.

Once Mrs. Rao's guests began eating, I had nothing to do but wait in the kitchen. I browsed the foodie and travel magazines, listening to the sounds of corks popping, glasses clinking, and cutlery tinkling in the dining room. Sometimes, when three or four bottles of wine had been opened, things would get loud quickly, and I'd hear drunken laughter from the men and high-pitched giggles from the women.

I'd wait in the kitchen, poring over recipes until the second buzzer summoned me. This was the signal to have chai tea and sweets ready to serve. After dinner and dessert, the guests would retire into the massive living room, where they'd open decks of cards and bottles of whiskey, and the games would begin.

One night, while I was cleaning the dinner table, I peeked into the living room through a crack in the door. Everyone was huddled around the coffee table, some guests lounging on cushions on the floor. Mrs. Rao was pouring glasses of port for her guests and the proboscis man was smoking an expensive cigar. Everyone had cards in their hands, and there were piles of paper notes in the middle of the table. This was real money, and from the color of the bills, I could see they were not small denominations.

When I finally heard the engines of the Cadillacs, Mercedes, and BMWs rev up and pull out of the driveway, my next tasks began. I emptied the dishwasher for the third time, took out the garbage, and vacuumed the dining room, the living room, and the kitchen. By the time I'd finish, it would be two in the morning, and Mrs. Rao and Mr. Raj Kapur would be sound asleep upstairs.

This was my life now. Housework, and sticking to house rules.

Mrs. Rao had four house rules. One, I couldn't leave the house grounds without an escort, which meant her. Two, I couldn't speak with any of her guests even if they initiated a conversation. Three, I couldn't pick up the phone.

Mrs. Rao had two handsets, one in her bedroom upstairs and the second in her office den near the library. The telephone rang incessantly every day, and she always ignored it. On my second day, the phone rang while I was vacuuming her bedroom, and I glanced over to see the words "West End Collection Agency" scrolling on the telephone's display. I paused for a minute. That name sounded familiar. Then, I remembered. One of my jobs was to empty the shredding machine in the library, and right next to it had been a pile of unopened letters from the West End Collection Agency. But the ringing soon became background noise.

The fourth house rule was the strangest. I had to stay in my bedroom with my windows and curtains closed whenever Mrs. Rao asked. It took me a few months to realize she only asked me to do this once a month.

And it was always on nights when the moon was full.

Chapter Twenty-seven

H*iccup!*

I looked up. *Where did that come from?*

I'd just finished washing Mrs. Rao's Cadillac and was wiping it down with a terry cloth. She had two vehicles: the beautiful black Cadillac in which she'd picked me up at the airport, and an enormous white Land Rover I had to climb up high to get into. The Rover was for winter, she'd said, but I had to clean it every week even when she hadn't driven it at all.

I'd been at Mrs. Rao's for six months, and as immense as her home was, it felt claustrophobic. It was heaven to be outside, to feel the wind on my face, to hear birds chirp, and see squirrels chase each other across the lawn I'd just mowed. Car cleaning was a relaxing job, almost like meditating.

I daydreamed as I cleaned. *One day I'll have my own shiny new car*, I told myself as I wiped a wet spot off the Cadillac. *When I become famous like Chef Pierre, I'll buy a car just like this and take Preeti and Aunty Shilpa driving across India.* I was lost in my thoughts, fantasizing about driving my own fancy car through the streets of Goa, seeing the astonished faces of my old classmates and the admiring looks of my teachers, when I heard the hiccup. It was loud enough to startle me out of my daydream.

Hiccup!

There. Again. I straightened up and looked around the yard, but saw no one. I peeked inside the garage. No one there either.

"Did you just move in, my dear?" a slurred voice asked.

I jerked my head up. The voice had come over the cedar hedge. Two wrinkled gray eyes gazed down at me.

"Who...who are you?" I asked.

"I heard noises, so I thought I'd pop over and see," the eyes said. "Come to think of it, I've been hearing quite a lot of funny noises lately. More than usual."

I peeked through the seven-foot hedge. Either the gray eyes belonged to someone impossibly tall, or she was standing on something high.

"How did you—?"

"It's called a stepladder, my dear. My gardener left it out. I thought to see what's going on over"—*hiccup!*—"here." The eyes roamed, taking in Mrs. Rao's front yard.

Mrs. Rao's yard was now a beautiful mosaic of fall yellows, oranges, and reds. The garden looked vibrant and alive, except for one anomaly. There was always a mysterious rusty shipping container at the end of the yard. This one had a faded decal plastered across one side with a picture of a basket overflowing with papayas, mangoes, and bananas. "Super India Fresh Fruit and Vegetable Exporters of Goa" read the colorful lettering.

The container changed every month with different decals, but the name remained the same. It had taken me a while to notice that it switched on those full-moon nights when Mrs. Rao asked me to stay in my room—those nights when I'd imagine footsteps on the floor above my basement room.

"Just got back from my other home in the South of France. Had a lovely long vacation."

I stared at the eyes above me.

"If you ask me," the eyes said from over the hedge, "Mrs. Rao needs to hire a professional landscaper."

"I try my best...," I said.

"Oh, I meant no disrespect, my dear. You've done a wonderful job. Um, a wonderful job indeed."

There was an awkward silence.

I shuffled my feet and glanced over my shoulder. At the beginning, Mrs. Rao took her cars out of the garage herself. After a few weeks, she taught me how to move them, so she didn't have to come outside every time. Some days, I'd see her portly shadow at a window on the second floor observing my work, but this afternoon, I knew she was fast asleep in her bedroom upstairs.

I looked back at the eyes over the hedge. There was a mop of curly gray hair on the stranger's head. Her forehead had a thousand wrinkles, and her eyes looked kind, smiling even.

"Who are you?" I asked.

"I asked first," she said, her eyes crinkling at the corners. She suddenly wavered. A pale bony arm shot out and grabbed onto the hedge as if she was trying to steady herself.

"Oh, my!" she said.

"Oh, my god!" I said, my hand on my mouth. "Are you okay?"

"Of course, I am, my dear."

She sounded exactly like Mrs. Rao's Saturday night dinner guests at around one in the morning, but this was just after lunch.

"A few glasses of good Scotch never hurt anybody," she said as if reading my mind. *Hiccup!*

I had no idea how to respond. "My mother always said water stops hiccups."

"Oh, they'll go away"—*hiccup!*—"eventually. Tell me now, where are you from, young lady, and when did you get here?"

"Me?" I said, pointing at my chest. Silly question because I was the only other person in the vicinity.

"Yes. You. Not that I'm saying you're not from here. I mean, who's from here anyway?" She laughed, a forced, embarrassed laugh.

"India."

"O-o-o-oh." The eyes opened wide. "How lovely. You must be Mrs. Rao's niece, the one she's been gabbing on about?"

"I guess so. I mean, yes."

"What's your name?"

I hesitated. Franky and Mrs. Rao had been clear about the house rules. I looked back at the eyes. They looked friendly, and it had been months since I'd spoken with anyone other than Mrs. Rao, and I never had a proper conversation with her.

"Asha."

"What a pretty name."

"Thank you."

"I'm Jacqueline." A hand came over the hedge carrying a short glass filled with a golden liquid. She raised the glass. It glinted in the sun.

"Nice to meet you, Jacqueline." I put my hands together and gave a quick bob of my head.

"The pleasure's all mine," Jacqueline said. "How old are you?"

"Fifteen."

"Where are your parents?"

"I don't have any. They...um...passed away."

"Ooh, I'm terribly sorry, my dear."

"It's all right." I shrugged my shoulders. There was nothing else to say. I remembered my mother every time I picked up the cake mixer, and I remembered my father every time I opened a book. I still kept the red sandals they gave me as a memento even if they no longer fit. That uncomfortable knot in my stomach after the car crash had never gone away, and there were nights I had trouble sleeping, but in my mind, my parents were in Tanzania, waiting for me to return, waiting for me to visit them at their graves. *One day I will,* I told myself every day. *I will return. Soon.*

"Well then, it seems we have something in common. I'm a poor widow and you're a poor orphan. My husband passed away from liver cancer five years ago. My children moved to the US and don't care to visit me anymore." A pause. "I have no one here now."

"I'm sorry," I said. I stared up at Jacqueline, wondering what the rest of her looked like.

"You poor girl. You don't want to listen to a lonely old woman commiserating about her misfortunes."

"No, that's fine," I said. "It's nice to chat." I didn't tell her that I also felt like Alice in Wonderland having a conversation with the crazy Cheshire Cat.

"Well then, what about the noises?" Jacqueline asked, her head bobbing over the hedge. "Does she make you work all night? Is that it?"

"Not really," I lied. "It's quiet here."

"Really? You don't hear the noises at night?"

I looked away. It was true I heard noises of cars coming in at the middle of the night or heavy things being lifted or dragged, on those nights I wasn't allowed to come out of my room. Then again, I had an active imagination. My life had been too topsy-turvy that sometimes I was no longer sure where my imagination ended and reality began.

I remembered a week ago, on a full-moon night, how I had to mop up muddy footsteps from the main hallway to the guest bathrooms. It looked like a herd of elephants had bathed in the tubs the night before. It had been a chore to clean it all and my sore muscles the next day confirmed I hadn't dreamed that up. But I hadn't dared ask Mrs. Rao.

"Is Mrs. Rao having wild parties?"

"I don't know," I said, "except for her Saturday night dinners."

"Aah," Jacqueline said, nodding wisely.

"Tell me, little one, which school do you go to? Is she forcing you to go to that uppity private school down the road?"

"No...er...I don't go to school."

"What? You don't go to school?" She gave me a piercing look. "That's scandalous."

"It's only for a year." I stopped, realizing I was saying too much.

"Have you *ever* gone to school? Do you even know how to read?"

"Of course, I do." I squared my shoulders. *Does she think I'm an illiterate like Grandma?* "I went to international schools in Africa. I also went to a girls' school in Goa. I know how to read and write in English and Konkani. I also know a bit of Sinhalese and Hindi. And I'm pretty good at chemistry and math. I'm going back to school when I finish my year at Mrs. Rao's. I promised Papa I'd go to university, just like he did."

"My, my." Jacqueline's eyes grew wide. "What an impressive young woman you are. I speak only English, I'm afraid. My husband was French Canadian, always badgering me about learning the language. Pestered me for years, but languages are simply not my forté. Gets difficult as you get older, you know?"

"I guess so," I said.

"Is that all you do then? Wash cars for Mrs. Rao?"

"I cook and clean too."

"Just like the other girls," Jacqueline mumbled, more to herself than to me.

"What other girls?" There was something strange about Mrs. Rao and her house. I felt it in my bones. The dinner parties, the nighttime footsteps, the used uniform that was a size too big. A shiver went through my spine. "What other..."

"What a busy girl you are," Jacqueline said, changing topic. She took a sip from her glass, watching me thoughtfully. "What a very busy girl indeed."

I glanced quickly over my shoulder to make sure Mrs. Rao wasn't watching. She should be getting up anytime now. "I'm sorry, Jacqueline, but I've got to finish the cars or I'll get into trouble."

"We can't have that now, can we?" she said. "Well, it looks like you're done, aren't you? Look at how those cars are gleaming. The boys I hire to detail my cars don't do half as good a job as you've done. Maybe I should ask Mrs. Rao to let you help me one of these days."

I smiled. *I have enough work as it is,* I thought, but I didn't say anything.

Jacqueline gave a sly smile and whispered loudly, "Then, maybe, I can rescue you." *Hiccup!* Her head wobbled and one of her arms shot over the hedge. "Oh, goodness me!"

"Are you okay?" I asked, but it was too late.

I saw the twinkle of the glass tumbler as it fell over the hedge and crashed on the ground. The smoky smell of whiskey filled the air. Jacqueline was still up on her ladder, holding on to the hedge with both hands. "Oh, my goodness! What have I done?"

I looked at where the glass tumbler had fallen and my heart skipped a beat. It had bounced off the car's bonnet and broken into smithereens on the ground. When I bent over to wipe the few drops of whiskey off the hood, I saw the scratch. An ugly gray mark on Mrs. Rao's shiny Cadillac.

My heart stopped. "Oh, no!" I put a hand to my head. "Oh, no."

"Goodness me," Jacqueline said, looking terrified. "What have I done? I'm so sorry, dear child, ever so sorry. Please forgive me."

I wiped the spot with the terry cloth, but that just made it worse. A glass shard had scratched the paint to the primer. It was not a large scratch, but right then, it looked like I'd put a bullet hole through the sleek black panel.

I heard a rustle from the hedge. The eyes had disappeared, but I could hear Jacqueline's voice warbling from the other side. "I'm coming over, right now, to apologize to Mrs. Rao. I'm going to do so right away."

"No!" I shouted despite myself. "Please don't do that! Come back!"

Silence for a few seconds. Jacqueline's eyes popped over the hedge once again, her face a bright pink.

"Everything's fine," I said, gesturing for her to stay where she was. "No need to come over. Mrs. Rao will kill—." I stopped. *I've said more than I should already.*

"Let me talk to her," she said.

"It's not a big deal. Really. It's best you don't. *Please.*"

Silence.

"I do hope this doesn't put you in trouble. You tell me if it does, you hear?" she said.

"I gotta go."

I picked up the water pail and walked quickly toward the garage, my legs feeling like they were about to give way any moment.

Chapter Twenty-eight

It was a week later the front doorbell rang in the middle of the day. I was in the kitchen baking pecan muffins and jumped to get it. But before I could get to the hallway, Mrs. Rao rumbled out of the living room like a steam train.

"Get back in the kitchen and shut the damn door," she snapped, brushing me aside. Mrs. Rao didn't normally swear, but she had become increasingly impatient, ever since the scratch on her car.

Only a week earlier, I'd dragged myself back to the house after parking the Cadillac in the garage, feeling like I'd committed a major crime. Inside, I found Mrs. Rao standing in the kitchen, arms crossed, a dark look on her face.

That was the day those warthog tusks of hers came out.

As soon as I walked in, I blurted, "I scratched your car, Mrs. Rao. It was the water pail. I bumped it on your car. I'm so sorry."

With an angry snort, she brushed past me and stomped over to the garage. I trailed behind her, trembling in fear. Her face flushed bright red when she saw the scratch. I braced myself.

"What the in good Shiva's name did you do?" she screamed. It was the first time she'd shouted since I'd arrived at the house. "What did you do to my husband's beautiful car!"

A mistake, I said. I pleaded for forgiveness. I almost got on my knees, but her yelling didn't stop. Her oversized bosom heaved like she was hyperventilating. I cowered in a corner of the garage, behind the car, trying to hold myself together against the barrage of insults she lobbed at me.

I offered to take it out of my wages. I had no idea what she was paying me because it went straight to Franky's office in Goa, but I was sure something could be arranged.

She barely heard me. "This is my husband's car! I promised him I'd take care of it, and now you've gone and desecrated this, you useless runt! He's probably turning in his grave right now."

"I'm so sorry...."

"Do you realize how much this car cost, you wench?"

I shook my head.

"Almost a hundred thousand dollars, more than you'll ever see in your entire lifetime, you idiot!"

"I'm so sorry, Mrs. Rao. I'll do whatever I can to fix...."

"Do you think your stupid sniveling can fix this? Are you so dumb to think you can say sorry and get away with it?"

I looked at the floor, wishing it would swallow me up.

"I bring you all the way here to help you and your family, and this is how you repay me? You stupid, stupid village girl!"

Her screeching didn't stop for half an hour until her voice started to get hoarse. I stayed balled up in my corner, not daring to look up, not daring to move.

"How do you think you're going to pay me back for this, you imbecile?" she shouted.

"I'll work harder, Mrs. Rao," I mumbled.

"Not good enough."

"I'll work longer if you want, Mrs. Rao."

She took a deep breath and put her hands on her hips. "I'm going to add twelve more months to your contract. That's still not going to pay for this beautiful car, but I'll take that." Her voice was still angry, but at least she'd stopped screaming.

"A year?" I asked, shocked.

"I'm being generous, you dolt!" she screeched. "I can make you stay two years to pay in full!"

"I'm good for twelve months," I said quickly, without even thinking.

The next day, she drove the Cadillac to an auto body repair shop and it came back three days later in pristine condition. I had no idea how much it had cost. All I knew was I had promised to stay for another year.

The doorbell rang again.

"I said get back in there!" Mrs. Rao snapped, pointing to the kitchen. "Now!"

I turned around and fled down the corridor. I was just about to shut the kitchen door when I heard a female voice.

"Good morning, Mrs. Rao. I'm here to see about the girl."

I took in a sharp breath.

"Aahh, thank you for coming," Mrs. Rao said in an unusually syrupy voice. "Come in. Please do come in."

I tiptoed out of the kitchen and peeked into the hallway. A middle-aged woman stood at the doorway, dressed in a smart tweed suit with a blue scarf around her neck. She was carrying a briefcase like she was ready for the office. A ray of sunshine flashed off a silver badge on her lapel, but it was too far for me to read. I'd never seen her at any of Mrs. Rao's weekend parties. *Who is she?*

I tiptoed back toward the kitchen. There was a nook outside the kitchen door where no one could see me, but from where I could hear everything going on in the dining and living rooms.

It was a good place to hide on Saturday evenings after I served dinner to Mrs. Rao's guests, especially on those days I dreamed up a new recipe. No one ever complimented me directly, but from my hiding spot, I could hear the clink of forks and knives against plates, and the *oohs* and the *aahs*, and the mumbles of "delicious," "what a treat," and "she's good," between mouthfuls.

"May I get you tea? Coffee? Orange juice?" Mrs. Rao said.

"No, thank you," the guest said. "I don't have much time today, I'm afraid. I only have a few questions and then I need to run to my next appointment."

"Of course, of course. Make yourself comfortable," Mrs. Rao said, leading her guest to the living room. There was silence while they settled down. I could imagine them sitting in Mrs. Rao's prim empress chairs.

"About this girl now." The woman said.

"Of course, of course."

"First, we need to know what relation she is to you."

"The girl is my niece. You see, my youngest sister died last year in a car crash in India."

I felt a stabbing pain go through my heart as she mentioned the car crash.

"Oh? I'm so sorry to hear that."

"Yes, it was heartbreaking news. She was my closest and dearest little sister. We spent all of our childhood together in India. In our culture, family is the most important thing, you know. The only thing. We live and breathe for our family. Life is strange sometimes, isn't it? How it can so easily take away those most precious to us." Mrs. Rao sniffed loudly.

I felt my cheeks burn.

"I'm truly sorry, Mrs. Rao. I didn't know."

"I'm doing my best to take care of the little girl now. My lonely niece, an only child, you see. I sponsored her as a family member. That was the best I could do for my dear sister. In our culture, we never leave our family behind, no matter what."

I heard a tissue being pulled out of a box. Like an elephant trumpeting, the sound of Mrs. Rao blowing her nose reverberated through the house.

"I'm sure you're doing your best." The woman's voice had taken a softer tone. "I'm sure the girl appreciates having an aunt who cares so much for her. I usually have trouble finding families for our orphans. They get shunted from one foster family to another. I wish they all had generous aunts like you."

"Oh, I only think of that poor girl. She sleeps next to my room, and some nights, I hear her cry, you know. I know she misses her mother, but I can never replace her. It's truly heartbreaking. I get my strength from Lord Vishnu." More pitiful sniffs from Mrs. Rao.

What lies, I thought from my hiding spot. *What horrible lies.*

"The thing is, and this is what I came to talk to you about, she's a minor, and we must ensure she's going to school. You do know, education is compulsory until eighteen in Ontario."

I perked up.

"For girls too?" Mrs. Rao asked.

"We don't discriminate, Mrs. Rao."

"Oh, I knew that," Mrs. Rao said quickly.

"I'm sure you did. When we get reports of unattended children who don't go to school, we have to investigate. I understand this is a difficult time for your family, but the law is the law, as you know, and it is there for good reason."

"Of course. Of course. You see, the girl's still adjusting, especially after that painful accident. I was waiting for her to settle down a bit and get over the trauma before finding a suitable school. It isn't easy to lose your parents like that, you know? The girl was very close to them, you see."

How dare she talk about my parents? My hands clenched into fists.

"I can fully understand."

"The problem is she doesn't speak English very well, so it's important to be selective, you see. Didn't want to shock her, you see."

What? I speak better English than she does.

"We have English-as-a-second-language classes for new immigrants, especially children who are sponsored here. They're offered for free. My office will do whatever we can to help you and your niece."

"Well, that's very kind of you. Thank you for thinking of my little girl. I have so much going on that I am not doing everything I should be doing. I am a terrible aunt."

"I understand perfectly. You're struggling through a loss, and that must be truly difficult. Let me know how we can help you. You can find the information you need on our website. We even have someone you can call during the day if you have questions about our services."

"Thank you so much. The girl is a bit nervous about going to school, you see, but this may help her adjust. I am glad you came today."

Nervous about school? Me?

"So, where's the girl today? I'd like to talk to her."

"She's sleeping in her room. Not too well today, I am afraid. A bad period, you know."

I cringed. *Couldn't she have picked a better excuse?*

"Perhaps next time?" Mrs. Rao said, her voice seeping with honey.

"Here's my card. Don't hesitate to call if you have any questions or need any help."

Noises of chairs being scraped back came from the living room. I scooted into the kitchen and closed the door gently, my heart beating fast. I couldn't decide whether to be angry or worried. *Who's this woman? Does she work for the police? How did she know I lived here? Does she really mean it about school?*

Mrs. Rao barreled into the kitchen so abruptly, I nearly jumped out of my skin. I grabbed a dishcloth and pretended to wipe the counter. The phone rang in the background for the hundredth time that day, but we both ignored it.

"Next Monday, you will come with me to register at school," Mrs. Rao said, her face puffed up in fury.

I looked at her in surprise. *Is she serious?*

"Don't you think I'll be sending you to that private school like the Jones' girls. I don't throw away my hard-earned money on servant girls, you hear?"

"Yes, Mrs. Rao."

"And don't think you'll get out of work. I didn't pay to bring you all the way here to play. I don't do charity. You'll finish your task list every day, like now. That's the contract, you understand? Otherwise, you and your family won't get paid a dime."

"Yes, Mrs. Rao."

She stomped toward the door, her face contorted into a nasty scowl. She stopped at the doorway and turned around so quickly, I jumped again.

"I know about Jacqueline," she hissed.

I gulped.

"That nosy, interfering old bag," Mrs. Rao growled. "Don't think I'm stupid. I know everything that goes on inside this house and outside. You hear me?"

I nodded, feeling numb to the bones.

"You'll work in this house till the day you drop dead."

Chapter Twenty-nine

Ashok appeared out of nowhere.

I was getting ready for my first day of school. It was seven in the morning, and I'd already vacuumed the house and cleaned the bathrooms and the dining room. I was tired but happy. *I'm going to school again!*

For the first time in six months, I got a whiff of freedom. I was going to see the world again, the world outside this house. I pushed Mrs. Rao's threat to the back of my mind, the threat I'd work for her forever. That can't be true, I thought—she'd been really angry when she said that. So I woke up that morning, feeling a slight sense of relief. While things were bad, not all was lost.

But that morning, Mrs. Rao wasn't in a good mood.

"Ashok!" she yelled over my head, making me jump.

The kitchen door creaked open. To my surprise, a lanky Indian man, barely in his twenties, wearing baggy gray pants, a threadbare shirt, and open-toed slippers, appeared at the kitchen doorway. I stared at this apparition. He shuffled over self-consciously, his slippers making sticky noises and leaving traces of dirt on the white kitchen tiles I'd just mopped. His back was slightly stooped and his face cast down as if he was walking into the den of a lioness.

No one came into the kitchen other than Mrs. Rao and me, and no one visited the house during the day. The only people I saw inside, other than whoever belonged to those mysterious footsteps every full-moon night, were the well-heeled dinner guests who came on Saturday nights and filled the house with expensive smells of whiskey, cigars, and French perfume. Those people owned exotic cars and yachts, unlike this man who looked like he'd just stepped off a rickety fishing boat.

"You take this girl to this address like I showed you, okay?" Mrs. Rao spoke to him in Hindi as she flung a slip of paper onto the counter. "Then you pick her up exactly at two this afternoon, do you hear? The car has a GPS and a clock. Use them."

Ashok nodded at his slippers.

"The girl can't go anywhere other than school and the grocery store. You hear me?"

The man nodded again, not making eye contact with Mrs. Rao or me. He picked up the car keys and the slip of paper. Putting his hands together, he bowed low and shuffled back out of the kitchen door, closing it gently behind him.

"Who's that?" I asked, turning to Mrs. Rao.

"None of your business," she snapped. "He's a mute, dumb as a doorbell, and only understands Hindi, so no use making him talk, you hear?"

I stared at her. *How'd she manage to conjure up someone like that out of the blue?*

I vaguely recalled being woken by the sound of a car engine in the dead of the night before. Unlike the sound of trucks coming in and out on full moon nights, the noise had dissipated within two minutes, and I'd gone back to sleep not thinking much of it. It could have been a passing car or a brief stopover by one of the private security guards who did their rounds at the nearby mansions.

"No need to wash the cars anymore. I'll give that job to Ashok from now on. But you need to clean Mr. Raj Kapur's room tonight. He's made a mess again. After that, I need you to clean the swimming pool in case my guests want to use it this weekend. And here's what I want you to make tonight." She threw a piece of paper at me. "Ashok will drive you to get groceries after school. When you get back, I want to see good cooking, you hear me? No slacking."

"Yes, Mrs. Rao," I stammered. I took her grocery list and stuffed it in my pocket. I reached for my bag and followed Ashok's steps out.

Outside, the white Land Rover was parked in the driveway, ready to be taken out. Ashok was squatting beside the driver's door like I'd seen bus drivers do at the station in Goa when they were on their breaks. He had an unsophisticated look about him, but there was a glint in his eyes that made me wonder if he saw and heard more than he let on.

He stood and climbed into the driver's seat as I approached the car. I stepped in next to him, a whirlwind swirling inside my head. Life was going to be different from now on, I thought.

Yes, very different.

Part SIX

If we had no winter, the spring would not be so pleasant
Anne Bradstreet

Chapter Thirty

Tim's soft lips felt like sweet honey and fire. I shivered with pleasure.

"Happy birthday, cutie," he said, looking into my eyes, his arms circling my waist. I was standing on tiptoe, leaning against his broad chest, melting like butter. I reached up half-nervously, half-excitedly, searching for another kiss.

Mrs. Rao was having a late supper by herself in the dining room above us. She'd been a little distracted lately. I'd noticed the letters from the West End Collection Agency came in more frequently recently. I wasn't sure if it was my imagination, but the unanswered phone calls had become even more incessant as well.

I'd cooked dinner exactly as Mrs. Rao had asked. That night, she'd wanted curry and something "sweet and alcoholy" for dessert. So, I'd cooked up a Thai red curry and served it with steamed Jasmin rice sprinkled with black mustard and scallion. On the side buffet, I'd left a white ramekin of caramel pudding spiced with cloves and cardamom, and a glass of blood-red port. She was going to be happy with her supper, I was sure.

Like every evening for the past year and a half, I knew exactly what Mrs. Rao was up to in the dining room. Every time I brought dinner up, Mr. Raj Kapur would hop onto a free chair next to her. A slight wag of the tail and a well-timed big-brown-eyed look was all he needed to persuade her to hand-feed him bits of food, despite the vet's advice.

He was as overweight as his owner, but Mrs. Rao didn't care. Even if she did, she'd be too preoccupied to notice him licking her plate.

As usual, I'd turned on the giant flat-screen TV on the dining room wall to the Bollywood satellite channel. I'd discovered it on my third day at Mrs. Rao's house when I'd come up an hour after serving her meal only to find a half-eaten plate and Mrs. Rao sobbing into her napkin. I'd glanced at the screen.

Two star-crossed lovers were being separated by warring families, each forcefully held back by parents, siblings, and who-knew-what relatives in a remote village somewhere in Bollywoodland. Threats of murder, plunder, and suicide rang out with passion from the sur-round-sound system—the typical hyper-drama I remembered my mother loved to watch.

Seeing me, Mrs. Rao had quickly dabbed her eyes with her napkin and scowled. She hadn't been pleased with my intrusion. From then on, I left her alone after dinner and cleaned up first thing in the morning instead. And I left a box of tissues next to the dining table every night.

Since Bollywood made the longest movies in the world, Mrs. Rao would be fixated on the screen for at least three hours every evening, twice that, if she decided to watch a second movie. This meant suppertime was the best time for Tim to visit.

Tim caressed my neck and removed a strand of hair from my cheek. His chocolate-brown eyes melted into mine. My heart skipped a beat. Kissing Tim was heaven, sweeter than licking a pineapple ice pop because of the way it made my heart beat wildly and my legs go squishy.

With his dreamy eyes and buff body, I knew the other girls thought him cute, which made me feel lucky he'd even said hello to me.

When I'd walked into school the first day, no one talked to me. No one even noticed me.

But I was accustomed to this. I'd always been the invisible black sheep everywhere I went, and after having lived in almost a dozen countries, I was used to being the one everyone ignored and kept their distance from. This didn't mean it was easy. I cried on the first day of school, every time, and this school was no exception.

So, I was surprised Tim had even looked at me, let alone sat next to me in the school cafeteria on the second day. Then, I learned it was his second day as well.

Tim's true name was Tsing Tong Hank. He got his first name from his Chinese mother and his last name from his German father, a mix that gave him the best looks from both continents.

At his old school in Seattle, his classmates had laughed hysterically every time the teacher called his name during roll call. That was a slight improvement from grade school where the other kids had followed him around singing "Ding Dong." So the day he started high school in Toronto, where his parents had moved to take care of Tim's grandfather, he changed his name.

We'd been dating officially for two whole months now. Hanging out with Tim was an escape from the weird world at Mrs. Rao's house. I had a calendar in my basement room, on which I counted the months, weeks, and days till I'd leave this place. But when I was with Tim, all those troubles melted away, and I lived, just lived, even if my heart knew it wouldn't be forever.

We'd been in my basement room fooling around, forgetting time. It was close to nine at night, and time for my first high school party, a party my new friend Katy had organized for my sixteenth birthday. I'd stopped celebrating my birthday since I was twelve since it coincided with my parents' funeral.

Now, four years later, all I wanted was to spend this day with people I cared about, even if it was people I was only beginning to know.

"Hey, can I have one before we go?" Tim said, eyeing the cake tray on the bedside table. "I'm starved."

"Sure, if you can't wait for the party," I said. I'd made twenty-four raspberry cheese cupcakes, each one with a red raspberry crown and brushed with edible snow-white glaze from Mrs. Rao's pantry.

With Tim in my life now, the world was bright, and everything was possible. I'd stayed up the night before, after my chores were done, and had skipped across the kitchen floor, trying not to make too much noise and wake up Mrs. Rao or Mr. Raj Kapur.

I'd hummed softly as I'd mixed the batter and swirled the icing into the wee hours of the night, fantasizing about kissing Tim again the next day. It wasn't only flour, honey, and milk I added to the cakes. I'd also poured in boundless cups of teenage puppy love.

"Yum," Tim said, picking the biggest cake and downing it in two bites. His arm snaked behind me toward the tray. "Can I have another one?"

"No, Tim," I said, gently slapping his hand away. "These are for the party, remember?"

"Hey, I've got something for the celebration too." He pulled a square bottle from his pocket. "Look what I got," he said, grinning. I took the bottle and turned it in my hand.

"Jamaican rum," I said, reading the label. I remembered my father used to drink the occasional glass of rum after work. Unlike whiskey, with its bitter, smoky smell, rum smelled sweet. I'd always wanted to try it, but he'd never let me.

"Have you had rum before?" Tim asked.

I shook my head.

"I'm gonna mix this with Coke for ya. You'll like it, I promise." He lowered his voice. "It'll be your get-out-of-jail drink."

"But I'm not supposed to...."

"Hey, you need to learn to have fun."

I removed myself from his embrace and opened the wardrobe to find a top for the party. "I'm really happy Katy's putting this on for me, but I feel like everyone knows everyone at school, except me."

Six months had passed since I'd started school, and though I was slowly being accepted, I still felt like an outsider because I couldn't hang out with anyone after school, couldn't use the phone, and couldn't go to any of the parties. Other than Tim and Katy, not many said hello.

"Don't I count?" Tim gave me a mock insulted look. "I'm new too, remember? Besides, Katy's fun, and she puts on amazing parties. You should've been there last Saturday. It was awesome."

A tiny jealous pang went through me. Tim and Katy got along well and he'd been to her house parties many times before. I shook my head, trying to get rid of my green feelings, but it wasn't easy. Katy wasn't only the school's most popular party maker, she was also drop-dead gorgeous.

If it hadn't been for her upturned freckled nose, she'd have been selected by the teen model company that visited our school last month. Katy was as tall as I was short. Bouncy red curls framed her freckled face and fell gently on her shoulders. Her green eyes looked like those of a beautiful, exotic kitten. She wore cute miniskirts to show off her long legs, but what every girl in school envied the most, and what I coveted too, were her pretty red heels. She always had on a shiny pair of two-inch red heels, and she seemed to have one of every kind, with bows, sashes, buckles, and even shiny fake stones.

The red sandals I'd loved so much were worn now, held together by staples and Sellotape. They no longer fit and made me feel like I was still a schoolgirl back in Africa, back in that musty school library surrounded by books. Katy was surrounded by cool friends everywhere she went. All the boys wanted to be with her and all the girls wanted to be her, and I wanted nothing more than a pair of sexy red heels just like hers.

Like Tanya, Sophie, and Shanti, the cool girls at the international school in Dar es Salaam, I'd expected Katy to snub me, but she always had a friendly smile on her pink lips.

In East Africa, buxom was beautiful. In North America, skinny was in style. I remembered Mrs. Ngozi pinching my cheeks and saying to my mother, "This girl's skin and bones. How will she ever find a good husband one day? You need to feed her more of those cakes of yours, I tell you." I was glad to finally be the size everyone else craved to be.

I still spoke with a funny accent and everyone still asked me where I was from, but then, everyone here came from somewhere else or many places, all at once. The best thing about this new school was there was no über-strict school monitor watching my every move. This meant I was free to let my hair down and dress as I wished. I wore the hand-me-down jeans and faded T-shirts I found in my closet at Mrs. Rao's. They didn't fit, but they were not much different from what everyone else wore to school.

Katy was the only one in our class to have a real job, a company van and a shiny shirt badge that said "Assistant Manager." Every afternoon after school, she drove her old van to the Next Day Catering Company downtown. Compared to her, my work at Mrs. Rao's home didn't sound like a real job. I had no title or badge or company car, and I was on call twenty-four hours a day.

Every evening, Mrs. Rao immersed herself in smelly bath salts and gooey gels of all kinds in her tub, surrounded by candles. That meant, every morning before school, I had to scrub and remove the candle wax and leftover gel stuck to the tub, and return the bathroom to its glory before cleaning up the dining table from the night before.

That day, I'd woken up at four thirty to clean the bathtub, do the laundry, and make Mrs. Rao's breakfast. After school, I'd vacuumed, mopped, and made dinner. My muscles ached just thinking about everything I'd done that day.

But now, I had to get ready for the party. My party. I changed into a clean T-shirt and fastened on the ankle bracelet Preeti had given me. I removed it only when I was cleaning the house but otherwise wore it all the time, even to bed. It was my only link back to Preeti, back to my family, and to Goa. It jingled pleasantly as I moved.

"Mrs. Rao will throw a fit if she ever finds out I'm gone tonight," I said.

"She's not your *mother*," Tim said.

"She's my aunt," I said, looking away. It was a lie, but an essential one. I hoped he didn't notice.

"Doesn't mean she can dictate your life," Tim said. "It's time I saved you from your wicked step-aunt."

I laughed. Tim made me feel giddy like I was the most special girl in the world. It was one reason I was risking a lot by going out this evening. I ran a brush through my hair and put on the dangly earrings I'd bought at a street stall in Goa in my previous life. "Okay, I'm ready," I said, checking myself one more time in the bedroom mirror.

"Aren't you a sight for sore eyes?" Tim said, admiring me from the bed. "Can I kiss you now?" He pulled me close. I cuddled up to him.

Buzzzzzz!

We sprang apart like we'd been shocked by an electric prod.

Chapter Thirty-one

"What the heck was that?" Tim asked, stunned.

"The buzzer!" I jumped on the bed to reach it. Mrs. Rao had a buzzer on every floor to summon me when she needed something and I had to answer without delay. Being asleep or being in the washroom were no excuses.

I glanced at Tim and put a finger to my lips. He nodded with a dazed look on his face. I pushed the white button.

"Asha?" Mrs. Rao's deep voice came through the intercom. I could hear Mr. Raj Kapur chomping loudly on something, leftover fish on her plate, most probably.

"Yes, Mrs. Rao."

"I don't want you leaving your room tonight. It is the full moon. Do you understand?"

"Oh? Ah—"

"What's the matter?"

"Nothing, Mrs. Rao. I mean, yes, Mrs. Rao."

"Good. I will see you at seven in the morning, then. Please have my breakfast ready, as usual."

"As usual, Mrs. Rao," I said and lifted my finger from the button.

"Oh no," I said, sinking into the bed, feeling like a deflated balloon. "I totally forgot. I'm not allowed to leave my room tonight." I wasn't normally allowed out any other night either, but during full moon night, it was a specific house rule.

"Why the heck not?" Tim asked. "It's your birthday!"

"Because it's a full moon."

He gave me a look that said, *Are you mad?*

"I mean, it's a bad night to go out..." I added in a lame voice.

"Are you gonna turn into a werewolf or something?"

"Don't be sill—."

"Is *Mrs. Rao* gonna turn into a werewolf tonight?"

"Tim...."

"You can't just not show up to your own party. Katy's gonna be pissed!"

I sighed loudly. This wasn't just my first birthday party since my parents died, it was also my first real going-out-together date with Tim, and a chance to get to know Katy and maybe even make new friends. I couldn't bear the thought of missing all this.

"It's my job." I gave Tim a doleful look.

"Your job?" He gave me a puzzled frown.

I looked at the floor. *Where do I even begin to explain?*

"She sounds like a nutcase."

"It's a house rule," I said. "Whenever there's a full moon, I'm not supposed to leave my room. And I completely forgot tonight's one."

"That's crazy shit. This is not normal. Doesn't she know it's your birthday?"

I sighed again. Of course, Mrs. Rao didn't know. She couldn't care less.

"That's it," Tim said, picking up his jacket and putting it on. "You've been cooped up way too long. Your aunt's batty and you're going nuts too. We're leaving now and I'm gonna bring you back by two a.m. By then, she'll be snoring away." He stood near the window, motioning me to follow him out with the other hand. "Come on, Cinderella. Let's go."

My room was in the sunken basement at the back of the house. Mrs. Rao slept two floors up in the master bedroom. The windows in my room were at ground level, so it was easy to sneak in and out using the bedside table as a giant stepping stool. After that, all you had to do was climb over the back steel fence, which had bars at just the right height. That was how Tim had got in that evening, and every evening before that. I could just as easily follow him out. No one would hear me coming in later, not even Mr. Raj Kapur. His yappy barking could wake up the world, but he'd slept through every time Tim had sneaked in and out.

I hesitated, my heart beating a tad faster at the thought of disobeying a major house rule. I knew what Mrs. Rao's wrath could be like. "What if she buzzes and finds out I'm gone?"

"Does she buzz you during full moon nights?"

I shook my head. "Never. Not even for a glass of water."

"She'll never know you're gone then."

"Yes, but…" I stammered.

"I can't believe how shitty she treats you," he said. "She's a slave driver."

"I'm not a slave," I said, feeling slightly offended that he'd think I'd stooped that low. "She pays me for my work. Well, not me exactly. It goes into my account in India."

"What?"

"It's to help my aunty who's sick and my cousin who needs to go to school back in—"

"She's lying," Tim said with a snort. "You're a slave."

"I've got a contract to prove…." I stopped, realizing how much I've been sharing.

"A contract? You have a contract with your own aunt? What a weird woman. How can you stand her?"

I looked away. "Things are good here. Plus, I get to go to school."

That was true. I had a safe place to live and even my own private bathroom. I had barely enough space to move in it, but after sharing a dirty communal toilet with twenty other women for two years, this was heaven. I even had a small desk for books in my room. Best of all, I got to go to school. Though they didn't have a martial arts program like at my international schools in East Africa, they didn't have strict dress codes or a nasty school monitor like in Goa either. They also didn't have a mind-boggling hierarchy of middle students, senior students, junior teachers, and superior teachers like in India, all of whom reminded you of your very small place.

What I liked best was there was less memorizing and more real learning here. My new teachers encouraged questions and ideas, and gave points for participating, unlike in India where school girls got points for obeying orders and staying silent. Even with my back-breaking work schedule, I'd never felt freer.

With my new promise to Mrs. Rao, I had twelve more months to go before returning to India. I dreamed of making enough money that I could first fly to Tanzania to visit my parents' graves, then fly back to Goa and buy a house as big as Mrs. Rao's, where Preeti and Aunty Shilpa and Grandma could live with me. I'd already written to Franky about it.

"Mrs. Rao's not all that bad," I added, thinking of my alternative. If I were back in Goa, I'd have been married off to that disgusting Kristadasa. A shiver ran through me at the mere thought. "She's a bit strange, that's all."

"If it was me," Tim said pointing at his chest, "I'd call the Social Services people."

Everybody seemed to be interested in my life these days.

My science teacher had asked about my home life the week before when she found out I hadn't finished a take-home exam on time. It was because I'd spent the evening prior cleaning Mr. Raj Kapur's bathroom after he'd eaten too much hot curry and thrown up, not once but twice, and growled whenever I tried to get close to clean up. Mrs. Rao said I couldn't go to bed until the dog and the room were clean and Mr. Raj Kapur was happily tucked in bed.

My teacher hadn't been impressed when I'd told her I'd stayed up all night to take care of a family pet. She didn't buy it because that wasn't the first time I'd used that excuse.

When she called home that night, Mrs. Rao had explained in her sweetest voice how I was helping her out because she was an "invalid." I was in the kitchen when the call came, so I heard everything. But I didn't care what Mrs. Rao told my teachers, or how much work I had to do for her. Franky had already written to me to say Aunty Shilpa was taking her medicine and getting better every day, and Preeti was doing well in school and had even applied to university to become a medical doctor. I kept reminding myself, every day, why I was here.

I'd also written to Preeti and Aunty Shilpa many times, telling them about my new life, Mrs. Rao's beautiful house and garden, the fresh air, the expansive boulevards, and the changing seasons in this grand country. Mrs. Rao had even given me fancy writing paper and offered to mail my letters for me. Grandma's apartment complex didn't receive any postal service, so all letters had to go via the Good and Fast Immigration Broker office. I never heard back from Preeti or Aunty Shilpa, but then Aunty couldn't write, and I knew how Preeti could get caught up in her books, especially if she was on her way to med school. Mrs. Rao also said it was because the Indian postal service was so slow.

"I like it here," I said to Tim, guardedly. "She treats me well. Better than anyone else."

"Whatever you say." He was looking at me with raised eyebrows, half-turned toward the window like he couldn't wait to get out. "You'll only have one sixteenth birthday in your whole life, and you're gonna stay stuck here alone because of that bat? Coz, I'm not staying here. I'm going to the party!"

I stared at Tim. Suddenly, my need to escape this claustrophobic house overpowered my fear of disobeying the rules. I got up and grabbed my jacket.

"Now we're talking," he said with a grin. "Let's get outta here."

We stepped toward the window.

That was when my window rattled like an earthquake had begun.

Chapter Thirty-two

"What's going on?" Tim asked, peering outside the window. I walked over and peeked out. It sounded like a large truck was coming up the driveway.

"They're early tonight," I whispered.

A shadow fell on the wall. We instinctively took a step back.

We didn't hear voices, only sounds of the truck engine, doors opening and shutting, creaking hinges, something heavy being dragged or moved. Doors slamming shut. Then urgent footsteps. We strained to listen, but it was hard to make anything out. Whoever was out on the driveway wasn't talking.

"What the hell?" Tim said.

"Shhh," I whispered. "It's the full moon crowd."

"Who the heck are they?"

"I've no idea."

"Does this happen every full moon night?"

"Yes, but usually after midnight."

"This is freaky, you know that, eh?" Tim asked.

"Yes." I looked at him desperately. "I know."

"I think your aunt's in the drug business."

"Drugs?" My eyes widened.

"Maybe we should call the cops."

"No!" I said too quickly. "I don't want to get into—I mean, I don't want her to get into trouble."

Tim raised an eyebrow.

"Maybe she's just having friends over for a late supper," I said.

"Seriously?"

"Maybe they're having a secret full-moon dinner out on the lawn," I said, grasping at straws.

Tim's eyes widened. "Is your aunt into crazy full-moon orgies?"

"Well...."

"I don't care what they're doing, as soon as these old geezers quiet down, you and me are getting out."

"But they'll spot us."

"Not if we get out on the quiet," Tim said. "I'm not staying stuck down here, while they're partying it up upstairs. We've got our own party to go to, remember?"

He's right. I didn't want to stay cooped down here either.

"Hey," I said, "let me make sure everyone's inside first and the front door's closed, so we don't bump into anyone in the yard, okay?" I whispered, signaling him to be silent.

He nodded.

I walked over to my door and put my ear to it. Not a sound from outside. No one came to the basement other than me anyway. All I had to do was tiptoe up the stairway and peek into the kitchen to see if I could see or hear anything. I quietly turned the doorknob.

Will I finally get to see these full-moon strangers?

"There's gonna be a w-e-r-e-w-o-l-f," Tim sang in a low voice behind me.

"Shhh...." I said, trying not to giggle.

"If I see one, I'll knock it out," Tim said with a wink. He stationed himself behind me, holding out his bottle of rum like a weapon. I pulled the door open. And my heart jumped straight into my mouth.

Standing outside the door with her hands on her hips and her dog at her feet was the formidable Mrs. Rao.

Behind her, Ashok was holding my kitchen mop upside down.

Seeing Tim, Mr. Raj Kapur let out a volley of barks.

"Oh my god!" I cried out, horrified.

"I knew it!" Mrs. Rao roared, pointing at Tim. "I knew we had an intruder! Get out before I set my dog on you!"

Mr. Raj Kapur didn't waste a second. He rushed toward Tim, barking like mad. Tim jumped onto the bedside table near the window. Mr. Raj Kapur balanced himself on his short hind legs and jumped on the table after him.

Tim struggled to open the window. Now on the table, Mr. Raj Kapur jumped once, then twice. The third time, he sunk his teeth into Tim's left bum cheek, which I'd found oh so cute only minutes earlier.

"No!" I cried. "Get down, Mr. Raj Kapur! Let him go!"

"Get him!" Mrs. Rao shouted, gesturing madly. Ashok waved his mop with a wild look in his eyes but didn't budge from his safe spot behind Mrs. Rao.

"Argh!" Tim said, clutching his bottom. "Damn dog!" He let out a wild kick.

Mr. Raj Kapur went flying across the room with a piece of Tim's jeans tucked tightly between his teeth. He smacked right onto Mrs. Rao's stomach. She doubled over from the force and slammed into Ashok, knocking them both down to the floor.

She sat on the floor on top of Ashok, her legs spread apart, her chest heaving, her hair askew, looking half-shocked, half-enraged. The mop was now on her head and Mr. Raj Kapur was on her lap, a fiery, barking ball of fur.

Squashed underneath them both, Ashok looked terrified. With considerable effort, he squirmed out from under his heavy-set boss and stood up shakily. Then he put his hands together and started to prance around Mrs. Rao like he was engaging in a strange worship ritual. I guessed that was the closest he could come to saying sorry.

Mr. Raj Kapur wasn't done yet, though. He jumped off his owner's lap, spat out the cloth, and, snarling like a mini tiger, ran back to the table as fast as his stubby legs could take him, and readied to take another shot at Tim's bum cheek.

"Get away, you piece of crap!" Tim shouted, half-way out of the window now. He twisted his body a few times to wiggle out. The bottle of rum in his pocket slipped out and came crashing on the floor, sending glass shards everywhere.

"Shit," Tim said, looking down at the mess. The smell of cheap rum filled the room and the red booze oozed across my carpet. Mr. Raj Kapur stopped his barking immediately, sniffed the spill, and started to lick it.

"No-o-o-o!" Mrs. Rao screeched, waving her hands, still on the floor, her face a dark crimson now. "Don't touch that! Come here, my baby. Come here!"

I looked up to see Tim almost out of the window, his feet dangling on the ledge.

"Be careful, Tim!"

"Get out of there, Asha!" he yelled. "Follow me! Get out!"

His shirt tore on the window ledge.

"Jeezus!"

"Tim!" I brought my hands to my face. "Oh my god."

When he'd come into my room through the window earlier that evening, he'd looked debonair, like a knight in shining armor coming to rescue me. Now, he looked like a scruffy thief trying to make an ungainly escape.

"If I see you again, I'll have you arrested! You hear me!" Mrs. Rao shook her fist at Tim's disappearing back. "You criminal! You thief!"

Mr. Raj Kapur stopped for a second to bark half-heartedly at no one in particular and went back to licking the spilled liquid.

Mrs. Rao struggled to get up. Ashok gingerly offered a frail hand to help her up, almost getting pulled down as he did.

"It's Tim from school, Mrs. Rao," I said to her. "He's not a thief. He's harmless. He's my friend."

"Oh, is that right?" Mrs. Rao snapped. "Is this what happens when I let you go to school? You let intruders in? You ungrateful tramp! I never let any of the other girls go to school. This is how you repay me for treating you so well? Well, I don't ever want to see that boy or any other boy in my house again, you hear me?"

I nodded, trembling, worried what punishment she would mete out on me now.

"And when I say, stay in your room, I mean stay in your room!" She glared. "I don't want to see your face till seven tomorrow at breakfast, you hear!"

Something outside banged, startling us all into silence.

Chapter Thirty-three

"There's some weird shit going on in your house," Tim said, splitting open a dark chocolate cupcake.

Katy, Tim, and I were sitting in the school cafeteria during lunch the next day. Katy had been upset we hadn't shown up to the party. The chocolate cupcakes were my way of saying sorry.

"Sounds like you guys had a real crazy night," she said, shaking her head.

Crazy was right, but I'd expected worse. Much worse.

To my surprise, Mrs. Rao simply picked up her dog and marched out of my room in a huff with Ashok at her heels, trailing the mop behind him. Then, in the morning, she acted as if nothing had happened. I wasn't sure if she was prolonging my fear and holding off the punishment till later or if something more urgent occupied her mind. I dared to wonder if she'd forgiven me and moved on even. I highly doubted it would be the latter, but she and I had run out of excuses for me not being in school, so she had no choice. Ashok took me to school as usual the next morning.

"I thought someone shot you or something," I said, looking at Tim. "I didn't sleep at all last night."

"I'm alive, aren't I?" Tim said, puffing his chest slightly. "Won't let a bunch of batty fogies bring me down. Can outrun them any day."

"I didn't know you could jump out of a window that fast. I was worried you'd break your neck or something."

"I did break something. My good bottle of rum."

"It didn't go to total waste. Mr. Raj Kapur licked all of it."

"You guys wanna know what happened after I got out of your room?" Tim asked, reaching for another cake. He seemed to be relishing keeping us in suspense. I'd been asking him all morning how he got out okay.

"Yes!" Katy and I said at the same time.

"Thought I'd slip out through the front because the wall is short-er and easier to climb," he said. "But I bumped into that probo—that orangutan you keep complaining about."

"It's a creepy old man who comes to Mrs. Rao's dinners," I ex-plained to Katy.

"Yeah, I'm sure that was him," Tim said. "This guy had the biggest, fattest nose I've ever seen on a man. He was standing near the shipping container with another dude. This other guy was wear-ing this weird pajama shirt, just like that dude with the mop in your room last night."

"Really?" I said. "There were more people like Ashok?"

"Did they see you, then?" Katy asked.

"Oh yeah, they did, but I was half-way up the wall by then. The fat nose dude started shouting, 'Intruder! Get out! Call the dogs!' and all that."

Katy and I listened with wide eyes.

"Didn't you hear them?" Tim asked. "They were loud enough to wake the devil."

"No." I shook my head. "Mr. Raj Kapur was getting drunk and Mrs. Rao was having a stroke. It was a circus in my room."

"You guys have got to be kidding," Katy said, shaking her head again. "You were having way more fun than I was last night, and the party was at my place."

"This was no party, I can tell you that," Tim said. "The fat-nose guy came rushing to me. He was shaking his fist and shouting. The other man hiked up his shirt and ran over with a two-by-four piece of wood in his hands. I was sure they were gonna kill me."

"What happened?" I asked.

"That shirt dude tried to hit me with the two-by-four, but he swung too far and hit the other guy instead."

"Oh!"

"He tried again but missed me and hit the wall. There was a huge bang."

"That was the sound we heard?"

"Probably. Didn't look. I climbed over real fast. Think I left my jacket on your lawn, but I didn't look back. Just ran like hell all the way home."

"That's wild," Katy said. "Like something from a movie."

"You know what I think?" Tim said, looking at me pointedly. "Your aunt's not an innocent widow like you say she is. She's not a crazy old dingbat either."

"Oh?"

Tim leaned over. "I tell you, she's doing serious crime."

"Crime?" I said.

"Don't you find it strange?" Tim asked. "This moonlight shit and these crazy dudes?"

"It's a house rule."

"House rules?" Katy raised an eyebrow.

"Whatever she's up to, she doesn't want you to know," Tim said. "That's why she makes you stay in your room like that. Don't you see?"

"Ah..." My mouth had dried up.

They were looking at me with strange expressions on their faces. I looked down and wiped a cake crumb off the table. I wasn't ready to share my story yet. They didn't know about my forced engagement to Kristadasa. They didn't know about Aunty Shilpa's terrible sickness, or that Mrs. Rao wasn't really my aunt, that I was only here to make money, and return home. I knew Mrs. Rao's antics were making my new friends uneasy, but the last thing I wanted was to scare them off, the only two people I knew at school.

"Asha," Katy asked after a long silence. "Does she, like, ever, like, hurt you?"

"No," I said. "Of course not."

"Oh no," Tim said, rolling his eyes. "She only treats her like a slave. That's all. She even has a contract to do housework, can you believe it?"

Katy looked deeply concerned. "Has she, like, ever done anything weird to you?"

"Especially on those full-moon nights?" Tim said, wiggling his eyebrows.

"This is serious, Tim." Katy gave him a withering look.

"Look, I'm fine," I said with a sigh. "No one's ever done anything bad to me. I help around the house. Indian kids have a lot of house stuff to do and rules to follow. It's expected. It's something to do with family duty..." My voice trailed.

"Do you want to talk to a counselor, maybe?" Katy asked gently as if she was afraid she'd offend me. "Or maybe a teacher?"

"No!" I said more forcefully than I expected. "You guys are really overreacting."

"Well, I think you need to get the hell outta there," Tim said, pointing a chocolate-icing-covered finger at me. "And real fast too before anything real bad happens."

"And where will I go?"

"Come stay with me," Katy said.

I looked at her in surprise.

"If you promise to help with my rent," she said with a smile.

"You live on your own?"

"It's not my apartment. It belongs to my boss, but I'm the only one who lives there. It's a tiny studio but two can live there. And I need help with the rent."

"That'll be a riot," Tim said, with his mouth full.

"You bake, right?" Katy asked, picking up a cake and twirling it in her hand.

I nodded. I noticed she had looked longingly at my cakes all morning but she never took a bite.

"You can work with me," she said. "My boss is a bit of a pain, but he's okay."

"Isn't that your boyfriend?" Tim said with a wide grin. "Your sugar daddy? The Mafia man?"

"Don't be silly," Katy said, turning red. She turned to me, ignoring Tim. "We're looking for a baker right now."

"You work at a bakery?"

"Kind of. They do other things too. The baking business seems to lose money all the time, and he's always trying to find a good baker."

"That's because he hasn't met Asha yet," Tim said with a wink.

"Whenever we lose a baker or Dick fires one, he keeps trying to shove me in the kitchen," Katy said, "but I just want to stick to my own job."

"What do you do?" I asked.

"Bookkeeping and client stuff. I hate working in the kitchen. Can't even boil an egg, so I'd love some help."

"I wish I could." I sighed. As appealing as this was, I had other priorities and a family to take care of back in Goa.

"If you ever feel like you need a place to stay, call me, okay?"

I smiled at her. "That's really nice of you."

"Hey, that's what friends are for. Life can be weird sometimes, so I totally understand."

How true. Life can be weird.

My short fling with Tim ended as quickly as it began. He said he was too scared of my "wacko aunt" to date me anymore. I knew what he really meant was I was too wacko to date. Four weeks later, I caught him kissing Monica, the cute new girl from Quebec. They were behind the locker rooms where Tim played tennis. That was the day my teenage heart broke into a million pieces and I cried all night.

After that, I kept to myself. I had to focus on finishing school and getting back to Goa. Every time I strayed from that goal, I paid the price, it seemed.

But things had turned stranger at Mrs. Rao's home.

A chilled stream of Arctic air had settled over the Rao mansion. The few conversations I'd had with her before seemed gregarious compared to the atmosphere now. She didn't even look at me anymore and left instructions on a notepad stuck to the fridge door.

Ashok was, as usual, petrified of his boss, the house, and sometimes, I suspected, even of me. He never made eye contact and was always engrossed in his slippers. He only came out of the shipping container where he slept when Mrs. Rao pressed the buzzer to call him. I made sure to leave him a plate of food on the kitchen counter. It disappeared when I wasn't looking, and the dirty dish reappeared mysteriously in the dishwasher, again when I wasn't looking. It was like having a live ghost in the house.

While Ashok went through the motions of picking me up and dropping me off at school, I could see he was nervous around me, like I had the power to hurt him. Once, he jumped when I came out of the kitchen. I couldn't fathom what he was scared of.

One other peculiar thing happened a few weeks after the crazy incident in my room.

Strangers in suits started knocking on our door every few weeks, leaving official envelopes on our doorstep when no one answered. I was no longer allowed to open the door or pick up mail. Then, I noticed the Saturday night dinners and full-moon visits stopped altogether. Mrs. Rao didn't explicitly ask me to stay in my room, no strange cars visited our driveway after midnight, and no one left muddy footprints for me to clean anymore.

Mrs. Rao slowly retreated to her bedroom. One day, she asked me to serve her breakfast in bed. Soon after, she asked for lunch in bed. Finally, she was taking all her meals in her room, on a tray in bed with the supersized TV across from her constantly tuned to the Bollywood channel. With Mrs. Rao cloistered away in her chambers and

Ashok skulking in the shipping container in the backyard, I had the whole house to myself.

I spent my days doing homework and housework, and eating in the kitchen alone. Cleaning had become cathartic. Instead of crying buckets over Tim, I scrubbed until my hands got callused. Instead of seething over Mrs. Rao's mistreatment, I focused on my school books. When I was done with both, I sat in the library and got lost in worlds of recipes and stories to forget the real world.

This zombie-like existence went on for several months until someone picked up the house phone for the first time since I arrived in Toronto.

Part SEVEN

They say when you are missing someone that they are probably feeling the same, but I don't think it's possible for you to miss me as much as I'm missing you right now.
Edna St. Vincent Millay

Chapter Thirty-four

I was dusting the mantelpiece when Mrs. Rao's home phone rang twice and stopped.

Strange. She never picked up her landline and normally let it ring forever. She talked at length on her mobile and avoided the house phone like it had an infectious disease, to the point I wondered why she kept it at all.

It was almost ten months after Tim's escapade from my room. At school, I'd kept my head down and focused on my books. At home, I'd kept my head down and focused on my chores. I'd passed my exams, not as well as I'd have liked, but I was progressing. By then, I'd learned to hum to Christmas carols, watched as days shortened and lengthened and had seen my first snowfall.

But my excitement over seeing snow had melted as quickly as the snow itself. Only two things kept me going now.

One was my father's voice in my head telling me to finish school no matter what. The other was my wall calendar that counted the days I had left till graduation from high school—exactly four weeks before my purgatory at Mrs. Rao's ended.

I marked each day off with a black felt pen. I couldn't wait to see Preeti, Aunty Shilpa, and even Grandma, again. I got butterflies in my stomach every time I thought of them. I daydreamed of the plane ride back and of seeing Preeti and Aunty Shilpa at the airport arrival area again. Unlike last time, I was going to run and fling my arms around them. I couldn't wait. My spirits rose steadily with every passing day.

Nothing Mrs. Rao could do would dampen my feelings now.

That day, when someone picked up the house phone, I'd just pulled the heavy vacuum into the library, the next stop in my cleaning routine. I was about to start the machine when the phone rang twice and stopped, and a muffled murmur come from upstairs.

Ashok had gone out on a chore so it couldn't have been him who picked it up. I listened to the low sounds coming from upstairs with growing curiosity until I couldn't help myself.

I tiptoed up the stairs with my duster in hand and walked toward Mrs. Rao's room. I stood outside her door, pretending to dust the great blue Chinese vase on the high table outside, catching snippets of words floating out of the room.

"...delivery not good..."

"...pay back money..."

"...if police find out..."

Police?

"...the girl...too much trouble..."

The girl? What's she talking about? Who's she talking to?

I remembered next to the library downstairs was a den where Mrs. Rao kept important papers, bills, and the only other telephone in the house. She never worked in this room and only used it for document storage. It was a room, she'd said, that never needed cleaning. I tiptoed down the stairs, walked over to the den, and slowly turned the doorknob. To my surprise, it slid open. I walked in and closed the door gently behind me.

An ebony black desk sat in the middle of the room, taking up more than half the space, an antique brought over from India decades ago. On my first day, when Mrs. Rao had given me a tour of her mansion, she'd opened this door and pointed at the desk. "See that? This is my husband's desk. It's a priceless piece of furniture, and I never, ever want you to touch it. If anything happens to it, it will cost you a fortune. You hear me?"

"You don't want me to dust it?"

"I don't want you to even look at it. In fact, you don't need to clean this room at all, do you understand?"

She'd shut the door, and that was all I remembered of that room. From the tour I'd had that day so far, I'd realized there was enough work to keep me busy for years. Not having to clean this one small room was perfectly fine with me.

The phone on the desk was blinking a green light, which meant a call was in progress.

I reached out to pick up the handset and stopped just in time. Mrs. Rao was sure to hear a click if I picked up the phone now. I pulled my hand back and glanced around the room. Other than the desk and the oversized leather chair, there wasn't much else.

For the first time, I touched the beautiful ebony wood. I ran my fingers over its polished surface. Ancient Indian motifs were carved into the wood and elaborate flowery designs were etched on each drawer. This desk belonged in a museum, not in an abandoned room hardly used by anyone. The only items on it were a dusty green banker's lamp, the telephone handset, and a legal-sized red file folder in one corner.

My curiosity got the better of me.

I reached for the folder and flipped it open. It contained official documents on loans, mortgages, and whatnot. I went through them quickly. A familiar logo caught my eye on the last piece of paper. It was a letter from the West End Collection Agency. I skimmed down the page. It was dated a week ago and contained one paragraph. My eyes opened wide.

Mrs. Rao was in trouble—deep trouble. She owed $1,432,965.43 to the agency—one-and-a-half million dollars, give or take. I gasped. I couldn't imagine having that much money, let alone owing it to someone else. *What did she do with all that?* For this amount, I could help not just Aunty Shilpa but all of Goa.

I kept reading. There was something about a "loan reprieve" months ago. I did a quick mental calculation. That was about the time Tim got caught in my room. *So this was why she'd been too pre-occupied to punish me then.*

The last sentence in the letter said something about "repossessing the property" in May. I looked at the date. That was three months away. The letter went on to say if Mrs. Rao repaid a partial amount by the end of February, they'd reconsider the terms of the loan. *Does this mean she'll lose her house if she doesn't?*

I glanced at the telephone. The light was still blinking. Without a smidgen of shame, I opened the first drawer. It slid out like it had been oiled with butter. *She must use this desk often.*

The drawer contained another file folder, a blue one, this time. I pulled it out and settled back on the leather chair to rummage through it. There were letters from the Super India Fruit and Vegetable Exporters of Goa. I looked at the first one. The purple-blue ink and the shaky handwriting were familiar, but I couldn't place it.

The letter said deliveries were to come from Goa to Mrs. Rao's home in Toronto, via Singapore and Vancouver. *That's a long way for fruit and vegetables to travel.* I rummaged through the other letters. Each gave the number of crates and a delivery date. Sometimes, a letter was sent to say they—whoever *they* were—lost a crate in Singapore or Manila. *How can you lose a fruit and vegetable crate?*

I looked at the delivery dates. Something nagged at me. One letter, dated exactly a year and ten months ago, said a cargo was to be delivered on 15 April. I stopped. I remembered that date like yesterday. That was the day I landed in Toronto.

Then, it came to me. All these dates, except the day I came to Toronto, matched the nights I'd been asked to stay in my room. I knew this because I'd written the dates of the full moons in a notepad to remind myself when I'd be stuck in my room. It had only been after I'd met Tim, distracted by his attention, that I'd forgotten to keep track of the days.

I peered at the letters again. This time, the handwriting jumped off the page. *Franky's writing!* It was unmistakable. *Since when did Franky run a fruit and vegetable exporting business?*

I went through each letter, my heart beating faster, organizing them in order of date.

Mrs. Rao's home was a waypoint. From here, cargo was sent to the United States, some to New York, some to Chicago, and others to Detroit. What a roundabout way to get bananas and mangoes to their final destinations. *Wouldn't they all turn bad before they reach the grocery stores?*

So, did those mysterious footsteps on full-moon nights belong to truck drivers? Crate carriers? Vegetable traders? Some days, they delivered one crate. *How many people did it take to move one box? Wouldn't that be expensive?* Something didn't make sense.

I shuffled through the papers and finally got to the end of the file. There was a bulky envelope in the back.

After a quick glance at the blinking phone to make sure Mrs. Rao was still occupied, I pried the envelope open. Slippery pieces of small black-and-white paper slid onto my lap and to the floor. *Photos.*

There must have been dozens and dozens of them. I picked one up and looked at the strange face. The photos were of Indian men and some young women. All were black-and-white and passport-sized. Among them, I found one of Ashok. I stared at his unsmiling face, willing it to tell me what was going on here. But it didn't give me any clues.

I thrust all the photos in the envelope and stuffed the folder back into the drawer. That was when I felt something else.

I peeked inside the drawer to see what it was. Right at the back, in a dark corner, was a small booklet with a blue-black cover and a golden embossed etch. *My passport!* I grabbed it and pulled it out, almost ripping the cover. I looked over it quickly to make sure it wasn't damaged or changed from when I'd last seen it, and thrust it in my pocket.

Together with my passport, I'd also pulled out loose pieces of flimsy paper from the back of the drawer. They flew out, one settling on my arm. I turned it around. It was a small, see-through, credit-card-sized paper with a shiny sticker in the shape of a maple leaf.

I pulled my passport out of my pocket and opened it to the last page that had been used. There it was—the same sticker with a shimmery maple leaf, with the words "Visa" in black letters on top.

I remembered my parents complaining about how long it took to get visas to travel to a new country. They had to first fill out applications and send them with our passports to the official embassy of whatever country we wanted to travel to, and then, we waited. And waited.

Many times it took months. I remembered because I was always fretting about which school I'd be going to next. If I hated my current school, the waiting took forever. If I liked my school, the visas came too quickly.

How did Mrs. Rao have all these visa papers in her drawer? Was she an official embassy of sorts? I remembered how quickly Franky had got my visa—within a week almost. *Is that even possible?*

That reminded me of a conversation my parents had over dinner one night, a long time ago. They'd been talking about "snake-heads." I'd sat quietly, listening, eating my food, conjuring up images of beefy men in sarongs with deadly cobra crowns in place of human heads. These snake-heads, my parents had said, charged thousands of dollars to poor villagers who wanted to escape their poverty-ridden lives to the free West.

I remembered my parents shaking their heads, talking about how these poor people were stuffed into shipping containers with no food, no toilets, and barely enough water. Some didn't survive the journey. Once on shore, they were smuggled by trucks and vans and forced to work in factories and farms to pay back debts to the snake-heads.

They had no choice because they could never go to the police who'd throw them in jail, anyway. They were trapped for life. "Modern-day slavery," my mother had called it.

A chill went down my spine.

It all came together now. The noises on full-moon nights. The shipping container in the backyard. Ashok's sudden appearance. Mrs. Rao wasn't transporting vegetables around the world. She was smuggling people.

Tim was right. She was a criminal. *A snake-head.*

I sat at the edge of the chair, feeling goose bumps on my arms and neck. *Is this why Ashok's so jumpy? Was he smuggled? Was I smuggled too? But I came in a plane. What about my visa? Is it fake? If the police catch me, will I go to jail?*

I had all the reasons to go through Mrs. Rao's drawers now.

The phone light was still blinking. I yanked open the last drawer. It was filled with stuffed envelopes that looked strangely familiar. I picked up the first and turned it over.

When I saw the writing on the front, I nearly dropped it. This was *my* letter, one of the many I'd sent to Preeti and Aunty Shilpa. I pulled out all the envelopes in the drawer with a sinking feeling in my stomach.

All the letters I'd written over many sleepless nights and passed onto Mrs. Rao, who'd promised to mail them—these letters to Preeti, to Aunty Shilpa, and even to Franky—were still here.

They'd been piled up in this drawer over the two years, addressed and stamped by me, but never sent. One of them had the address crossed out and "Shred" written on it. I guessed Mrs. Rao, a pack rat by nature, had been collecting these to be discarded but had forgotten them in here.

A hot flash of anger went through my body. *So this is why no one's replied.*

I sat glued to edge of the chair, feeling rivulets of sweat go down my back. Something was nagging at me. Something dark and frightening in the back of my brain slowly percolated up, and I froze.

Did Aunty Shilpa get my money and the help she needed? Is she still sick? Is Preeti fine? Is Grandma okay?

A door banged upstairs, making me jump.

I looked at the telephone. The blinking light was gone. Mrs. Rao had ended her call.

I looked around frantically.

The desk was strewn with papers. I had to move fast. I shoved the papers and files back into the drawers, taking care not to make any noise. My heart was thumping so loudly I was sure she could hear it from upstairs.

I was about to shut the last drawer when my eye caught a yellow envelope stuck to the bottom. I hadn't seen it before. I pulled it out. It bore an Indian stamp from an address in Goa. I recognized the handwriting.

I pushed it into my pocket with my passport and dashed out of the room.

Chapter Thirty-five

"Where were you, girl? Didn't you hear me call?"

Mrs. Rao was standing at the foot of the stairway in her fluffy pink bathrobe and matching bunny slippers. I got a whiff of ratty, unwashed smell mixed with the bitter odor of whiskey. Though she had a choice of three oversized, luxurious bathrooms, Mrs. Rao had stopped taking showers weeks ago. She was beginning to look and smell like a homeless person.

I opened my mouth to answer only to discover my voice had disappeared.

Ten seconds ago, I was madly stuffing papers back into her desk drawers. I'd just picked up the vacuum hose in the library when she walked down. My chest was heaving, my heart was thumping, and I was sure my face gave everything away.

"What's wrong with you? Have you gone dumb like Ashok?" she snapped.

"Sorry, Mrs. Rao." I barely got the words out.

"The TV remote in my room is dead. Fix it!"

"Okay," I squeaked.

Mrs. Rao shuffled back up the stairs, into her bedroom, and banged the door shut. I stood frozen for a whole minute before I realized I had got away free.

It was late at night, after finishing all my chores and crawling into bed, that I remembered the yellow envelope in my pocket. I pulled the letter out.

The dated stamp told me it had arrived a year ago but it hadn't been opened. The letter, addressed to me, had originally been sent to Franky's office in India, but someone had scratched that address out and written Mrs. Rao's address on top of it.

I opened it with trembling hands.

Pink paper. A jolt went through my heart. Preeti always used pink paper to write her letters, soft paper like this. When I spotted her signature scrawled at the bottom of the letter, my heart jumped to my throat.

I began to read, holding my breath.

Dearest Asha,

I don't know if you will ever receive this letter. You haven't replied to our earlier ones. I am hoping that's because you have found a good life and moved on. I'm sad about that but hope all is well.

Franky told us you are back in Tanzania now. That sounds so far away, I can't even imagine what it is like there. Is it too hot for you? Have you found your old friend Chanda again? Franky said you were soon going to marry a rich Indian businessman over there and that you were doing very well. I am so happy for you. I know that if anyone deserves a good life, it is you. I hope that your new husband is treating you well.

After you left, Grandma got quite angry. She declared to everyone that she disowned you from the family, that you can never come back. Kristadasa came to our home with the marriage broker and said if I didn't marry him, they will throw us out of our house. I told Grandma I will marry that man, but on one condition, that she can't disown you, her own granddaughter. I want you to know that. No matter what you have heard or anyone has told you, you will always be part of my family. But in a way, her words don't matter anymore, because she has left us for the afterlife.

It has been a very difficult marriage for me. Some days I wished to kill myself, but it was Aunty Shilpa who kept me going, who kept me alive.

I miss her a lot. Even though we knew it was coming, it was still very difficult. The disease wrecked her body. When she died, she was thinner than a rake and looked like a skeleton. She could barely speak. But she asked for you every day.

She lay in her bed for weeks before she took her last breath. I was with her that last day, holding her hand. She was not scared of death. She was scared of leaving me behind, alone. I told her not to worry, that you were doing well and that you will come and rescue me one day. She smiled when I said that.

Five days after we buried her, Grandma's heart gave away. Hers was a quick and painless death, or so the sadhus in the temple told me.

I am now alone here. I miss you and wish you would join me again. You are my only family and friend. Please write back. Even if you don't, I will keep writing, dreaming, and hoping that I will see you again, my dear cousin.

With all my love,

Preeti

I sat on my bed, staring into space for a very long time.

My mind had gone blank and my body had gone numb. When I finally came to, my muscles were stiff and I was still clenching Preeti's letter—so tightly my fingertips had turned white.

Did I imagine all this?

I looked down at the letter in my hands. No, the words were still there in Preeti's neat handwriting on her favorite pink paper.

It had been almost two years since I'd left Goa. I had two months to go before I'd have paid my dues for Mrs. Rao's car damage. I looked up at my calendar. It seemed too long to wait to return home, to see Preeti again.

A tsunami of memories rushed in.

I remembered Preeti's pretty eyes, her innocent face, and that brilliant mind of hers that impressed our teachers and even the school monitor. I remembered her funny hobby of collecting chocolate wrappers in her scrapbook diary, and how we'd curl up under the ratty old blanket on the sofa bed giggling over some silly joke or the other.

I remembered Aunty Shilpa's sad but beautiful eyes, and how her face lit up whenever I'd read from a book. I remembered how much she'd tried to help us, how she'd always been there for us.

I recalled Grandma's wrinkled old face as she'd stooped over the heavenly smell of her curry pot on the stone stove.

Precious memories. They were my family, my only family.

The image of the dirty, drunk Kristadasa looming over me in the apartment corridor flashed across my mind. A wave of nausea washed over me. This was the life of horror Preeti was going through every day. And it was all because of me. Because I ran away like a coward.

I got up and walked unsteadily to the bathroom. I collapsed in front of the toilet and threw up.

Chapter Thirty-six

I didn't leave my room the next morning.

I couldn't face Mrs. Rao. I couldn't eat or sleep either and wished I'd stop breathing.

I lay in bed, curtains drawn, devastated at what I'd done.

Aunty Shilpa had died, and Grandma too. I didn't even want to think of what Preeti's life must be like with that vile man.

When Mrs. Rao buzzed me the next morning, I told her I was sick. She didn't inquire after my well-being. She was only irritated she had to make her own coffee. I stayed in bed in a haze of sadness and despair, getting up only to drink from the tap in my bathroom.

After one day, I began to feel weak and dizzy. After two days, I thought of killing myself. On the third, I fantasized about murdering Franky and Mrs. Rao, poisoning them with my cupcakes laced with something bad. Meanwhile, the intercom buzzed every morning. Each morning, I told Mrs. Rao I was sick. Each time, she hung up, annoyed.

On the fourth day, I decided to get up.

The previous night, as I'd lain in bed with Preeti's letter still tucked under my pillow, I'd thought of her and only her. She was still alive somewhere in Goa. I had to find her. I had to help her. How, I didn't know, but I knew I couldn't save her lying in bed, feeling sorry for myself.

With the remaining strength I had, I took a shower and stumbled into the kitchen for something to eat.

"Ah, you're back," Mrs. Rao said sharply. "I need the laundry done. It's been piling up for heaven's sake!" With a snort, she walked out, got in her car and left. I watched her leave, an unspeakable anger gnawing inside me.

Over the next few weeks, I didn't sleep much. I lost my appetite and got tired easily. When my teacher asked me what was wrong, I told her I had a bad case of the flu and was just recovering. My hands shook so much, I had to redo the icing on the cakes Mrs. Rao had demanded I make. I couldn't bear to look at her anymore, so I kept my eyes down and went through the motions.

But my mind was racing a million miles a second.

How do I get out of here? How do I get back to Goa? Who can I call for help? How can I tell the police what Mrs. Rao's up to without getting myself thrown in jail first? An image of a white-and-blue police car rushing to our house with sirens blaring haunted me every night. The thought of prison sent cold shivers down my spine. *If I'm in jail, how can I help Preeti?*

Two weeks after I got out of bed and started work again, the landline was picked up for the second time during my stay at Mrs. Rao's house.

Ashok was gone somewhere. Mrs. Rao was upstairs cloistered in her bedroom as usual. There wasn't much time.

I dropped the icing tube on the counter, the pink splattering everywhere, but I didn't care. I dashed to the den as fast as I could and closed the door gently. I leaned across the big desk and slipped the phone out of its cradle.

Buzzz whirrr buzzzzzz. I nearly dropped the handset. *What's that?*

"Hello? Hello?" Mrs. Rao was trying to speak through the crackle and hisses coming down the line.

More static.

"Hello? Hello?" She sounded anxious now.

A crisp female voice cut through the noise with a lilting Hindi accent. "Will you please accept a collect call from India, madam?"

"Yes, yes." Mrs. Rao's voice was unusually strained.

"You can go right ahead, mister," the female voice said from far away.

"Mrs. Rao?" This time, I dropped the phone. It slid down to my lap. I picked it up gently and brought it back to my ear.

"Hello, Franky," Mrs. Rao was saying in a subdued tone. "May Lord Vishnu smile upon your family. I hope all is well."

"Yes, yes," Franky said. He sounded hurried. No, he sounded irritated. "Let's get to the business, shall we? We have to make arrangements very fast now."

I clutched the telephone to my ear, not daring to breathe.

"I will find the money, I promise," Mrs. Rao said. "Please be patient, Franky, please."

"You ran out of chances. I gave you six months to solve this problem. What did you do?"

"I...er..." I'd never heard Mrs. Rao speechless. "Please, Franky. Give me time."

Is Mrs. Rao begging?

"No!" Franky yelled so loudly I had to pull the headset away from my ear. "I already made other arrangements. I am fed up, very much fed up. Do you understand?" He sounded furious.

"I'm only asking for one more week. You have to understand. I promise over my dead husband's grave—"

"That stupid husband of yours was no better. Pretending he was a Brahmin from New Delhi. I paid him well, but he gave me trouble, just like you. You owe me."

Mrs. Rao let out a whimper. "My husband, rest his soul, did his best for you. He worked so hard. Please do not insult him, Franky."

Did I have this all wrong? Was Franky Mrs. Rao's boss? Was he the real snake-head?

"Oh yeah, bless him. Lost all the money he left you to those rich friends of yours, eh?"

"My friends are all I have," Mrs. Rao whimpered. "They won't come if I didn't feed them and entertain them. I'm just a lonely widow, Franky."

"Don't think I don't know what you're up to over there, Mrs. Rao. You gambled all the money we made. Now you're losing your house and you're ruining my business. We'll be finished, and this is all your fault!" Franky sounded like he was frothing at the mouth.

"You know I am a good woman. I always give a little something to the animal society. I'm a very good person—"

It was strange to hear Mrs. Rao so meek. I imagined her in bed upstairs, cowering.

"You can't even do a simple job." Franky wasn't done shouting yet. "I sent you the girl as a favor, and you let that footloose tramp run around like a *gora*. How many times did I tell you to be careful? You couldn't even do this one simple job."

"But someone told Social Serv—"

"Stop making excuses, Mrs. Rao!"

I listened in shock, my heart pounding.

"How hard is it to keep a schoolgirl locked up when we're making deliveries? A few thrashes to the back of her head was all that was needed. Make them bleed a bit and they will listen. You're a coward, like your husband. Even Ashok could have done a better job."

"Franky," Mrs. Rao said in her most endearing tone, which she reserved for outsiders, like my teachers and our neighbors, "you know the Arabs pay very good money for young girls. I have a friend who can help us make a deal. The girl is still very fresh, healthy, only sixteen."

The hair on my neck stood straight. *Is she bartering me off?*

"Ha!" Franky said. "The Arabs don't like them over twelve. Besides, have you seen that girl? The color of over-brewed tea. You could have at least used that skin-lightening lotion on her that I sent you. We could send her off for domestic work, but even then, we won't get much for her."

I looked down at my arms and turned them over. I hadn't realized I was the color of over-brewed tea.

"I've tried my best, Franky. If you had sent a girl version of Ashok, we wouldn't have these problems, you know. An illiterate, dumb girl from a village wouldn't gossip with the neighbors, ask to go to school, or bring boys into the house. She is so much trouble. What can I do, Franky? At least that boy and her didn't call the police."

"Enough! I already found a businessman from Tamil Nadu who is ready to pay to solve both of our problems. He needs to leave the country for a while, and we have to get a marriage visa for him. I know he will pay, not like the rich Arabs maybe, but he will pay something. We can get rid of her and solve our immediate problem."

"Does this mean," Mrs. Rao said in her sweetest tone, "that I get to keep my house? This is all I have. My memories of my dear husband, our life together—"

"I don't give out free money, you understand? You will be paying back with big interest for the rest of your life. You were too busy stuffing yourself and playing cards with your rich friends to do your job. It was my mistake to even start this business with you."

Silence from Mrs. Rao.

"Any more boyfriends around?" Franky snapped. "I don't want more trouble."

I nearly choked. I clenched my fists. *I should have trusted my gut when I first saw Franky's yellowed hyena smile back in Goa.*

"No. No boyfriends," Mrs. Rao said quickly. "I keep her very busy here at home."

"That, at least, is good news."

"She cooks excellently. My friends think she cooks better than those fancy restaurants on Queen's Quay. That's why they always want to come to my house. I've taught her very well."

Taught me? How dare she?

"Good, that was your job anyway," Franky said, apparently satisfied. "Balasubramanium, this man I found, is fifty and already has a wife, so he will know how to give a good thrashing if she misbehaves. Maybe you need to learn something from him."

With that, Franky hung up with a click. With a huge sigh, Mrs. Rao followed suit.

I stayed still for a minute holding on to the phone, listening to the dead monotone. My shoulders felt tighter than a bow drawn taut.

When I finally put the phone back on its cradle, there were red marks on my palm from clutching the handset too tightly.

Chapter Thirty-seven

"**F**ranky's sending the man from Tamil Nadu next week."
I heard Mrs. Rao's booming voice from the living room. My head jolted, banging on the table. I winced from the pain.

It was two weeks after the fateful phone call from Franky. Mrs. Rao and her friends were playing their usual game of cards after dinner, chatting over cigars, port, and a pile of money on the coffee table.

If Mr. Raj Kapur hadn't made a mess under the table after stealing a slice of chocolate cake, I'd have been cloistered in the kitchen. I'd only spotted it after I'd cleaned the table and almost finished vacuuming the room. I'd been scrubbing with one hand for a while, using the other to cover my nose.

I hunkered under the table next to Mr. Raj Kapur's vomit and listened in.

"Maybe it's time you got remarried, Mrs. Rao," the Proboscis Man said, "to solve all your problems."

"Never!" Mrs. Rao snapped. "I will never betray my dead husband."

"You found a solution then, Mrs. Rao?" someone else asked.

"I get to keep the house. But it would have been so much easier if the girl had been younger. Much easier to handle."

"Like that last one you had," someone else said.

"She was older, but an illiterate. I arranged a marriage for a good sum and she didn't say a word," Mrs. Rao said.

I involuntarily shivered in my corner.

"If you had a second girl who could cook like this one, you could pay all of your debts."

The guests laughed.

After the phone call from Franky, Mrs. Rao had slowly turned back to her normal self. She shed her bunny slippers and dressing gown and started eating at the dinner table again. One day, I walked up with her dessert tray to hear her tell Mr. Raj Kapur in a gleeful voice, "We get to keep the house, my daaarling. We get to keep our home."

After a week, she had become jovial, even. She started taking long baths again and watching Bollywood movies over supper in the dining room with Mr. Raj Kapur. She invited her friends to dine, wine, and gamble that first weekend. It was a merry party when they all got together as if the guests were celebrating Mrs. Rao's good fortune with her.

But while she was on an upswing, I was running downhill fast.

Every time the bell rang, my heart jumped. I'd bitten my nails to the quick wondering when the old man from India would force me to marry him and give me a good thrashing, as Franky had threatened. Other days, I worried myself sick about the police coming to cart me off to jail or do whatever they do to illegal immigrants.

I wanted to run away, and fast, but I had one more day before my exams ended, and I was desperate. I didn't care about the prom, the dresses, the dates, or the after-parties. I had other things on my mind, like returning to Goa to rescue Preeti. But I had to finish school for my parents, to honor my promise, no matter what.

Taking a year off to get out of a forced marriage and get medicine for Aunty Shilpa had been understandable then. Not finishing school with a few days remaining was unthinkable. I had come this far—I couldn't quit now.

"So, when's the wedding?" said a woman's voice from the living room.

Wedding? I dropped my wet rag on the carpet, got up carefully so as to not bang my head again, and tiptoed over to the entrance. I stood with my ear to the door, still as a statue.

"Wedding?" Mrs. Rao said with a snort of derision. "Ha! She's drained me enough. I even paid for her immigration application and test."

"You only did that so you could negotiate more with Franky," someone said with a guffaw. "You're a clever one, Mrs. Rao."

"But look at all I've done for her," Mrs. Rao said defensively. "I fed her, I clothed her, I even sent her to school. I treat her practically like my own daughter."

"The immigration department will ask for wedding photos, Mrs. Rao. You need one whether you like it or not. You now my neighbor Mr. Jagmit Singh? He got caught last year because he couldn't offer proper proof for one marriage he was trying to arrange."

"Ah yes," the Proboscis Man said, " I remember this. He even tried to convince the officer to change his mind with some nice cash, but you can't do that with these Canadians. They're gullible but so dastardly by the book, if you ask me."

"Well, the groom can pay for the wedding." Mrs. Rao sniffed. "I've done my part."

"What about us, Mrs. Rao?" someone asked in a slurred voice.

"You?" Mrs. Rao said. "What about you?"

"Who's going to make our Saturday evening suppers now?"

"Yeah, where are we going to go for a good meal, wine, and card games?" someone else piped up.

"I hate going to Queen's Street. Last time I had to wait for a table for fifteen minutes. Ghastly," the Proboscis Man said.

"And don't get me started on the service. It's not like how it used to be."

"I like coming here because it's private. I can say what I want without worrying about gossipy ears."

"Me, too. I can sit back and have a cigar and no one will notice. No annoying journalists to worry about."

"Mrs. Rao, you *must* do something for our sake."

"Look, my priority is to get out of this sinkhole." Mrs. Rao sounded irritated. "Once this man gets what he wants, his visa to stay, he'll discard her like a dirty rag. She'll be back in my kitchen in no time. She'll be thankful to me then, I tell you. She'll be begging me to take her in and I can pretend to save her." She laughed a throaty laugh.

"That's so true. Mrs. Rao, you think of everything," a woman's admiring voice said. "All he wants is a visa to Canada."

"Plus a compliant young girl in the sack," Proboscis Man said, chortling through his nose. "One that can cook well, too. What a bonus for this guy!"

Raucous laughter all around.

Leaving the dirty rag on the carpet and the vacuum still plugged into the socket, I walked down the basement stairs to my room.

I opened my clothes drawer and picked up my schoolbag.

Chapter Thirty-eight

T he next day, when the school bell rang to signal the end of exams, I stayed inside. No one noticed.

Everyone was in a tizzy about the upcoming prom. It had been
the only topic of the week. Everywhere I turned, I heard what someone was going to wear, who was taking whom, whether they were going in a limousine or a car, and where the after-parties would be. I
had major plans too, but of a different kind.

I climbed up the fire stairwell so no one would see me, and
slipped into the empty art classroom on the top floor of the school
building. There, I walked into the large art supply closet, found a
painter's stool and took a seat between the canvasses, paintbrushes,
and rolls of paper. I leaned against the back wall and closed my eyes,
thankful to have finished my last exam. I was officially done with
school. Just as I'd promised my parents.

I slipped my hand into my pocket to feel Preeti's letter. I carried
it everywhere I went. I desperately wanted to see her, hug her, cry
with her, and ask about Aunty Shilpa's final days.

Over the past few weeks, my mind had focused only on one
thing; how to contact her. There were no telephones or mailboxes
in Grandma's apartment complex. Any messages, letters, or parcels
had to be delivered care of a business nearby, like Franky's office.
I couldn't risk him finding out I knew about his lying, scheming
games. I also had no idea who else was working for him in Goa. No,
I couldn't risk writing to Preeti and getting her into more trouble.

After fifteen minutes in the closet, when things had quieted
down in the building, I opened the door slowly making sure no one
was in the room, and walked over to the window that overlooked the
parking lot.

The stragglers were getting into waiting cars or riding away on
their bikes. But there, parked right in the middle of the lot, was

Ashok in the white Land Rover, waiting for me. My heart skipped a beat. *What's he doing here this early?*

I told him school was going to finish an hour later that day due to exams—an excuse to give me time to get away before he came to pick me up. *Did he forget?* I wondered if he knew of Franky and Mrs. Rao's shady business. He must, if he'd come with the moonlight crowd. *Did Franky or Mrs. Rao warn him to be on the lookout?*

I stared at the Rover wondering what to do.

The cleaners didn't come till later in the evening so I could stay here for the next few hours, undiscovered. The school building had a back door, but the caretaker locked it at four every afternoon. I had no choice but to wait for Ashok to leave.

I took a seat at the art teacher's desk, chin on my hands, hoping to hear the sound of a Land Rover engine roar to life. For the next half an hour, I stared at the paintings on the walls, looking at the squiggly lines and abstract cubes done by budding artists, not seeing, not thinking, just waiting, counting time.

After fifteen minutes, I looked out the window once again. The jeep was still there. It was more than half an hour since the school bell had rung, and everyone had gone home. Ashok had more grit than I thought. As I watched, he opened the driver's door and gingerly stepped out of the car. I quickly drew my face away from the window and peeked from a corner.

He walked up to the windows on the first floor and peered in. Then, he began to rattle every doorknob he could find.

I watched him, anxious, but knowing, thankfully, the main building doors automatically locked from the inside when school was over. Realizing he couldn't get inside, he began to investigate the yard. He poked his head around concrete walls and walked around the maple tree. He even peeked behind the cedar bushes. *Did he think I was hiding behind that?*

He cut a strange figure in his gray, baggy clothes and open-toe slippers, stepping this way and that, hesitating, like a lost dog seeking its master. Even from the fourth floor, I could see his face lined with worry. I felt sorry for him. I knew how deathly afraid he was of Mrs. Rao. He was, without doubt, fearful of returning home empty-handed.

It was five thirty in the afternoon when Ashok finally drove away. As soon as the Rover pulled out of the parking lot, I opened the classroom door and ran down the stairs, two steps at a time. I opened the main door slowly, heart pounding, wondering if Ashok could have turned around and come back.

But the parking lot was deserted.

I stepped out to a cool breeze and stood on the stone steps of the main entrance, taking in deep breaths of the chilly air. The sky was painted a forlorn gray. The sun had disappeared for the day, but there was still some light left.

When I had mapped my escape the night before, it had sounded easy.

All I had to do was tell Ashok to come later than usual, leave the school grounds with the rest of the stragglers, and hop on the first bus that came my way. Once I got some distance from the school, I'd find the main airport bus and get myself to the airport, where I'd find a way to Goa. Simple.

If they stopped me and told me my visa was fake, I'd tell them I hadn't known, that I hadn't meant to break the law. I'd think of something. Anything was better than hanging around Mrs. Rao's house waiting to be married off to another Kristadasa—a much worse fate than any prison cell the police could put me in.

But now, standing alone in the front porch of my school, I felt like an idiot. *Did I really think this half-baked plan would work?* I had a total of seven dollars and fifty-three cents in my purse, saved up from coins left over on Mrs. Rao's kitchen counter. *How much did a ticket to Goa cost?*

I felt utterly alone. Working for Mrs. Rao meant I'd been grounded indefinitely since day one. I'd never been able to go to parties, hang out with classmates, or make friends. I kept to myself mostly, purposefully alienating myself, to the point I think my classmates found me strange. Tim had moved on quickly, to several other girls.

The only person who talked to me was Katy, but we didn't hang out much anymore. We couldn't, because I had to run home as soon as classes ended, and she had to get to work. But she always found time to ask how things were, and I'd always reply with "fine."

A gust of wind swooshed around the maple tree that stood proudly at the school entrance. I stared at it mindlessly through the dimming light, watching the leaves whirl around, dancing to a song I couldn't hear. Katy drove her company van to school every day and parked it under that tree. She said her boss allowed her to drive it because she worked early mornings, and she had to make deliveries during lunchtime some days.

"Company van" was a fancy term for the ancient VW camper Katy drove. It had green and yellow psychedelic paint that had faded decades ago, now overtaken by rusty splotches. The van had a large decal on the side that read, "Next Day Catering Company. Call 1-800-522-6969, 4 Avenue de Libre. *We'll be there when no one else will.*" Even Katy agreed it was the lamest slogan ever.

Standing alone on the school steps with the wind whipping my hair and the night growing around me, it didn't sound so lame anymore.

Chapter Thirty-nine

"Katy!"

A dog barked somewhere in the neighborhood. Night had set in fully and I couldn't see much.

I threw another pebble at the window. "Katy!" I hollered as loud as I dared.

I didn't know when her shift ended or who else she'd be with. All I knew was she was working that evening and missing the pre-prom party everyone else was going to.

The front of the bakery was dark except for the dimmed security lights outside. There was a faint light at the back where I guessed the kitchen was, and that was where I was aiming my small stones.

I waited a few minutes and tried again.

"Katy! It's me, Asha."

Not a flicker of life inside.

I wondered if she'd finished her work and gone to the party already. I walked up the stairs and knocked on the door. Not a peep. After waiting a minute, I jiggled the handle like Ashok had done at the school an hour ago. Just like him, I had no luck.

I looked at the windows. They were similar to mine in Mrs. Rao's home, close to the ground and large enough for someone small to sneak through. I tried the first window. It didn't budge. I tried the second window. After some rattling, it slid open an inch.

If Katy or anyone else was inside, they'd get a fright, so I knocked gently on the pane. Not a sound from within. With my heart beating fast, I pushed the window up as silently as possible, parted the curtains, and slipped inside one leg at a time, like how Tim used to enter my basement room.

A flickering fluorescent light hummed above me. I sneezed. The place reeked of cigarette smoke and something sweet.

I waited for my eyes to adjust to the light.

It was a kitchen, but what a kitchen. A vast, industrial-sized kitchen. The counters, the stoves, the double-door fridges, the two oversized ovens, and the massive microwaves were all made of stainless steel. The biggest cake mixers I'd ever seen sat on the counter, calling out to be tried. I stepped toward them and peeked inside. *Gross.* They still had leftover batter in them.

I looked around. On the shelves lining the walls were rows of see-through plastic containers with all kinds of cake toppings—stars, hearts, balloons, baby shapes, glittery balls, snowflakes, and more. The containers were dusty like no one had touched them for a while. Watermarks and dirty spots made the counter look like it hadn't been wiped in days if not weeks. I'd been so impressed by the mammoth size of this place I hadn't noticed the fingerprints and splotches of dried goo everywhere.

I rotated slowly in one spot, careful not to touch anything. If this place got cleaned up, it could be a dream kitchen, I thought. While Mrs. Rao's kitchen was upscale and luxurious, it didn't compare to the industrial strength of this place. This was built to bake hundreds and hundreds of cakes and pies and puddings and breads. It made my head spin.

I put down my schoolbag on the cleanest part of the counter, walked over to the cabinets and opened them one by one. Sacks of different kinds of flour were stowed inside—white flour, brown flour, pastry flour, and all sorts of cheap cake mixes. Smaller bags containing brown sugar, cane sugar, white sugar, and icing sugar lay haphazardly, ripped apart, used, and thrown back in a hurry. I could see trails of sugar inside the cabinets.

Containers with baking powder and cocoa powder lined the top shelf in helter-skelter fashion, tossed carelessly in between bottles of vanilla and coloring. Some didn't have lids and others were past their due date. *Shouldn't these be in the fridge?*

I got on a stool to reach the row of cupboards on top of the shelves. They were filled with grungy, used things that belonged in a chemistry lab rather than a kitchen. Crammed in the cabinets were glass beakers, boxes of baking soda, and cast-iron pans that didn't look like they'd been cleaned well. Right at the back were stacks of something in brown paper bags, which I couldn't reach. Everything looked dirty, so I closed the cupboard doors and stepped down.

I opened the fridge, trying not to touch the gook on the handles. Other than two sticks of butter and seven eggs, there were bottles of rubbing alcohol, two half-filled bottles of wine, and twenty intact bottles of rum. Someone here was seriously using alcohol for baking.

I twisted off one of the wine toppers, sniffed the contents and nearly gagged. The wine had turned—it was worse than vinegar now. I'd taught myself how to bake with alcohol using Chef Pierre's recipes and knew it was a myth you can cook with cheap wine. I put the bottle back and closed the fridge gently, shaking my head.

And that was when I saw it—in one corner, standing tall and proud—a white chef's hat. There was a large dab of brown something on it. On closer inspection, I saw it was a smudge of chocolate icing. On the floor nearby was an apron streaked with yellow and brown marks. It had faded lettering that said, "I'll tell you the recipe, but then I'll have to kill you."

I placed the chef's cap on my head, feeling like I was putting on a crown. I picked up the apron and tied it around my waist. I puffed out my chest, walked over to the main counter, and put my hands on the cold steel. I looked around me, imagining what it must be like to be the chef here. *How come Katy never told me about this place?*

Still in my chef's hat and apron, I walked toward the front of the shop. To my left was a washroom with a mini-washer and dryer next to a large sink. To my right was an office with a view to the strip mall outside. I stepped inside and looked around. On the scratched

Ikea desk sat a brass nameplate with "Domenico Benedetti Valentini" etched in a flowery print. *This must be Dick's office—Katy's boss.*

Like Mrs. Rao, Dick was a pack rat. Fridge parts and old stove pieces were strewn all over the floor. Brown cardboard boxes covered one wall from the floor to the ceiling. I peeked into a half-opened box at the bottom and saw bottles of cheap Jamaican rum inside. On the box was a sticker that said, "Buy ten, get two free."

In between these boxes, were crates and crates of cigarettes with the words "USA" stamped on them. *This is why the place smells so bad. Dick must be the biggest chain-smoker and rum drinker in the world.*

While Mrs. Rao was a neat pack rat, Dick was a cluttered one. Papers littered his desk. On one corner, sat a sad houseplant with droopy yellow leaves, like it had been fed rum instead of water. On the other corner, sat a locked safe, one of those portable ones you can buy at the local drugstore. Coiled around the desk lamp's base were a dozen rosary necklaces, covered in so much dust it was difficult to know their original colors.

On the shelf behind the desk was more school chemistry paraphernalia, all dusty. There was a blue suede sofa in the corner where some of Dick's jackets had been thrown carelessly. The armrests were brown with overuse or dirt. I shuddered in disgust. I would never sit on that.

"Hello?" a garbled voice said behind me.

The hair on the back of my neck sprang up. I turned around slowly, expecting to see a stranger, but there was no one in the room. My heart sped up. With legs like jelly, I walked over to the doorway and looked out. Not a soul.

"Helloo?" the croaky voice said again.

I whirled around. *Who's that?* Whoever it was had a cold, or something strange stuck in their throat.

"Goddammit!"

I jumped.

"Shit!"

I felt goose bumps on my arm. The voice was coming from *inside the office*. With my heart pounding, I looked around and around. I peeked behind the shelves, under the desk, and finally looked up to the ceiling.

There.

Perched high on top of the bookshelf, next to an ivory statue of Jesus, was a multicolored parrot with a tail as long as its body. It was a beautiful bird with feathers of purples, blues, and reds. I would have thought it magnificent if I hadn't heard it swear like a sailor a second ago.

"It's you who's talking," I said, staring at it in wonder.

"Hello-o-o-o?" replied the parrot, cocking its head to one side. "Get ba-a-a-ck to work!"

This must be Dick's unofficial watchdog. It had been quietly watching me all along. It dipped its head a few times and opened its beak again.

"Go to hell!"

I blinked. "That's rude," I heard myself say.

"How a-a-are you?" it replied, giving me a piercing look.

"I'm... er..." I caught myself in time. I was standing in the middle of an empty bakery, late in the evening, talking to a rude bird, while I was on my way to the airport and out of this country. If this wasn't crazy, I didn't know what was. I had to get out. I had to find Katy. *Maybe her phone number's here somewhere. Didn't she say I could stay with her? She wouldn't mind me staying over one night, would she? At least until I sort out a ticket to Goa.*

With one last glance at the bird, which was now busy scratching its head and studiously ignoring me, I walked out of the room and closed the door. I didn't want to take a chance on it flying out and following me. The main reception desk was in front. It was as messy as Dick's office. I spotted an alcove next to the front desk and peeked inside.

This little den was the tidiest place in the entire store. A simple wooden table and chair were tightly wedged into this small space. An old laptop sat in the middle of the table next to a stack of ledger books. I opened one of the books and recognized Katy's handwriting. *So this is where Katy spends her time after school.*

It was strange to imagine the red-heeled, miniskirt-wearing, party animal Katy sitting for hours doing bookkeeping. I looked through the papers on her desk and those posted on the wall, searching for her telephone number. She'd given it to me once, but in my rush, I'd left it in my room at Mrs. Rao's house. All I had on me was a pair of jeans, a white T-shirt, a change of underwear, my passport, and my purse filled with a few dollars. And Preeti's letter.

I plopped onto Katy's chair, touching the computer mouse as I did so. The computer came alive without asking for a password. I hesitated a few seconds, then opened a web browser and punched in Air India's website address.

It took a minute to get flight schedules and prices. It was a good thing I was sitting. The cheapest flight from Toronto to Goa, with four stops along the way, was $1,500. That was one thousand, four hundred, and ninety-two dollars and forty-seven cents more than I had in my purse—more than I'd had in my entire life.

I swiveled around in Katy's chair, desperately trying to think of what to do next. I needed a better plan. I also needed a good story to tell the police if they stopped me at the airport. So many questions gnawed at me. *Where am I going to find the money? How am I going to get to Goa? Where am I going to sleep tonight?* I sat in Katy's chair for half an hour collecting my thoughts, too tired to be hungry, too anxious to fall asleep.

Then I made a decision.

I got up and walked back to the kitchen, ignoring the annoyed croaks coming from Dick's office.

There was one thing I could do. I looked under the sink and pulled out a pair of oversized rubber gloves.

Chapter Forty

"Who the hell are you?"

I jumped and came down hard on the wooden chair. It was like a bull had bellowed right next to me. The roar was still ringing in my ears.

"I said, who the hell are you?" the bull thundered again.

The room spun. I shook my head to clear it.

"Hello-o-o-o?" a familiar voice said nearby.

I wiped my bleary eyes. *Where am I? Who are these people? And why is everyone shouting?*

"I said, who the hell are you, and what have you done to my kitchen?"

I squinted up at the bull roaring in my face, my heart thumping like mad.

I knew it was Dick the moment I saw him. There couldn't be too many Mafia goon lookalikes in town. He was wearing a rumpled gray suit with a white T-shirt and around his neck was a thick gold necklace with a cross pendant.

His face was flushed a dangerous maroon; I could almost see steam rising out of his ears. A thin cigar dangled from his lips, and the parrot I'd locked up in his office the night before was casually perched on his shoulder. It regarded me with disapproving eyes.

"I can he-e-ear you!"

I stared at the feathery apparition.

"Go-to-hell," it said.

"Shut up, Jim!" Dick spat, without taking his eyes off me.

"Shu-u-u-t-u-u-p," echoed the bird softly. "Go-to-hell."

"I..." I tried to speak, but I'd lost my voice. My throat felt dry and cracked. I looked around me. I'd fallen asleep on the most uncomfortable chair in the bakery kitchen. "I was—"

"And what the hell is this?" the man thundered again. My head started to throb. *Does he have to yell?*

I looked in the direction of his angry finger. A dozen cupcakes stood on a stainless-steel tray on the table. They were topped with chocolaty swirls and dusted with multicolored sugar crystals. They looked pretty and proud, I thought.

Then, I remembered. This was why I felt exhausted. After having cleaned for Mrs. Rao day and night for months on end, I couldn't stand the sight of an unclean room, especially an unclean kitchen the magnitude of this one. It was in my blood now. Too stressed to sleep or think about more important matters like how to get my hands on an expensive airline ticket and how to evade border guards with my fake visa, I'd done the only thing I could do.

I'd scoured the kitchen, scrubbed the counters, and cleaned the cabinets. I'd washed the steel appliances until they shone and I'd dusted the shelves and organized the flour and sugar sacks, containers, and tins according to their contents. I'd vacuumed and mopped the floor until the early hours of the morning, and I'd opened the windows to air out the smell of smoke.

This was nothing compared to what I'd done at Mrs. Rao's every day on top of keeping passing grades and finishing my graduating exams. I'd enjoyed the massive cleanup just to see the final results.

Once done, the kitchen had gleamed so clean I couldn't bear to see it go to waste. Whoever inhabited this place during the day was sure to ruin my hard work and return it to its dirty state tomorrow, so I'd donned the apron and chef's hat and baked a dozen cupcakes. When the cakes were done, I'd promptly kicked off my shoes and fallen asleep on the chair closest to the oven radiating warmth and sweet baking smells.

"What did you steal from my goddamned kitchen?" Dick shouted.

"Steal?" I sat up quickly. "No, I didn't take anything...er...I made these for *you*."

"Asha?"

I glanced over Dick's shoulder to see Katy. Her eyes widened as she saw me.

"Katy!"

"What are you doing here?"

"You know this hobo?" Dick pointed at me, like I was a piece of rotting garbage.

"She's my friend."

"How the hell did she get in?"

"Through the window," I answered.

"Through the window?" Dick bellowed so violently it unsettled the bird on his shoulders. "Through the window?" I was sure he was going to have a heart attack.

"That's what I said." My head was throbbing again.

"Who the hell do you think you are to walk in like this?" He turned to Katy. "And why the hell was the window not locked?"

"Dammittohell!" Jim said, not wanting to miss out on the debate.

"She didn't know I was here," I blurted. I couldn't get her in trouble. "I came through—"

"Thru-u-u the window! Thru-u-u the window!" echoed the parrot. I stared at it. I couldn't decide whether it was too smart, or too annoying, or both.

"Dick, I know her," Katy said, getting in between the angry bull and me. She stood with her hands clasped in front of her, worry lines on her face, eager to please her boss. "She's a friend from school."

"Oh, yeah?" Dick didn't seem convinced. "You'd better have a good explanation why she's in my kitchen chair."

"Yes, I do," I said adjusting my chef cap. My brain was starting to wake up. "Katy said you were looking for a baker."

He turned to me with a frown.

"A good one, too," Katy said. Our eyes met briefly.

"Well, here I am." I spread my arms bodaciously. Katy slipped behind my chair and grabbed me by my weary shoulders. "Ta-da! Best baker in town for your money." Her voice was strained and not totally convincing, but I was glad she was playing along.

"You know I always come through, Dick," she said. "You won't regret this. She's not like the others."

Dick stared at her with a frown, then looked me up and down, scratching his chin. I sat up and squared my shoulders, hoping I looked like the best baker in town for his money.

"She's already made samples for you," Katy said, "Here, try one." She was all sunshine and sweetness though the catch in her voice was still there.

"If you're my new baker," Dick said, turning to me, "then why the hell are you drinking my rum?"

"Rum?" I looked at him, startled. That was when I noticed the half-open bottle of rum on the table. "Oh, that. I used it in the cakes."

"You cooked with my good rum?" he bellowed.

"Good" was a stretch, but I kept a straight face. "Good chefs always cook with good rum," I said.

"R-u-u-u-m," Jim rolled his tongue.

"Damn it to hell!" Dick said abruptly. "I've had enough of this yakking. Get back to work, both of you!"

He was about to turn and stride out of the room when he stopped. I watched him warily, fearful he'd yell in my ear again. Or worse. I pulled back, bracing for a slap or a punch. He bent over me, scooped up a cupcake, and limped out of the room, muttering to himself. The bird wavered on his shoulder, trying to keep its balance.

"Wasting my time and money. These frigging girls..." Dick mumbled.

"Friiiggingirls," the bird practiced, excited to learn a new phrase. "Friiiggingirls."

I waited till they left the room and looked up at Katy.

"I'm so sorry."

She shook her head. "His bark's worse than his bite."

"I guess I owe you an explanation, eh?" I said, removing my hat and sheepishly putting it on the table.

Katy gave me a sad look. "Mrs. Jones said you needed an intervention."

"An intervention?" I stared at her wide-eyed. *My biology teacher thought I needed serious help?* The teachers at my school were an overworked, underpaid lot who had barely enough energy to teach our classes, let alone worry about each of us on a personal level. Other than the one teacher who'd called Mrs. Rao about my late homework, most of my teachers had been happy with my progress. "Why?"

"She said you looked like you were either being hounded by a killer gang or suffering from a terminal illness."

"Really?" She was partly right on the first point, but I couldn't tell her that.

"Latoya heard you throwing up and crying in the toilet stall for a few days in a row, and Mrs. Jones asked me if I knew anything was wrong."

It was true I'd been acting odd lately, especially after finding Preeti's letter.

"You're trying to get away from that mad aunt of yours, aren't you?"

"I guess I needed a place to stay," I said. "But I didn't know anyone...."

"Stay at mine," Katy said, with a shrug. "You can work here and help me pay rent like the other bakers before."

"Seriously?" I stared at her.

She nodded.

"Th...thanks."

"I should warn you, though. Dick fires a baker every few weeks." She paused. "But I have a funny feeling he'll like you. Just don't expect him to be nice or anything."

"How much does he pay?" I asked, feeling dazed. Things were happening too fast to process.

"Minimum wage," Katy said.

"Okay," I said, nodding, feeling slightly elated. I had a place to stay and a way to make money. All in one morning. I desperately wanted to ask what the minimum wage was—that way, I'd know how long it would take me to make $1,493—but I didn't want to sabotage anything now.

"I was in your shoes once," Katy was saying.

"You were?" I looked at her, startled. *Was she forced to get married to an older man too? And run away from a country with a fake visa?*

"I was twelve when I left home," Katy said. "So I totally know what it's like."

We were quiet for a while.

"Hey, you need new shoes," Katy said suddenly, peeking at my feet under the table.

I looked down at the flat black shoes I'd found in the basement in Mrs. Rao's home, a pair bought for five dollars at a dollar mart for a girl before me, most probably.

"I have an old pair of red heels you can have," she said. "They're a bit too small for me, so I've never really worn them."

"Really?" My spirits rose. Katy had the nicest shoes in town. That she was even thinking of letting me borrow a pair from her was a small but happy spark to a difficult night. Week. No, month. Okay, a year.

"Welcome to the Next Day Catering Company," Katy said with a smile before walking out of the kitchen.

I noticed she didn't touch my cakes.

Part EIGHT

We must be willing to get rid of the life we've planned, so as to have the life that is waiting for us.
Joseph Campbell

Chapter Forty-one

"Where the hell are you?"

I was running toward the party hall with a plate full of frosted blueberry cupcakes in one hand and my mobile glued to my ear with the other. I didn't need to hold the phone so close. Dick's voice boomed through loud and clear.

He was going to kill me for being late again.

It had taken me ten minutes to find parking for our van, and in the rush, I'd forgotten to pull the handbrake. I had to jump back into the rolling van to take control while trying not to upset the cake tray. It had been a rough morning.

"Just outside, Dick. Be there in half a minute," I said, prying the door open with one foot. "Ouch!" My ankle bracelet had caught on a splinter on the door. I bent down and noticed a white scratch mark on my heel.

"Oh, no."

I was wearing my own red heels, a pair of hand-me-downs from Katy when she was younger and skinnier. I wore them every day and would have worn them into the shower if I could have. I didn't care they were old or the heel was slightly worn. They were fiery red and made me feel beautiful and powerful—just like the sandals my parents had bought me had made me feel, just like I'd hoped the ruby red sandals I'd stolen for Chanda, oh so long ago, had made her feel.

"Oh, no?" shouted Dick on the phone. "You're fifteen goddamn minutes late and all you have to say is "oh, no"?"

"Sorry—"

"One more time and you're demoted!"

My heart sank. I'd heard his threats before, and every time, he'd make me feel two inches tall.

I hated my boss. Dick, as everyone called him, was CEO of Toronto's Next Day Catering Company, which had minimum wage slaves for employees and a 1-800 number for clients who called us as a last resort. That usually happened when their own caterer had bailed and they had no other options. When it came to local catering firms, we were at the bottom of the pile.

In the eight months I'd been with Next Day, Dick had promoted me from Catering Trainee to Assistant Manager of Desserts, Baked Goods, and Sweets. It's true what they say. The longer your title, the smaller your job and the bigger the chance your boss is a dick.

The "manager" in my title was Dick's way of getting me to work day and night without overtime, so I ended up getting paid even less. He said managers got a special bonus at the end of the year if we did well, so I kept trying. I had more than my seven dollars in my purse now, but not enough for a one-way ticket to Goa.

Preeti's letter was always in my right-hand pocket and, whenever I had a bad day, I'd reach in, feel the soft pink paper, and remember why I was doing this. It was her letter and the ankle bracelet she gave me so long ago that kept me going.

My getaway from Mrs. Rao and Franky had been a lucky break. I'd been even luckier they hadn't tracked me down. Toronto was a big city, but not that big. The longer I stayed, the closer they would get to me, but my departure date depended on my boss's generosity and mood.

And he was not in a good mood that day.

I could imagine him now, pacing up and down the hall, yelling into his earpiece and glancing at his Rolex knockoff every few seconds. Dick looked the quintessential used-car salesman, slightly overweight and always wearing the same ill-fitting suit with a liter of cheap cologne. His dark hair was slicked back with grease and a skinny cigar always dangled precariously from his lips. His unique smell warned us of his approach from a mile away.

Tim had got one thing right. With that hint of Italian accent Dick put on to impress the girls, he'd have made an excellent goon in a Mafia movie. Because he went to the racetrack with other strange men in dark suits every afternoon and then to church every Sunday, I was one hundred percent sure he had connections to the local mob.

When I finally managed to open the church's basement door a few inches, it banged shut on me. My plate of cakes nearly smashed in my face, and I struggled to balance the tray.

"Can't you get your crap together for once?" Dick shouted.

"This order came close to midnight, Dick, and I've been up since four, trying to make this happen," I said to the phone. "It's a miracle I got it all done."

"It's a miracle you're still my assistant manager. That's what, goddammit! Get in here *now*!" The phone clicked dead.

I hung up. Dick wasn't helping. He never did. Taking care to balance the cake tray, I pushed the door with a gentle shove of my shoulders and propped it open with one leg, not the easiest maneuver in Katy's hand-me-down miniskirt and heels.

I took a deep breath and stepped inside, faking calm. That was when I saw Dick at the other end of the corridor, shaking a fist at Katy.

Her beautiful red curls drooped onto hunched shoulders, looking as limp as their owner. With anyone else, Katy would have rolled her eyes. I once saw her stick her tongue out at the back of another driver who'd cut her off. She could be a firecracker when she wanted to. Now, she was a nervous, quiet girl with downcast eyes taking a verbal beating from our boss. Dick was the only person in the world who could do this to Katy.

Though she didn't like to admit to it, Katy got an automatic crush on every power figure she met, from our grade-twelve gym teacher to the security guard at school. Dick was no exception. For months after starting the job, Katy dreamed of the day Dick would whisper sweet nothings in her ear, shower her with flowers and jewelry, sweep her into his strong arms, and carry her away into the sunset.

One day, her daydream came true, but instead of a romantic date, it was a quick one-night affair after work and a few drinks, one that left Katy dangling over a cliff. Dick knew how to rein her in now. Some days, he'd bring her flowers and tell her she was the most beautiful woman in the world; other days, he'd tell her she was an idiot. After one particularly nasty day, I gave him a new nickname—Dick the Douche. I told Katy he was no sugar daddy, just a jerk from hell, but she wouldn't listen.

"Eight! Not eight goddamn fifteen!" The Douche's voice rang through the corridor. This was how I knew his Italian accent was fake. When he got mad, he reverted to his mundane inner-city drawl. "Can't you read the goddamned time? Where's your brains, girl? There's nothing up in there, is there? You're only good for one thing!"

Katy's face went beet red.

I was stunned.

"I should fire your ass."

Just when I thought my job was so bad I couldn't stomach it anymore, it had gotten worse. My mouth opened before my brain kicked in.

"Hey, stop picking on her!"

Dick whirled around and glared. "You!"

My heart began to beat faster. "Can't you see we're trying our best? What's the point of shouting at her like that?"

"Telling me how to do my job, eh? I can hire any chick off the street in two seconds flat to take over your work. Don't need two-bit girls telling me how to do my job!" He stepped toward me. His six-foot frame towered over me but I didn't budge, rooted out of fear more than anything else.

The cake tray wobbled in my hands. I clutched it tightly, wishing I didn't shake when I was nervous.

"If we lose this order, I'll have your head," Dick said, sticking a finger an inch from my eyes. "I've got debts to settle. People to pay back. I need this money. You think this company runs on icing sugar?"

"I'm not telling you how to do your job," I said trying to keep my voice firm. I wished I could rustle more pluck to tell him how I truly felt. "I'm just asking you to stop yelling at Katy and me. We'll get the job done, okay? We always do."

"Trying to be a smart aleck, eh? You come here late and think I'd give you a bloody raise? Or keep you employed?"

I heard a cough behind me and turned my head. The entire birthday party was silently staring at the spectacle through the open doors of the party room. I hadn't even noticed. The adults looked embarrassed at what they were witnessing, the kids curious.

It was true I'd asked for a raise for both Katy and me the day before. I'd known it was going to be an uphill battle, but I hadn't expected it to come with public humiliation.

I turned to Dick and said in a softer voice to avoid attracting any further attention, "It's because we've been working extra hours. I think..."

"Don't *think*!" he yelled. "Just do, like I tell you! You're good for nothing, I tell ya!"

Something snapped in me.

Ignoring him, the curious crowd, and my flaming face, I drew myself up to my full five feet and strode into the room holding my head high. My legs were shaking, but they kept moving, and that was all that mattered. As soon as I put the cake tray down on the buffet table, I turned around and looked Dick in the eye.

"Show us some respect, Dick."

Dick pointed at the door. "You're fired!"

Chapter Forty-two

Dick's voice was still ringing in my ears as I walked into Katy's apartment.

It wasn't the first time he'd fired me, and it wasn't the first time he'd yelled at me. Insulting Katy and me was like drinking rum for Dick. He thrived on it. There were days I wished I could quit.

Working at the Next Day Catering Company felt like a dead end. I was making just enough for food, heat, water, and a half of the rent. My plans for buying a one-way ticket to Goa seemed to get further and further from me.

I closed the door behind me wondering how Katy was coping back at the shop.

Katy hated working in the kitchen. Whenever I offered to teach her how to bake a cake or make the icing, she became busy with something or the other—a spreadsheet had to be balanced or a client had to be called. She didn't just hate cooking, she didn't enjoy eating either.

Often, after she ate a meal, I'd find her locked up in the toilet. And if I'd walked by the door, I'd hear her retching. I only asked about it once, because I'd been worried she was sick, but she brushed me off so brusquely, I didn't mention it again. In the end, I gave up, and our shop duties became more distinct as the months went by. I was the chef of the kitchen and she was the chef of the books, while Dick did nothing, but lorded over everything.

He spent many late nights at the bakery after Katy and I had gone for the day, but given the magazines of half-clad women stacked up on his desk alongside the open boxes of rum, I didn't think he did anything productive. Right now, I hoped my friend wasn't getting the brunt of his anger. Though he yelled at her as well, I knew he liked Katy in his own twisted way and would never really fire her or harm her.

To calm myself down, I decided to make walnut banana cakes. With a hint of rum, they were the ultimate cheer-up food, easy to make, comforting to eat, and the calories didn't count, especially on bad days.

The meals I'd made at Mrs. Rao's home had been a fusion of East and West, made with my imagination, partly following Chef Pierre's recipe books, partly listening to my mother's voice in my head. Each dish had been different—a new recipe, a new idea put to the test.

Mixing spices and whisking sauces were fun, but my passion was baking cakes. It was how I kept memories of my mother alive. Her cupcakes were to me the queens of all desserts. In a few sweet bites, they could mend broken hearts, heal wounds, and make you forget mean bosses, even if only for a day.

As I mixed the batter in my bowl, my mind wandered to that morning. *Did he really say, "You're only good for one thing?" What a scumbag.* I mixed faster, wishing I could make him pay for his nastiness. The pale yellow mixture thickened quickly. When I got mad, I was more efficient than my electric mixer.

An urgent knock at the door jolted me out of my reverie.

I placed the bowl on the kitchen table as quietly as I could, and stayed silent as a mouse, hoping for it to go away. The knock came again, insistently this time. I wiped my hands on my apron and tiptoed over to the door with a frown. *Who can that be?* No one was home at this time of the day.

I'd lost sleep many a night over the past months, worried sick Mrs. Rao would snatch me away and force me to get married to another vile old man. The reason she hadn't come after me yet, and the reason no one had reported me missing, reaffirmed my worst fears. *My visa is a fake.* I was sure of it now. Mrs. Rao would never call the authorities or bring attention to the illegal activities she and Franky were involved in.

But that didn't ease my worries. It was only a matter of time before they found me.

I laid low and hadn't dared to venture near my school again, even to pick up my high school diploma. Katy had gone to the graduation ceremony by herself and picked up my certificate with hers. I restricted my movements and wore shades, even on cloudy days. I badly wanted to find a second job, but I worried they'd ask too many questions. I felt lucky Dick had hired me with just a referral from Katy.

Katy told me I was being paranoid and that it would be hard for anyone to track me in a city of almost eight million. But every morning, I got this strange feeling of eyes watching me. I couldn't shrug that feeling off.

The knock came again, much louder this time.

I opened the door slowly, keeping the chain intact. I peeked outside with one eye.

Randy's face came into view.

He was our apartment building's caretaker, a reedy man in his thirties who dressed like he was nineteen and smelled like pot. With a sigh of relief, I pulled out the chain and opened the door.

"Hey, Randy."

"Saw you come home early," he said, thrusting something toward me. "Here."

"What's this?" I asked, taking the brown envelope and opening it.

"Rent change."

"Again? How much?"

"Read it yourself. This apartment's for one person. Since you're two now, rent's been raised."

The letter was short and to the point.

"Nineteen percent? It's difficult to pay our rent as it is."

"That's your problem. Should have thought of that before moving in, eh?" Randy sniffed loudly and swiped his nose. "By the looks of it, management's generous. If there's two of you, I says we hike it by fifty."

"You can't do this to us," I said. "Is it even legal?"

"Them's the rules. Not me who made 'em up." Randy shuffled off, sniffing to himself.

I watched his disappearing back in dismay. I closed the door and leaned against it.

Katy's apartment was really Dick's apartment. He'd rented it out for her, under his name, with the express agreement she paid all rent and utilities. It was an informal arrangement between the two, and Dick never seemed to care about the cost of the rent and how fast it was going up. He was doing her a favor as far as he was concerned.

This small studio, located in the cheap student district above a Chinese takeout shop, was only a few square feet bigger than Grandma's home in Goa. The main difference was while Grandma's kitchen belonged in the nineteenth century, Katy's came with appliances from the seventies. Instead of smells from the communal toilet in Goa, smells of Chinese fried rice came wafting in, which I had to admit was a million times better.

On my first day at Katy's, I craved spring rolls all day long, salivating at the thought of biting into a crispy wrapper filled with mint leaves, shredded carrot, and sweet dipping sauce. After five days, the smell became less alluring. By the tenth day and onward, I didn't want to have another Chinese spring roll for the rest of my life.

At night, I slept on the sofa while Katy slept on her single bed in the corner. Other than that, there was enough space for a kitchenette table and two chairs. After living in Mrs. Rao's spacious mansion in the northern Toronto suburbs, Katy's apartment felt like a shack in a shantytown. But compared to how I'd lived in Goa, this was a roomy place with a full bathroom for the two of us, a luxury compared to Grandma's old home. I had nothing to complain about.

I threw the letter on the kitchen table with a sigh and walked over to my mixing bowl. Katy wasn't going to be happy to hear this news. Just as I picked up my spoon, the telephone rang.

What a busy day.

"Hello?" I said.

Frrzzzz. It was static coming down the line.

"Hello?"

I heard the faint sound of someone breathing, mixed with the buzz of static.

"Is anyone there?" I said.

"Is this Asha talking?" It was a distinct Indian accent. A man.

My heart skipped a beat. "Who...?" I swallowed. "Who's this?"

More static.

"Who are you?" I said, my heart beating faster now.

The line went dead.

I stared at the handset for a few seconds before placing it back on its cradle. No one knew I was staying here. No one had this number except for Dick, and he didn't have an Indian accent. Within seconds, the phone rang again, making me jump. I yanked the phone to my ear.

"Who's this?" I barked. "You better tell me or—"

"Asha?"

"Katy?" I said in relief.

"I'm so glad you're home. I was worried. What's going on?"

"Oh, nothing," I lied.

"You sound funny."

I hesitated. "Just got a call. Wrong number I think."

That strange feeling of being watched came over me again and I gave a quick glance at the window. But no one was looking in from our second-floor apartment window.

I'm getting paranoid.

"Reason I'm calling," Katy was saying, "is because Dick says he didn't mean it."

"Didn't mean what?"

"To fire you."

"Again?"

"He's really sorry this time."

"Sorry? Dick? Why can't *he* call and say sorry?"

"He's under a lot of pressure these days. He owes Jose a ton of money, so he's totally stressed out. He told me to tell you that."

"Who's this Jose you keep talking about?"

"His business partner from Detroit. Dick's borrowed a lot of money from him and is in pretty bad shape. I did the books this month, and things don't look too good. It hasn't looked good for a while now really. That's why he can't give us a raise."

"Maybe Dick should stop his trips to the racetrack and strip clubs and pay his partner back," I said, feeling my face getting warm. "Anyway, he shouldn't be taking out his frustrations on us. Especially on you."

"He's begging you to come back."

"Really, Katy?" I couldn't imagine Dick begging anyone for anything.

"Okay, *I'm* begging you to. There's a big order tomorrow, and they want a batch of fifty cupcakes. And I truly believe he's sorry."

How she couldn't see his bad side was baffling.

"He needs me now? Maybe *I* don't need him," I said, more out of spite than anything else.

"Please, Asha? Please?"

I sighed. I could never leave Katy hanging.

"Well...," I hesitated.

"It's not like we have much choice anyway, do we?" she said.

I thought about that for a second. Katy had half a point. *She* had a choice. I didn't.

Chapter Forty-three

"'Scuse me, miss, have a light?" asked the man, leaning toward me. He waved a half-chewed cigarette in front of my nose.

"Sorry," I said, looking away.

Even if I had one, he wouldn't have been allowed to use it on the bus. I quietly inched toward the edge of the seat. The man's face looked blotchy and sickly, and he reeked like he'd downed a bottle of Jack Daniels for breakfast.

I was taking my usual morning bus to work and hadn't been too careful where I'd taken my seat. Other headaches had crowded my mind. I was worried about Katy, who'd told me she had to work late doing the books the night before, but I suspected spent the night at Dick's apartment.

Then, that morning, I'd woken up to a puddle of water in the kitchen. The roof was leaking again, right onto the kitchen table, which was already on its last legs. I soiled my best skirt trying to clean up the mess. I made a mental note to call Randy to get this fixed once and for all. We couldn't afford any more money trouble.

The man next to me in the bus sneezed. Loudly. A stream of snot oozed down his face. I crept further down the seat. That's when he let out an undeniably loud and smelly fart. I gagged.

A few people were staring now. *Do they think it's me?* I squirmed in my seat. I clutched my purse, cringing, waiting for a polite moment to get up and find another seat. I was just about to stand when the bus took a sharp corner and threw me against my smelly seatmate. He'd been looking sickly throughout, and now it all came out.

The vomit squirted like a broken sewer gushing out. I sprang up. It smelled so bad, I wanted to throw up. The bus lurched to a stop at a red light. I didn't think twice. I sprang down the steps, pushed the doors open, and jumped out. I heard a surprised yell from the driver, probably not too happy someone had jumped out at a non-designated stop, but I didn't care. The air outside was a welcome relief.

From the corner of my eyes, I briefly noticed someone else jumping off the bus behind me, but I was too busy trying to think of what to do with my soiled skirt. I looked down at the splotches of yellow goo and shuddered in disgust. I reeked of puke.

I scanned the surrounding area. I was too far from home, but I remembered a big-box store nearby that sold everything from candy bars to lawn mowers. I plodded in its direction, ignoring the strange looks people were giving me.

The greeter at the store noticed me the minute the main glass doors slid open.

She gave me a suspicious look as I walked in, trying to hide the wet patch on the front of my skirt. Pretending not to see her, I hurried toward the women's department. I was really late for work now. That morning, after cleaning the mess in the kitchen, I'd called to let Katy know I wasn't going to get in on time. Thankfully, Dick had gone to the track for the day, so he wouldn't know. At least I had one thing going for me.

I walked rapidly down the clothing aisle looking for the smallest sizes. My frenemies at school used to taunt me with "stick insect." When they felt particularly generous, they called me "tiny chick." Katy had always defended me, but most of the time, she'd played things down. She used to call me an *exotic* tiny chick. "Hey, you're lucky you don't have to worry about hips. Guys love tiny girls," she'd say. *Right, and that's why I didn't have any boyfriends after Tim.*

Good thing my love for cakes over the years had helped fill me out. It still didn't make me look like a respectable baker, like Chef Pierre did on the cover of magazines, but at almost eighteen, I finally had hips and a couple of bunny hills on my chest. It was a step toward womanhood. I looked desperately around the store and realized they didn't sell clothes for exotic tiny chicks here, even those with a hint of hips and bunny hills.

I slouched against a clothes rack in frustration, badly wanting to get out of the stinky skirt. As I stood there, a young man, an Indian man, ambled by, glancing at the blouses. I straightened up. *Who's he?* I automatically pulled down the sunglasses that had been sitting on my head.

It was strange to see a lone man fingering women's clothes, early on a weekday morning in a big-box store. I looked around but didn't see any signs of a female companion. The man walked casually into the lingerie section, not even glancing my way. *A cross-dresser?*

A knot began to form in my stomach. *Is he following me? Did Mrs. Rao send him here? Or is he with the police?*

I shook my head. *Just because he looks Indian doesn't mean he works for Mrs. Rao.*

I never came to this store. I was far from both my home and my workplace. No one could have known I'd be here. Besides, I never went shopping, taking Katy's hand-me-downs and fixing them to save money. I gave another shake of my head. I was becoming paranoid, and I couldn't hang around here all morning.

That was when I noticed a small clothes section in the back with a sign above that said, "For Teens—Sale Today Only." Perfect. *Why didn't I think of that before?* Without wasting a second, I skipped over and picked a plain black skirt and a white shirt and took it to the cashier.

The woman at the checkout counter was too busy chatting with her coworker to notice me or smell me for that matter. She scanned my items and went back to gossiping with her pal while I pulled out and counted sixteen dollars from my purse. When I asked her if I could change in the washroom, she nodded and waved me off. I ran into the toilets and tore off my disgusting clothes.

I walked the rest of the way to work though it was going to be a long walk in my heels. My clothes in the bag stank so badly, I was sure no bus driver would have let me in any way, and I didn't even want to try. While I walked, I glanced behind me a few times but no one was following me. There was no sign of the Indian man from the store either. I'll go mad if I keep this up, I thought.

By the time I got to the office, I was already two hours behind. If Dick had been around, he'd have given me a good yelling. Luckily for me, it was the slow season. By the end of the summer, party orders fell as people stayed home to pay for their bills and their sins of the season. I walked in to see Katy sitting in her chair in the alcove and chewing her pencil, which was never a good sign. She wrinkled her nose as soon as I came through the door.

"What's that smell?"

"Long story. I need to wash up," I said, walking toward the washroom with my stinky bag in tow.

"You won't believe who just called," Katy said, following me to the back of the store. "With an emergency."

I stopped and turned around. I knew there was more bad news somewhere.

"Who?"

"The Pasty sisters."

Chapter Forty-four

"Oh, no, please not today," I said with a groan. "Jeez."

"Jeeeez," said a voice from a corner of the bathroom.

"Not now, Jim," I said, throwing a napkin in his direction. Jim wasn't allowed in the kitchen or the bathroom, but he, like his owner Dick, was as stubborn as a donkey. I was sure if a health inspector ever visited, they'd shut us down in an instant.

Katy picked him up.

"Jeeeez," Jim repeated, settling on Katy's sleeve. Once he caught on to a new word, that was all we heard for weeks. Some days I wondered if he enjoyed annoying us like this. "Jeeeez."

"They want us to cater to a party of forty by ten thirty this morning," Katy said. "That gives you exactly, oh, an hour and a half, tops."

"Forty! By ten thirty?"

"For a charity event—cupcakes, tea, and coffee."

"Do we have a choice?"

"Not if we don't want to get fired. Again."

Katy walked out of the kitchen to lock Jim in the office and returned as I was getting ready to wash up.

"Do you want to hear the list of their needs?"

I turned around to see her consulting a piece of paper in her hand.

"There are a few guests with allergies to milk, one to strawberries, another with gluten issues, and nothing we bring should have touched any nut of any kind, whatsoever." She looked up and made a face.

"Makes our lives easier, doesn't it?" I said, shaking my head. "What excuse did the sisters come up with this time?"

"Their caterer got poisoned."

"Poisoned?"

"Allergic reaction of some sort," Katy said as she walked back to her office. "To the sisters, I'm sure. I'll come and help you in a sec."

Dick's business had two kinds of clients.

The first were those who needed regular catering services. If we did our job well—that is, with minimal interference from Dick the Douche—they gave us repeat business. Then, there were clients who called us at the last minute because their principal supplier had bailed, or whoever was in charge of the committee for catering had forgotten to place the order in the first place. It was surprising how often this happened. These clients were one-offs, driven by one emergency or other—except the Pasty sisters.

Katy once compared the sisters to unhappy bulldogs. They were both big, buxom ladies in their sixties who liked garish makeup and didn't seem to realize the colors only accentuated their jowls. They liked flowery, showy clothes with lots of eye-stinging colors, ruffles, and folds, which made them look larger than they were. They were the event planners at Dick's church and operated in perpetual crisis mode.

How they called themselves planners with a straight face boggled my mind. Katy and I hated dealing with them, but Dick refused to drop them from our roster because he had a "reputation to uphold at church."

After a two-minute shower and getting back into my brand new clothes, I walked into the kitchen, feeling slightly refreshed and less stressed.

I surveyed the counter carefully before touching anything. It was a habit I had from the time I started work here. Every morning when I walked into the kitchen, I got this uncanny feeling someone had been working on the counter or in the sink the night before. Every morning, I discovered one or two things had moved overnight. It was strange, and I couldn't imagine Dick making a midnight snack here. But I didn't have time to think about that now. I had work to do. I opened the cabinets looking for the ingredients I needed.

Working at lightning speed, I rustled up forty hypoallergenic nut-less, plain vanilla cupcakes, one pot of black tea, and another pot of coffee. Katy came out of her bookkeeping cave to help me with the drinks and packing. We piled everything into our delivery van and dashed to the church.

There, the Pasty sisters were waiting impatiently at the basement door. They were quite the sight, and as usual, they didn't look pleased to see us.

"My good Lord! Could you come any slower? What kept you, girls? Hurry up!" one of them said, clapping at us like she was ushering in children.

"We've waited an hour. You could get organized, you know," the other sister said, her badly painted lips set in a scowl. Katy and I looked at each other. We always paid for the chaos they created for themselves.

I walked in carrying the cake tray, but just as I was about to step into the doorway, I heard a yell. I swiveled around to see one of the sisters flapping her ruffled sleeves like a deranged tropical bird. I looked at her in alarm.

"Are you okay?" I asked her.

"You can't walk in like that!" she shrieked.

"What? Why?" I stared at her. Did I still smell? I sniffed the air. I'd washed up thoroughly before I started cooking. *What's wrong?* I noticed Katy gawking at the back of my skirt.

"Hey, what's going on?" I asked her.

"You're unbelievable," Katy whispered to me.

"What did I do?" I whispered back in alarm. My new skirt was an inch above my knees. It wasn't a nun's black habit, but I hadn't realized it would be a no-go for a church's basement. "What's wrong with it?"

"*What's wrong with it?*" Katy's eyes opened wide.

"Yes, what's wrong with everyone?" I said.

"Your skirt says 'Booty for Hire' in the back."

Chapter Forty-five

"N o!" I said, horrified.

I craned my neck but couldn't see a thing. "Why didn't you tell me?" I whispered fiercely.

"I didn't notice!" Katy whispered fiercely back. "Besides, I don't go around looking at the back of your skirt."

"You're not going inside the good Lord's house dressed like a hooker!" squealed one of the Pasty sisters, pointing a finger my way.

I stared at her open-mouthed. *Hooker?*

"We don't care how you dress for your night job. You can't come in here dressed like that!" squawked the other.

I raised my eyebrows. "Night job?"

"Here, let me take that for you," Katy said, putting her coffee pot down and grabbing my cake platter. "You go wait in the car, okay?"

I let her take the tray and stumbled back to the van with my head down. My back tingled as if the world was watching and laughing. I yanked the driver's door open, jumped in, and slammed it shut. That's what I got for buying in the teen department.

"Did you see their faces when they saw your skirt?" Katy said with a grin on our way back to the office. I'd laid low in the van the whole time Katy had done the delivery. It was a relief to head back to the shop. "It was hilarious."

"Hilarious?" I was still smarting. "They were mean. I didn't even know. Who makes skirts for fourteen-year-olds with 'Booty for Hire' in the back? Seriously?"

"That's nasty. You should look before buying," Katy said. "I guess we're off the Pasty Sister's emergency list now. At least there's that."

I sighed. Dick wasn't going to be happy. Again.

"Real bulldogs are nicer than those two." Katy giggled.

"And better looking," I said.

Katy flapped her arms around like the Pasty Sisters did. "Come on, it was funny," she said, nudging me. "Admit it."

Soon, we were collapsing in giggles. We laughed till tears streamed down our cheeks, and we were no longer sure if it was because of what had happened or from hearing our own cackles.

When we got to our destination, we pulled into one of the parking spaces in front of the Next Day Catering Company. Our office was a hole in the wall, huddled between a sleazy video rental store and a pawn shop. It wasn't in the best of neighborhoods, so I was surprised to see a brand-new black Mercedes with Michigan plates parked next to Dick's car.

"Who's that, you think?" I asked.

"That's Jose," Katy said.

"Jose? The guy Dick owes money to?"

"Yup. He's Dick's business partner from Detroit. He moved from Colombia to the States a few years ago, I think."

"What does he do? Other than lend money."

"He's in the car business and a big shot down south. He always drives up in fancy cars. Tony, Dick's brother, works for him. Jose's much nicer than Dick."

"C'mon. *Everyone's* nicer than Dick."

"You know what he did once?" Katy said, not hearing me. "Jose saved a kid from drowning in a pool. He jumped in and saved the boy's life. He's a super nice guy." She paused. "Though Dick's not half-bad."

"How in the world can you find Dick anywhere near not-half-bad?" I said, looking at my friend. "He looks like a hit man and acts like one too."

"Have you ever met a real hit man?"

"No, but...."

"A cute hit man then," Katy said with a giggle. "But Jose's the real hot one, you'll see."

I shook my head. My friend's taste in men was something I'd never understand.

We got out and walked into the building. I'd planned to use one of Katy's scarves to cover my skirt. It was in her office and I couldn't wait to get my hands on it. I followed her inside and turned to close the door.

"Oy! How much?"

Someone was hollering from the dark corner of the corridor. I looked over my shoulder to see a younger, thinner, slimier version of Dick staring at the back of my skirt. I felt my face go warm.

"How much for a ten-minute job, eh?" said the slime with a wink.

I looked away, embarrassed.

"I got cash, honey."

"That's not a nice thing to say," I heard my voice say, the smartest comeback I could think of.

"Don't get all pissy with me," he said with a smirk. "You're the one advertising booty." The man grinned at his own bad joke.

Before I could say anything, he turned to the office at the back and hollered. "See you at the track tomorrow, Dick. And bring your bimbos with you. They're cute." He threw a cigarette butt into the garbage can and swaggered out passing us.

I didn't move. I couldn't.

"Tell me that didn't happen," I said finally.

"That's Tony for you," Katy said with a grim look on her face. "He could've been worse."

"Not possible," I said.

"Are those damn girls back?" The roar came from Dick's office.

Katy and I looked at each other in alarm.

Dick limped out, his face flushed like he'd been drinking for a while now. Behind him was a drop-dead-good-looking, olive-skinned man with curly black hair. He was dressed in a finely tailored pinstripe suit and looked sharp except for—*is that one of my pink vanilla cupcakes in his hands?* Next to me, Katy took a sharp breath when he strutted out. I looked at her. She was staring at him with starstruck eyes. This had to be Jose.

I was about to nudge her when Dick bellowed at us.

"Guess which dimwits just called?" he yelled, waving a piece of paper in front of him. "The blasted Thompson sisters, that's who!"

"Oh? You mean the Pasty Sis—" I caught myself in time and closed my mouth. Dick glared at me.

"Jeeeez!" Jim said, flying out of the office and settling on Dick's shoulder to get a better vantage point of the ruckus.

"What the hell were you girls thinking, going to my church dressed like whores?"

Katy and I stood rooted on the spot, speechless. Jose stood next to Dick looking cool. It was unnerving to see the two together, one raging mad like a bull in a rodeo and the other as collected as a proud peacock.

"If I wanted you to dance at my nightclub, I'd have hired you there. You're running a bakery for me here! A bakery! Are you stupid or what? Jeezuz!" Dick's eyes looked like they'd pop out any moment. The veins on his neck bulged. He was going to die of a heart attack one of these days, I was sure.

"Jeeeezuz!" Jim said, delighted to hear his master use his new word. "Jeeeezuz!"

"Come on, man, don't be so mean," Jose said in a soft southern drawl. "You're being hard on the girls."

"These women called me ranting about insulting their church. *My* church, goddammit!" Dick said, not paying one iota of attention to his friend. "Is that true?"

"Well... er..." *What do I even say? All I've got to do is make sure I don't turn my back to him.*

"You made me lose two hundred bucks today because they refused to pay." Dick was still shouting. "Do I look like I can afford crap like that? Are you proud of yourselves now?"

"I'm so sorry," I said, my heart sinking. When he didn't get paid, we didn't get paid. "I didn't mean to make us lose a sale."

Part of me wanted to throw my tray at Dick's head and run away, get out of this hellhole forever. But if I did that, how would I ever get back to Goa? Plus, I couldn't leave Katy alone with this crazed man.

"Hey, you heard her," Jose said, his mouth half full of cake. "She said she's sorry."

"I can hire any idiot off the street to work for me," Dick said. "I don't need these two ruining my business."

"You won't find cute ladies who can bake like this. Seriously, you gotta try one."

Dick growled in reply.

"Man, you got a heart of steel," his friend said, shaking his head. "I vote they stay."

"Don't you start with me now," Dick snapped as he turned to leave.

"Hey, don't you still owe me on that loan?" Jose asked in a quiet voice.

"So?" I noticed a slight waver in Dick's voice.

"So?" Jose said. "The deal was, until you pay me back, I own half the company."

Silence. Even Jim was listening intently now.

"And that, my good friend," Jose said, "means you've got to consult me in every major company decision. And I say no to firing these lovely ladies."

Dick's glare could have wiped out the entire city of Toronto. "You'd sell your mother for a buck if you could. What are *you* getting out of this?"

"Just making a smart business decision," Jose said, with a wink in our direction. "The ladies stay."

Katy blushed.

Without a word, Dick swung around and strode back to his office with such force Jim lost his balance.

The bird fluttered desperately for a few seconds before catching air. A deafening parrot screech and colorful feathers filled the room. He circled over our heads, making us all duck, before following his master into the office.

Chapter Forty-six

Four weeks after Jose turned up in our lives, Katy told me what really happened to her.

Jose had transformed Katy into a bubbly schoolgirl again, high on the attention he was giving her. Dick seemed happy to hand over the management of the catering company to his partner. He spent his days at the track, his nights at the strip clubs, and all Sundays at church, reciting Hail Marys for whatever he did during the rest of the week. He'd never been serious with Katy and had enough girls to play with at his nightclub, so he didn't seem to care what was happening right under his nose. That, or he knew he was no longer the alpha dog, and ceded his place to avoid a fight he knew he'd lose.

On our way home from the bakery after a hard day of work, Katy and I decided on takeout from the Chinese restaurant downstairs. It was late when we walked in and the place had just closed for the night. The entire family was sitting around a table having supper. Everyone was there: grandparents, parents, uncles, aunts, cousins, and kids. Despite us trying to leave quickly, the grandmother got up and insisted on serving us a plate from their dishes. She refused to take any money and sent us on our way with one of the few English words she knew, "Enjoy, enjoy."

We took the container upstairs, kicked off our heels, and sat at our kitchen table to feast on a delicious chow mein meal.

"What a nice family," I said. "They always have dinner together."

"Lucky them," Katy said.

"Fun family dinners stopped after my parents died," I said, remembering how supper with Grandma had always been a silent affair, not knowing what she'd spring on us.

"Mine were living but we never ate together. Ever."

I turned to Katy. "Hey, you never told me why you ran away from home."

"Didn't I?" she said. I couldn't help notice she wouldn't meet my eyes.

I shook my head.

"My uncle raped me when I was ten."

It took a second to get what she'd just said. I stared at her open-mouthed.

"For two whole years."

My chopsticks fell on the floor, spilling warm noodles on the table. As if she'd said the most normal thing in the world, Katy got up, took a dishcloth from the kitchen sink, and wiped the table. I sat gaping at her, unsure how to react.

"Close your mouth or a fly will get in," Katy said with a soft smile. "Mom used to say that when I was a kid."

"Oh my god, Katy, I'm so sorry," I said finally.

"Don't be. Wasn't your fault. Wasn't mine either. It took me a long time to realize that."

"How...what did you—?"

"My father left way before I was born and my mom made a living sleeping with men. Her brother moved in when I was nine and he was nasty. He lazed around all day, kicked my puppy and took whatever he could from us, including me. What could I do? I was just a kid. I think Mom knew, but she said nothing."

Katy busied herself at the sink while I stayed frozen in my chair, trying to digest this.

"But I made him pay before I ran away," Katy said.

"What do you mean?"

"He was sleeping on the couch that morning. So I took one of Mom's empty wine bottles and smashed it between his legs. Really hard too."

I stared at her. I didn't know she had this in her. "Good for you," I stammered. "I'm glad, I mean, oh my god—"

"He woke up screaming, and I ran away. Just ran out the door and never turned back. A cop found me on the street that night, but I refused to tell him my name or anything. Mom never cared to call, so they put me in a shelter. After a few months, they moved me to a foster home. I moved from one home to another, and I hated it. No one was nice because all they wanted was the money."

All I could do was shake my head.

"I couldn't wait to grow up and get my own place. I'd have cleaned bathrooms with a toothbrush if Dick had asked me to, I so badly wanted to be on my own."

I opened my mouth to say something to make her feel better, but nothing came out. Instead, I felt hot tears running down my cheek.

"Hey, hey, why you crying, girlfriend?" Katy asked, leaning over to wipe my tears with the dishcloth.

"I'm so sorry you had to go through that," I spluttered. "I didn't even ask you. I didn't even know. I'm so sorry—"

"How'd you have known anyway?"

I guess so."

"Do you know what I feel bad about the most?" Katy said with a sigh. "That poor pup I left behind. I always wonder what happened to him after that."

I looked down at my half-eaten bowl, my mind whirling. Behind those sassy red heels and cute miniskirts lay a sweet and gentle friend. Katy worked hard, treated everyone around her well, and wanted nothing more than a safe life for herself.

"Jose's here now," she was saying. "He'll take care of us."

I swallowed. It took me a few seconds to speak up. "About Jose," I said and stopped.

When Jose sauntered down the street, every woman turned to look. And every man pointedly ignored him, but no one ever seemed to hate him, not even Dick. Jose was polite, well mannered, and charming, but something about him didn't feel right. Then again, I was suspicious about everyone and paranoid at everything.

"What about him?" Katy asked.

"Are you, er, sure about him?"

She nodded. "He's so much nicer than Dick."

True. Anyone would be better than Dick, but I couldn't tell her that.

"You know Mike, that really nice cute delivery guy?" I said, trying to change the topic. "I saw him checking you out the other day."

"Really?"

"Yeah, why don't you say hello sometime? He's nicer and better looking too. Plus he's our age."

"Cute guys like that don't want girls with big hips like me."

"You don't have any hips, Katy." I still hadn't approached her about her habit of running to the washroom after dinner every night, but there were more pressing issues to talk about at this moment. "You're way too critical about yourself, you know that?"

"Jose's always telling me I'm pretty." Katy's face flushed a light pink. "He makes me feel real good."

I was silent for a while. "You really like him, don't you?"

"Yes. Hey, want to know what he asked me today?"

"Out for dinner?"

"He told me to get my passport."

"Passport?" A jolt of electricity shot through me. I sat up and looked at her in alarm. "Why? Are you going somewhere?"

"Cancun!" The biggest smile spread across Katy's face. "He's gonna take me to Mexico. Can you believe it?"

"Oh, my gosh," I said in surprise. "That's wonderful." I paused. "It's a bit fast, don't you think?"

"He showed me the brochure. We're staying at a five-star luxury resort. This place has four buffet restaurants and we can walk to the beach. It's gonna be my first holiday ever!" Her eyes shone in anticipation. "Can you imagine?"

"That's awesome. I'm happy for you." I didn't sound convincing even to my own ears. I wanted her to be happy, but something about Jose made my stomach feel strange.

"I know this sounds like a schoolgirl crush." Katy put a hand on my arm. "He's my boss. He's from Detroit. He's ten years older—"

"Fifteen!"

"Okay, fifteen," she said, shrugging. "But he's nicer than anyone I've met before. And he's an amazing kisser."

"All that matters is he treats you right," I said. "I'm just worried maybe he's already mar—" I swallowed.

"Married?" asked Katy.

I nodded with a sigh. "Yes. It's just that he's, er—"

"What?"

"A bit too suave," I said. Jose was just the type of guy to have a different girlfriend in every city, but I didn't know how to tell her, or if I should tell her at all.

"Oh, you're way too paranoid. Besides, I asked him."

"You asked him?"

"He swore on his mother's grave he's not seeing anyone. He even asked me to check with Dick and Tony if I wanted to."

"I'm glad to hear that," I said, wondering how impeccable his references were. "I just don't want you to get hurt."

"I won't," Katy said, beaming at me. Her cheeks had turned a rosy color. "He told me I was his queen."

"That's good." I nodded. "He's doing the right things, I guess."

"You worry too much, Asha," Katy said, smiling over her bowl.

I tried my best to put on a smile for my friend. *But why did I feel afraid all of a sudden?*

Chapter Forty-seven

"Let me show you ladies how a real business is run," Jose said with a wicked grin.

Jose had jumped into the Next Day Catering business with far more ease and enthusiasm than Dick had ever shown in his life. And it looked like he was staying for the long haul.

In his first week, he responded to a newspaper ad by the Department of Diplomacy, Development and Foreign Affairs. Maybe he exaggerated slightly, maybe he inflated our capabilities somewhat, but a month later, he was proudly waving an official email in front of us. It was an invitation to an interview at the department.

I read the email, eyes wide in disbelief.

"Did you lie about us?" I asked warily.

"What did you tell them?" Katy asked breathlessly.

We were in Dick's office. Jim was fast asleep on his perch above the bookshelf, and Jose, in another one of his custom-made pinstripe suits, was sitting at Dick's desk in front of the computer screen. He looked like the quintessential CEO, respectable and knowledgeable, unlike Dick, who was off at the track with Tony again.

I wondered if Dick was trying to avoid the bakery and Jose, or whether he was having fun while his brother visited. Either way, we hardly saw him anymore.

"Don'tcha think I can make a good business case?" Jose said, giving Katy a teasing look.

Katy was sitting on the desk in her miniskirt, long legs crossed and a pretty smile on her face. "Just wondering what you promised them," she said, returning his look, her hand toying with her hair.

"Told 'em we had the best baker in the city," Jose said with a quick wink at me.

"Hey," I said, holding my hands up. "I bake for people who eat hot dogs and fries before my cupcakes. These people have caviar and champagne for lunch."

"So?" Jose said.

"This is different."

"Can you bake good cakes or not?"

"I cater to church meetings and birthday parties. This is way too fancy for me."

"No way," he said, shaking his head. "You can do this."

"Yes, you can, Asha," Katy said, nodding. "No one bakes like you. All the bakers we had before you were awful, and look, you've out-lasted all of them."

"Ladies," Jose said, swiveling his chair around to face us. "We've been playing with this business for a long time—too long. We've got to stop dabbling in small potatoes and start thinking big. Forget Dick. I'm taking this company to the big leagues. Are you with me or not?"

"Of course, we're with you," Katy said, fluttering her lashes. Jose looked at her with a grin. His eyes ran down her legs. Katy put a strand of hair in her mouth and looked at him coyly. I tried to swallow something that was threatening to come up.

"And how are you planning on taking us to the big leagues?" I asked.

"I'm a serious businessman," Jose said, straightening his tie. "I run five businesses back in the States—real businesses, not mom-and-pop joints like this. Dick dabbles here and there so he can play the horse tracks. I'm here to make money, real money."

Real money?

That made me stand up straight. With what Dick was paying me, I was going to be stuck in this job for a while, barely eking out a living. Paying rent was hard enough. Making enough to buy a ticket back to Goa seemed like a lifetime away.

"You really think this invite from Department of Diplo-whatever is serious?" Katy said, her head cocked to the side.

"Yessiree," Jose said with a grin. "Asha, if you're up for it, your job is to make a dozen of your best samples. Our appointment is at two tomorrow. Can you do that?"

"Absolutely," I said, an idea forming at the back of my mind. I looked at Jose squarely. "On one condition."

"Condition?" He sounded surprised.

"Condition?" Katy echoed.

"I'd like a raise."

"A raise?" Jose looked startled.

"A raise?" Katy repeated.

"Katy, you said I was the best baker in town, didn't you?"

"Of course, you are," Katy said with a bright smile.

Jose let go a low groan.

"I deserve something for my hard work, don't I?"

Another groan.

"Or, you can find someone else for the job." I pretended to turn around to leave.

"No! You can't go!" Katy said, throwing her arms up. "We need you! *I* need you."

I stopped. I felt bad for leading Katy on like this.

Jose shook his head. He was silent for a moment. "Okay, instead of a raise, how about a commission? I'll give you a percentage of every sale we make, but remember, you only get paid if we make a sale."

"Wow," Katy said.

"Sixty percent," I said to Jose. "Or nothing."

"Are you outta your mind?" he spluttered. "Who can afford to give anyone that kind of a commission? Are you trying to kill me?"

"Okay, here's the deal." I leaned forward. Jose leaned back like he was afraid I'd hurt him or something. I knew what I was doing. I grew up going to the markets after all.

"Forget the raise. Instead, I'll take a fifty percent cut of all sales, and I will do the work. Baking and sales." I paused. "That's a very generous offer. Deal?"

There was one reason I wanted an in on the sales. I wanted to know exactly what the numbers were. No one was going to cheat me again.

While Katy kept the books, I had a sneaking suspicion the men fed her lies and false numbers. I was also reading as much as I could about everything from visas and immigration to contracts and business, all of which occupied my mind twenty-four hours, seven days a week. One thing I learned was I couldn't sign any business contracts in Canada till I was eighteen years old.

Until then, I was at the mercy of Dick and Jose's business.

Jose looked gobsmacked. "You're not serious!"

"Take it or leave it," I said, and paused. "And Katy gets a fifteen percent raise."

"Ooooooh." Katy clapped her hands. "Thank you."

"That's nuts!" Jose sat back in his chair and let out a breath. "You're totally, royally nuts."

"And *I* will go to the screening tomorrow." I didn't trust him. I was bamboozled once, a long time ago in Goa, and I wasn't going to let that happen again.

"You? But you work in the kitchen."

I straightened up and looked him in the eye. "Your call."

He let out a big sigh. I looked at him squarely, my chin up and face firm, but my insides were churning, worried I was pushing him too far.

Katy had shown me the books a few weeks earlier. Since I'd started at Next Day, our orders had gone up four hundred percent. Jose was right. We'd been dabbling in small potatoes for too long. And I'd given away my time and talents for too long. It was time I took credit for bringing in the cash. It was time to take a risk. I whirled around and stepped toward the doorway.

"Deal."

I turned back.

Jose was holding his hand out. I looked at him in surprise. I didn't think he'd give in so quickly. But before I could take his hand, Katy slipped hers into his.

"Oooh," she said with a smile, clasping his hand. "Isn't this wonderful?"

Jose took her hand and brought it to his lips. Katy's face went crimson.

Chapter Forty-eight

I smelled her before I saw her.

The screening was held in a spacious hall on the top floor of the Department of Diplomacy, Development and Foreign Affairs.

The windows were covered with forest-green curtains that fell to the floor. The lush green-and-yellow carpet and empress armchairs were the images of retro luxury. A gold-framed photo of the queen and the prime minister standing side by side adorned one wall. On another was the prime minister with the president of the USA, shaking hands and smiling.

There were seven of us in the room. And everyone was dressed for a job interview. I was glad I'd listened to Katy. I didn't own a proper suit, so she and I had headed to the thrift store the day before, to see if we could find something professional. After an hour of trying dozens and dozens of pieces, I'd finally found a boy's black jacket which had presumably been worn to a wedding and a smart black skirt, this time without any slogans on the back. Together, they didn't look too mismatched or consignment-like.

"You look so like a professional caterer," Katy had said, giving me the thumbs-up. "Like a real bakery saleswoman." But now, in this plush room, with everyone dressed in designer suits and carrying Michael Kors handbags, I was painfully aware of how hand-me-down I looked.

Each of us had placed our wares lovingly on the table in the middle of the room and were seated in a row of chairs, waiting for the games to begin. At the head of the table was a place set for one, with a gold charger plate, silver cutlery, and a white napkin with the department's logo. In front of this setting was a lineup of cakes and pastries waiting to be judged like contestants at a beauty contest.

The first tray held a lemon cream cheesecake topped with colorful berries. Next was a triple-layered butter cake covered with an intricate icing-sugar design of flowers that had taken an entire day to do—I knew because the woman who brought it told everyone about it. Next was a chocolate log on which sat miniature handmade marzipan fruit, perfect to the detail.

In the middle of the table stood the fairest of them all, a majestic three-tiered cake with white fondant icing, perfectly manicured and impeccably designed, like those dazzling wedding cakes that graced the covers of Chef Pierre's foodie magazines. I looked at it in awe.

All the way at the far end, dwarfed in so many ways, sat an aluminum tray of my homemade cupcakes. I'd brought one sample of each of my best recipes: pineapple cupcakes with creamy white swirls; black forest cupcakes with raspberry chocolate topping; blackberry cupcakes with cream cheese swirls on top; and finally, my favorite, nutty mango cupcakes.

Next to the traditional pastries and the top-supermodel of a cake in the middle, mine looked fit to cater to a second-grade birthday party rather than a swanky diplomatic function.

My competitors were chatting in muted voices. They looked comfortable and confident as if they'd done this before. Some even seemed to know each other.

This place was seriously official. Two women in strict navy suits and sober expressions sat across from us at a side table, doing paperwork and conferring with each other in whispers. They checked their phones every few minutes, furiously tapping at the screens as if they were answering calls on national emergencies. Given they worked for the Department of Diplomacy, Development and Foreign Affairs, they might as well have been, except at that moment, they were surrounded by cakes, pastries, and bakers.

Outside the door, a security guard stood at attention in a smart blue uniform, with a dark scowl on his face. I glimpsed a handgun on his belt. *What are they expecting? An uprising of sugar and spice?*

I sat back and waited. My plan had sounded great when I was bargaining with Jose. I'd been excited at the thought of taking control over my work and making more money, but now I felt like I'd come in vain. My cakes didn't belong. The worst thing was I was now on commission, which meant I wouldn't even get my regular paycheck if I didn't win this gig. *What was I thinking? It's time to quit this charade and go back to Jose and ask for my regular job.* I quietly pushed my chair back to leave. That was when I smelled the expensive perfume.

It filled the room, overpowering everyone. The security guard gave a sharp salute. The two suited women immediately scraped back their chairs and stood up. Everyone craned their necks to look as a tall and slender woman entered the room with the slow grace of a runway model.

The hum of conversation trickled to silence within seconds. The remarkable balance with which this woman stood on her stilettos defied her age. Statuesque and lithe, with her shiny white hair swirled into a bun, she was nothing short of dignified. I sat back down on my chair quickly, my heart racing.

When I'd called to confirm my appointment with the department, a grave voice at the other end had told me the wife of a distinguished former ambassador may come to judge our samples.

He'd said the department had been disappointed with their caterers lately, and this "VIP" had been invited to fix an embarrassing diplomatic problem. "She's got expensive tastes from the old days," he'd warned me. "You must remember she's a relic from the diplomatic era when ambassadors were royalty."

"Okay," I'd said, taking this all in. "Anything special I need to know?"

"For one thing, you have to remember contractors are the untouchables."

"Really?" This was news to me. "You have a caste system in Canada, too?"

"Huh? What are you talking about? I'm merely sharing with you the office hierarchy."

"Oh, okay."

"Consultants are at the bottom of the ladder. After them come civil servants like me. A few steps over us are the attachés and consuls, who make up the majority of the bureaucracy. Then several echelons above are the almighty ambassadors. What I'm trying to say is you'll be meeting diplomatic royalty. Got it?"

"Got it."

"And remember, she's not called the Diplomatic Dragon Lady for nothing," the man had said before hanging up. I didn't even get the chance to thank him for the mini-orientation to the diplomatic corps.

"Good afternoon," the Diplomatic Dragon Lady said.

"Good afternoon," we prattled back in unison, sounding like a bunch of kindergarten students.

She stood in front of us, panning the room from one end to the other, quietly surveying each one of us. Everyone had been lounging in their seats, relaxed and comfortable before she walked in. Now, everybody was sitting up straight with perfect posture, looking earnest.

Spellbound, we watched her watching us.

The Dragon Lady looked like she'd written the book on dress and decorum. Immaculate in a black-and-white Chanel pantsuit and with exquisite white pearls wrapped around her wrinkled but elegant neck, she was obviously dressed for a formal dinner. Seeing her, I felt severely underdressed, like I'd come to a fancy ball but had forgotten to wash my sooty face.

In a voice that displayed superior elocution, the Diplomatic Dragon Lady began the proceedings of the day.

"Ladies and gentlemen, I've been invited to help restore this institution to its former glory and move us away from this gray bureaucratic shell it has sadly become." She paused and wrinkled her brows. "I learned last week, to my utmost horror, that our events serve coffee and donuts from a local franchise. From a local franchise! Unimaginable. I remember when we hosted events that served delicacies with such fanfare that our guests would talk about them for days. Those were the days, as they say in common vernacular."

No one said a word.

"I am here to remind you that the winner of this competition will be catering to the diplomats of our country and those of other countries. Diplomats, ladies and gentlemen, not construction workers." She gave us a piercing look. I wished I could sink into the floor. Construction workers and their families were, exactly, my target market.

"I do not wish us to be mediocre. If I wanted mediocre, I would walk into any local catering company. What I am seeking is creative brilliance, the crème de la crème with a twist our guests will taste on their tongues for hours afterward and wish to come back for more. Your products must be of extraordinary quality. I will expect nothing less." She spoke those last few words with extra vehemence.

"Now, where are these samples, please?" She looked around her. The two suited women scurried to the table and began removing the cake tray covers one by one, with brisk efficiency. The Dragon Lady walked around the table with her hands behind her back, inspecting the cakes. When she got to the end, she gave a cursory glance at my tray, turned around with her nose high in the air, and walked to the head of the table, where one of the women was waiting to pull out her chair.

The Dragon Lady sat down and unfolded the napkin on her lap, precisely and deliberately. The two women didn't miss a beat. One of them poured her a tall glass of water. The other carved a thin slice of the butter cake and handed it to her on a gleaming white dessert plate.

"Traditional butter cake with handmade icing-sugar flowers," explained the woman in a low, deferential voice.

The Dragon Lady took a bite.

We watched, not daring to breathe.

"Hmmm..." she said. "Not bad."

She put her fork down, wiped her mouth and took a sip of water. That was the signal for one of the suited women to pass her another sample. I heard a slight rustle to my side. The woman sitting next to me had a nervous twitch in her foot. I looked at her. She was staring at the unfinished cake on the plate with a horrified look on her face. *Why's she worried? Didn't the Dragon Lady say it wasn't bad?*

"Hmmm..." said the Lady, as she took a second bite of the lemon cheesecake. "Good. Quite good." This time I heard a gulp from behind me. That must be from the maker of the cheesecake. Two bites, I thought, were better than one. She didn't even look at my cakes.

When the royal white cake was pulled to the center of the table, gasps went off around the room—and for good reason. The cake gleamed under the bright lights. This was crème de la crème material.

"Aaahh," said the Dragon Lady. "Well done, indeed." The wedding cake got three bites. I looked over at the man—the only man in the room—who'd brought in this beauty of a cake. He sat with a smug look on his face.

I began to sweat. *Will she notice if I sneak out now?* I wiggled in my seat, wondering how to signal to the suited women and ask them not to bring out my tray, to put it aside, throw it under the table—anything but reveal my desperate cupcakes to this grand woman. Ignoring my flustered looks, the women got to the end of the table and brought out my cake tray. I wished I could disappear.

"What's this?" the Dragon Lady asked, screwing her face as one of the women brought a peaches-and-cream cupcake on a plate. She took the plate and turned it around, scrutinizing the little cake with a puzzled look. She put it down gently, picked up her fork and hesitated a second before slicing into the icing. I closed my eyes tight and stopped breathing.

"You say there are more flavors?"

I popped open my eyes and looked at her.

"I'll bring the papaya and coconut next, madame."

"Did you say *papaya and coconut*?" the Dragon Lady asked, looking incredulous at just the thought. I thought I heard a mocking tone in her voice. I cringed.

"Yes, madame," the suited woman said, looking sheepishly at the offending cupcake. "That's what the label says."

The Dragon Lady looked at us, her eyes wrinkled as if daring the person who'd brought it to stand up and be shamed.

I sunk further into my seat, but I couldn't help take my eyes off the scene. I watched her like I was watching a macabre car crash happening in slow motion in front of me. She lifted a morsel from the plate to her lipsticked mouth, opened her lips ever so slightly and pushed the small piece of cake inside as delicately as the Queen of England would have. I didn't see her chew or swallow. I only knew she was done when she reached for the glass of water.

"These are different," she said. "Certainly different."

Certainly different? As in who-let-this-riffraff-in certainly different? I was dying in my seat, wishing I were anywhere but there. My face was warm and my armpits were moist.

The Dragon Lady signaled to one of the suited women, who brought the next cupcake. And so, the Lady took a small bite from each of my cakes, her face straighter than a poker player's, giving nothing away.

Finally, she dabbed her lips with her napkin and asked, "Might I ask what you put in these cakes other than the traditional ingredients?" She scanned the room with a serious expression on her face, while the suited women looked at us sharply. I sat quietly. I couldn't form a coherent thought, let alone speak.

"Which one of you brought these, please?" one of the suited women asked.

"Er..." Just when I wanted to speak, the cupcake fairy had got my tongue. I put my hand up, feeling like a kindergarten kid who'd been asked to come to the front of the class.

"Yes?" the Dragon Lady said, in the tone of a strict schoolmarm.

I stood up and cleared my throat. "It's my mother's recipe mixed with Chef Pierre's."

"Chef Pierre?" Her eyebrows arched up.

I nodded, feeling like I'd committed a crime.

"What have you done to Chef Pierre's sublime recipes?"

My mouth had dried up. It took effort to speak. "I...er...added spices."

"What kind of spices?"

I gulped. "Er...cinnamon with the pineapple cake, cardamom and cloves in the chocolate, and...er...maple syrup and nutmeg in the peaches and mango cake."

The Dragon Lady raised a beautifully groomed eyebrow and regarded me.

"And the black forest has lots of rum in it." My nervous mouth had opened before my brain did. I almost kicked myself.

"*Rum?*"

"Jamaican rum."

"*Jamaican rum?*"

Is that a smirk on her face? I stood quietly, feeling everyone's judging eyes on me, feeling more self-conscious with every passing second. I desperately glanced over at the two businesswomen for any signs. They were regarding me with shocked expressions on their faces.

I shuffled my feet. *Do I leave now? Am I supposed to curtsy before I go?*

The Dragon Lady picked up the remaining piece of my chocolate cupcake with her fingers and put it into her mouth. She swallowed noticeably this time and licked the icing off her fingers. She looked elegant, even when licking her fingers.

"Would you be able to make these with cognac?"

"*Cognac?*"

"Indeed," she said, looking thoughtfully at the ceiling. "A hint of Rémy Martin Black Pearl, perhaps?"

The night before, I'd raided one of Dick's half-empty liquor boxes and poured a generous serving of his cheap rum into my chocolate cake batter. I'd never heard of anything remotely sounding like Pearl, let alone Black Pearl. *Did she mean a real oyster pearl?* That reminded me of when Shanti, my Indian schoolmate back in Tanzania, had boasted about eating gulab jamun sprinkled with real gold flakes.

"Sure," I stammered. "I can do that." I couldn't say no. Not to her. Either way, I was sure as dead now. Nothing I would say would save me anyway.

The Dragon Lady was watching me closely.

I put my hands in my pockets to hide my nervousness and instantly felt Preeti's letter between my fingers, the letter I carried with me everywhere I went.

What's happened to me? What about my plan to make enough so I can go back home to Preeti? I stopped fidgeting. I could almost feel Preeti's words come through my fingertips. I'd read that letter so often, I remembered every word by heart. I straightened my spine and looked the Dragon Lady in the eye.

"Madam, I can bake with black pearls if you'd like. I can bake with white pearls too, if you want," I heard my voice say. "I am the best baker in town, and I promise you will not regret hiring me."

The Dragon Lady looked at me with a half smile. It was not a smile you smiled back to.

No one spoke.

"You have absolutely no clue what Black Pearl is, do you?" Her crisp voice cut through the silence.

I heard a low snicker behind me. I looked down at the ground. I couldn't lie.

Just like moons and like suns,
With the certainty of tides,
Just like hopes springing high,
Still I'll rise...
Leaving behind nights of terror and fear
I rise
Into a daybreak that's wondrously clear
I rise
Maya Angelou

Chapter Forty-nine

The phone rang at the worst time.

Dick was the only one who called in the mornings and he called only in an emergency. I hoped our order hadn't changed at the last minute.

"Hello?" I mumbled through a mouthful of toothpaste.

But there was nothing but silence on the other end of the phone. *Did they just hang up?* The dial tone kicked in. *Why can't people check before dialing?* I thought as I hurried back to the bathroom.

I had a long to-do list that morning, including a run to the specialty grocery store before heading to the bakery. My forty-fifth catering order for the Department of Diplomacy, Development and Foreign Affairs was due that morning, an order for two-hundred-and-fifty Cognac and Coffee Cupcakes.

The faceless man at the department—the one who'd explained the diplomatic caste system the other day—told me, with sufficient awe in his voice, the defense minister, herself, was to preside over this fund-raiser. The order was a big deal for my client and me.

Jose had reluctantly bought the smallest bottle of the highest-priced cognac I'd asked him to buy the week before. He was as cheap as Dick, but he had no choice. We had a contract to follow. It wasn't exactly Rémy Martin Louis XIII Black Pearl, Limited Edition, of which I'd learned only a hundred cases existed in the world, but it was miles ahead of Dick's cheap rum. With two hours to get the order ready, I now had everything, except for one main ingredient. I'd run out of ground coffee beans.

My life had taken on a new urgency after meeting the Diplomatic Dragon Lady. The Department had asked us to sign a yearlong contract that was as long as it was detailed. It even specified the quality of flour and type of organic sugar I was allowed to use for baking, obviously an inclusion from the Dragon Lady herself.

Ironically, just as Mrs. Rao used to, the Dragon Lady sent me a menu with special instructions before every diplomatic event. Unlike Mrs. Rao, the Diplomatic Dragon Lady's demands were beautifully crafted and handwritten on stiff paper with the department's official insignia. It was a pleasant surprise to not be subjected to condescending barks or dismissive snorts for once.

I wondered for a long time why she'd picked me over the others, especially the self-assured baker of the gorgeous top model of a cake. That is, until one day, the faceless man on the phone at the department explained. The Lady, he said, had been tired of the same predictable menu items. She had wanted pizazz and zing, but with a Goldilocks quality—not so crazy it would unsettle their sophisticated guests, but not so understated that people wouldn't notice. My cakes gave just the right unexpected twist to the department's parties, a twist that got everyone talking afterward.

But there was something more which I suspected clinched the deal. She'd been looking for a caterer who wasn't only good at the job, but also obedient enough to take detailed directions every week. The baker of the top-model cake was superb, the man on the phone told me, but everyone in town knew he was a drama queen.

I never spoke with the Diplomatic Dragon Lady again.

But after six months on the job, I got a hand-delivered letter on official paper, thanking me for my service to the department. It was the first time anyone had formally acknowledged my talents. When I showed it proudly to everyone at the bakery, Jose slapped me on the back with a "Good on ya," and Dick grunted his approval. Katy promptly made a copy, enlarged it, framed it, and hung it up in front.

A few times when I was making a delivery, I caught sight of the Dragon Lady getting ushered out of her white limo by the chauffeur. Whenever she noticed me, which was rare, she'd give me a brief nod with a queen-like wave. She never smiled. I knew her by then—she wasn't one to show petty emotions. Her focus was on getting the job done and getting it done right. Regardless, I'd wave back enthusiastically with my brightest smile, suppressing the itch to run over and say *thank you, thank you, thank you!*

The word was spreading. My small cakes were becoming popular, and one day, we got the ultimate compliment.

Katy took a call from the French embassy, with the caller saying the referral had come from the Diplomatic Dragon Lady herself. New world cupcakes for the old world of croissants, chocolate éclairs, and Chef Pierre's headquarters. When Katy told me about the call, I pinched myself to make sure I wasn't dreaming and did a happy dance around the kitchen while Jim eyed me with suspicion from the top of the door.

From there, we got three more contracts. Before I knew it, five embassies were offering us catering jobs. Jose was pleased. I was bringing in clients and cash. I was also doing most of the work, baking and making deliveries with Katy. Neither Jose nor Dick lifted a finger. Either way, the two men seemed busy with other things.

I was getting close to my goal. I'd passed my eighteenth birthday and had spent over three and a half years in Toronto by now.

Thanks to my arrangement with Jose, in eight months I had enough to buy an airline ticket. And in three more months, I'd also have enough to pay off Kristadasa, Franky, the marriage broker and anyone else who might lurk around, making it difficult to get Preeti out of her marriage. I was now working for insurance money. I didn't want to arrive in Goa unprepared and penniless, so I worked furiously every day, saving every dollar in a box under my bed.

Saving wasn't easy though. Our rent had been hiked again, and if we were late by a day, we paid hefty interest charges, which Randy refused to reconsider. "You pay or you go," he'd say whenever we pleaded our case. The apartment was getting expensive. I was thankful Katy kept paying her half though she spent more nights at Jose's place these days.

When I suggested we give up the apartment altogether—that Katy officially move in with her new boyfriend and I move into the shop and sleep on Dick's couch to save money—it fell on deaf ears. Neither Jose nor Dick nor Katy wanted to even discuss it.

I wondered about Katy. Though she was still starry-eyed about Jose, I got the distinct feeling something was not right. She kept saying she wanted to keep the apartment in case she needed to move back *quickly*.

"Why?" I'd asked. "Is everything okay?"

"You never know," she'd said, with a shrug. "Just good to have my own place." Then she'd changed topic. Katy was a private person, so I knew she'd tell me when the time was right.

Thirty seconds after I'd put the phone down, it rang again.

Again?

"Hewwo?" I answered, my toothbrush still in my mouth.

Whirr... buzzzz... Static.

I had little time for pranks that morning. *This time, I'm calling the phone company to blacklist this number.* I was about to hang up when a crackled voice came through.

"Is this Asha?"

My heart sank.

It was the same voice as the previous mysterious caller. The same Indian accent. I hadn't dreamed it up, I was sure now. The voice was muffled as if the caller had a bad cold or something. With the head-set stuck to my ear, I ran to the bathroom, pulled out my toothbrush, and spat into the sink.

"Who's this?" I asked.

"Someone pay very good money for visa."

"Who...who are you?"

"You cannot run away all the time." There was something famil-iar about the way he spoke. "You're a very bad girl, you know."

"I said, who are you?" I demanded.

"Franky is disappointed, very disappointed with you."

The bathroom felt suffocating. I stepped through the door, half expecting to find the intruder inside our apartment. It was early and Katy was still asleep; it being one of those rare nights she'd slept at our apartment.

I walked toward the kitchen with the phone glued to my ear, my legs wobbly. I leaned against the table and clutched the back of a chair to steady myself.

"Tell me who you are." I tried to sound as authoritative as I could. "If you don't, I'm going to call the police."

To my surprise, I heard a chuckle. "If you want to go to prison, go ahead. Go, right ahead. Otherwise, we are waiting for you here."

A chill went through my spine.

"Waiting for what? Where?"

"You must keep promises."

"I never made any."

The phone went dead before I could say anything else. The buzz and crackles ceased, leaving a monotonous dial tone.

"Morning."

I jumped and whirled around. A sleepy Katy was stumbling into the kitchen in her pink pajamas, her hair askew.

"What's the matter?" she said stopping to squint at me. "You look like you saw a ghost."

"Nothing. It's...er...just a prank call." I put the phone down quickly and picked up the kettle with shaking hands. "Want some tea?"

"Sure, thanks," Katy said, pulling out a chair to sit down. "Must have been a heck of a prank to make you shake like that."

I stood still for a full minute, before turning around.

"Katy, there's something I need to tell you."

Chapter Fifty

"**M**issus Rao!"

My head jerked up so fast, the egg whisk flew out of my hand.

It was four days after the mysterious phone call, four days after I'd spilled my guts to Katy and told her everything. Sharing my story had been a relief, but doing so had brought back memories—memories I'd rather have forgotten, and now, I was all nerves. I hadn't slept for days and I was starting to hear and see things everywhere.

With three months to go before I returned to Goa, my mind was buzzing with mixed feelings of hope, worry, relief, and nerves, tumbling through my mind, day and night. I thought I spotted Ashok at the grocery store, Franky at the gas station, and someone who looked suspiciously like Kristadasa at the bakery parking lot. I shook my head. I had to get rid of these wild imaginings or I'd end up in a straitjacket.

I picked up the whisk, threw it in the sink, and plucked a clean one from the drawer. My hand was shaking. *Stop it.* I shook my head to clear my mind. *I'm working too hard and I've become paranoid. What do I have to be so worried about?* Sure, Dick was the worst boss in the world, but he'd not let anyone hurt his best baker, would he? I was bringing in good money now.

And Jose, who'd started to date Katy in earnest, was turning out to be tolerable—nice, even. I knew he thought me demanding, but he respected me. *He'd help if I'm in trouble, wouldn't he?* Maybe, I thought, it was time to stop mistrusting everybody and ask for help for once.

I continued to mix my batter, but my mind was elsewhere, back in the past, remembering Mrs. Rao's home, those odd moonlit nights, Tim's crazy escape, Ashok's sudden arrival, Franky's call, Preeti's letter.... My mind got stuck on Preeti's letter. *What did last week's call mean? What did he mean when he said they were waiting for me? Who? Where?*

"Misses Rao!"

I put my whisk down and listened. The sound was coming from the front of the store.

"Raoooo!"

This wasn't my imagination. This was real.

I tiptoed toward the front trying not to make any noise, glancing around as I went. *Did someone come in?*

But the front door was locked and I was the only one in the bakery. Katy always locked the front door when I was working alone in the kitchen and everyone had stepped out. It was Friday afternoon and Dick, while telling us he was at a church fund raiser, was really with his brother at the local strip joint having a beer and ogling women swinging naked around poles. And Jose had taken Katy on a lunch date at a fancy restaurant downtown.

No one should have been in the store other than me. And Jim, of course.

I peeked inside Dick's office.

"Hellooo!" Jim said, cocking his head at me.

"You silly bird. Is it you making all this noise?"

He gave me a condescending sniff and looked away grandly like I wasn't worth the effort.

He was perched on top of the safe on Dick's desk. Next to him was a glass tumbler half-filled with dark rum. While I watched in surprise, Jim casually slipped his curved beak into the glass and took a sip. He tipped his head back and swallowed expertly. This was the first time I'd seen a bird drink liquor. *Hiccup!* Oh, no. I looked at him closely, hoping he wouldn't get sick.

Right next to the tumbler was a magazine turned upside down. I didn't have to turn it right-side-up to know what it contained. On the back cover was a platinum blonde holding a leather whip and wearing nothing but tiny black panties. It was one of Dick's magazines. I looked at the bird sitting nonchalantly next to it, one claw over the woman's breast and the other scratching his head.

I shook my head. This bird was something. Jim seemed to agree. He rustled his feathers proudly and opened his beak. "Rao!" he cried out, nearly splitting my eardrums. I jumped.

"What did you say?"

He gave me an innocent look and blinked.

"Heeellooo," Jim replied solemnly.

"Where did you learn that name?"

"Dammittohell."

"Tell me. Where'd you learn that new word, Jim?"

He cocked his head and scratched it with a claw.

"Come on, talk to me, Jim. *Please.*"

I sighed. I was trying to have a conversation with a parrot. I considered the possibilities. Jim had never met Mrs. Rao, so he must have heard the name from somewhere or someone else. Or had he met her? At a meeting after Katy and I had left for the day, maybe? Someone calling on the telephone? I stared at the bird. He stared back.

"Why can't you speak intelligently for a change, you silly bird?"

Squawk! he said with contempt in his eyes. He glared at me as only an annoyed parrot can glare. Then, he turned around and preened his feathers. *Squawk... squawk...*he muttered softly to himself, as if in disdain he had to talk to a lowly human.

The front door banged open, making me jump again. I turned around and stepped out to the front.

"Hi," Katy said, her face pink from the crisp air outside.

"Hey, you're early."

"Is Jim giving you trouble again?"

"You could say that." *She'll think I've gone bonkers if I tell her what I'd heard.* "What happened to your lunch date?"

Katy looked crestfallen. "Jose had a business meeting, so we just went to the corner café."

"Oh, I'm sorry." She'd been looking forward to the fancy outing and had even dressed up for it.

"Yeah, me too," Katy said plopping down on her chair in the den, letting out a big sigh.

"Everything all right?"

"Not really."

"What's wrong?"

She paused before speaking. "Things have kinda changed."

"Why do you say that?"

"It was great at the beginning, and then, he started to act kind of like..."

I looked at her expectantly.

"Not very nice," she said finally. "Sometimes I wake up in the middle of the night and he's gone off."

"Gone off? Where?"

"I dunno." She shrugged. "When I ask him, he tells me he's got insomnia or something and goes for long walks to shake it off, but every time he comes back to bed, he smells of cigarettes and rum. Just like Dick used to. But he never lets *me* go out at night. I have to stay home alone while he's out."

I looked away. *Why did sweet, lovely Katy always have to pick the wrong kind of man?*

"He got mad at me today for leaving fingerprints on his car."

"What?"

"Called me useless."

"Katy!" I looked at her, shocked.

"And yesterday, he told me he's going to make me work from home because he thinks I'm checking out other guys."

"*What?*"

She nodded forlornly. "And that trip to Mexico..."

A series of red flags were going up now, one by one. I crossed my arms and stared at my friend, half-wishing Jose was here so I could tell him what I thought of him.

"What about your trip?"

"He said I've got work to do and he doesn't want to waste time or money on trips."

"Are you serious?"

"I know," Katy said, looking down at her shoes.

"He sounds controlling. Totally controlling. This isn't right." This was the guy who made a big fuss of calling us "ladies" and even opened doors for us like a gentleman. I knew he had another side.

"He was mean to me at lunch today. Was on his phone the whole time and didn't even look at me when I left."

"Oh my god," I said. What I really wanted to say was "Drop him now!" but those words didn't come out.

"Ever since he started that important project with the Indian company, he's been acting strange."

My eyebrows shot up. "Indian company?"

"That's his twelve thirty meeting."

"Who's he talking to?"

"I dunno," Katy said, shrugging her shoulders. She started to mindlessly straighten her ledger books. "He doesn't tell me much anymore. Anyway, I guess I'm not important enough to be at the meeting."

"Why are they meeting at a coffee shop? Don't customers normally come to our office?"

"Think they had a few meetings already here last week after our shift ended. Saw them on Jose's phone calendar," Katy said, looking slightly guilty. "I thought he was seeing someone else at night, so I peeked."

"I don't blame you."

"That's why I've been sleeping at our apartment because he's working late here."

I stared at her.

"Come with me," I said.

"What?" she asked, not getting up from her chair.

"I want you to hear this. Come."

I walked into Dick's office with Katy shuffling behind me. Jim was half-asleep on the desk now, the tumbler next to him empty.

"What is it?" Katy asked, looking around the room.

"Shhhh," I said, putting a finger to my lips.

"Hello, Jim," I said in a soft voice, stooping in front of the bird.

"Helloo," said a slurred, sleepy voice.

"Hey Jim, wake up, sweetie, and tell us what you learned recently," I said.

"Helloooo," the bird said softly, without opening his eyes.

"That's good. What else, Jim? What's the new word you've learned?"

"Dammittohell," Jim said happily to himself.

"Come on, Jim. Try once more. Please." I looked around, wondering how to prompt his memory. *Ply him with more rum? Give him another porn magazine?*

"Missus Raooo!" the bird called out.

"Ha!" I said, whipping my head around. "Did you hear that?"

"What?"

"How many people do you know called Mrs. Rao?"

She shook her head.

"Missus Rao," Jim said again softly, cocking his head and regarding us warily with one open eye.

"See? I know I'm not imagining this," I said, pointing at the bird. "I don't know where he's heard it, but it has to be recent. You know how he likes to repeat his new words? Who knows what goes on here when we're out making deliveries or after our shift ends?"

Katy's face was blank.

"Mrs. Rao must have been here for Jim to hear her name. Or someone called her a few times and Jim heard the name."

Katy's face looked strange like she was remembering something.

"What's wrong?" I asked.

"At lunch today—"

"Yes?"

"Jose took a call. He was talking to his phone, but I was close enough to hear. It was a woman on the other end, a woman with an Indian accent. I didn't think much of it because he said he was meeting an Indian company, but I remember the photo avatar on the screen now. It was an Indian woman with a short bob haircut and warts on her face. I couldn't help notice the warts."

My blood ran cold. "They've found me."

Chapter Fifty-one

"That's him!" I said and ducked in my seat. "That's Ashok!"

We'd just driven to the café where Jose was supposed to have his meeting with the Indian company. And there in the parking lot was Mrs. Rao's unmistakable white Land Rover with Ashok squatting beside it.

I peered above the dashboard. Yes, it was him and he hadn't changed a bit. And right next to the white Rover was Jose's black Mercedes.

"Stay down!" Katy said in a fierce whisper.

An unearthly squeal came from underneath us. The old bakery van always squeaked like a giant mouse, but right now it sounded like the rodent had a megaphone. We were announcing our arrival to every living thing in the vicinity. A month ago, Jose had slyly asked me for half of my commission so we could get a new van and "do even bigger business together." I refused.

"Can we try not to make so much noise, please?" I whispered, glancing up at Katy from the foot well.

"It's the brakes," she said. "The van's dying."

"Let's park far away," I said. "There's only one van like this in the whole city. Everyone will know it's us."

Katy drove slowly through the parking lot toward the back of the café, with me hunched low in my seat. In the back, there was a semi-truck with a photo of a giant iced donut plastered on its side. No other vehicles or people were around.

"Right behind the truck," I said, pointing. "Good place to hide this."

Katy swung in and pulled the hand brake. We got out, closed the doors quietly, and scanned the area. Traffic was swooshing by on the busy highway next to the café. We could hear the hum of voices talking near us, but saw no one. I signaled to Katy to follow me and stepped toward the back door of the café.

"Do we go in?" Katy whispered, when we got to the door.

"I don't know," I whispered back, looking around. I didn't have a plan, except I wanted to find out who Jose was meeting with without them seeing us.

"What if they see us?" Katy asked, reading my mind.

"Then we'll—" I didn't get to finish. The back door opened with a bang, almost bowling us over.

Katy and I shrieked at the same time.

"Sorry!" said a skinny, pimple-faced man in a café uniform. He had a broom in one hand and a dustpan in the other. He stopped and eyed us. We stared back. My heart was pounding. *Does he know why we're here? Is he going to rat us out?*

"Hey, you gals have a lighter?"

"Oooh." Katy looked visibly relieved. "Sorry, left mine in the car."

"I'm totally desperate for a smoke," he said. "Is your car here?"

"Right there," Katy said automatically, pointing at our hideout behind the semi.

I shook my head. "I think you forgot to bring—"

"You'll so totally save my life. I'm dying here. Can I use your lighter please?"

"No problem, I'll go get it," the ever-pleasing Katy said, turning to return to the van.

"Oh, thanks, man. Sweet."

He followed her with his broom dragging on the ground. I followed them both, racking my brain to think how to tell Katy to stop drawing any more attention to us. The problem was she was always too nice.

"Here you go," she said, opening the glove compartment of the van and bringing out a silver lighter. "It's not mine," she said, when she saw me shaking my head in warning. But it was no use. "It's Jose's," she said. "Don't worry, I haven't started smoking."

"Dammit to hell!"

We jumped.

"That's not a fair deal!"

Katy and I looked at each other in alarm.

"Dick?" I said in a hoarse whisper.

"You know these dudes?" The café man pointed in the direction of the voices. "These guys have been hogging my smoking spot for hours." He bent down to light his cigarette. "What a bunch of asses," he said through his teeth.

"They're inside the truck?" I asked in a low voice.

"Not inside. In front of it," the man said, handing the lighter back to Katy. "Thanks, eh."

I tiptoed around the truck and peeked. There was a large "No Smoking" sign over a wooden bench, right in front of the great big truck concealing our van. Sitting at this outdoor makeshift boardroom under a cloud of cigarette smoke were Dick, Jose, and a third man, a thin man with a dark complexion wearing a brand-new Rambo T-shirt.

My heart jumped to my throat.

Franky? I stared at him in shock. *What's he doing here?*

"They didn't even leave a tip," I heard the café man say behind me. "Cheap bastards. Hey, you gals wanna join me for a smoke? I have two more in my pocket. Maybe we can go kick those guys out." He waved his broom menacingly in their direction.

"No, thanks," I said quickly, giving Katy a warning look.

"We'd love to," Katy said, giving him one of her sweet smiles. "Gotta get our coffee fix first."

"Suit yourself," he said, sauntering back toward the café.

I waited until he was out of sight and motioned to Katy to join me. We crouched down low next to the truck, straining our ears.

"You almost fired that chick! If I didn't stop you, we wouldn't even be here!" That was Jose's voice. And that was the first time I'd heard him use the word chick. *What happened to "these lovely ladies"?*

"I was the one who found them in the first place. If it wasn't for me, you'd be kissing this commission goodbye!" Dick snapped. "You owe me for that."

"It was my idea to turn your cigarette and crack-smuggling racket into a baking business," replied an angry Jose. "If it wasn't for me, you'd have been screwed as hell the first time an inspector checked out that kitchen of yours. It'd be your fat ass in the big house right about now."

Katy and I looked at each other with wide eyes. *Crack-smuggling? Is that why Dick had such a big kitchen?*

I remembered the dirty chemistry equipment stashed away on the top shelves, shelves I couldn't reach and had never opened except the first day I'd explored the kitchen. I also remembered how things mysteriously moved around at night. *Is that what they did at night at the bakery?*

"What and how I run my business is none of your business," Dick snapped. "I kept everything respectable. I even got us a baking gig with my church."

"I got a gig with the federal government. Beat that!" Jose shouted.

"I did all the work around here until you came strutting, so shut the hell up."

"The hell I will. I'm the one who loaned you money so you don't have to close up shop. You were so happy I came to save you from your screwups, you didn't even mind me sleeping with your chick!"

I felt Katy give a start next to me. I leaned over and squeezed her arm.

"If I hadn't hired the girl, both of you wouldn't be here now. I need the bigger commission."

I peeked around the corner. Though he was giving a good fight, Dick looked a little scared of Jose.

"Okay, okay, very good, please, good gentlemen. Let us not fight. Please. We can solve this in the most civilized fashion."

My stomach turned.

That was Franky, overly polite and scheming nasty, as usual. I felt nauseous. I wanted to run out, shake him, slap him and scream at him and ask what he did to my cousin Preeti and Aunty Shilpa. I glared with dagger eyes from behind the truck. I should have never trusted that hyena face.

"Listen to me, most respectable gentlemen. My man in India wants a good visa, and for that, we need a girl. He's in hurry to get out, and he will pay good money." My memory clicked. It was *his* voice I'd heard over the phone, disguised, screened with a cloth or something. That was why I hadn't recognized it at first. My heart sank. Katy must have noticed because she reached over and squeezed my arm.

"How much?" Jose asked.

"You give me girl in good condition, and I give you two percent."

"Two percent! You take us for morons, man?" Jose banged his palm on the table. I hadn't realized how much of a Jekyll and Hyde he was—sugar and sweetness to our faces, a nightmare behind our backs.

"No, no. I have utmost respect for you, mister," Franky said, his voice sweeter than gulab jamun sprinkled with gold. "As you can understand, I have to give a cut to Mrs. Rao as well, you know. She's the one who arranged to find the girl, and that cost her a lot of money. She will tell you this herself, but she is not well today."

"That's her problem," Dick muttered. "She took her time, didn't she? Could have used this money sooner, I tell ya."

"You know, we have to all be supremely cautious in this business. I don't have to tell you that," Franky said, giving that genial Indian head nod. "Mrs. Rao only knew where the girl was when she went to that Indian embassy party and saw the cakes. Also we want to make sure police is not watching. All this took time. Patience is virtue, as I say. Very good virtue."

"Just give us a decent deal, man," Jose said. "I've been in this business for years. You can't fool me. I can get a Russian chick for nothing and sell her in Morocco for five grand. Now, that's good money."

I heard a gasp from Katy.

"Is that what you been getting from those sleazy Russian bride catalogs?" Dick said with a leer in his voice.

"None of your goddamn business," Jose growled. He turned back to Franky. "If I help anyone to come over here, I charge them no less than a hundred grand—two grand for the girl and the rest for the visa. Easy-peasy. That's what I'm negotiating for the redhead."

Katy jerked back like she'd been slapped. She clutched my arm tightly, her face a ghostly white.

"How could he?" she asked in a whisper. "*How could he?*"

I was speechless. I'd never fully trusted Jose, but this was too much.

"My man can only offer seventy," Franky was saying. "Five hundred for the girl and the rest for the visa. Very good deal, no?"

Five hundred dollars? That's what I'm worth? I glared at the men who were haggling our lives like used cars.

"Peanuts!" Jose said.

"Highway robbery!" Dick said.

"Indian men aren't that rich, misters," Franky said. "This is not an Arab sheik. This is poor village man who worked very hard to save money to come abroad. He's a good family man, you know, with a wife and six kids to feed. Think about that, please."

"For a man who's rustled up enough to come here on a fake marriage license, he must have very good reasons for leaving the country,"

Dick said with a smirk. "So, who's this bugger, Franky? Big shot in Indian Mafia? Crooked Indian politician?"

"I am just the honest middle man. I cater to demand and supply. I don't ask any questions."

"Enough," Jose said. "We're quibbling over chicken feed. Let's close this deal, gentlemen. We've got bigger fish to fry than these girls."

"Such as?" Dick asked, giving his partner a suspicious look.

Jose looked at Franky. "I'm glad to have met you, Franky, because I think you're just the right man for a new job I need to do."

"What kind of job, mister?" Franky asked after a cautious pause.

"What are you talking about now, Jose?" Dick asked.

Jose gave a quick wink to Dick as if to say, *I've got this*. "I need a fast and secret UPS service to South Asia, no questions asked."

The other two men leaned in.

"I need to get packages from Colombia, also no questions asked. And I need someone who can make visas, passports, and travel for a few people who can deliver these packages for me. Your line of work, no?"

Franky was silent for a few moments. "I help move people for work and girls for marriage," he said slowly. "I don't do drug business, mister. That's dirty business."

"What the hell!" Jose exploded like a grenade. Katy and I crouched lower behind the truck. "Are you calling me dirty? Are you—"

"No, sir! You misunderstand me at the utmost!" Franky said, waving his arms in protest. "Please, *please*."

"Keep it down, you idiots," Dick said, "or we'll all be in real trouble."

Franky looked around him as if searching for something. "Look, what I mean to say, sir, is girls are cheap and easy to manage. No one takes them seriously even when they run to police. What you're proposing now, this business is much more difficult. Much more dangerous. It will be much, much work, and it will cost me a lot more."

"How is that?" Jose growled. "Instead of people, it's packages. Should be even cheaper."

Franky gave an exaggerated sigh. "I have to give big cuts to my connections at the borders, at the airports, and to the police. This is a very big and costly operation, you know sir, and not such a fast-fast job. I can't afford to pay more and more, and your proposal is going to be super sensitive and super expensive. That is all I am saying, sir."

"If you can figure out the logistics, I'll pay for these extra steps you have to make."

Silence as Franky contemplated the offer.

"All you have to do is take care of the supply chain logistics," Jose added. "For that, I'll give you fifteen percent. Deal?"

"Deal," Franky said, with a smile. "And I'll take the girl for four hundred then."

Chapter Fifty-two

I tugged at Katy's sleeve. "We've got to get out of here. Now."

She didn't budge. Her hands were clenched into fists, and her face had turned a deep, dark red.

"They'll be done soon," I said, nudging her.

"All I wanna do right now," she said, her voice quivering, "is slap that lying man and scratch his eyes out."

I'd never seen her this angry before. I didn't realize she could get angry.

"He was playing me all along and now he wants to *sell* me?" Her voice rose.

"Shhhh," I pulled her up by the shoulders. "If they find us here, we're dead."

"So we let them play us like this? Treat us like, like—*animals*?"

"No, no." I shook my head and motioned her to keep her voice down. "I've got a plan."

"I've got one too," Katy said loudly.

I cringed. "Shhh."

"I'm gonna *kill* him."

"No!" I pulled her away from the truck. "Please get in the van. We gotta leave now."

Katy shrugged me off and marched toward the café's back doors.

"What're you doing?" I whispered hoarsely after her.

She grabbed the café guy's broomstick which had been leaning against the side of the building, and turned to me with a venomous look on her face.

I ran toward her.

"Katy, stop! Whatever you're thinking right now, it's not a good idea. Please listen to me."

"I told him I loved him yesterday. How stupid was that, huh?"

Tears welled up in her eyes.

I put my hands on her shoulders. "I totally understand, and I'm so sorry, Katy, but right now, right now, we've really got to get outta here."

Just then, I heard footsteps around the corner. I froze.

Ashok's face popped around the building. We stared at him. He stared back at us. His eyes widened when he saw me. He pointed a silent finger at me and waved frantically.

"Shhhh." I put a finger to my lips. I knew he was mute, but at that moment, he looked like he was about to yell out to the world. "Please don't say a word, Ashok."

"You!" Katy snapped. "You're in this racket too? Trying to sell us? How much is your cut?" She waved the broom at him. Ashok took a step back, his mouth open, confused.

"You disgusting, nasty piece of... I'm gonna start with you!" With her red hair frizzed up and the pointy broomstick in her hand, she looked like a madwoman on the war path. Ashok's face went white.

Before I knew it, she lunged at him. I saw him duck, but I didn't wait to find out what happened next. I looked around for our best way out. I didn't dare return to our van, as it was too close to where the men were congregated. They'd probably heard us scuffling and were already coming this way.

Then I remembered Ashok always left the car keys in the ignition.

I didn't wait another second. I ran to the Rover, yanked the door open, and jumped in. *Shoot.* I'd forgotten Mrs. Rao's Jeep had manual transmission. The only times I'd driven this were to take it in and out of the garage to clean it. In total, I must have driven it exactly ten yards.

I pressed the clutch to start the engine. *I can do this. I can do this.* The engine turned and just as quickly shuddered to a stop. Behind me, I heard crashing and banging. A car alarm went off and it sounded like a riot had begun. *One more time.* With my heart beating wildly, and praying that Katy was okay, I pressed down on the clutch and tried the ignition once again. It took three tries for the Jeep to purr to life.

From the side view mirror, I saw Ashok turn toward the Jeep, his arms waving frantically, with Katy in hot pursuit, the broom still in her hand. His mouth was moving but no sound was coming out. I swung the steering wheel and gunned the jeep toward Katy, almost hitting Ashok. I slammed on the brakes and screeched to a stop.

"Get in, Katy!" I shouted. "Now!"

Katy jumped in and slammed the door shut.

"That did it," she said in a satisfied voice.

I glanced quickly at her hands and face. *No blood. Thank god.*

I slammed the accelerator, throwing both of us against our seats. Through the rearview mirror, I saw Ashok jumping up and down, waving his arms maniacally. I lurched across the parking lot, and his frantic face disappeared in our dust.

I only started breathing after we got on the main road. "Are you okay?" I asked giving a quick glance at my friend.

"Good. Real good." Katy's voice was quiet but smug. She threw the broom in the backseat and buckled up.

I kept my focus on the road and on maneuvering this beast of a car. My hands were shaking, and I was having a hard time keeping the steering wheel steady. I also had one eye on the rearview mirror to make sure we weren't being followed.

"What *happened* back there?" I asked, when we'd finally put the café well behind us.

Silence.

I glanced at Katy to see her smiling.

"Did you hit Ashok?"

"I didn't touch him."

"Did he hit you?"

"He wouldn't know how to, even if he wanted to."

"What was all the noise then?"

"I smashed Jose's lights and mirrors."

"You did *what*?"

"All of them. Then, I scratched his doors. All of them."

"Oh my god."

"He'll have bigger things to worry about than my fingerprints now."

"Wow."

"Should have done it yesterday. If I had more time, I'd have smashed his windows too."

I'd never seen this side of her before.

A nervous giggle escaped her lips.

"I can't believe you did that!" I said, letting out a nervous laugh.

"Me neither!" She giggled some more. I laughed out loud, and soon we were both convulsed with laughter and tears, a release from all the tension.

"Where are we going now?" Katy asked, wiping her eyes.

"Home."

"Then what?"

"We're going to pack our bags. Grab my cash and our passports," I said, bolting through a yellow light, holding on to the steering wheel with a death grip.

"Passports?"

"Uh-huh," I said, maneuvering around a yellow cone on the side of the road.

"Why passports?"

"Did you get yours for your Mexican trip? Please say yes."

"Sure. Last week," Katy said. "Why?"

"Good." That was one major hurdle out of the way.

"Why do we need passports?"

I'd just pulled up to a four-way stop sign when the car shuddered to a complete halt. "Darn, darn, darn!" I said, shifting through the gears, looking for neutral. I pressed the clutch and turned the engine over again. The car jerked back to life, and we lurched through the intersection, sweat pouring down my back.

"Oh god, I think I'm going to be sick," Katy said, holding the door handle with both hands. "Stop the car."

"This thing's hellish to drive. If I stop now, we'll be stuck forever," I said. "You can throw up inside."

"Asha!" Katy said. "Why do we need passports? Tell me!"

"Because we're going to India."

"*India?*"

Katy was silent for a full minute. I hoped she wasn't going to be sick.

"My passport's on my desk," she said in a quiet voice. "At the bakery."

"Oh, no! Don't say that!"

I had no choice.

I swerved the car around, making an illegal U-turn, and headed toward the bakery, a few minutes from where we were. With my heart pounding, I screeched to a halt right in front of the store. Other than one car at the pawn shop next door, there were no other cars or people.

"Hurry!" I yelled. "Hurry!"

Katy had already opened the door and was running out.

I maneuvered the Jeep around to face the street so Katy could jump in and we could dash out. This way, I also had a good view of the street and anyone coming our way. I waited, the car running, my fingers drumming on the wheel, ready to gun it as soon as Katy got back.

Why's she taking so long?

That was when it dawned on me. I had cash for only one ticket to Goa with a bit left over. *How were we going to pay for Katy's ticket?* I turned off the engine and ran inside.

"Hey!" Katy jumped when she saw me.

"How much is in the safe?" I asked.

"What safe?"

I pulled her by the elbow into the office and pointed at the safe on which Jim was now having a nap.

"Do you have the combination for this?"

She gave me a wide-eyed look. But only for a moment. Within seconds, her fingers were deftly maneuvering the lock, much to the annoyance of Jim. The lock clicked, we pushed Jim off and opened the door. We peered in. Inside were papers, envelopes, and plastic packets.

"Drug money," Katy whispered. "That's what this is."

I picked up the packet on top and unzipped it open.

"Oh my god," I said, staring at the contents.

"Wow," Katy said.

"Let's get out of here."

She banged the safe door shut, making Jim squawk.

We ran outside. And soon, we were speeding across the parking lot and onto the road.

We drove silently for a while, Katy lost in her thoughts, me focusing on my driving.

"Wanna see?" I heard her say, after a few minutes.

"What?"

A wad of hundred-dollar bills fluttered in front of my face. I almost bumped into the car in front of us.

"How much is there?" I asked.

"Twenty grand."

"Twenty thousand dollars?" My throat went dry.

"This is back pay," Katy said, with a grim look on her face. "Do you know how long I worked for less than minimum wage for those asses? It was you and me that kept the bakery running. They used us like slaves."

I kept my focus on the road, trying not to think too much. *Do you get jail time for stealing from bad guys? What happens when you take money tainted with crack and who knows what else?*

"Oh my god," I said, suddenly realizing what we'd done. "We're going to the airport. We're going to an airport, Katy!"

"So?"

"Take a thousand for your ticket and throw the rest out with that packet. Throw it to the side of the road or something. We can't take that through security."

With a huff, Katy stuffed the money back in the packet, zipped it up and slipped it into the breast pocket of her jacket. "Dick uses these packets to take money when he flies," she said, "I know because I used to pack his suitcase for him. Security won't catch it. This might even be X-ray proof."

"Are you sure of that?" I asked. "Do you know what they'll do to us if they find out we're carrying that?" I had enough problems with my fake visa. I didn't need this extra worry.

"They won't find out." Katy sounded super confident. *She's still seething over what she heard,* I thought. *She's keeping this money just to get back at Jose.*

"This is our blood money," she said, as if reading my mind.

"*Blood* money?"

"We're keeping it."

There was no use arguing, and I had other things to take care of at the moment.

As soon as we got to our apartment, we dashed up the stairs. I pulled the shoe box out from under the bed where I'd squirreled away all the commissions I'd earned. I counted my money—my hard-earned, *legal* money. There was just enough for one ticket to Goa, but that was it.

"Ready?" I jerked my head up. Katy was standing in front of me with a carry-on sized suitcase filled to bursting. "Since Mexico's out, why not India? Or Tanzania? Or Australia? Or even the South Pole? I'm up for whatever now."

I looked at her. Her hair was tangled like a ball of flame over her head. Her face looked tired. We were both being traded to unknown men like cheap cars, but at least I hadn't fallen in love with the man who was planning to sell me.

"Hey, are you okay?"

"Just don't mention his name, okay?"

"Promise."

I stuffed as many clothes as I could into my backpack, zipped it up, and tucked the envelope of money in the front pocket. We raced back down the stairs and into the Rover. This time, I got it right the first time. The engine started without a hitch, and we dashed off in the direction of the airport.

"Can you check for flights?" I asked Katy once we were on the road.

She pulled out her phone and started clicking, muttering to herself.

"Is Islamabad in India?"

"Um..." I was preoccupied with passing a truck on the road.

"I'll take that as a yes," Katy said, swiping the screen.

"No! That's a whole different country."

"Okay, okay. What then?"

"Try Delhi—D-E-L-H-I. Or Mumbai. M-U-M-B-A-I."

"There's a flight today to Mumbai, but I don't know if they have any seats," Katy mumbled to herself. "Maybe if you stopped jerking around, I'd be able to read my phone."

The Land Rover was grouchy—snarling and screeching as if it knew it had a new manual driver at the wheel. I was making a routine check in my rearview mirror when I noticed the black Mercedes weaving in and out of traffic behind us.

"Hey, Katy," I said in the calmest voice I could muster. "Are there many black Benzes in town like the one Jose has, you think?"

"Why do you ask?" she said, not taking her eyes off her phone.

"Think I saw something. Wasn't in good shape, like the mirrors were all out or something."

Katy sat bolt upright. "What? Where?"

"They don't know where we're going, right?" I said, racking my brain to think if we'd left any clues at the bakery.

"Where do you see it?" Katy's voice was rising in panic. "I don't see it."

I squinted at the rearview mirror again. We were in the middle of afternoon traffic, but the black Mercedes was nowhere in sight.

"It's gone."

Katy slammed back in her seat and let out a huge breath.

"False alarm," I said. "My mind's playing tricks on me."

Chapter Fifty-three

"Watch out!"

I swerved the Rover to avoid hitting the golf cart. It dashed within inches of us, beeping a high-pitched horn. The uniformed driver gave us a nasty glare as she sailed by.

"What was that?" I asked, after catching my breath.

"Airport security shuttle," Katy said. "She could have got killed."

"Us, too," I said, looking at the disappearing cart, bolting so fast its wheels hovered above the pavement. "That was close." I looked around us and moved the Rover slowly forward, scanning the area.

"What are you doing?" Katy asked.

"Looking for parking," I said, searching for a spot to fit this immense beast.

"Let me get this right," Katy said, speaking slowly. "Dick and Jose are plotting to sell us. We just stole their money and Mrs. Rao's car and broke every speed limit in town. Plus, they're probably right behind us. *And you're looking for parking?*"

"Gosh," I said. Katy did make sense sometimes. I needed to listen to her more often. "You're right." I turned the car to stop.

"Look out!" Katy shouted, pointing in front.

The airport golf cart was zipping by again, this time from the other direction. "Oh, no!" I turned the steering wheel to a hard right, slammed on the brakes, and crashed right into a light pole. I heard a bang.

"Help!" Katy cried out, pinned behind the airbag, her arms flailing.

"Oh my god, Katy!" I pried myself out between the seat and the bag and jumped out. The cart was now five hundred yards away. The driver hadn't even realized what she'd done.

With my heart in my mouth, I ran to her side and opened the passenger door. For a split second, the images from another car crash from long ago flashed across my mind. My throat choked up. *If anything happens to Katy—*

"I'm okay, I'm okay," she said, as I pulled her out of her seat.

"I'm so sorry."

"Good thing we weren't driving fast or we'd be toast now."

We pulled out our bags from the backseat and surveyed the damage. The pristine Land Rover, the one I'd spent many hours polishing, was now crumpled, the front part anyway. I looked up at the light pole. The sign posted above our heads said, "No stopping under any circumstances—Airport Security." Katy and I looked at each other and shook our heads.

"Let's get outta here," I said.

We ran toward the airport building, leaving the jeep where it was. It took several minutes to find the Air India counter, and that's when we heard the bad news.

"Five in the morning!" Katy said in shock.

"That's almost sixteen hours from now," I said.

"I'm afraid that's the earliest we have available, and it will be standby so I can't promise you anything," the counter attendant said. "Otherwise, you can book a direct flight on Friday. We still have plenty of seats later this week. Shall I look into that option?"

"No!" I said louder than expected. "We've got to get out as soon as we can." The attendant looked at me with raised eyebrows. "It's a family emergency," I explained quickly. That was partly true. No, fully true.

"Do you want to take these two standby seats then?"

"How much is it?"

"Two thousand six hundred and eighty dollars."

I looked at her, shocked.

The attendant looked from Katy to me and back again. "Do you want the seats or not?"

I nodded.

She punched in more keys.

"Any baggage to check in?"

"No, we're good, thanks."

"Passports, please," she said, hammering away at her keyboard.

"Will the owner of a white Land Rover, license number AGK 6X8, please report to the security desk." The PA system reverberated throughout the airport.

Katy and I looked at each other quickly, as the announcement repeated. *Did it have to be so loud?*

"Asha," she whispered, but I motioned for her to wait.

I had bigger problems on my hands right now and could feel the sweat beading on my forehead already. I watched helplessly as the attendant went through my passport and punched the numbers into her computer. *Is she going to find out my visa is a fake? Will she call the immigration police?*

"Asha!" Katy called again. I turned and shook my head, and mouthed *not now*.

"Okay, ladies," the attendant said, peering into her screen. "The best I can do is this. First leg is from Toronto to London, second from London to Delhi. In Delhi, you will transfer to Goa. Not a fun flight, but everything else is booked today."

"That's fine," I said, relieved. "This is really, really fine. Thank you so much."

"It's six hours from Toronto to London, and then seven from London to Delhi. The layover in London is twenty hours," the attendant continued. "This is all standby. Are you sure you want this?"

"Yes, we'll take it," I blurted, and passed her the cash.

"Asha!" Katy said, this time tugging my sleeve.

"I know, I know," I whispered. "They found the Jeep."

"Forget the Jeep. Look behind." She gave a barely perceptible nod of her head.

I glanced back and froze.

"Don't move," she whispered.

I didn't think I could. "How did they know we're here?"

"Must have followed us."

"That Benz behind us was Jose's, right?"

"Excuse me," the attendant said, turning from her computer toward us with two pieces of paper and our passports in her hand. "Here are your tickets. Your flight departs at five a.m. Make sure to be at the gate at least an hour ahead. Remember this is an international flight."

"Thank you," I said.

"Next, please," the attendant said, turning her attention away from us.

"What do we do now?" Katy whispered. We kept our heads down and stayed close to the airline desk, pretending to be busy stuffing our tickets in our bags. The next person in line rolled up with three large suitcases and a golf bag. We couldn't hang around here forever.

The airport was getting crowded. A couple with a screaming baby was trying to calm their kid down, and a group of teenagers with long hair and musical equipment rolled into the lineup. Even if we got lost in this crowd, we'd only get so far. To get to the security gate, we had to cross miles of corridors, giving ample time for Jose, Dick, and the gang to ambush us.

"Where's the washroom?" I whispered.

"You need to use the washroom *now*?"

"No. I mean, yes. Just look for the sign."

We both scanned the area, desperately trying not to make eye contact with Ashok, who was hovering near the edge of the lineup, scanning the crowd. From where we were, we could see Dick and Jose walking the length of the corridor, looking here and there, searching for us.

"Over there," Katy whispered. "To your right, near the bookstore."

"Go!" I grabbed Katy and pulled her with me.

Chapter Fifty-four

"**N**ow what do we do?" Katy asked.

We'd only sprinted a few yards, but my heart was thumping like I'd run the hundred-meter dash. I looked around me. This wasn't the best hiding spot, but the men couldn't walk in without others noticing. For now.

"We can stay here until they get tired of looking."

Katy didn't look convinced.

"I've done this before—outwaited Ashok, I mean."

"*This* is your plan?"

"Do you have a better one?"

She shook her head.

I pulled a bunch of paper towels from the dispenser and wiped the floor nearest the handicapped stall. I plunked down my backpack and sat on my bag. Katy watched me, threw down her suitcase next to mine, sat on it with a thump and put her chin on her hands.

Every fifteen minutes, I snuck toward the washroom door to see if the coast was clear. After an hour, Jose and Dick disappeared, maybe to haunt another part of the airport, leaving Ashok to keep vigil at the main departure area.

He was sitting on his haunches on the floor at the back, with a mobile phone in his hands. Though he couldn't speak, all he had to do was dial a number when he spotted us and the others would be after us in a flash.

"Do you think they saw us?" Katy asked.

"Don't think so," I said. "Dick and Jose wouldn't leave him alone like that if they knew we're in here."

"He can't sit like that forever," Katy said.

"Oh, trust me, he can wait for a long time."

"What if they're still here tomorrow morning?"

"We'll think of something," I said, settling on my bag.

We sat silently for a few minutes.

"You know what?" Katy said, studying the ceiling with a distant look on her face, "I've lived in the same place...in the same country, the same city, the same neighborhood all my life. This is my home."

"Home?" I whispered, realizing I didn't know what that word meant. By then, I'd lived on three continents, in as many countries, and with as many families. I had no idea where home was anymore.

"I'm giving it all up and coming on this crazy trip halfway around the world with you," Katy was saying.

"Well, he did one good thing."

"Who?"

"Jos—" I caught myself. "I mean, that guy...."

"Him?" Katy's faced flushed red. "You mean that mean, lying bastard?"

She's being generous, I thought. "What I meant to say was," I said quickly, "it's a good thing you got your passport. Otherwise, we'd have had to think of something else."

"Where'd we go, then? The North Pole to see Santa Claus? Since Mom died, I don't have anyone to go to."

"Me neither—just you and my cousin Preeti."

"You can't wait to see her, eh?"

I nodded.

"What are we going to do when we get there?"

"We'll figure something out," I said. "Maybe we'll get our own place, the three of us."

"In Goa?"

"Or Tanzania," I said. *That's my home*, I thought. My home was where my parents lay buried and where I had to return, eventually.

A glint came to Katy's eyes. "Hey, maybe we can start a business and charge money to give a good whopping to men who treat their girlfriends bad."

"That'd be illegal but fun."

"A good whopping to their cars then. I've got experience on that front now."

"Still illegal," I said. "But I bet we'd make a ton of money."

"We could get some cool uniforms, you know, like Wonder Woman."

"With red heels."

"And ankle bracelets. I want one like yours."

"Preeti gave this to me before I left. I'll ask her where she got it."

Seconds became minutes and minutes became hours. Katy and I had all the time in the world now, to chitchat about the past and our imagined future.

Women came into the stalls and left. After a while, we began to see a pattern. There was a time when most flights departed, bringing in a rush of women desperate for a last-minute pee break before they got on the plane. Some women marched in, did their job, and left. Others stayed for fifteen minutes, brushing their teeth, washing their faces, grooming their hair, touching up their makeup. Most ignored us in the corner. One old lady asked if we were okay. A few glared at us, especially during those packed times, when there was little space for the lineup.

We settled against the wall, tired and hungry, but safe for the moment.

Sometime after midnight, Katy drifted off to sleep. I was exhausted too but couldn't sleep. My brain kept spinning, thinking of the hair-brained schemes those men might try to get inside the women's washroom.

They could barrel their way in with guns or they could slip in disguised as cleaners or airport officials. After that last thought, any woman in a uniform, from cleaners to stewards to pilots who happened to stroll in through the doors, looked highly suspicious to me.

I kept a sharp eye open all night.

Chapter Fifty-five

H*onk.*
 I jerked awake, banging the back of my head against the wall.

Where am I? My head was heavy like I'd drunk too much rum. My mouth felt cakey and my legs felt numb. It took a few seconds to situate myself.

We were still inside the airport bathroom, and the clock on the wall said it was four thirty in the morning. Our flight was leaving in half an hour. I sat up, panicking.

Next to me, Katy was snoring gently. "Katy," I whispered, but she didn't budge. "Katy, wake up!" She was dead to the world.

Other than the strange sound that woke me up, things were quiet outside. Deadly quiet. It was that eerie time which was no longer night, but not fully morning either. I got up, feeling stiffer than a plank, and tiptoed to the door.

Outside, I could no longer hear the hum of people or announcements over the PA system. One lone security guard was patrolling the corridor. I watched him walk up and down, his mouth moving rhythmically like he was chewing gum. His station was a few feet from the entrance to the washrooms. From the corner of my eye, I saw a movement.

It was Ashok. *He's still here?* He sat looking like a long-distance traveler waiting for the next flight on his itinerary. We'd been very lucky. Without the security guard, the men would have barged in here without a moment's hesitation.

Honk!

A golf cart driven by a second guard, a female guard, swung into the corridor and screeched to a stop next to the patrolling one. The two chatted for a while, heads bowed. I leaned in to hear better.

That was when I realized what we had to do.

I turned around and dashed back inside. I shook Katy by the shoulders. "Wake up!" She stirred but didn't open her eyes.

"Lemme sleep."

"Get up! We gotta go!"

She turned away and snuggled deeper into her jacket.

I let go of her shoulders and ran back to the door. The female security guard had already got back in her cart, ready to leave. She waved at her colleague and gunned her engine. Just as she took off, I dashed out of the bathroom, waving my arms and yelling.

"Help!" I said. "Hey! Help!"

From the corner of my eyes, I saw Ashok, like a cat sighting prey, pounce in my direction. The security cart screeched to a halt within inches of me. At the same time, I saw Dick grab Ashok by his shirt collar and pull him back. *Dick's here too?*

"Help!"

"You tryna kill yourself?" barked the guard in the cart.

Her colleague ran over. "What's going on here?" he asked, a frown on his face.

"Please help us," I said. "My friend's really sick." I pointed toward the washroom. "She's in there."

"Oh, yeah?"

The female guard got out of her vehicle, gave a nod to her companion and said, "I got this." I dashed into the washroom, shouting, "Katy! Katy!" The guard followed, the key chain on her belt jangling loudly with every step.

She stopped when she saw Katy asleep on her suitcase on the floor.

"What are you two doing here at this time of the night? You can't sleep in here."

"She's not feeling well. We have a plane to catch and we're really, really late."

The guard stood with her legs apart surveying us. With her dark paramilitary uniform, spiky blonde hair, and pudgy jowls, she looked more like a prison guard than someone who worked for an airport whose slogan was "Welcome on Board." Suddenly, I wasn't sure I'd made the right decision.

Katy blinked her eyes and sat up slowly. She gave a start to see the guard. "What's going on?"

The guard surveyed her closely. "She looks sleepy, not sick. What's the matter with you?"

Katy gave her a confused look. "Nothing," she mumbled.

"A bad period," I said quickly. "A really bad one."

The guard raised an eyebrow. "Sick from weed more like it," she said. "Open up, ladies. Show me what you have in there."

Katy and I stared at her.

"I said open up. You can't hide these things from me."

"You think we have *drugs*?" I said, shocked. "But we don't have any."

"That's what they all say. Let me be the judge of that." She pushed Katy off her suitcase, ripped open the zipper, and started pulling things out one after the other, some falling onto the washroom floor.

"Hey, don't do that!" Katy said. "Asha, what's going on?"

I couldn't do anything other than watch the guard do her job, knowing the minutes were ticking away.

The guard was thorough.

She went through Katy's clothes one by one, picking them up with the tips of her fingers, holding them out, and sniffing them like a bloodhound. She kept rooting around Katy's bag until she found something. She triumphantly held out a granola bar.

Katy and I exchanged glances. *When did it become illegal to bring granola bars to the airport?* The guard turned the bar over, inspected the unbroken wrapping, brought it close to her nose, gave it a few official sniffs, and placed it back in the bag with a look of disappointment.

"Hold your arms out."

"Sorry?" Katy said, with a look of alarm on her face.

"Up."

Katy got up shakily and stood on her jacket, which she'd been using as a pillow until now.

"Arms out."

I looked on aghast as the guard patted Katy down. I glanced around us in panic. *Where's the money packet?* I could have sworn Katy had it on her when we came in.

"You're clean," the guard said. Katy sat back down on her jacket with a thump and a glazed look on her face. I realized then the money bag was in the jacket pocket. For some reason, the guard hadn't picked it up.

"Your turn, missy," the guard said, pointing at me.

Before she could scatter my contents on the floor, I opened my bag myself, my mind a whirlwind. *How do I get her to help us get to our gate? Can we catch our flight on time?* The guard went through my things with the same hound-dog efficiency, except with me she couldn't find even a bubble gum wrapper. I spread my arms and legs apart and stood perfectly still for her to pat me down.

"Okay, you're clean."

She hooked her fingers in her belt and surveyed us while we squatted on the ground, pushing our things back into our bags and zipping them shut.

"Girls," she said, clearing her throat and speaking in a softer tone, "airports have lounges for a reason. It's so passengers such as yourselves can sit and wait. Bathrooms are not appropriate places for sleeping. And if you're not well, there's a twenty-four-hour clinic you can go to see a nurse."

"Officer," I said, not sure what to call her, but "officer" sounded good. I gave a quick glance at Katy and crossed my fingers. "Our flight leaves in fifteen minutes, but we couldn't get to the gate earlier 'cause she was too sick. Can you help us?"

The guard rocked on the balls of her feet and squinted at Katy.

"Oooh." Katy clutched her tummy and screwed up her face into a pained look. "The cramps again."

I sighed in relief, glad she was finally following my lead.

The guard frowned at her.

"It's this horrible pain, like a knife turning in my stomach." Katy put a hand on the wall to steady herself. "Worst pain I've ever had in my entire life."

I prayed she wouldn't overact.

"Maybe you shouldn't be flying, if you're that sick," the guard said, concerned now. "Maybe I need to get you to the clinic."

"She's feeling better now," I said quickly. "We just need to get to the plane and get her to her seat so she can sleep. Would you mind giving us a ride in your golf cart?"

"My what?"

"Your shuttle?" I swallowed.

She hesitated a few seconds. Then, she turned around in sharp military fashion. "Come on, girls. Get your bags. Hop to it. A bathroom's no place to hang out when you've got your period."

She marched out of the bathroom, jangling her key chain loud enough to wake the dead. Katy and I picked up our bags and quickly followed her outside. I hesitated at the door.

Outside, Ashok and Dick were waiting, watching us. They glared when we came out, but they couldn't make a move in front of the two guards.

We were safe, at least for the moment.

"Hop on board," the guard said, taking the wheel of her cart. I took Katy's bag and mine and jumped into the backseat. Katy still clutching her stomach, climbed laboriously into the front. The guard started the engine and we lurched forward.

I took a quick look behind me. Dick and Ashok were standing near the bathroom door, mouths agape. I couldn't help but wave. They didn't wave back.

We weaved in and out of the corridors, honking at the occasional airport worker on their night shift. The guard drove like she was in the home stretch of a NASCAR race while Katy and I hung on to the handlebars for our lives.

Katy didn't need to pretend she was sick anymore; her face had gone white. We turned one corner so quickly I was sure we were on two wheels. That was when we bumped into two familiar men: Franky and Jose, carrying coffee cups.

"Oh, my god!" Katy screeched when she saw them.

"Watch where you're going!" the guard yelled.

The two men jumped out of the way and we charged on. Clutching the bar to keep my balance, I glanced behind me to see them gaping at us, their coffee splattered on the floor. I sank into my seat feeling exhilarated.

No. Liberated.

Chapter Fifty-six

"This is the final boarding call for Air India Flight Eight-Six-Three to London."

"That's us!" I yelled.

We were finally at our gate, and we'd been lucky. Very lucky.

The security guard had taken us under her wing and escorted us all the way to the boarding desk, bossing her way through security. The skeleton staff at the security gate hardly glanced at our papers or bags and let us through quickly.

I went through security check with my heart in my mouth, while Katy played up her sickness to anyone who'd look at her. If anyone had seen what she had in her jacket or had scratched the surface of my passport, it would have been over. Somehow, the money packet in Katy's jacket had not raised any eyebrows, even as it slid through the X-ray machine.

The security guard handed us to the check-in desk and said goodbye with a friendly, "You girls take care now."

We trundled into the plane with a couple other latecomers and found our seats in the back.

"Oh, god," Katy groaned as soon as we sat down. "I really need to pee."

"We were stuck in a washroom all night and you didn't go?" I asked with half a smile.

She gave me a dark look.

"You'll have to get used to different toilets in India," I said with a grin, remembering the open pit holes at Grandma's apartment complex. "Indian toilets are not places you wanna get stuck for seven hours."

"Your cousin will find us a decent place to stay, won't she?" Katy looked hopeful.

"Flight attendants, prepare for takeoff. Cabin crew, please take your seats."

I put on the seat belt. "Look on the bright side," I said. "We're leaving a horrible situation, I get to see Preeti again, and you get to visit India."

"Then what? What are we going to do there? Where are we going to stay? Thank god, we've got enough to—"

"We're not touching that stuff unless it's an absolute emergency," I said, giving her a warning look.

"How are we going to eat, then? Where are we going to sleep?"

"You know what we're going to do?"

"What brilliant idea do you have now?"

"We'll bake cakes in Goa."

. . . .

—THE END –

Read the first chapters of the next Red Heeled Rebels book here.

The Girl Who Made Them Pay
Red Heeled Rebels Book Two

· · · ·

CHAPTER ONE

· · · ·

THE MAN IN THE BLACK suit pushed Katy toward the airport doors.

"Hey!" I shouted. "Stop!"

Two smartly dressed women walking into the Heathrow business lounge glared at me as they passed by.

Why can't they see what's happening?

"Let her go!" I yelled louder, waving my arms. "Someone help!"

I wasn't watching where I was going and hit a trolley piled with luggage. The handle bar whacked into my stomach and I doubled over.

The trolley rolled toward a man reading the flight display screens, but I didn't stop. I couldn't. I straightened up and kept running. I dodged a bunch of kids walking through the terminal with their noses stuck to their phones. They didn't move an inch. Didn't even look up.

"Stop!" I shouted again, my voice getting hoarse.

Who's this guy? Where's he taking her?

From the corner of my eyes, I saw the vague shape of a man in a blue uniform at the other end of the corridor. It was a British cop.

For half a second, I thought of turning around and sprinting that way to ask for help, but the brief distraction cost me. My heel buckled and I tripped. I caught myself before I hit the floor and looked up to see the man in the suit pull my best friend outside.

Why isn't she fighting back?

Ignoring the searing pain in my ankle, I crashed through the main doors, just as he pushed Katy into a black London cab.

"Katy! Come back!"

The cab door banged shut, catching Katy's bright red scarf on the door well. The man jumped in front and the car pulled out.

"No-ooo!" I screamed. Everyone turned to look. "Stop that car! Help!" I spluttered, pointing.

A group of businessmen waiting in the limousine line looked over with smirks on their faces. Others turned away as if embarrassed by the spectacle. I didn't care. I dashed across the road.

With a sinking feeling in my stomach, I watched as the cab gathered speed. Katy's red scarf fluttered from the door well like it was giving me the finger.

"Katy!" I screamed as the car turned the corner and disappeared from view.

Chapter Two

• • • •

NONE OF THIS WOULD have happened if Katy had followed me inside the café.

But a fancy shoe store had distracted her and shoes for Katy were like crack for addicts. She didn't make a lot of money at Dick's Next Day Catering Company back in Toronto, but she'd rather starve than forgo a pair of sexy new heels even when the world was crashing around us.

Only a day earlier, four men had chased us across the city of Toronto to the airport, where we'd hunkered down in a women's washroom overnight. We'd barely evaded them on our way to the boarding gate.

On the plane, I tried to forget our worries while Katy switched on the little screen to get lost in the movies. But I never relaxed, and I saw Katy's eyes flit from the screen to the aisle and back again as if she was afraid the men would somehow appear in midair. When the plane finally touched down at London's Heathrow Airport, we stumbled out, burnt-out and nerve-racked.

My hastily packed backpack weighed me down and the wheels on Katy's fake Louis Vuitton suitcase made a racket to wake the dead. It was a relief to find our departure gate to Goa, but that was when Katy spotted the flashing red sign over Air India's check-in counter.

"Oh, no!" she cried out.

We'd been so desperate to get out of Toronto, we'd taken the only seats available, which were standby. This meant everyone else had first dibs and the airline could bump us as they wished.

I ran up to the desk. I hated these high service counters because they made me feel even smaller than my five feet. I got on my tiptoes. "We've got boarding passes, but they're standby. Could you find seats for us, please?" I asked, with a smile on my lips and hope in my heart.

The attendant didn't even touch my ticket. She wrinkled her nose like it smelled of bad cheese. "Do you not see the sign?" she said, pointing up. "The flight's full." Her tone was crisp. Final.

"Is there any way you can squeeze us in?" I asked, unbeaten. "It's just two of us."

"We'd fit anywhere. We're on the smaller side," I heard Katy say from behind me.

The attendant didn't look amused.

"It's an emergency," I said. That wasn't a lie. Dick and Jose, who owned the bakery in Toronto where I baked cakes and Katy kept the books, had plans to sell us like we were nothing more than lemon tarts or plum pies. I had no idea how far their reach was, but I didn't want to hang around to find out. "It's really, really urgent," I said to the attendant.

She sighed and snapped her fingers. "All right, passports and boarding passes please." Her fingers flew across the keyboard while we stood by, our own crossed tightly.

"Sorry," she said, turning to us. "There are absolutely no seats on this one. But—" She stopped to squint at the screen. We waited, holding our breath.

"I see a couple of seats in the next flight departing to Delhi. You won't be sitting together and I can't promise anything because you're on standby. That flight's tomorrow at thirteen hundred hours."

"Tomorrow?" I said. That would give Dick and Jose ample time to figure out where we'd run off to and catch up.

"Don't you have anything today?" Katy asked, in a plaintive voice.

"Booked passengers get priority," the ground attendant said. "Here are your new boarding passes, and ladies, don't be late tomorrow."

I took back our papers with shaking hands.

"If you need a place to stay the night, the airport Sheraton's right up—" She paused and looked us over. Our wrinkled, hand-me-down clothes were a dead giveaway. Lowering her voice, she said, almost sympathetically, "Girls, there are quiet lounges in Terminal Three if you need some rest for the night."

She glanced at the line that had formed behind us and snapped her fingers. "Next, please."

Katy and I stumbled to the closest waiting area and collapsed.

I swung my feet out and leaned against the back of the seat, my right foot clinking as I shifted. My ankle bracelet had been a gift from my cousin Preeti, a gift for my wedding day three years ago, back in Goa, the day I made the biggest escape of my life. That was also the last time I saw Preeti.

"What're we gonna do now?" Katy asked.

Dark circles ringed her bloodshot eyes, making her look years older than nineteen. I was only six months younger than her but I must have the same ragged look, I thought.

I pulled my bag off my back and rubbed my eyes. "Find a place to sleep, maybe?"

"Way too stressed for that."

"We could go hide out in the washroom again," I said with a weak smile.

"Don't even think about it," Katy said.

We sat silently on the stiff bench seats for an hour, leaning against each other, not sure of what to do or what to say.

Around us, businesswomen and men in sharp suits marched up and down, pulling their laptop bags behind them. Families hurried by with fussy kids in tow, toward departure gates. Couples with arms intertwined walked by on their way to honeymoons or romantic destinations. Occasionally, a harried soul stumbled by looking as jet-lagged and beat as we were, but they were few, and they seemed to know where they were heading, unlike Katy and I who felt totally lost and alone.

We must have looked a strange pair.

She was a sinewy redhead in a miniskirt and her signature three-inch red stilettos, all found in a consignment store, but as good as new. She'd dressed for a date with Jose, a date that never took place. And never will, now she's found out what he really wanted to do with her.

I sat next to her, a petite half-Indian girl in a hand-me-down miniskirt and more sensible red pumps. I couldn't afford to wear high heels like Katy, because while she sat at her desk in the book-keeping anteroom most of the day making client calls, I spent most of mine bustling between the bakery's kitchen counter and oven.

Right now, my skirt was streaked with white because I'd had only enough time to throw off my apron before running out of the bakery. After that, more important worries had crowded my mind than flour on my skirt or icing sugar in my hair.

Katy let out a loud sigh. She looked like she was asleep, but I could see her scan the crowd from under half-closed eyelids.

"Hey." I nudged her gently on the elbow.

"Hmm?" She stirred and opened her eyes. Her face looked pale and drawn and I could see visible lines on her forehead.

"We can't lounge here all day."

"I can."

"They've probably got a shoe sale over there."

"I'm tired, Asha."

"For *shoe sales*?"

She sat still for a minute, surveying the surrounding area. People were pushing trolleys, pulling suitcases, heads lost in phone conver-sations. Announcements blared from the loudspeakers: pre-boarding calls, boarding calls, final calls, final-final calls. It seemed like this air-port never stopped.

Katy sat up. "I'm beginning to spot Jose and Dick everywhere."

"Me too," I said. "But I don't think they'll come here."

"Why not?"

"Because—" I paused to find the right words. I'd been ruminating over this for the past few hours. "They only picked on us because we were right there in their store. They won't spend a fortune flying all the way here after us."

Katy raised an eyebrow.

"We were convenient," I said. "Plus, you and me have nobody to call for help. They knew no one's gonna notice if anything happens to us."

"You think so?"

"Who'd we call for help?"

Katy looked down at her hands and shook her head.

"We're not worth the trouble. They probably already found other girls to make money off of."

"What a bunch of basta—"

A loud bang resonated inside the terminal. We both jumped.

A gunshot?

But it was only a suitcase that had dropped from a luggage trolley to the floor. Katy and I sighed in relief.

I sat up. We had to find something to do, a distraction, *any* distraction, or this paranoia would overtake us both.

I touched her shoulder. "Hey, let's get out of here. Come on."

With another sigh, Katy unraveled her legs and stood up slowly.

We spent the next two hours strolling the length of the airport. We had time on our hands now. We stopped for a sandwich and tea at a takeaway booth and walked through the terminals, mindlessly window-shopping.

Very soon, we'd left the airport's security zone and stepped into the shopping plaza to gawk at the high-end clothing stores, luggage shops, and shoe boutiques that carried gorgeous things we couldn't afford even if we worked a lifetime. But looking at them helped us to forget our worries if only for a little while.

We'd just stepped out of one of these luxury shops when I spotted the café.

I grabbed Katy's arm. "Look!"

• • • •

CHAPTER THREE

· · · ·

"WHAT?" KATY WHIPPED her head around. "Are they here?"

"Over there." I pointed at the red-and-white striped awning of the bistro in front of us.

She looked confused. "You still hungry?"

"No, but—"

I paused. I'd seen photos of Chef Pierre's cafés in the glossy magazines at Mrs. Rao's upscale, suburban house in Toronto.

Her home was where I first landed after I ran away from India. I wasn't the first girl to become a slave housekeeper and cook to Mrs. Rao who'd promised my wages would be sent back to my family in Goa. She'd known how to keep me under her thumb. Experimenting with the recipes in Chef Pierre's magazines had been my only escape from that hell.

But I never dreamed to see his cafés in real life.

The lettering on the window was unmistakable. Inside, pastries of all kinds weighed down glass shelves that extended the length of the store. Golden croissants, colorful fruit tarts, shiny sugar buns, mousse cakes, cheesecakes, caramels, and éclairs sat side by side looking rich and pompous. The heavenly smell of oven-fresh baked things wafted my way. I took a deep breath in and closed my eyes.

It was my mother who came to my dreams every night, bringing memories of us baking together on lazy Sunday afternoons in Tanzania a long time ago. She'd been in my life for only a short time, but I never forgot her captivating smile, her contagious laughter, and those sweet cakes she loved to make.

When I was confined to Mrs. Rao's house and later, when I was stuck at Dick's bakery, it was Chef Pierre's recipes I immersed myself in. I could get lost in his cookbooks and foodie magazines for hours. He'd kept me company on days when I felt like the whole world was against me. Everything I learned about the art of baking after my mother died, I learned from him. And it was this skill that had saved my skin every single time.

"What's so special about this place?" Katy asked, walking over and pressing her face against the window.

I stepped up next to her. "It's Chef Pierre's café."

"Who?"

"He's famous. I used his recipes at Dick's place."

Katy pulled her face from the window and gave me a dubious look. "Six euros for a ping pong-sized sugar ball? Seriously?"

"They're good. You liked them."

"Don't remember," she said, frowning at the cakes on display. If Katy could go through life without eating so she could preserve her skinny thighs, she would, so I forgave her for saying that.

I peered inside. "Wish I could work here. I'd wash their floor if they'd let me in."

"Who needs all this sugar and fat?"

"All our clients loved them, remember?"

She made a face. "I'm gonna gain ten pounds just by looking at these. How you stay so small with the sweets you stuff yourself with, I don't know." She sniffed as two thin European women walked into the café. "You and those French girls."

"Small portions," I said with a smile. Katy always complained about her hips, her thighs, and her waist, which was ironic because she'd been the prettiest girl at our Toronto high school. She was almost selected by a modeling agency and all the boys would have given an arm and a leg to date her. I worried on those days when she locked herself up in the toilet after supper. If I pressed my ears to the door, I'd hear her retching, but I never knew how to bring the topic up.

"Yeah, right." She turned away from the coffee shop. "Oh my god, look!" Her eyes flashed. She'd caught sight of the shoe store next door. "Jimmy Choo!"

It was her turn to grab me and pull me away. She marched inside and toward a pair of four-inch black boots studded with Swarovski crystals. They had a sticker price that could have bought a used car.

"Can I try these on?" she asked the store attendant, who barely acknowledged us. Katy didn't seem to care. She plopped down on the nearest bench with the boots in her hands and let out a happy sigh. This was her heaven. Mine was next door.

"Hey, Katy," I said, "I'm going to check out some of the pastries, okay?"

"Join you soon as I'm done," she said, but she was already lost among the crystals and plastic.

I felt goose bumps on my arms as I crossed the threshold of the café.

Chefs in Europe are like royalty. They usually come from regal lineages with noble blood and even nobler connections. They grace the covers of flashy magazines and hang out with fashion moguls and film stars. Chef Pierre, though, was an anomaly. He was the son of a coal miner from the south of Belgium who'd fought his way to the top, armed with his grandmother's recipes, a whipping whisk, and a big dream.

His story had a happy ending when he finally made it big and married his true love, Andre from the Netherlands, in the biggest, fattest, gayest wedding of the century. In those snazzy magazine photos, handsome and buff Andre looked like he'd just stepped out of *GQ*. Next to him, plump Chef Pierre looked like a village boy, out of place in any high society club.

Like him, I was different. I didn't fit anywhere. I was born in Africa but wasn't truly African. My parents were from Asia, but I wasn't truly Asian. I'd lived in Canada for the past three years, but

I wasn't really Canadian. I was a strange, mixed-up girl who'd been everywhere but belonged nowhere. And just like Chef Pierre, all I carried with me were a whipping whisk and a big dream.

I dreamed of the day when my cousin Preeti, Katy, and I would set up our own bakery in Goa near the beach among the waving coconut trees. With the first money I'd make, I'd return to Tanzania and visit my parents' graves. That was my plan.

At the back of every Chef Pierre's coffee shop was a rack that showcased his foodie magazines. I walked over to it and picked up the latest edition. Following in the tradition of Oprah, Chef Pierre's magazine covers featured only him in his signature hat and apron, holding the pastry of the month. This month's cover had him showing off a beautiful soufflé. The side caption read, "Perfect dessert for the perfect royal party."

I picked up a copy and stepped up to the shelves. My mouth watered as I wondered which to try first. The éclair covered with dark melted chocolate or the cheesecake with fresh raspberries on top?

I'd been so preoccupied I hadn't noticed the tall man in the black suit sidle up to Katy in the shoe shop next door.

• • • •

...TO BE CONTINUED

• • • •

CONTINUE THE ADVENTURE...

Do you want to know what happens to Asha and Katy next? You'll find out in the second book of the Red-Heeled Rebels series.

The Girl Who Made Them Pay is a gritty tale of crime and revenge that will take you on a feverish race from the underbelly of London to the cobblestone squares of Brussels, and to the medieval land of Luxembourg where castles and fortresses can hide the unimaginable.

Asha and Katy are fleeing a fate worse than death. They think they are finally safe in London, but one girl is snatched into a waiting black cab...

Yes! The Red Heeled Rebels are going to the fairytale land of Luxembourg.

Go to www.RedHeeledRebels.com[1] to get the next book in the series. Enjoy the read.

Your Gift

• • • •

If you'd like to know what inspired the Red Heeled Rebels series, in particular this novel, you can read **The Girl with No Hands,** a short story by the author.
Get your exclusive copy of the short story here: **The Girl with No Hands**[2].
www.BookHip.com/PBRRAS

---

2. http://www.BookHip.com/PBRRAS

The Red Heeled Rebels Novel Series

In a world where justice no longer prevails, six iron-willed women rally together to seek vengeance on those who stole their humanity.

This is a story where the thrill of *Kill Bill* meets the wrath of *The Girl with the Dragon Tattoo*.

If you like gripping thrillers with flawed but gutsy heroines, vigilante action in exotic locales and twists that leave you at the edge of your seat, you'll love these books by multiple award-winning Canadian novelist, Tikiri Herath.

Pick up the Red Heeled Rebels books for a heart-pounding international adventure without having to get a passport or even buy an airline ticket!

· · · ·

WHAT READERS ARE SAYING on Amazon and Goodreads:

- "Fast-paced and exciting!"

- "An exciting and thought-provoking book."

- "A wonderful story! I didn't want to leave the characters."

- "I couldn't put down this exciting road trip adventure with a powerful message."

- "Another award-worthy adventure novel that keeps you on the edge of your seat."

- "A heart-stopping adventure. I just couldn't put the book down till I finished reading it."

• "Kept me mesmerized and captivated with the rich descriptions which made me feel like I was actually inside the story."

• "This is a fantastic read that will have you traveling the globe. I absolutely loved this book. You won't be able to put it down!"

• "A real page turner and international thriller. Reminds me of why I've always loved to read. Because I can visit worlds and places I wouldn't ordinarily get to see."

To learn more about this addictive series, go to www.RedHeeledRebels.com[1]

• • • •

PREQUEL: THE GIRL WHO Crossed the Line

A reckless girl. A grave mistake. A fateful destiny.

All she wanted was to belong. Then, she committed an unforgivable crime...

• • • •

BOOK ONE: THE GIRL Who Ran Away

An estranged orphan. A treacherous plot. A perilous journey that could kill her.

She'd just survived a fiery car crash in the middle of nowhere. Both her parents are dead, but that's nothing compared to what she would face next...

• • • •

BOOK TWO: THE GIRL Who Made Them Pay

---

1. http://www.redheeledrebels.com/

A kidnapped friend. A forbidden house. A precarious journey to escape their captors.

They are fleeing a fate worse than death. They think they're finally safe in London, when one of them is snatched into a waiting black cab. And now, she will do anything to find her friend...

• • • •

BOOK THREE: THE GIRL Who Fought to Kill

A lost cousin. A heinous crime. An impossible rescue that risks it all.

She was ready to cross oceans to hunt down her stolen cousin. But she didn't know the terrifying stakes waiting for her on the other side that will test her resolve and courage...

• • • •

BOOK FOUR: THE GIRL Who Broke Free

A sweet sixteenth birthday banquet. A missing diplomat's daughter. A menacing family secret.

She thought she'd finally made it when she was invited to cater for the swankiest party in upscale Manhattan. But she didn't realize the birthday girl's family has other plans and the banquet is a ruse for something more perilous than she could ever imagine...

• • • •

BOOK FIVE: THE GIRL Who Knew Their Names

A glittering Hollywood gala. An actress with a dark vendetta. A cold-blooded murder among the stars.

She thought she'd snagged the most coveted catering job in Los Angeles, and a chance to meet A-list celebrities. But she didn't realize she was about to confront the most powerful predator in town on her first day...

• • • •

BOOK SIX: THE GIRL Who Never Forgot

A girl from the swamps. A family gripped by darkness. A killer on the loose at the Mardi gras.

She was invited to cater a lavish ball where New Orleans' blue-blooded families celebrated Mardi gras in style, away from the cacophony of common street parades. But she didn't realize a murderer was lurking in the shadows, waiting to frame her for their deed...

• • • •

AWARDS & PRAISE FOR The Red Heeled Rebels books:

- Grand Prize Award Finalist - 2019 Eric Hoffer Award, USA
- First Horizon Award Finalist - 2019 Eric Hoffer Award, USA
- Honorable Mention General Fiction - 2019 Eric Hoffer Award, USA
- Winner First-In-Category - 2019 Chanticleer Somerset Award, USA
- Semi-Finalist - 2020 Chanticleer Somerset Award, USA
- Winner in 2019 Readers' Favorite Book Awards, USA
- Winner of 2019 Silver Medal - Excellence E-Lit Award, USA
- Winner in Suspense Category - 2018 New York Big Book Award, USA
- Finalist in Suspense Category - 2018 & 2019 Silver Falchion Awards, USA
- Honorable Mention - 2018-19 Reader Views Literary Classics Award, USA
- Publisher's Weekly Booklife Prize – 2018, USA

Truth Is Harsher than Fiction

- 130 million girls around the world are missing from school.

- Two-thirds of the 774 million illiterate people in the world are female.

- One in seven girls in developing countries is married before the age of 15 (excluding China).

- In 2012, 70 million women 20-24 around the world had been married before the age of 18.

- The second most common cause of death for girls between the ages of 15-19 is complications from pregnancy and childbirth.

- Girls between the ages of 10-14 are five times more likely to die in pregnancy or childbirth than women aged 20-24.

- 75% of HIV-infected youth between the ages of 15-24 are girls.

- 50% of all sexual assaults worldwide are against girls 15 or younger.

*Source:

2017 Statistics from United Nations Foundation Inc Girl Up - www.girlup.org/impact/why-girls

. . . .

"Cultural acceptance does not mean accepting the unacceptable."

~Jasvinder Sanghera, British Human Rights Activist.

· · · ·

AS I RESEARCHED, PLANNED, and wrote these novels, I spoke with women and men from around the world, some of whom I'd never met before. They included women who are tirelessly fighting for equality and dignity in South Asia despite the push back and hostility from their own families and communities.

They included former military officers and peacekeepers who had been deployed to conflict zones and saw the heart-wrenching plight of children, but had neither the resources nor the permission to assist them.

Regardless of where they came from, they all shared with me their stories. They read mine. Most importantly, we discussed the difficult topics in these books frankly and without prejudice. I gained many insights through these chats, but one lesson I took away was there are good people everywhere.

These are the good people who do not apologize for harmful traditions nor tolerate cultural dogma. These are the good people who yearn to change age-old customs that subjugate our daughters and alienate our sons. These are the good people who desire to create a better world for all humanity, for now and for the future. I was surprised to see how much of our world views we share, regardless of differences in gender, vocation, political views, sexual orientation, or nationality.

We all have more in common than not. And this gives me hope, hope for a wiser, kinder, open, and more connected global community that uplifts us all.

How would you like to write your own life story?

The Rebel Diva Self-Empowerment Series
www.RebelDivas.com[1]

The Rebel Diva books are life-changing practical guides that take you on an adventure of a lifetime. Uncover your purpose, your passions, and your talents to create a step-by-step masterplan to achieve your life goals.

You'll create a story in these Rebel Diva books and that story will be yours.

What readers are saying:

- *"One of the most motivational and thought-provoking books I have ever read."*

- *"This book is phenomenal! This book is written for real people; no platitudes or empty promises."*

- *"A very inspirational read. This is highly recommended, especially if you're seeking to do and make a difference."*

- *"The author is teacher and cheerleader. She gives solid guidelines to help you figure out your goals and action plans, and she truly comes across as someone who cares."*

- *"This isn't just another self-help book—instead, this incredibly useful book includes a clear method and helpful exercises to help you uncover your dreams, passions and purpose."*

---

1.   http://www.rebeldivas.com/

● *"Very inspiring. Even though I am older, this book made me want to go after some of my dreams that I thought I was too old for. The book comes with a link that you can download a 100-page workbook. I plan on giving my daughter a copy too."*

● *"Proudly considering myself a Rebel Diva after taking this journey to self-discovery!"*

Sign up to get your exclusive Rebel Diva gift!

The Fear Buster is a short Rebel Diva workbook that shares three essential tools to help you overcome any fears or doubt and make both small and big decisions quickly. Go to the Rebel Diva site to get your personal copy as a gift.

www.RebelDivas.com/FearBuster[2]

---

2.   http://www.RebelDivas.com/FearBuster

Dedication

This book is dedicated to all the girls in the world wherever you are, whether you live in the slums of Asia, the villages of Africa, the favelas of South America, or the inner cities of America. I thought of you every day as I wrote this book. Every day, I wondered how many of you are standing up for your rights to learn, to play, to live a life of your own design, filled with happiness. I want you to know that no matter what happens, no matter what anyone says, you matter to this world, more than you realize.

Rise up. Be brave. Stand strong. Above all, stay in school.

Acknowledgments

To my fantastic international team of beta readers who helped me through this adventure, who cheered me on as I toiled, and who gave me their frank feedback, thank you.

(In alphabetical order)

- Adrienne Benson Scherger, USA
- Amanda L. Webster, Author of the Valley of the Bees series, USA
- Betsy Boyte, USA
- Bill Joyce, Author of the Shadow Soldiers series, USA
- Carla Chiodi, Brazil
- Carolyn Pennett-Staresinic, Canada
- Cyndi Wannamaker, Canada
- Jan Reatherford, Canada
- Janet Angelo, USA
- Laurence French, UK
- Lindsey M. Albright, USA
- Mikaela Kate Hennessey, USA
- Nadia Brown, USA
- Nadine Hutchinson, Author of Beyond the Khrysalis,USA
- Otivbo Akhigbe, Nigeria
- Rene Fomby, Author of the Moose McGillicutty Mystery series, USA
- Vivian Maxwell-Onwunali, USA

· · · ·

TO MY AMAZING, TALENTED, superstar editor, Stephanie, thank you for coming on this literary journey with me and for helping make these books the best they can be.

• • • •

TO ALL THE GENEROUS readers who take the time to review my novels and give their frank feedback, thank you. I owe you all a debt of gratitude and a glass of wine (or several) when you come to Vancouver next!

About the Author

Tikiri Herath is a multiple-award-winning Canadian author. Born in Sri Lanka, a tropical island in the Indian Ocean, she spent her childhood in South East Africa, and has lived and worked in Southeast Asia, Continental Europe, and North America.

She started her adult life as a lone immigrant girl, but went on to receive a bachelor's degree from the University of Victoria, British Columbia and a master's degree from the Solvay Business School in Brussels.

For fifteen years, she worked in risk management in the intelligence and defense sectors, including in the Canadian Federal Government and at NATO.

Tikiri's an adrenaline junkie who has rock climbed, bungee jumped, rode on the back of a motorcycle across Quebec, flown in an acrobatic airplane upside down, and parachuted solo.

When she's not writing or plotting another thriller scene, you'll most probably find her baking in her kitchen with a glass of red wine in hand and jazz playing in the background.

To say hello and get free travel stories from around the world, go to www.TikiriHerath.com.[1]

1. http://www.tikiriherath.com/